PRAISE FOR MATTHEW FITZSIMMONS

PRAISE FOR *CONSTANCE*

"What a book! Like all the best speculative fiction, FitzSimmons's compelling thriller *Constance* takes elements of real science and spins them up into a novel and terrifying premise."

—Blake Crouch, *New York Times* bestselling author of *Dark Matter* and *Recursion*

"*Constance* is a blistering, balletic read—silky-smooth world building that effortlessly grounds a wonderful, harrowing tale of mystery, suspense, identity, friendship, and redemption. This is, for all its twists, turns, and tricks, a novel that does what a novel *should* do: examine what makes us human after all. Genuinely one of the best books I have read in a long, long time."

—Greg Rucka, *New York Times* bestselling author and creator of *The Old Guard*

PRAISE FOR *ORIGAMI MAN*

"FitzSimmons brings Gibson Vaughn and an old enemy full circle in *Origami Man*—an intricately plotted, rapid-fire thriller guaranteed to hook you from page one. Easily the best Gibson Vaughn installment to date."

—Steven Konkoly, *Wall Street Journal* bestselling author

"Matthew FitzSimmons's rapid-fire novels are loaded with twisted plots, explosive action, and dialogue that crackles with wit and emotion. His bighearted characters keep me coming back, book after book. Grab this thriller with both hands because *Origami Man* is a total blast."

—Nick Petrie, bestselling author of *The Drifter*

PRAISE FOR *DEBRIS LINE*

"Matthew FitzSimmons writes the kinds of thrillers I love to read: smart, character driven, and brimming with creative action sequences. If you're not yet a fan of FitzSimmons's Gibson Vaughn series, strap in, because you soon will be. *Debris Line* is tense, twisty, and always ten steps ahead. Don't miss it."

—Chris Holm, Anthony Award–winning author of *The Killing Kind*

"Matt FitzSimmons continues his amazing literary feat of creating an ensemble cast of troubled heroes and shooting them through page-turning thrillers with his latest, *Debris Line*, continuing the fast-paced adventures of Gibson Vaughn and his crew as they battle to stay alive and find some measure of justice in this unforgiving world. The Gibson Vaughn series is on its way to being a classic franchise of thriller fiction, with a unique voice and an unusual approach that keep the stories as appealing as they are entertaining. Highly recommended."

—James Grady, author of *Six Days of the Condor*

"*Debris Line* . . . doesn't waste a word or miss a twist. It's always smart, always entertaining, and populated top to bottom with fascinating and unforgettable characters."

—Lou Berney, author of *November Road*

PRAISE FOR *COLD HARBOR*

"In FitzSimmons's action-packed third Gibson Vaughn thriller . . . fans of deep, dark government conspiracies will keep turning the pages to see how it all turns out."

—*Publishers Weekly*

"*Cold Harbor* interweaves two classic American tropes: the solitary prisoner imprisoned for who knows what and the American loner determined to rectify the injustices perpetrated on him. It's a page-turner that keeps the reader wondering—and looking forward to Gibson Vaughn number four."

—Criminal Element

"There are so many layers and twists to *Cold Harbor* . . . FitzSimmons masterfully fits together the myriad pieces of Gibson Vaughn's past like a high-quality Springbok puzzle."

—*Crimespree Magazine*

PRAISE FOR *POISONFEATHER*

An Amazon Best Book of the Month: Mystery, Thriller & Suspense Category

"FitzSimmons's complicated hero leaps off the page with intensity and good intentions while a byzantine plot hums along, ensnaring characters into a tightening web of greed, betrayal, and violent death."

—*Publishers Weekly*

"[FitzSimmons] has knocked it out of the park, as they say. The characters' layers are being peeled back further and further, allowing readers to really root for the good guys! FitzSimmons has put together a great plot that doesn't let you rest for even a minute."

—*Suspense Magazine*

PRAISE FOR *THE SHORT DROP*

"FitzSimmons has come up with a doozy of a sociopath."

—*Washington Post*

"This live-wire debut begins with a promising lead in the long-ago disappearance of the vice president's daughter, then doubles down with tangled conspiracies, duplicitous politicians, and a disgraced hacker hankering for redemption . . . Hang on and enjoy the ride."

—*People*

"Writing with swift efficiency, FitzSimmons shows why the stakes are high, the heroes suitably tarnished, and the bad guys a pleasure to foil."

—*Kirkus Reviews*

"With a complex plot layered on top of unexpected emotional depth, *The Short Drop* is a wonderful surprise on every level . . . This is much more than a solid debut, it's proof that FitzSimmons has what it takes."

—Amazon.com, An Amazon Best Book of December 2015

"Beyond exceptional. Matthew FitzSimmons is the real deal."

—Andrew Peterson, author of the bestselling Nathan McBride series

"*The Short Drop* is an adrenaline-fueled thriller that has it all: political intrigue, murder, and suspense. Matthew FitzSimmons weaves a clever plot and deftly leads the reader on a rapid ride to an explosive end."

—Robert Dugoni, bestselling author of *My Sister's Grave*

CONSTANCE

OTHER TITLES BY MATTHEW FITZSIMMONS

The Short Drop

Poisonfeather

Cold Harbor

Debris Line

Origami Man

CONSTANCE

MATTHEW FITZSIMMONS

Published by Thomas & Mercer, Seattle

www.apub.com

Amazon, the Amazon logo, and Thomas & Mercer are trademarks of Amazon.com, Inc., or its affiliates.

ISBN-13: 9781542014267 (hardcover)
ISBN-10: 1542014263 (hardcover)
ISBN-13: 9781542014274 (paperback)
ISBN-10: 1542014271 (paperback)

Cover design by Faceout Studio, Spencer Fuller

David Bowie interview quoted by permission of ConcertLivewire.com

Printed in the United States of America

First edition

For Alison

PART ONE

UPLOAD / DOWNLOAD

She died—this was the way she died;
And when her breath was done,
Took up her simple wardrobe
And started for the sun.

Her little figure at the gate
The angels must have spied,
Since I could never find her
Upon the mortal side.

—"Vanished," Emily Dickinson

CHAPTER ONE

The little purple Christmas tree had a lot to answer for. Con hadn't celebrated Christmas in the three years she'd lived in Washington, DC. Hadn't meant to this year either. But then on the way home from the corner store, she noticed the tree in a box of junk left on the sidewalk outside her building. She couldn't say what made her rescue it, but it felt right playing Charlie Brown in her very own melancholy Christmas special.

She took it up to her apartment and set it on a table, where it twinkled at her hopefully. Other than being two feet tall, and purple, and not smelling a bit of pine, the little tree was virtually indistinguishable from the real thing. But it put her in an uncharacteristically festive mood, and she poured herself into decorating. She even baked Gamma Jol's fruitcake, which sat untouched on the kitchen counter but made the apartment smell like home back in Texas.

However, her spirits, like the tree, proved artificial. Celebrating the holidays alone was like setting a bonfire in her living room. One that cast unwelcome light into all the dark, carefully disregarded recesses of her life. The delicate truce she'd recently established with her depression unraveled overnight, and she woke on Christmas morning feeling low as hell. She worked remotely for a small nonprofit, which made it far too easy to avoid human contact if she chose. But how had it been a week since she'd left the apartment for anything other than food?

Einstein should have spent more time investigating the uneven way that time passed in December, the supermassive black hole of the Gregorian calendar.

Perhaps that was why she accepted the invitation to the dinner that night—an orphan potluck for people with no way to get home for the holidays. Not that she would've set foot in Lanesboro even if she could afford the ticket. She hadn't been home in close to five years, not since the beginning of her sophomore year in college when Mary D'Arcy, her mother and righteous servant of God, had informed Con that she was going straight to hell. Con had looked her mother dead in the eye and with nineteen years of pent-up fury answered that she'd meet her there. They hadn't spoken since, not even after the accident.

The party started well enough. But a tableful of lonesome people and their press-on good cheer only reminded Con of how isolated she'd become. She compensated by accepting an invitation to go home with a burly white New Zealander. His name was Oliver, which he pronounced in a way she found delightful. Oliver had thighs like Doric columns, a mane of curly black hair, and a laugh that made you want in on the joke. She had no intention of actually going home with him— these days it felt better to be wanted than to be had—but she enjoyed the confidence of his attention.

To a point.

After dessert, she extricated herself from the table to the living room and fell into a conversation with a musician who Con discovered shared her Mick Ronson obsession. And like that, Oliver and his tragic thighs were forgotten. How many people even knew the name Mick Ronson anymore? Much less could hold a knowledgeable, geeked-out conversation about his guitar work on early Bowie albums like *Aladdin Sane* and *Ziggy Stardust and the Spiders from Mars*. It was like discovering a shared, secret language, and the two women huddled in a corner for the rest of the night talking guitars and exchanging songs and tidbits of musical lore—somehow Con never knew that Ronson had played guitar on

John Mellencamp's "Jack & Diane." That blew her mind a little. For the first time in a long while, she wished she'd thought to bring her guitar.

At an uncharitable hour the next morning, the bleating of the alarm woke her. Groping around on the bedside table, she found her LFD and slipped it behind her ear to find out why.

Today, December 26, 2038, will be sunny and clear, with highs in the mid-nineties.

Another scorcher. The eighth consecutive day and far from a record for late December in Washington, DC. A calendar notification reminded her about her appointment at Palingenesis. Groaning, she rolled onto her side, trying vainly to get comfortable enough to fall back asleep. She was overdue for her monthly refresh and remembered thinking how clever she was scheduling it for the day after Christmas when the place would be deserted. Well, this was what cleverness got her.

From the other side of the apartment, the little tree twinkled forlornly at her like a friend who'd spotted her across a crowded room. She felt that she'd let the tree down by not trying hard enough to lift herself out of her gloom. Talking music had been nice, but it had left her with an emotional hangover. Mick Ronson had been Zhi's favorite guitarist (tied for first with Nile Rodgers), and it brought up too many memories. It also reminded her that she owed Zhi a visit. She could stop by on her way to Palingenesis, but that would mean getting out of bed right now.

But did she? Want to see him?

What difference did it make, really?

Ashamed of herself for even thinking it, she forced herself into a sitting position and rubbed her right leg, which always ached first thing in the morning. Ugly scars crisscrossed her knee where the surgeons had reattached it after the crash. A medical miracle by all accounts.

Picking out clothes from a mountain of dirty laundry—a pair of black jeans and her vintage Rihanna T-shirt from the Anti World Tour (2016, the year of Con's birth)—Con gave each a forensic sniff and deemed them passable. *Keeping it classy, Miss D'Arcy.* From the corner, the purple tree watched her silently, speculatively, as if wondering how it had been dragged into this janky scene. That was alright. Con wondered the same thing all the time.

———

"Who are you here to see?" the nurse at the front desk asked. He was a tall, Nordic-looking man with shaggy alpine hair and eyes too small for his face that gave him a perpetually suspicious squint.

"Zhi Duan," Con replied.

It spoke volumes that the nurse didn't recognize her. The first year after the accident, Con had rarely left Zhi's side. She'd been on a first-name basis with the entire staff, who'd taken pity on her and let her sleep on the chair in the corner of his room. She didn't remember the exact moment she'd become a disloyal piece of shit. At first, visits had been every other day, then once a week, and now she dreaded even the thought of seeing him.

The nurse asked Con for her name and entered it into the system. He informed her that she was not family. Con would argue that point. Rock band might not be a legally recognized family unit, but it sure as hell should be. Zhi Duan, Stephie Martz, Hugh Balzan, Tommy Diop—they were her family. The family she chose. Bound in love and music and shared tragedy. Now and forever. Even if they were all gone, one way or another.

"Check the exception list. I should be on there," Con suggested. She'd been on it the last time she'd visited, but when had that been? The summer? The spring? Zhi's parents lived in Dallas and had always been grateful that someone who cared about their son still visited. Had they found out that she'd stopped coming and revoked her permission?

To Con's relief, the nurse found her name. "I'll need your ID and three biometrics."

"Have as many as you like." She dutifully submitted a handprint, eye scan, and speech sample, which the nurse compared against the data stored on her ID as well as the facility's records. The facility had long-running issues with fans sneaking in to take pictures and steal mementos from Zhi's room. One sixteen-year-old had been caught shaving Zhi's head, planning to sell locks of his hair online.

Since the accident, a romantic mythology had sprung up about Zhi like weeds around an untended headstone. How his band, Awaken the Ghosts, had been heading into the studio to record its debut album once the tour wrapped up. How their van had jumped the median after a show, killing keyboardist Tommy Diop and bassist Hugh Balzan, and leaving their lead singer, Zhi Duan, in a coma. How they'd been on the verge of stardom and greatness. Con didn't know about that, but the obsession with Zhi was real. Bootlegs of the band's shows and demos were shared back and forth online among the fervent. Thousands of posts had been written in fan forums, especially about Zhi, who had been transformed into a tragic poet-musician god. A generational talent cruelly taken before his time.

Fans of the band—*cult members* when Con wasn't feeling generous—pilgrimaged from all over to pay their respects. The site of the crash had become a graffiti-stained shrine. The uber-creepy ones with boundary issues even tracked Con down to ask intimate, presumptuous questions about Zhi. They talked about him like they'd known him, which made her vaguely ill. Her memories weren't roadside curios, three for a dollar, to be pawed through by grubby-fingered tourists. When confronted, she always kept her answers vague and extracted herself quickly, aware that some of the more hard-core fans resented her and Stephie for not having the decency to die in the crash.

The nurse handed over a visitor's pass. "Lucky timing. He's been up at Johns Hopkins for the past few weeks. Only just got back a few days ago. Looks like his parents enrolled him in some study the university is running on long-term-care patients."

In the elevator, she tried to talk herself into leaving. She'd signed in at the front desk. Didn't that count as visiting? No one would know if she didn't actually see him. Least of all Zhi himself. When the elevator opened, she meant to get off, but her feet refused to move. It wasn't until the doors began to close that her hand shot out to hold them open. With a sigh, she got off and went down the long hall.

Zhi's room was silent apart from the machine that breathed for him and the rhythmic beeping of the monitors. Seeing him like this always broke her heart all over again. She hurried to the window and opened the curtains. Why did they keep it so dark in here? There was a tree in the courtyard, tall and sinewy, that Zhi would have loved. Con made a circuit of the room, straightening up. Not that it was necessary—the staff did an excellent job—but this was her routine to make herself feel like she still played a part in his life. When she had finished tidying, she pulled up a chair beside the bed and took Zhi's hand. Once, they'd been the calloused hands of a guitarist, but now they were as soft as a newborn's. She squeezed. He didn't squeeze back. He never would again.

Persistent vegetative state.

She didn't think she'd ever heard three uglier words. The first year, she'd clung to the fantasy that if she kept talking and singing to him, her devotion would be rewarded. The more doctors tried to convince her that Zhi's brain damage was irreversible, that he would never regain consciousness, the more radicalized in her certainty she became. He was special. He had a destiny. They didn't know him, know his strength. Not like she did. So it would be up to her to help him find his way back. She'd made herself his lighthouse, resolved to keep watch until he came back to her. One day his eyes would flicker open. He would look over to her and smile and ask when they could blow this place. Like in a fucking fairy tale. *Could you imagine anyone being so naïve?* But here was the thing, she still was. A pathetically stubborn woman who refused to listen to reason.

It was why she couldn't get out of bed some mornings and why her friends had run out of patience with her. After the crash, people had respected her grief, indulged it, even admiring its spiky resilience. Their hearts and thoughts and prayers went out to her. But the luster of any tragedy eventually wore off. The narrative changed. It wasn't as if she and Zhi had been married. Three years was long enough to mourn. Too long, some whispered. She needed to quit milking it and move on. She'd felt herself being reclassified from grieving to depressed. And depression, unlike grief, was treated as a character flaw. Not that anyone said it aloud, but who wanted to deal with some sad girl and her bum knee? Con didn't blame them. She didn't much want to deal with herself either.

"Merry Christmas, Zhi," she said and put her head down and cried.

The band had played a show in DC that night and were on the way to North Carolina at the time of the accident. Con had been curled up asleep in the back, no seat belt, and woke in a hospital bed with no memory of the crash. No one could say for certain what had happened. Not even Stephie, who had improbably walked away without a scratch. All that was known was that the truck had hit them head-on and their van had been totaled. Hugh had died instantly. Tommy hung on for two days before succumbing to his injuries. Zhi had never regained consciousness. Her Zhi. Con was in the hospital for two months recuperating from multiple surgeries and missed both funerals. She hadn't spoken to Stephie, her best friend in the world, in years.

Without noticing that she was doing it, she put her hand on her right knee and rubbed the scars beneath her jeans.

Zhi had been driving that night as he had throughout the tour, clocking unhealthy hours behind the wheel. Without discussing it with anyone first, he'd bought the band a self-drive '27 Chevy van. The new laws required vehicles to be auto-drive but had grandfathered in older models. It was an expensive hobby. Parts were harder and harder to find, and the cost of a self-drive insurance policy was stratospheric. None of their families had that kind of money, except for Zhi's parents, who could afford to underwrite their only child's reckless flight of fancy.

Before leaving Texas, Con had been nominated by the rest of the band to try one last time to convince Zhi to trade in the van and get something newer. Something reliable. She was the band's chief negotiator and had done her best, but no one ever won an argument with Zhi. Not when he dug in his heels and got that look in his eyes, talking about how a band being driven around America by computer would never truly understand where it came from. It was all soulful bullshit, but it sounded so good when Zhi said it. Everything always did. That had been Zhi's gift. The reason Con had fallen in love with him in the first place, why she loved him even now, though it didn't feel good anymore, and she wished that she knew how to make it stop.

Her LFD chirped with yet another reminder of her appointment. Con wondered what Zhi would think if he knew that she had a clone waiting for her at Palingenesis or that the crash was the reason she kept these monthly appointments. Death had always been an abstraction, but after the crash, nothing frightened her more. The clone was cowardice, pure and simple, cowardice that had seeped into her groundwater like a toxin.

She would give anything for him to sit up and remind her that she didn't have to be afraid every minute. He'd once told her that she was the bravest person he'd ever known. Where had that woman gone?

CHAPTER TWO

Only ten in the morning, but already it was on the mean side of ninety. Con fought her way through the scrum of grim-eyed protesters chanting their defiant, rip-cord slogans outside Palingenesis. She'd scheduled the appointment for the day after Christmas hoping it would be quiet for a change, but the protesters were out in force. There had to be three times as many as she'd ever seen before. Maybe they didn't have anywhere to spend the holidays either.

The protesters were a permanent fixture, rain or shine, huddled beneath the black umbrellas that had become the unofficial symbol of their cause. These were the shock troops of the CoA—the Children of Adam—the single largest anti-cloning organization in the United States. They picketed every Palingenesis clinic in the country, but the headquarters here in Washington, DC, held a particularly intense fascination for them. In their minds, this was the point of origin. The birthplace of human cloning. Where the species had begun to disentangle itself from its humanity.

The umbrellas pulsed excitedly as word filtered through the crowd—the front doors of the clinic had opened. Everyone knew what that meant. A client was arriving. Two white security guards emerged into the sunshine. Both wore ballistic vests and didn't venture far from the doors as they scanned the crowd for Con.

She didn't dare call out to them. Not yet anyway. Not until she was much, much closer. She knew exactly how the protesters would respond if they realized that the enemy walked among them. The main entrance was rarely used, so these protests were a frustrating, thankless vigil; they would be eager to put a face to their rage. Con pulled the brim of her cap low over her eyes. Not that anyone was likely to recognize her, but the possibility scared her enough to keep photographs of every outfit she wore to her monthly appointments, careful never to wear the same thing twice.

The crowd surged forward, lifting Con off her feet and knocking the wind out of her. She'd been in enough mosh pits to know better than to fight against the tide. Safer to be carried along, conserving energy, and wait for an opportunity to swim for shore.

"No birth, no soul! No birth, no soul!"

"God doesn't want you!"

"Pretentious meat!"

With each chant, the crowd took another step forward. By law, protesters were required to remain forty feet back from the clinic doors, but the police, who mostly sided with the demonstration, had better things to do than enforce the legal buffer zone. Normally it didn't matter. No one who could afford Palingenesis's services arrived on foot. The clientele was nine-digit wealthy and preferred the private underground parking garage to avoid all the ugliness out front.

Except for Con, of course. Her bank account rarely broke three digits and some days barely two. She couldn't even afford a new used scooter after her last one had been stolen. So to keep her monthly appointments, she had no choice but to run this gauntlet. Not that running was something she did well anymore, but she still had a little fight left in her. Elbowing her way through a gap, she emerged at the front of the protest. The doors, and the safety of the guards, beckoned only a short distance away.

Con made a break for it, hobbling for the door and pleading with her reconstructed knee not to lock up. Realizing they had been deceived, the demonstrators roared. It was a terrible, prehistoric sound, and Con braced for the hands that would drag her back into the protest's maw. This was the part she hated most. When all eyes would be on her. Ironic considering how much she loved to be on stage. She had sung for audiences as large as five thousand, yet this crowd, no more than four hundred strong, made her stomach seize up. But then the guards spotted her and rushed forward, each taking an arm, and bundled her inside as the crowd howled for blood.

The soundproof doors sealed closed behind them, silencing the din of the protesters. In the abrupt calm, Con looked questioningly at the guards.

"What's going on out there?" she asked, trying to catch her breath.

"You didn't hear?" the taller of the two said. "Abigail Stickling died last night."

"Died?" his partner said. "You mean base-jumped off the Monroe Hotel without a parachute."

Con was stunned at the news, but it explained why there were so many protesters this morning. Dr. Abigail Stickling, the mother of human cloning and co-founder of Palingenesis, the bogeyman who haunted so many conspiracy theories, was dead. A suicide. This would be a day of triumphant celebration for the CoA and anyone else who believed human cloning to be an abomination.

"Either that or she forgot her broomstick," the first guard said.

His partner snickered and made a whistling noise of something plummeting to the ground. Con walked away without a word, and the guards fell silent behind her. Good, she thought. Abigail Stickling might be a controversial figure, but she was also Con's aunt. So the hell with the guards and their petty cruelty. The irony, though, was that Con shared similar thoughts about her aunt, a woman she barely knew beyond what she read in the media.

The last time she'd seen her aunt had been the commotion at her father's funeral. An ugly fight had erupted between her mother and her aunt before the service. To this day, Con didn't know what had set her mother off, but having grown up with her, she knew it wouldn't have taken much. The Sticklings were a large clan—two sisters and four brothers—that enjoyed the spectacle of taking sides. Con's uncles had all rallied around the grieving widow and against Abigail, who everyone agreed had put on airs since moving to Boston for school. It was also agreed that her interest in human cloning, still in the theoretical stages, was a sin of pride—a wretched befoulment of God's design.

In the end, Abigail had been permanently disinvited from her parents' home. Her name wasn't to be spoken, her existence not to be acknowledged in any way. Everything Con knew about her aunt she'd learned either from the media or else from Gamma Jol, her father's mother. Gamma Jol had never wanted anything to do with the Sticklings in the first place, her son's courtship of Mary an enduring mystery. Perhaps that was why she took such pleasure in answering all the questions her granddaughter couldn't ask anyone else.

For her part, Abigail had taken her shunning in stride and left West Texas, never to return. It had made her an inspiration of sorts to Con six years later when she'd rebelled against her mother's strict expectations and gone to live with Gamma Jol. She'd resolved to follow her aunt's example by getting out of Lanesboro and making something of herself, only her route would be music, not science. Her aunt had gotten out alright. She'd become both world famous and phenomenally wealthy, and she'd never spoken to anyone in the family again.

Not one solitary word.

Until the letters arrived.

Two years ago, lawyers had turned up at the doorstep of every member of the family, bearing legal paperwork gifting each with a clone. Con had to hand it to her aunt. What was the market price of an individual clone? Twenty-five, thirty million? No one in the family had ever had money, so to an outsider, it would've looked like an extraordinarily generous and extravagant gesture. To the family, however, it was

Abigail rubbing her success in their faces by offering the one thing that none of them would ever accept.

If there was any doubt of her aunt's intentions, the accompanying letter was a masterpiece of score-settling that perfectly encapsulated the resentments that had riven the family for decades. Con remembered the last sentence verbatim: *I hope this small token of my affection allows you all to live long, long lives wallowing in your collective mediocrity.* Apparently, Con's mother wasn't the only one in the family who could hold a grudge.

Con alone had accepted her aunt's gift despite, or perhaps because of, it being wrapped in an emphatic *fuck you*. The mixed-race daughter of a fire-breathing white evangelical and a half-Black, half-Vietnamese army corporal, Con had grown up an outsider, contending with tormenters of every age and race. She'd had to fight her way through school. Too small to win most of them, she'd learned the art of survival instead. Stubbornness was a rich vein of ore running through both sides of her family, and Con mined it for the will to endure anything. Setting her jaw, she willed her way through childhood following three simple rules: never cry in public; never ask for help; never, ever give them the satisfaction of knowing they'd gotten to her. So when the taunting letter from her aunt had arrived, Con recognized the work of a bully. She tore up the letter and took the clone even though she wasn't sure why she wanted it.

Since Con had been in DC, her aunt had never once reached out to her. Not even when Con was convalescing in the hospital following the operations to reattach her leg. And in the two years that she had been coming to Palingenesis to refresh her upload, Abigail had never emerged from her laboratories to say so much as hello. Outside Palingenesis's windows, the great tent of umbrellas trembled in frustration, and once again, Con thought of birds. Only, this time, it was of the ravens that sometimes gathered along the Texas highways of her childhood, waiting on a dying animal to give it up. What had Gamma Jol called a group of ravens? An unkindness? Yes, she thought, that sounded about right.

CHAPTER THREE

The genius of Palingenesis was that it felt more like an upscale day spa than a clinic. Instead of a sterile waiting room, Con was let into a sweeping atrium that was always a sun-dappled dawn, courtesy of photosensitive skylights that adjusted throughout the day. The sound of a waterfall cascading gently into a koi pond set into the center of the floor echoed soothingly off the rough-hewn limestone walls. Shallow alcoves displayed arrangements of sclera-white orchids in blue china pots and willow branches in glass vases. No hint that, deep in the bowels of the building, the laws of nature were being systematically rewritten.

The atrium had no reception desk, but Con knew the drill. She sat patiently on the ledge of the pond, skimming her fingertips across the water and watching the orange-and-white fish cavort beneath emerald lily pads. She hummed part of a tune to a new song she'd been working on. It had no lyrics yet, but the guards' jokes about her aunt kept coming back to her: *a witch without a broom, a witch without a broom.* Words began to string themselves together in her mind as they always did when she felt inspired, and she sang quietly to herself, testing how they fit the melody. There might be something there. She wondered if she'd get in trouble if she brought her guitar next time. The acoustics were spectacular.

Curious what the rest of the world was saying about her aunt's death, Con searched for articles on her LFD. In the weeks to come, there would be time for long-form opinion pieces about Abigail Stickling's impact on American life, but it had only been a matter of hours, so most news outlets carried only bullet-point accounts of the suicide. The gist was that at 11:34 p.m. on December 25, contentious inventor of human cloning Abigail Stickling had taken her own life, jumping from the roof of the historic Monroe Hotel. Witnesses reported that Dr. Stickling had sat at the bar of Skyline, the popular restaurant overlooking the White House, chatting with bartenders and drinking champagne. After paying her tab, she'd gained access to the roof, where she jumped to her death. There were links to security camera footage from the restaurant, but Con had no desire to click on any of them.

One article noted that Abigail had never married, nor was she close to her family. That was putting it mildly, Con thought. A second article said that her aunt had been battling depression in the last few years (something else they had in common). It went on to mention that, as a child, Abigail had been diagnosed with Wilson's disease, a rare genetic disorder that caused a buildup of copper in the body and brain. It could be managed with medication, but the copper interfered with the cloning process, so, the article took unseemly pleasure in explaining, unlike Palingenesis's clients, Abigail Stickling would not be coming back. Con shut off her LFD, unsure why she suddenly felt protective of her aunt.

On the far side of the pond, a silver-haired white man in a terry-cloth robe struggled to fill out the client paperwork on his LFD. Con gave him points for trying. A lot of people over forty had a hard time with next-gen light-field devices and clung to their legacy smartphones rather than adapting. She watched him adjust the fit of his LFD, which rested behind the ear like an old-fashioned hearing aid and projected data to a floating point six inches in front of the user's eyes. When that didn't solve his problem, he reached out with both hands like he was trying to feel his way in the dark. It really wasn't necessary. LFDs were paired to their users and would read hand movements from any position. Kids who had grown up with the technology were blindingly fast, all ten fingers working independently, hands fluttering at their sides. But for older users like the silver fox over there, the need to "touch" the screen was hard to break. The results could be hilariously uncoordinated. Exactly why kids mocked their parents as "zombs" for the way they flailed their arms in front of their faces.

The man noticed Con watching and frowned as if he'd caught her peeking in his bedroom window. He looked at her worn-at-the-knee jeans and black T-shirt, deciding everything about her that needed deciding. The wealthy sensed poverty the way other people smelled something that had soured at the back of a refrigerator. Con had read somewhere that the average net worth of Palingenesis's clientele was five hundred million—cheating death didn't come cheap.

Her LFD buzzed, and Con checked the ID. *Kala Solomon.* At this hour? It must be an emergency, and Con could guess what kind. Against her better judgment, Con resisted the urge to let it go to voice mail. LFDs transmitted sound via bone conduction, sending vibrations directly to the inner ear, which as a musician, Con didn't think she'd ever get entirely used to.

"Con?" Kala sounded like the last survivor of a sinking ship. "I'm really sorry for calling so early."

"Hey," Con said, conscious of how voices traveled in the atrium.

"Can you hear me? You're really faint."

"Sorry, I'm in a waiting room."

"Everything okay?"

"Yeah, just my annual," Con lied. Having a clone wasn't anything she talked about to anyone. Not everyone was a member of Children of Adam, but the subject was a third rail and it was impossible to predict how anyone felt about it. "What's up? Everything okay with you?"

"It's Trina," Kala answered, confirming Con's suspicions.

Trina was the singer in Kala's band, Weathervane. They weren't bad. A little green, but Con dug their sound, a wild blend of country and go-go—Lucinda Williams meets Chuck Brown—that worked better than it had any business doing. Trina was gorgeous. A magnetic presence on stage with a huge voice, but she was also the Mayan apocalypse of lead singers. Kala spent half her time micromanaging Trina's mood swings and supernatural pharmaceutical intake.

"What happened now?" Con asked.

"I don't know. I can't find her."

"Any sightings in New York?" The last time, Kala had tracked Trina down in Harlem after a two-week bender.

"She'll turn up when she's ready," Kala replied diplomatically. "Thing is, we have gigs every night between now and the thirtieth. So naturally, Trina would pick this as the time to bug out."

"The holidays are hard," Con commiserated, bracing herself for the inevitable question.

"So will you do it?" Kala said. "I know it's short notice again, but you killed last time. It was unbelievable. The crowd ate you up. Everyone's still talking about it."

Con rolled her eyes. She'd been the guitarist in one lousy band. A band that hadn't ever gotten around to recording its debut album. Yet despite that, or perhaps because of it, she got her ass kissed by every musician in DC who had bought into the morbid hype surrounding Awaken the Ghosts. Personally, Con thought the band was overrated, tragedy lending them more significance than they deserved. Or maybe it was just easier to believe they never would have amounted to anything because now they never would.

"Please?" Kala said, on the verge of begging.

Con had been scrolling through her list of prefab excuses, so it surprised her when her mouth opened and said yes. She hadn't been on stage in a while. Maybe that was part of the reason she'd been so down. Performing always buoyed her spirits; hopefully it would help shake off her holiday depression.

"You will?" Kala said and thanked her a hundred different ways.

"But only until the thirtieth," Con qualified.

19

"Of course," Kala said, relieved and excited. "Oh man, I owe you so huge." She filled Con in on the details and promised to send her the set list for tonight.

Before Con had time to think about what she'd just gotten herself into, seams appeared in the far wall. A door swung open silently, and Laleh Askari emerged. Although she was a registered nurse, her official job title was steward. Instead of hospital scrubs, Laleh wore a sapphire-blue pencil skirt and an egg-yolk-yellow blouse, lustrous black hair piled high on her head, held in place with a single surgically positioned gold pin. Her heels made no more sound than ballet slippers on the stone floors. Con admired Laleh's dedicated retro flair. It wasn't a look Con could pull off, but Laleh made it look effortless. Con was a master of the dark art of looking like she was too cool to care how she dressed. Women knew the difference, of course, but men were never any the wiser.

"Hello, Constance! Happy holidays," Laleh said, her accent a silken blend of British and Iranian. Palingenesis prided itself on its personal touch. Laleh had been Con's steward since her first appointment and always greeted her as if they were old friends unexpectedly reunited. Except that Con's friends knew not to call her Constance. Con hated it—a family name from her mother's side, which had a tradition of saddling girls with old-timey names: Chastity, Charity, Faith. It made her sound like a pioneer settler trudging wearily across the Great Plains in search of a simple life. She hadn't gone by her full name since the day she'd stopped singing in the church choir. She'd been a star since she was a precocious seven-year-old, but it hadn't been until her twelfth birthday that it occurred to Con that her voice was the only value her mother saw in her. Con had quit to test the theory, and nothing that followed had done anything to change her mind.

"I'm so, so sorry about your aunt," Laleh said. "We can absolutely reschedule."

"I'm fine," Con said, although she was a little taken aback. She didn't know why she assumed no one at Palingenesis knew her relationship to their founder. Laleh had never mentioned it before now.

"I understand. It would just be a shame if you had to repeat the procedure because your refresh was corrupted."

To make an accurate image of a human consciousness, a subject had to be both consenting and in a calm frame of mind. Palingenesis covered this ad nauseam during orientation, but Con didn't see how it applied in this situation. It wasn't as if she and her aunt had been close.

"Honestly? I haven't seen my aunt since I was six. It's sad, obviously, but I'm not upset. It's not like I knew her."

Laleh nodded and led her to the changing room. In the time it took to refresh Con's neural record, her clothes would be pressed and waiting for her. Dry-cleaning jeans and a T-shirt seemed a little excessive, but the service was complimentary, so she went with the flow. Stripping to her underwear, Con examined herself in the mirror. She'd put on fifteen pounds in the years since the accident and didn't like how it looked or felt. Tentatively, she flexed her right leg, which was already sore from her mad dash through the protesters. Her scars twisted like barbed wire—the reason she hadn't worn a skirt since the wreck. After she'd been discharged from the hospital, Con had blown off physical therapy and allowed her new knee to atrophy. Like everything else, it was her own damn fault that her leg was chronically stiff and uncooperative, but maybe after New Year's, she'd try again to get into some kind of a workout routine.

Absently, she ran a hand down her left arm—the sleeve of tattoos was almost complete; only a few gaps remained. If you knew how to read it, the sleeve told her story and that of her family going back generations, spun from threads reaching across three continents. At her wrist, a lion held a yellow flower in its jaws and clutched a red lotus in its talons—the Barbary lion, the official symbol of England, where her mother's family originated. The red lotus represented Vietnam, and the yellow trumpet was the national flower of Nigeria—the ancestral homes of her paternal grandfather and grandmother, respectively. Circling her bicep was her father's story, which she'd learned not from her mother but from countless hours at Gamma Jol's kitchen table. After her grandmother passed, Con had hated the idea of that history being lost. The tattoos were one way of keeping it alive while adding her own chapter. She traced the pattern on her shoulder, where she had memorialized the tragic car crash that had changed her life.

Con slipped on a backless hospital gown and then a monogrammed bathrobe and slippers. She loved these bathrobes. It was like being swaddled in a warm cloud. She would have stolen one already had it not been too luxuriously bulky to hide. Funny thing was, Con was sure Laleh would've been delighted to give her one, only her pride wouldn't allow it. She was too keenly aware of her poverty to ask for gifts.

Back in the atrium, Laleh settled Con in a plush armchair and threw today's menu from her LFD to Con's. It popped up in Con's field of vision, and she gave it a quick read despite already knowing exactly what she wanted. Out in the real world, Con couldn't afford to splurge on sushi, but Palingenesis kept a chef on staff. They never used a food printer and served authentic farm-grown tuna. She ordered rainbow rolls and edamame. She would have killed for some warm sake to take the edge off, but alcohol was prohibited twelve hours before a refresh. She winced and counted backward. What time had she quit drinking last night? She should be fine by the time the procedure began.

"Mani-pedi?" Laleh asked. Another of the many amenities provided to distract clients from the real reason for their visit. Better to focus on freshly pressed clothes, cozy bathrobes, and the soothing beauty of Japanese koi. It had taken a while to come around on someone touching her while she was unconscious, but waking up to her nails being done was too good to pass up.

"I was thinking maybe a light orange."

Laleh noted Con's selection, then hesitated. "Confession."

"That sounds ominous."

"I looked up Awaken the Ghosts and listened to some of your old songs."

"Oh yeah? You didn't have to do that," Con said, although what she meant was *I wish you hadn't done that.*

"Seriously," Laleh said. "You guys were amazing. I get why there was all that buzz around your band. Your voice is beautiful."

"Thanks," Con replied, hoping that would be the end of it.

"Do you still sing?"

Con nodded, reluctant to get on this subject. She'd tried to quit music after the accident, but it was a part of her that she found impossible to leave behind. It would have been easier to live without her leg. Still, she avoided the kind of music that had landed Awaken the Ghosts its recording contract, instead gigging with local bands that didn't have a prayer of making it. That kept her safe, or so she told herself.

"Will you tell me the next time you've got a show? I'd love to come."

"I will," Con said, neglecting to mention the shows she'd just agreed to do with Weathervane.

Laleh smiled, sensing she'd crossed a line. "Okay, well, anyway, I really loved it. I'll be back in a few. Why don't you get started?"

Before every refresh, there were always the same forms to fill out, the same waivers to be signed. *Initial here to indemnify Palingenesis in the event that the refresh accidentally turns your brain into a three-cheese omelet.* It went on for pages and pages like that in mind-numbing legalese. Laleh threw the forms to Con's LFD and excused herself. Con took off her slippers, tucked her feet under her, and opened the first page, the medical questionnaire.

Name?

Constance Ada D'Arcy

Age / Date of Birth?

22 / January 10, 2016

It informed her that her last refresh was forty-four days ago. An exhaustive, boilerplate disclaimer popped up, stating that Palingenesis strongly recommended gaps of no more than thirty days between refreshes to avoid neurological and psychological complications with the clone. In the event of the client's untimely death, Palingenesis would not revive their clone if it had been more than ninety days since their last refresh. In legal terms, you'd be shit out of luck. Con skipped to the bottom and checked the box affirming that she had read and understood the risks.

She did understand and lately had begun to wonder why she kept taking them. That was the reason she was two weeks late for her monthly refresh. She'd been debating whether to quit outright and move on with her life. But she couldn't quite bring herself to do it. She knew it had something to do with the crash. Having a backup at the ready felt reassuring even if the ethics of human cloning troubled her. And she couldn't be the only client who felt this way. There was a reason why Palingenesis worked so hard to make you forget why you were there. She couldn't remember a single time she'd heard or read the word *clone*. Everything was dressed up in euphemistic language: *backups* and *stewards* and *refreshes*. All designed to dance clients away from the disconcerting fact that, close by, their inanimate doppelgänger waited in the event that disaster struck.

Laleh returned and set down a silver tray. Five pills were arranged tastefully on a cloth napkin—the *Alice in Wonderland* meds that would put Con's mind in a relaxed and conducive state. Even with the drugs, an upload couldn't be made of an unwilling consciousness, but the drugs smoothed the way. Laleh waited until Con had taken the pills before excusing herself again, saying she would return after Con had finished her paperwork.

"All set?" Laleh asked.

Con's head jerked up. She'd been daydreaming when she should have been filling out the forms. Her eyes felt too small in their sockets.

"What? No, I still haven't eaten yet," Con said, pointing to a serving tray that was empty apart from sliced ginger and a dollop of wasabi. Who ate her sushi? She looked around for the culprit. The old man in the bathrobe had also disappeared. Coincidence? Con frowned. But on her LFD, a green halo indicated the forms were complete. When had she finished filling them out? She noticed how thick her tongue felt and smacked her lips together, enjoying the sound it made.

"You're so beautiful," she told Laleh. "You're the queen of pencil skirts."

Lowered inhibitions were a side effect of the drugs, along with short-term memory loss. Perhaps that was why she didn't remember taking the pills in the first place. Con wanted more than anything to yank out that gold pin and see Laleh's hair tumble down around her shoulders.

"Thank you," Laleh said sweetly, kneeling to help Con with her slippers.

"So you know how much this place sucks, right?" Con whispered conspiratorially.

"Alright, then," Laleh said with the indulgent chuckle you saved for a three-year-old who had stripped naked in a family restaurant. "Time for a little trip. Are you ready?"

"Sooo ready," Con said in a singsong voice.

She stood, swaying unsteadily on her feet, and all but fell into the waiting wheelchair. Laleh rolled her down a corridor that seemed to get longer the farther they went. The drugs again, flattening and lengthening her vision as if Con were standing between two mirrors. Laleh steered her gently into the refresh suite that would be her home for the next six hours until she was medically cleared to leave.

Laleh removed Con's LFD and helped her out of the bathrobe. Con fell happily into the ergonomic seat that looked like a dentist's chair no matter how hard Palingenesis worked to disguise it. Laleh began configuring the refresh, her fingers dancing in the air like she was practicing scales on a piano. Sensors snaked up from the headrest, attaching themselves to Con's neck and scalp like a giant millipede spooning her spine. It should have been creepy as hell, but the safe haze of drugs made it feel like dozens of fingers massaging her back. A smooth, featureless pillar descended from the ceiling and stopped twelve inches from her forehead. Con heard a gentle hum, and her vitals populated a screen set into the wall, which was only there to make the client feel secure.

Dr. Qiao appeared at her elbow and asked how she felt. Laleh was Con's steward, but Qiao ran this branch and oversaw every refresh personally. He linked to Laleh's LFD, double-checking her settings. His reassuring fatherly presence and practiced bedside manner always helped put Con at ease. She needed all the help she could get. They were about to upload a perfect image of her consciousness, her memories, everything that made her *her*, and store it in a quantum mainframe on the off chance that she died between now and her next appointment.

If she were to die, a biometric chip implanted in her neck would register her death and notify Palingenesis, which would immediately download her stored consciousness into her clone so that life could go on as seamlessly as possible. Con giggled at the thought. The drugs again. It wasn't funny, but it was. Life would go on. It was all so morbidly funny.

"Quiet now, Constance," Dr. Qiao said. "Remember your breathing."

"Sorry, Doctor," she said.

"Do you consent to the refresh?" he asked.

"I do."

"Good. We'll see you in a few hours."

David Bowie's "The Man Who Sold the World" began to play. Music had been found to be an effective lubricant during a refresh, and clients were encouraged to create a personalized playlist. Con couldn't think of a more appropriate soundtrack for making a copy of her brain than David Bowie. He had died the same day she'd been born. As a kid, that had seemed deeply significant, and like generations of outcasts before her, his music had reassured her that there was strength to be had in being different. She'd won her first talent contest performing a cover of "Heroes." It had scandalized her mother, but by then, Con was past caring. Or perhaps it was more honest to say that she was beyond admitting that she cared. If there was an art to hardening yourself entirely against a parent's disappointment, she hadn't learned it.

Zhi had loved David Bowie just as much as she did. Their shared love of the Thin White Duke had been what drew them together initially. They'd met the first week of her freshman year at UT Austin. Her new friend Stephie Martz introduced them on a Thursday, and by Sunday, they were inseparable. Zhi had been the first person who could keep up with her encyclopedic, esoteric musical tastes. They'd talked for twelve straight hours that first night, passing a guitar back and forth to play the other a song. It had been the best night of her life. The night that her horizons truly opened beyond the borders of her dusty, three-street hometown. On Sunday night, Zhi had confessed that he was putting together a band with his roommate, Hugh Balzan. Their guitarist hadn't worked out, and their first show was set for the following weekend. That's why Stephie had introduced them.

"So this was just an audition?" she asked, both exhilarated and disappointed.

"At first," he said, and then they'd kissed, warm in the glow of the possible. She was eighteen and her life had finally begun.

Trying to be cool, trying to play off that she'd felt the kiss dance down her spine like chain lightning, Con asked if the band had a name. Zhi shook his head and said that everything they'd come up with so far was terrible. Con suggested a quote from an old Bowie interview—how music awakened the ghosts inside him: "Not the demons, you understand, but the ghosts." Zhi had loved it. Awaken the Ghosts had played its first show the next Saturday at a small club on Sixth Street in Austin. It didn't go great, but they all felt the potential. When Tommy Diop joined on keyboards the following month, they established the sound that would set the band on its way.

It pained her that she could remember Zhi's first words to her but not his last. He had become both one of her ghosts and one of her demons, and she felt suffocated by his memory. God, how she missed him.

She felt her skin prickle as the refresh began, and her vision hollowed. The last thing she remembered was Laleh telling her that she would check in on her in a few hours.

Then came darkness.

CHAPTER FOUR

As Con clawed her way up the gray tunnel toward awareness, she knew something was very wrong. The hangover effect after refreshing her upload was rarely pleasant, but it had never been this bad before. Not even close. Her head felt waterlogged, and a steady pressure was building against her temples. Drip, drip, drip. Her brain felt as if it had been crammed into a soggy matchbox. No, not her brain. Her mind. And it wanted out, bad.

She yawned uncontrollably. That much was normal. Even though a refresh bore a superficial resemblance to slow-wave sleep, it wasn't restful. They'd explained it during orientation—how suppressing the prefrontal cortex simulated sleep while the rest of the brain lit up like a slot machine hitting a million-dollar jackpot. Which was why it felt less like waking up and more a guided tour of the world's largest tequila distillery.

When she opened her eyes, her eyelashes were crusted shut as though she'd been crying. It happened. Palingenesis called it *autonomic emotional response*, a side effect of the intense stimulation of the hippocampus. Con just called it draining. Though the lights were dimmed, their glare cut into her retinas like rescue flares. She raised her hand to shield her eyes, but her arm didn't respond. She couldn't even feel it. As if nothing at all existed below her shoulder. She tried to lift her head to confirm that she still had arms, but her neck wouldn't obey either. A terrible thought occurred to her. There'd been a malfunction. They'd fried her somehow. She squeezed her eyes shut and tried to remain calm.

Palingenesis billed uploads as routine outpatient procedures. Sure, there had been mistakes in the early days that had left smoking vegetables in the chair—cut and paste instead of copy and paste. But Palingenesis claimed it had resolved those issues and that the latest generation had upload errors of less than 0.0000004536 percent. Con had memorized the number because there was comfort in its infinitesimal smallness. There was a better chance of a shark attack on a mountaintop than of a neural lobotomy during a refresh. Or so Palingenesis assured its clients.

The sound of voices encouraged her to reopen her eyes. A man and a woman came gradually into focus. Con didn't recognize either of them, but more ominously, neither was Laleh Askari. Worse still, both wore white lab coats over hospital scrubs. No one dressed like a doctor at Palingenesis. Ever. It was part of their shtick to distract clients from thinking about where they were. That alone frightened Con more than how bad she felt. She opened her mouth to ask what had gone wrong, but all that came out was a low, grinding moan. *Wonderful.* The lab techs glanced briefly at her, then returned to their LFDs. Con decided to give establishing first contact one more shot.

"Where is Dr. Qiao?" she croaked. Not pretty, but progress.

The female tech looked at her partner questioningly.

He explained, "Qiao used to work here. Left before you hired on."

The female tech made an alarmed face. "How far back does this one go?"

"Eighteen months."

"No," the female tech said. "That's not possible."

"That's what her time stamp says."

"That's insane. Who authorized this?"

"The process is automated," he reminded her.

"Yeah, but there are safety checks in place."

"Well, someone screwed up," he agreed. "Royally."

Con hated being talked about like she wasn't even there. "Hello," she said. "Hello!"

The two techs fell silent.

"Would one of you explain what the hell is going on? What did you do to . . . ? Why can't . . ." She stuttered over her next word like a hiccup. ". . . move? Where's Dr. Qiao?" They'd said he'd left the company, but she must have misunderstood.

The male tech glanced at his partner before answering. "Dr. Qiao doesn't work here anymore."

"What are you talking about? . . . saw him this morning. Where is he?" Con demanded.

"He took a job in California."

"In the last six hours?" Her voice growing stronger by the word. Maybe she wasn't completely screwed.

"Nine months ago," he said, almost apologetically.

The hairs on Con's shoulders stood up. Ironically, the first sensation she'd felt below the neck since waking. They really *had* fried her. That was the only explanation. She looked around, taking in her surroundings. This wasn't the recovery suite. It looked like a surgical theater—white and immaculate. Machines and monitors everywhere. They'd fried her, and then they'd moved her here. Con tried to sit up, but her body still wasn't taking requests. Her fingers and toes began to tingle painfully as if all her limbs had fallen asleep and blood was beginning to flow back into them. Panic took hold of her. Alarms on the monitors began to squawk.

"She's going to stroke out," the female tech said.

"Miss D'Arcy? Miss D'Arcy! You have to try and calm down," the male tech told her.

"What did you do to . . . ?" Con stuttered again, unable to finish the sentence. It felt like a scratch in one of Gamma Jol's old records.

"Everything's going to be okay. But you have to calm down and breathe. Can you do that for me?"

"What did you do?" she repeated. "How did you mess up a simple refresh?"

The male tech cleared his throat, but his partner cut him off. "Don't. We're not supposed to be the ones."

"Well, where's the counselor?" he said. "Someone should be here already. She needs to know what's going on. It's cruel."

"Yeah, but not us. It's a huge break in protocol."

"She's at eighteen months. I'd say protocol's already broken, wouldn't you?"

"You're going to get us both fired."

"I'll tell them it was all me, okay?" He looked Con in the eye until she met his gaze. "Miss D'Arcy, this isn't an upload. It's your download. Welcome back."

Con stared at him uncomprehendingly. It wasn't that she didn't understand the words, but she was slow to make sense of what he was telling her. Or maybe it was that she didn't want to accept it, because she recoiled angrily.

"No," Con said. "No, there's been a mistake." They thought she was a clone. That was insane. She needed to tell them there'd been some kind of mix-up. Some kind of clerical error. She hadn't died. She was only here for a routine upload. She was right here. She was the original, not a clone. She was Con D'Arcy. *The* Con D'Arcy. This was a mistake.

"No mistake," he said. "I promise."

"No, listen to . . . It's a—"

The doors to the surgical theater were flung open by a white woman in a conservative gray suit. Both lab techs took a deferential step back.

"Dr. Fenton," they greeted her in unison.

Dr. Fenton ordered them out of the lab with a snap of her fingers; they fled without a word. Con let her head roll to the side so she could get a better look. The doctor was thin as a railroad spike and appeared to be constructed entirely of right angles. In her late fifties, she had a gaunt, unforgiving face that looked like it had been buffeted by the constant inadequacy of everyone around her. Three grim-faced doctors and a young assistant slunk in after her like beaten dogs.

"Why is it awake?" Fenton asked.

Con's left hand curled into a fist. She didn't think she and this Dr. Fenton were going to be friends.

"The download started automatically," said a tall Indian doctor. A sheen of nervous sweat coated his forehead. He looked around for confirmation from his colleagues, who offered none.

"I know *how* a download works, Dr. Pranav," Fenton snapped. "*Why* did it start automatically? Why wasn't this account locked out?"

"I don't know, Dr. Fenton. It just wasn't done."

"It just wasn't done?" Fenton said, eyes narrowing. "Say that again, Bob."

Dr. Pranav declined to say it again. "I know, I—"

"You are responsible for this branch and everything that happens in it," Fenton said, her voice gaveling him into silence. "Well, this is a goddamn mess."

No one disagreed with her assessment. Least of all Con, who listened with horrified fascination.

"Have every client's status reviewed," Dr. Fenton continued. "I want to know whether this was an isolated human error or if this is a system-wide glitch. Or if, God forbid, we've been compromised."

"That's impossible," Dr. Pranav said.

"Nothing is impossible until it's been ruled out," Fenton countered.

"Will someone tell . . . what's going on?" Con asked.

No one acknowledged the question much less answered her.

". . . talking to you!"

Still no answer. This was a living nightmare. She was like a specimen pinned down on a dissecting tray, unable to move, listening to these ghouls discuss her clinically. Her right hand spasmed, gripping the side of the examination table.

"Who is the steward?" Fenton asked.

The assistant pulled up the information on his LFD. "Laleh Askari. It's her day off, but she's on her way in now."

Relief flooded Con. Laleh would be here soon. Laleh would listen to her. She would explain to them how this was all some terrible misunderstanding.

"How are its stats?" Fenton asked.

"Inconclusive," the assistant said, throwing the chart to Fenton's LFD.

Fenton swiped through it with a manicured index finger. "How old are these neurologicals?"

"Initial readings, so twelve hours plus," Dr. Pranav said.

"Alright," Fenton said with a funereal sigh. "Rerun all of these tests every six hours. Let's see if there's any improvement after thirty-six hours."

"Yes, Dr. Fenton."

"Wait," Fenton said, something in Con's chart catching her eye. "This is Abigail Stickling's niece?"

None of the assembled doctors seemed to know, and all pulled up the chart on their LFDs.

"It appears so. She must have been a client of my predecessor, Dr. Qiao," Dr. Pranav agreed, clearly delighted to foist the responsibility off on anyone else.

For the first time, Fenton looked unsure. Everyone waited in awkward silence.

"Dr. Fenton? What is it?" Dr. Pranav asked.

Fenton waved him off. "I want to see Laleh Askari the instant she arrives. Until then, no one goes in and no one comes out."

"What about the client?"

Fenton looked at Con with dispassionate, calculating eyes. "Put it back under until I've had a chance to talk to the board."

The doctors murmured their agreement, but Fenton was already halfway to the door, leaving them to scurry after her. Con struggled to sit up, but her arms still weren't responding. She lay there in stunned disbelief as the doors swung back and forth, the sound of voices growing more distant.

"Wait," Con said, a terrible feeling of loneliness settling into her joints. The lab tech's words echoed in her ears: *It's your download. Welcome back.*

The female tech returned, alone now. She gave Con a wide berth. She reconnected her LFD to the surgical theater and kept her back to Con while she entered instructions.

". . . not a clone," Con told her, stuttering again.

The lab tech flinched but didn't answer. Con wrestled herself into a sitting position. This time, her arms pushed down obediently on the table. She felt a gentle tug and looked down at IVs inserted at the back of her hand and the crook of her arm. She had to disconnect them before the tech could sedate her again.

She froze.

Her tattoos were missing. All of them, the entire sleeve. Her left arm was bare. More than that—it was pristine. Her nails weren't orange either, but they were unnaturally long. How had they grown so fast? She put a fumbling hand to her earlobe and felt along the cartilage. Her piercings were gone too. She couldn't even feel where the holes should be. She checked her leg and hit a snag that threatened to unravel her. There were no scars on her knee. As though the accident had never happened. But it had, so what did that mean?

You know what it means.

A blanket of fog was settling over her thoughts, the sedatives taking effect. Her arms gave out, and she fell back on the table. There could only be one explanation. A terrible, unavoidable explanation.

She had died.

Not her.

The other her. The original her.

And if Con D'Arcy was dead, what did that make her?

Thankfully, the sedative did its work before she could answer.

CHAPTER FIVE

When Con awoke in the surgical suite for the second time, Laleh stood over her. Her hair had been cut short to her shoulders, which made no sense until Con remembered it had been eighteen months since they'd seen each other. It was hard to keep straight because her memories felt so recent. As if only a few hours had passed since she'd arrived at Palingenesis to refresh her upload. She could still taste the wasabi on her tongue, although that was quite impossible. It wasn't even the same tongue.

"Welcome back, Constance." Laleh was trimming Con's fingernails quickly and methodically.

"It's true, isn't it?"

"Yes, Constance." Laleh nodded, clipping the last nail.

"How did . . . die?"

"We don't have time for that right now, Constance."

"How?" Con demanded.

Laleh glanced nervously at the door. "I swear I don't know. Your biometric chip registered a death event twenty hours ago. The company doesn't wait to find out the details; the download begins automatically. You know that. We have to go now, Constance. Can you walk?"

". . . haven't tried," Con stuttered. "Why can't . . . say . . . ?"

"Can you do something for me, Constance?" Laleh said.

Con nodded rather than risk more stuttering. She had no idea why Laleh kept saying her name over and over. It had a ritualistic quality to it like a mantra or a meditative chant, and each time Laleh repeated her name, it sounded like a bell in her head, soothing and clear.

"Tell me who you are, Constance," Laleh said.

Con had expected some kind of physiological test. "That's all?"

"That's all, Constance."

Con opened her mouth but couldn't even force out the first syllable. Sweat broke out on her forehead. She shut her mouth rather than leave it hanging open stupidly.

"Con. Stance," Laleh prompted, breaking the name into more manageable pieces.

It didn't help.

"I . . . am . . . ," Laleh said, nodding along. She waited a moment and prompted her again.

On the third try, Con said it with her. Haltingly, like a rusted-out engine.

"I . . . am . . ."

"Good job. Now the rest," Laleh encouraged. "Constance."

Con could have sung "Station to Station" in the time it took her to say her own name. It was humiliating, and she was flushed and embarrassed when she was done.

Laleh smiled encouragingly. "Good. Good, that's a great start. I want you to practice on your own: 'I am Constance D'Arcy.' Work up to ten repetitions in a row."

"What's wrong with . . ." The word *me* caught in her throat.

"Personal pronouns. Names. They're difficult in the early going. We're not sure why, but you need to practice thinking about yourself as Constance Ada D'Arcy."

Con wanted to tell Laleh that was stupid. That she knew exactly who she was. But the words refused to cooperate. Her frustration must have shown on her face, because Laleh squeezed her shoulder reassuringly.

"It'll be alright, Constance. Everyone goes through this at first. Revival is not as seamless as they make it sound in the brochures." As she talked, Laleh helped her into a sitting position and began unhooking the IVs. "But in a couple of days, things will get easier. I promise. Your new brain grew twenty-four years' worth of neural pathways in a very short period of time. The mind-body relationship is incredibly delicate, and even with drug therapies, it's a massive shock to the system. Ordinarily, we would have a counselor to help you work through it, but there isn't time now."

"Why not?" Con asked, afraid of the answer.

"Because if we don't get you out of here, Dr. Fenton is going to delete you."

"Delete . . . ?" she stuttered.

"Can you stand up, Constance?" Laleh asked, helping her off the table.

Con didn't think so, but she found her feet and stood, rocking back and forth. A moment later, her vision filled with gray static and her knees buckled.

Laleh caught her. "It'll pass. It will pass."

"Head rush from hell," Con said woozily as blood pounded in her ears, although to call it a head rush didn't begin to do it justice. After all, she'd never stood up before. Not in this body.

When her vision cleared, Laleh helped her to a small footlocker, which all of Palingenesis's clients kept in the event of their untimely download. Like identical twins, clones didn't share fingerprints with their originals. Instead, the locker required an old-fashioned PIN and a cheek swab to open. Inside was a set of clothes, a key ring with a single fob, a physical copy of Con's ID, a backup LFD preloaded with her contacts and banking information, and a digital drive with her birth certificate and notarized legal documents proving that she was the clone of Constance Ada D'Arcy. Her new-life starter kit.

Laleh left her to dress and went ahead to scout the hallway. When she returned, Con was struggling to tie her shoelaces. Fine motor function was proving a particular challenge. Laleh knelt at her feet and finished lacing her shoes.

"Why does she want to delete me?" Con asked.

"Because you have eighteen months of lag. That's so far outside our safe range, we don't even have reliable data for it. The board is concerned that if they discharge you, and you become"—Laleh paused, searching for a diplomatic way to say it—"unreliable, it'll be a public-relations nightmare. Palingenesis can't afford to give anti-cloning advocates any more ammunition."

That was a lot of information to absorb all at once, but Con knew Laleh was right. In the early days of Palingenesis, there had been incidents of clones experiencing psychotic breaks. A tragic standoff with the Chicago police had ended in a clone murdering his entire family before turning the gun on himself. Right up until the end, he'd insisted that he'd only negotiate with David Lyons. The police tried and failed to convince him that he was, in fact, David Lyons. Critics still pointed to the "Chicago Massacre" as proof of the necessity for a federal moratorium on cloning. Palingenesis had worked tirelessly in the years since to reassure the public that such anomalies were behind them. If the company decided Con put that effort at risk, it would go to any lengths to protect its interests.

Laleh continued, "As long as you remain on premises, you're not a person. Do you understand? They can delete you and write it up any way they want. No one would ever know you'd been revived at all."

Con shivered. "Thank you."

"Don't thank me yet. This might be a mistake. The board could be right. I'll be honest, the chances that you won't have serious psychological issues are low."

"How low?"

Laleh glanced away. "I don't know. Palingenesis has run simulations for lag over twelve months, but it's purely theoretical. We know that as lag increases, it stresses the body's ability to accept a download. That's why we lock clients out after only ninety days, and you're at eighteen months without a refresh."

"What's the laggiest download that's been attempted?"

"You're it. By a mile, and there's no way to know for certain how it will affect you." Laleh hesitated. "Look, if you want, I'll put you back under. It'll be peaceful. No pain, I promise. But I figure you deserve to make that call for yourself."

Maybe if she'd had a better grasp of what waited for her, how hard it would be out there, Con would have climbed back onto the examination table and let Laleh reconnect the IVs. But despite how heavily her depression had worn on her of late, she'd never considered suicide. She wasn't ready to start now.

"Nah, I've already got my shoes on," Con said, hoping she sounded braver than she felt.

Laleh smiled, co-conspirators now. "Follow me, then."

She led Con out into a long, windowless hallway. It was slow going, and Con trailed a hand along the wall to help keep her balance. Walking felt more complex than she remembered, and she had to focus on each leg separately to complete a single step. Despite the bright lights and high ceiling, she sensed that they were deep underground. They passed a series of vault-like doors numbered "W1" through "W8" and stopped at a deserted nurses' station.

"Where is everyone?" Con asked.

"Sleeping," Laleh said. "Alarms wake the overnight staff if there's a problem. Don't worry, I deactivated yours."

"How's the security?"

"In the client wing, it's intense but outward facing."

Con gave her a questioning look.

"Designed to keep people out, not in," Laleh explained. "We've had some attempted break-ins by Children of Adam and other nutjobs. They want video of our inactive clones for their propaganda campaign. No one's ever broken out before, though, so we have that going for us."

The echo of boots snapped them both to attention. Security guards making their rounds and coming this way, by the sound of it. Laleh cursed under her breath and cast around for a place to hide. The nurses' station was too small, and there wasn't time to make it to the next junction in the corridor. Laleh dragged Con back the way they'd come.

The footfalls grew louder. There was no chance they'd be able to retreat all the way to the surgical suite—not with Con waddling like a drunk penguin. Laleh pulled up at the vault numbered "W7," swiped her ID badge, inputted her biometrics, and then slapped the door when it didn't swing open quickly enough.

"Come on," she implored. "Come on!"

With a petulant hiss, the door began to open slowly inward.

Laleh let out a sigh of relief. "Worried they'd locked me out of the system already." She pushed Con into the dark room. "Make yourself scarce, okay? I'll stall them, but they *will* check in here."

A man's voice called out, "Hey, who's there?"

Laleh stiffened. Through the gap, Con saw her turn and walk toward two guards, trying to sound upbeat and loose. "Gabe, hey, you startled me. Give a girl some warning?"

"Laleh? No one's supposed to be down here this late," the guard said, sounding almost apologetic.

"I know. But you heard about my epic screwup? Dr. Fenton is on my case to have it written up by the time she arrives in the morning. I need to check the settings in the vault for my report. Won't take me five minutes."

"You're not supposed to be down here," the second guard said, unmoved by Laleh's tale of woe. "Are you alone?"

Con took a step away from the door and cast around the vault for a place to hide. Computer monitors lit the room like phosphorescent algae in some underwater cave. She saw a series of identical pods lining both walls of the long, narrow room, the length of a city block. She paused, transfixed, realizing where she was. When a client signed up with Palingenesis, it took months to speed grow a clone that matched the client's current age. After that, the inanimate clones were stored in hyperbaric, self-monitoring medical pods—*wombs*, in Palingenesis-speak—where they aged in parallel to the clients, waiting to step into the lives of their originals should tragedy strike. She had read about the wombs but had never seen one. No one outside of Palingenesis had, not even the clients themselves. Staring aghast into the nearest womb, she understood why. If the outside world ever saw clones this way, it would sound a death knell for legalized cloning in America.

You're one of them.

The mere thought made her want to crawl out of her skin. No, she chided herself. She was from Lanesboro, Texas, northwest of San Antonio. She was twenty-four years old.

A voice like twisted smoke asked her if that was really true.

"I am Constance D'Arcy," she answered defiantly and pinched the skin of her wrist hard, the way she'd done ever since she was a girl, using the sharp pain to focus herself. Through the glass face of the womb, she could make out the shadowy outline of a naked man, his face sallow and vacant, skin the texture of raw chicken. In the next womb, a redheaded boy, no older than seven, lay dormant. Who would subject a child to this? Con gazed at the boy, a vacant Pinocchio, so realistic, so close to alive down here among all these other misfit creatures. Not people, not yet, the spark necessary to give them life stored on a fantastically large quantum computer elsewhere in the complex. So, what were they until then? What was she now?

Presumptuous meat. That was how Franklin Butler, the founder of Children of Adam and leader of the anti-clone movement, had described them at a rally on the steps of the Lincoln Memorial. At the time, she'd only caught the highlights on her feed and dismissed it as angry rhetoric. But now, from the other side of the divide, Con shuddered at its ugliness. The gulf between witnessing hatred and being its object was as wide as the ocean. Fortunately, or unfortunately, that was a problem for another time. If the security guards found her in here, then everything else was irrelevant. Problem was, despite the size of the room, it offered little in the way of hiding places. The only option she saw was to duck down between two of the wombs and hope the guards didn't give the vault more than a quick once-over. But, given the outrageous sticker price for even a single clone, she doubted they'd be that careless.

She paused before an open womb, staring up into the empty chamber. Could this have been hers? Out in the hall, the guards' voices grew louder. They were going to find her and delete her. There was one other place she could hide, although it made her skin crawl even thinking about it. Tugging her T-shirt and bralette over her head, she climbed into the empty womb. She pulled the lid closed, using the hem of her shirt to prevent the locks from engaging. She stifled a claustrophobic sob. Her fingers couldn't work the laces of her shoes, so the best she could do was to yank her jeans and underwear down to her ankles and pray the guards didn't linger for long.

A flashlight's beam swept across the room. Con shut her eyes and held her breath, wishing she could sink down into the gel-cushioned webbing that formed the back of the womb. It went fine until she began to question whether she'd heard the locks engage. What if she were trapped in here? Alive, aware, but mistaken for an inactive clone? Pounding on the glass with no one to hear her. No one to let her out. The thought was so vivid, so terrifyingly real, that spasms began in her hands, as if her fingers were trying to detach themselves and crawl away. She balled them into fists. *I am Constance D'Arcy,* she reminded herself as the guards neared. Repeating it silently like a prayer, she willed herself to lie motionless. The guard passed her womb without slowing down, but she didn't dare move until she heard the heavy vault door seal shut with a resolute thud. Only then did she open her eyes.

Zhi stepped out of the shadows and rapped his knuckles on the glass to get her attention. Con flinched, hands going to her face to cover her eyes.

"Where's Tommy?" Zhi asked, impatient to get on the road.

"Are you okay to drive?" Con asked half-heartedly, slipping effortlessly into the memory. She was eager to push on to Raleigh but had to admit Tommy was right: Zhi looked exhausted. They'd played five cities in six days, and they were all burned out. More than a little sick of each other after a week crammed into a van with all their gear. She loved them, but they were all starting to drive each other a little crazy. The way family could. Before the show, the band had voted to drive on to Raleigh rather than spend the night in DC.

It had been Con's idea, even though the Raleigh show wasn't for three days. If they drove straight through, she and Zhi would have forty-eight uninterrupted hours to themselves. They hadn't been alone in nearly two weeks, and her need for him had begun to ache. They were going to hang the "Do Not Disturb" sign on the motel door and not show their faces until it was time for the show. Two whole days in bed with Zhi. She could hardly wait.

Tommy had been the lone holdout, voting to stay and get a proper night's sleep first. Why the rush? he wanted to know. Majority ruled, however. Band policy. Although, in retrospect, hadn't Zhi always put up his hand straightaway so that everyone knew his preference? And didn't Con always vote with him, which meant that Stephie and Hugh almost always did too? That left poor Tommy to be the unwelcome voice of reason in the band.

"Yeah, I'm cool," Zhi said with a grin. "Stephie and Hugh are getting us some caffeine and snacks for the road. Just gotta find Tommy now."

"Haven't seen him," Con answered despite wanting desperately to warn him that maybe they shouldn't drive on to Raleigh tonight. But this was a memory, not a new experience, no matter how real it felt. She could only relive it the way it had been lived. There would be no revisions. No way to change the words any more than the outcome.

"Maybe he's having a smoke," Zhi said, turning to go. "I'll check around back."

"Raleigh!" she called after him. The way she had three years ago, when what she wanted to do now was tell him how Tommy's parents had paid to fly his body home. How even if she hadn't been in the hospital, she wouldn't have dared to show her face at the funeral.

"Raleigh," he answered with a melancholy half smile and dissolved into the gloom. Con yelled for him to wait and pushed open the lid. Her shirt had done its job after all, and she fell out of the womb, sprawling across the floor. She called for Zhi to come back, but he was gone. Had never really been there despite how real it felt. She shook all over. The gray static returned.

What was happening to her?

She lay there on the floor until her heart stopped trying to fall to its death. Then she rolled gracelessly onto her back and pulled up her pants in the dark. What the hell did she do now? On one hand, she hadn't been discovered; on the other, she was trapped inside a vault with the ghost of the man she loved.

Wonderful.

Her LFD vibrated in her pocket. An incoming message. She fought with her uncooperative hands to slip it into place behind her ear and toggled open a message window.

It's Laleh. Sorry about that. Are you okay?

Con struggled to type out an answer on her chest. Thank God for autocorrect. Creeped the hell out. Otherwise, decent. R u coming back?

Can't. Gabe here is keeping me company until Dr. Fenton arrives,
but I should be able to guide you out.

I'm kinda locked in a vault. Apparently she could type pronouns even
if saying them felt like she was being dragged across gravel.

The vault door clicked and began to open again.

How about now? Laleh messaged.

Less.

A floor plan appeared in Con's display. An *X* marked her current
location, and a dotted line showed a path to a door circled in red.

Give me access to your camera, Laleh messaged.

Con toggled her permissions.

Okay, that's better. Ready?

Is it safe?

No idea. Let's find out.

It took ten minutes to make it to the circled door because Con froze
every time she heard a sound. She felt strangely alienated from her body.
As if it were the avatar in a video game, and she didn't know how to
work the controls. Walking in a straight line proved a challenge, as did
spatial awareness. She had trouble judging the distance between herself
and objects, and bumped into more than one wall like a character out
of the old cartoons her grandmother had loved.

The door led to a stairwell that took her up to the underground
parking garage. It was mostly deserted, but Laleh guided her on a wind-
ing path to avoid security camera hot spots, then up a spiral vehicle
ramp. At the top, Laleh remotely unlocked a service-access door that let
Con out onto a loading dock. Maybe she should have felt more relief
at stepping outside. After all, she was now officially a person, at least by

Palingenesis's self-serving definition, and not some laboratory experiment scheduled for deletion. But it was hard to feel victorious—her head throbbed, her hands seemed to have a mind of their own, and her lungs burned from climbing the flight of stairs. Not to mention the vivid hallucination. She'd wait until she was safely home to start celebrating her escape.

A wall of summertime humidity hit her on the other side of the door. Her LFD said it was mid-June, which rationally she knew it must be, but that felt wrong, nonetheless. Her memory clung to the belief that it had to be December since it had been December when she got up this morning.

Reconciling the year and a half that had passed since was not proving an easy sell. In any event, she had definitely missed the Weathervane gigs. She hoped Kala understood. Then it occurred to her that her original hadn't missed the show. The original would have gone after the refresh eighteen months ago. But since that had happened outside the scope of the refresh, Con had no memory of it. Thoughts like that were going to make her lose her mind. What else had she missed in the last eighteen months?

Laleh directed her to a backpack hidden behind a dumpster. Inside were a box of protein shakes and five different bottles of pills.

The pills will help manage the transition, Laleh typed. It'll mask some of the side effects until you acclimate. Go ahead and take one of each now.

Acclimate to what? Con replied.

Being alive.

That brought Con to a halt. She stared at those two words. Being alive? What does that mean?

Sorry. What Palingenesis does is incredibly complex and delicate. Like any transplant, there is the risk of rejection. Except, in this case, it's a neurological and psychological rejection.

What kind of pills are these?

Mood stabilizers. An antipsychotic. The others manage the neurological adaptation.

AN ANTIPSYCHOTIC!? Con typed. She definitely didn't remember *that* from the brochure. Though it might explain her hallucination in the vault.

I know how it sounds, but Palingenesis has a very prescribed regimen for transitioning a clone into the world. And we just skipped all of it. The pills are part of that process, and hopefully they will get you over the hump. I wish I had more time to explain, but you have to keep moving.

Why are you helping me?

There was a pause long enough that Con wondered if their connection had been broken.

Because this is my fault. After ninety days, it was my responsibility to put a hold on your account. Honestly, I thought I had.

What's going to happen to you? Con asked.

They put me on administrative leave, pending a review. I'm supposed to write up a report, but they're going to fire me tomorrow. I would. Helping you will just speed up the process.

Thank you, Con typed. I mean it.

Hopefully you still mean it in a few days. Oh, and take it easy on solid food at first. Your digestive tract will take time to adjust. There's also a series of probiotics in the backpack for you to take.

I will.

Be careful out there. Palingenesis won't let this go just because you're out. They have too much riding on it.

What are they going to do? I thought they couldn't delete me now?

Probably not. But I wouldn't bet my life on how far they're willing to go to protect their interests. If it were me, I'd let as many people as possible know I was alive. Anonymity is not your friend right now.

It was good advice. Con thanked Laleh a third time and closed the message window. Then she shouldered the backpack and started for home, eager to put some distance between herself and Palingenesis.

CHAPTER SIX

Con lived in Takoma, a neighborhood in the northeast corner of the city on the Maryland line. The fastest way home was the Metro. Unfortunately, the way to the nearest Metro stop led straight past Palingenesis's front entrance. She didn't relish the prospect of dealing with the protesters again, not after the day she'd had; however, until her walking improved, she didn't think she should risk taking the scenic route. But when she turned the corner, everything was peaceful. The protesters had called it a night, and only a handful of righteous stalwarts kept a silent vigil. One lonely holdout rested a handmade sign on his shoulder. It read: "Clones ≠ Human." Succinct at least. She gave him a bitter thumbs-up, but it must have been too late for sarcasm because he smiled, grateful for her support.

She passed him, close enough to reach out and slap hands, but he never realized what she was. Why would he? She doubted he'd ever seen a clone in person before. Not many people had. That was part of the problem. Palingenesis had gotten its start as a contractor for the Department of Defense, making clone backups to support American soldiers, but those days were over. Since Palingenesis had gone private sector, only the extraordinarily wealthy could afford their services. The other 99 percent of Americans could only look on with a mixture of envy and resentment. Nagged by the sense of being left out, of being left behind. It was a volatile combination, and the Children of Adam had capitalized on that fermenting anxiety. *Great wealth doesn't give anyone the right to pervert the nature of the human race,* Butler had bellowed. *They enjoy the benefits while we suffer the consequences.*

When Con made it to the Metro, both the escalator and elevator were out of service as per the usual. By the time she made it down to the station, she was wheezing like a four-year-old was standing on her chest. She had the lung capacity and muscle tone of a newborn, which she supposed she was, but she took a moment to marvel that after all those stairs, her knee didn't hurt a bit. For the first time since the accident, nothing ached. Not her back, not her neck. Her knee felt great. Better than great—brand new. She wanted to run. She wanted to jump. It made her want to dance.

She went to buy a ticket at an automated kiosk, but it summarily rejected her banking information. *Transaction Declined* flashed on her LFD. *Wonderful.* The next kiosk returned the same error message. It was a cheap LFD that hadn't been synced in eighteen months, but when she couldn't even log in to the bank to check her balance, she knew it wasn't a glitch on her end. Her bank account had been closed. Why the hell had her original done that? How was she supposed to get home with no money? Walk all the way to Maryland?

She wondered if her body was coordinated enough to jump the turnstile, but as she got close, a heavyset Black cop stepped into view.

"Don't even think about it," he said, thumbs hooked casually into his utility belt.

"You could just let me through? No one would know."

He chuckled at her audacity. "That's not how this is going to go."

The thought of climbing all those stairs made her bold. She'd handled all the negotiations for the band for a reason.

"You're right," she said. "Someone would know. You and me. We would know. And it would mean so much. I would write songs about you. About how, on the weirdest day of my life, a police officer saw I was about at the end of my string and gave me a break. Saved me from walking the eight miles back to Takoma in the middle of the night. In June."

He looked at her impassively. "That's some speech."

"It's not a speech. I just really need to get home. Please," she said, not wanting to overdo it. Less was more here, she felt instinctively. Cops hated feeling played.

His fingers typed something in the air to his LFD. The turnstile gate snapped open.

"Alright," he said, with another chuckle. "Go on then and write them songs."

———

Despite being a three-hour walk, it was only four stops to Takoma. She used the time to take an inventory of the backpack. Along with the pills, Laleh had left instructions for when to take the various medications. After tapping a pill out of each bottle, Con popped one into her mouth. The pill immediately got stuck in her throat. She gagged until she coughed it up onto the floor along with the pink protein shake she'd tried to swallow it with. Thankfully, the train was nearly empty at this time of night. She took a minute to practice swallowing, which she had to consciously remember how to do. When she thought she had the hang of it, she tried again and this time managed to swallow each pill without throwing up. She really was like a newborn.

Looking out the darkened window as the tunnels flashed past, Con wondered again how she had died. As soon as the thought escaped, she knew it was dangerous to think about things that way. Besides, she wasn't dead. She was alive and traveling on a northbound Metro train toward home. But wasn't the only reason she was alive because she had died? Immediately, her mind scrambled to change the subject, as if she had stumbled onto a channel showing a scary movie. If she was alive, how could she also be dead? The two contradictory ideas struggled to coexist peacefully. She was a paradox and knew how the poor cat trapped in Schrödinger's box must have felt.

The truth was she felt like an imposter. Her last refresh was eighteen months old. How could she be Con D'Arcy if she was missing eighteen months of her memories? Without them, she was incomplete. A lie. She didn't even know how she had died. Wouldn't the real Con D'Arcy know that? She had a sudden, powerful urge to see the body of her original. It was morbid, but that would settle things. Wouldn't it? The train chimed and called out the stop for Takoma. Con hopped up from her seat and headed for the doors. That was quite enough thinking for now. Nothing good could come of it.

———

Her building was only a few blocks from the Metro stop. The lobby doors beeped when her LFD came in range but didn't unlock. Con cupped her hands to the glass and looked optimistically into the deserted lobby. It had been more than ten years since the building had employed a concierge. Built back in the teens during a spasm of overconstruction that had created a glut of rental units, it had fallen victim to the changing trends that had hit the DC region. The economic downturn hadn't helped matters either. Occupancy plummeted, prices followed, and now buildings like hers were run by cut-rate management companies eking out a profit from run-down money pits. Con couldn't complain, though. If they ever did fix up the place, she wouldn't be able to afford the rent.

Eventually an older Latino man who looked only half awake came out to walk his dog. She didn't know the man's name, but his dog was Jocko. Holding the door open for them, she knelt to greet the dog cheerfully so the old man would know she belonged. He looked her up and down suspiciously but said nothing when she slipped inside, unwilling to cause a scene in the middle of the night.

Con rode the one working elevator up to her floor. Most of the lights in the hallway were broken, and the remainders cast long shadows down the hall. It wreaked havoc on her nascent depth perception, and she needed to trail a hand along the graffiti-stained wall as a guide. The apartment doors had never been upgraded and still took a physical fob. Thankfully, hers still worked. Safely inside, she leaned against the door in the dark, savoring the air-conditioning. It was a relief to be home, and she debated what to do next. Bed. Sleep. No, she needed to eat. But first a shower—time to scrub off that new-clone smell. She wanted to hold her clean hair to her nose and smell artificial coconut.

She dropped her key ring on the hall table and heard it clatter straight to the floor. Flipping on the lights, she saw the problem. There was no hall table. She caught her reflection in a full-length mirror that hung in its place and froze as if she'd surprised an intruder. Who *was* that? She had put on weight since the accident, but it was all gone now. Her face was as thin as it had been in college. Stepping in close to the mirror, she touched her fingers to her cheek. The skin smooth and baby soft, undamaged by the sun or by life. No wrinkles or laugh lines. As if someone had sketched her outline but omitted any distinguishing features. It was horrible. Her hair hung halfway down her back in a rat's nest of tangles and knots. Behind her, a framed painting of Jesus gazed down with an expression that suggested he couldn't quite place her either.

Before she could contemplate when her original had found religion, a young Black boy, perhaps ten, padded out of the living room in a T-shirt and underwear. He yawned and gazed up at her through sleepy, hooded eyes. "Who are you?"

"Who are you?" Con replied.

"Where's my mom?"

Con looked past the boy and into the living room. None of the furniture looked familiar. And since when did she hang pictures of Jesus? Her spirits fell as she realized what had happened. She had moved out sometime in the past eighteen months. It hadn't even crossed her mind as a possibility.

The boy began to look worried. "How'd you get in?"

"I used to live here. Still have a fob. It's alright." A former tenant breaking in with a fob—Con didn't see how that made any of it alright. Why was she not surprised that the management company hadn't bothered to reprogram the locks?

"You should probably go. My mom will be back from her shift soon."

Con ignored his advice for a moment. "How long have you lived here?"

The boy shrugged, unsure. "Since last summer?"

A year. She hadn't lived here for at least a year. Moving hadn't even been on her radar eighteen months ago. This was the only apartment she'd ever had in DC, and she'd only just negotiated a rent reduction in November. So why the sudden move?

"Do you know what happened to the woman who lived here before?" she asked.

"Aren't you her?" the boy answered.

"Yeah," she said, although that feeling of being an imposter had returned.

"Then what're you asking me for?"

That was a really good question. One that Con didn't even know how to begin to explain.

"Are you okay?" the boy asked. "You look sick. Do you need to see my mom? She works at the hospital."

The question made her strangely emotional, and she had the urge to laugh and cry simultaneously. She did neither. What she had, his mother couldn't begin to fix. "I'm not sick. I'm just . . ." *New.* "Tired. Thanks, though. What's your name?"

"DeMarcus."

"Thanks, DeMarcus. I'm gonna go, okay? Sorry for waking you up." She handed him the key ring. Apologizing again, Con backed out into the hallway and shut the door behind her. She heard the dead bolt turn. Smart kid.

Con left the building and crossed the street to a small park formed by the intersection of three streets. She needed to sit down and gather her thoughts. She'd thought coming home would begin to provide some answers, but she was only accumulating more questions. If she didn't live here, where had she gone? Why had she stopped doing her monthly refreshes at Palingenesis? How had she died? Was it all connected?

First things first, though—what did she do now? Tonight? She felt exhausted. If she didn't sleep soon, she was going to collapse. But where? She was literally penniless. Maybe she could sleep here in the park. It had always been a place of refuge for her. Just a single bench, a small triangle of grass beneath a copse of oaks, but in the spring, she would sit against a tree with her guitar and a notebook.

She loved that guitar, a vintage Martin D-28. It was her most prized possession. Zhi had bought it for her at a little guitar shop in Detroit to celebrate signing the deal with the label. One of the last production runs to use authentic Brazilian rosewood. It had been through the wars with its previous owner. She could tell by the way the edges of the fretboard were rolled and rounded. Two of the bridge pins were mismatched, the headstock looked as if it had been used as a doorstop, and the back was scratched all to hell. From years of resting against a big ol' belt buckle, if she had to guess. But despite, or perhaps because of, the alchemy of time and wear, the guitar had a gorgeous tone, warm and familiar.

Zhi had been the principal songwriter in the band, but he'd always encouraged her to write. With him gone, writing had become her outlet and sole consolation. Not that she ever performed any of the new material. She'd never written anything as intimate or personal, and the thought of sharing it with an audience . . . well, she simply wasn't ready. But she had an idea that the songs she'd been hoarding in her notebook might be an album. One day. When she finally got her act together.

Across the street, an SUV glided silently up to the curb outside her old building. The doors opened almost before it stopped, and in unison three men dressed all in black got out. They trotted up to the front door and disappeared inside. Con sat up straight. How had they opened the building's door? They definitely didn't live there.

The SUV idled at the curb. Waiting. Watching. She had no way of proving they were from Palingenesis, but who else could it be? If they'd arrived only a little sooner, she would have been trapped inside the building with no way out. Laleh had been right that they wouldn't give up so easily.

The driver rolled down his window. His white face was gaunt and pockmarked, and in the glow of the dashboard, it looked like the surface of the moon. A thin chinstrap beard outlined his jaw. His head turned, scanning the small park, then swung back as if he'd caught a glimpse of something. He leaned forward, staring right at Con with the dull, lifeless eyes of a shark. She fought the urge to run, praying the shadows from the oaks would hide her, afraid even to breathe.

Two of the men emerged from the building. It broke the driver's spell, and he looked away. Silently, Con slid off the bench and pressed herself into the dirt.

"Anything?" the driver said, his voice carrying across to her in the night air.

"She was here," his man answered.

"When? How long ago?"

"Kid wasn't sure. Not long."

"How did she get on the train? How did she get here ahead of us?"

"She's being careful."

"Bullshit, she's just some girl. Someone's got to be helping her." The driver spat out his window. "Garcia stays put in case she comes back. You two are with me."

The two men grunted their assent and climbed back into the SUV. After a few minutes, it drove away. After a few more, Con slipped away into the night.

CHAPTER SEVEN

In the hours after the close call at her apartment building, Con stayed on the move, driven by a combination of adrenaline and fear. She felt stupid. Laleh had warned her that Palingenesis wouldn't give up easily, but she hadn't taken the warning seriously enough. Instead, she'd gone straight home, where, if she'd been a few minutes later, or those men had been a few minutes earlier . . . She let the thought trail off ominously. Bottom line? She'd gotten extremely lucky and couldn't afford to be that careless again.

Worried that Palingenesis might be tracking her LFD, she shut it down. Probably they'd simply followed her home, but better safe than sorry. Eventually, exhaustion brought her literally to her knees as she stumbled over an enormous tree root that had shrugged aside the sidewalk pavers like tissue paper. She had to find somewhere to sleep and was long past being picky.

She made her bed in an alley behind an Ethiopian restaurant on a stack of flattened shipping boxes, her backpack serving as a makeshift pillow. The restaurant's dumpster created a natural blind that blocked any view of her from the street. But it did have its drawbacks. The summer heat had turned the overflowing dumpster into a fetid Crock-Pot, and the simmering perfume of rotting food filled the alley. On the bright side, she figured the smell would discourage casual tourists.

Someone would need to be highly motivated to come looking for her here.

A car horn jolted her awake. Without her LFD, she could only judge the time by the hazy sunlight slanting down the alleyway. It didn't feel like she'd been asleep for that long, though. She lay on her side bathed in sweat, feeling nauseated and weak. Gamma Jol shuffled up in slippers and a housecoat. It was a bathrobe, but she had always called it her housecoat. As if that somehow made it alright to wear to the grocery store.

"When you going to stop getting in fights at school?" Gamma asked.

Con shrugged. She was twelve again and had just been suspended for the second time. Fighting again. This time with a white girl who'd run her fingers through Con's hair and pretended it was gross and dirty. She'd come here to Gamma's rather than face her mother.

Con shook her head, trying to chase away the hallucination, but Gamma just handed her a bag of frozen peas as if to say, *You're not getting rid of me that easily, child.* Con pressed the peas to her swollen cheekbone. The peas, frozen in clumps, felt so real. It all felt so real. The sweet, bubbling aroma of pork stew on the stove. Fela Kuti on the stereo—there was always music playing in Gamma Jol's home.

"You ever win any of them fights?" Gamma asked.

Con shrugged again. No, she never won. She was small and there were more of them. Always more. But winning wasn't even the point. You talked shit about her father who had died for his country; you made fun of how she looked; you put your hands on her—then it was on. Gamma clucked as if she could read her granddaughter's defiance.

"Will you braid my hair tonight?" Con asked. Let's see Amber Thornton run those pork-chop-looking fingers through her hair then.

"Oh, you get suspended—again—and you reckon your gamma's gonna fix that mess you got going on up there?"

"Can I stay here tonight?" Con said, asking her real question.

"Yes, but only for one night." Gamma Jol smiled and squeezed Con's face in her calloused hand, which Con loved and hated and loved to hate.

It would be two more years before Con moved back home. She'd recently announced that she'd no longer be singing in the choir at church. Con had become a star attraction in the last few years—this snippet of a girl with a voice larger than the sky—and her mother basked in the attention and praise it brought. Standing up to her mother had been the scariest thing she'd ever done and turned all the simmering tension that had been building between them to open hostility. Mary D'Arcy's house had never been a pleasant place to grow up, but since their argument, it had become downright poisonous. Twelve-year-old Con knew exactly how her mother would react to her being suspended. How she'd refer to it darkly as Antoine D'Arcy's "bad influence," even though the man had been dead for six years. Con was just old enough now to suspect what her white mother really meant by that and was afraid of what she might do if she said it again.

"Child, you are gonna be the death of me," Gamma Jol said with an exasperated eye roll. "Come on now and help me make up the couch."

Con wanted to chase after Gamma and take her hand but found she couldn't move. Gamma Jol disappeared from sight, the kitchen dissolving in smoke and haze, becoming an alleyway once again. Con knew it was another hallucination, but that didn't make it feel any less real or make her miss her grandmother any less. This was what Laleh had warned her about. Her new body trying to reject her consciousness. So far it felt like the world's worst breakup.

When she felt steadier, Con sat up and took another round of the pills Laleh had given her, washing them down with a protein shake. The shake did little but cause her stomach to rumble impatiently. She needed food. Real food. But food cost money she didn't have. Well, there was always dumpster diving in an emergency. Nothing like yesterday's Ethiopian to start the day off right. She meant it as a joke, but it landed with a thud—not nearly far-fetched enough for comfort.

The smart thing to do would be to ask her friends to loan her some money. She hated asking for help so much that dumpster diving actually sounded more appealing, but she was in trouble here. Real trouble. It might be time to suspend her first commandment, from the Book of Zhi-Left-You-All-Alone-in-the-World: Thou shalt not rely on anyone ever again. *Can a girl get an amen?* The only problem with asking for help was it would require turning on her LFD, which could bring Palingenesis's wolves down on her again. Laleh's parting words echoed in her ears: *Anonymity is not your friend right now.* Con was starting to see the wisdom in that. She needed to be seen and to establish that she existed in this world. So how could she kill two birds with this stone? Who did she know who lived around here?

Kala Solomon.

Con practically did a little dance of excitement. Kala lived nearby in Silver Spring, a neighborhood just outside the city in Maryland. Providing she hadn't moved in the last eighteen months. Con didn't know her exact address, but she'd been there a couple of times, so it should be easy enough to find. And Kala was a friend and would help. She had better, after all the times Con had bailed out her band.

Kala lived in an enormous house that she shared with a revolving cast of transient roommates. None of the people who had signed the original lease still lived there, but at any given time, there were between eight and twelve tenants. The ancient house had probably been a showstopper in its day, but that day was likely in another century. Years of neglect had left it in a state of indifferent decline. The landlord lived in Canada somewhere and did only the bare minimum maintenance to keep the rent flowing. White paint curled up in parchment rolls to reveal red brick beneath, and the front porch canted to one side like a ship in a storm. Con cut across the front yard, through the knee-high grass turned brown straw in the merciless summer sun, and rang the bell.

After a minute, a young white guy in a too-tight Knicks jersey and cargo shorts opened the door. He stood there holding a bowl of cereal under his chin waiting for her to identify herself. When she asked if Kala still lived there, he held up a finger and shut the door in her face. *Damn.* She checked her reflection in a window. By the most charitable of definitions, she was not having a good hair day. Gingerly, she extracted a candy wrapper that must have gotten stuck there while she was sleeping. *Wonderful.*

Before Con could finish finger-combing her hair into some semblance of order, the door reopened. Kala stuck her face through the crack. When she saw who it was, she made an expression that fell somewhere between irritation and indigestion.

Kala rested her head on the doorframe and waited. Con had a whole speech prepared, but she went immediately off script.

"Hey," she said instead.

"Hey," Kala replied, returning serve and nothing more. She looked surprised to see Con, but not you're-supposed-to-be-dead surprised. Maybe she hadn't heard the news.

Not knowing what else to say, Con repeated herself, only in more words. "How're you doing?"

"How am I doing?" Kala parroted. "I just got home from work, and I got to get to bed. That's how I'm doing."

"I'm sorry. I know it's really early, but it's kind of an emergency."

"Isn't it always with you?"

Her tone took Con aback. This wasn't Kala being tired and grumpy after a long night. She was angry. "What's that supposed to mean?"

Kala sighed. "What do you want?"

"Look, I'm in kind of a jam."

"So you came to me?"

"I really need your help," Con said.

"Bitch, are you kidding me right now?" Kala said, face going slack in disbelief. "You think I'm going to help you?"

Con felt like she was missing a page of the script. Obviously, Kala was pissed about something, but about what? And where did she get off, after all the times Con had bailed out Weathervane when Kala's lead singer was too hungover to go on? A familiar defiance welled up, the feeling she got when someone jumped to conclusions about her or heard some secondhand gossip and assumed it to be true without asking her to her face. She'd never taken that shit well and wasn't about to start now.

"What the hell is your problem?" Con snapped.

Kala's eyes widened first in shock, then fury. The front door opened the rest of the way, and she stepped out onto the porch. Her family was Samoan, and even barefoot, she had six good inches on Con. She jabbed a finger in Con's face.

"Don't play that with me," Kala said. "You know exactly what my problem is."

Later, Con would wonder why it took her so long to realize the obvious—whatever Kala was upset about had happened after her last refresh. Con couldn't remember because it wasn't part of her memory. She kept defaulting back to December 26 like a broken clock resetting to twelve a.m. But it was a year and a half later, and those shows she'd agreed to do for Weathervane were long in the past now.

"You know how badly we needed that New Year's Eve show," Kala said. "And you stood us up."

What? There hadn't been a New Year's Eve show on the list. The last gig had been for the thirtieth. She remembered it clearly. She ought to; it was yesterday's memory to her.

The confused look on Con's face wasn't scoring her any points with Kala. "So that's how it is? You need help, so, what? You've got amnesia now?" Kala flicked a finger at her own temple and made a hollow-coconut sound with her tongue. "So typical."

"I'm sorry," Con said, unsure what she was sorry for.

"Oh, you're sorry now, so we're supposed to be good? That it? We had the chance to play Glass House, and you freaked out and bailed on us."

"How'd you get a show at Glass House?" It was a reasonable if ill-advised question.

"What's that supposed to mean?" Kala demanded. "You think we couldn't book Glass House without riding the great Con D'Arcy's coattails?"

"I didn't say that," Con said, retreating a step. Glass House was a bigger venue and mostly booked regional or national acts. Honestly, she was surprised Weathervane could book Glass House, with or without her. It was a huge get for a band that size, especially a New Year's Eve show. What surprised her more was that she'd ever agreed to do it in the first place. Glass House was where Awaken the Ghosts had played its last gig. The manager had been pestering her for years with a ghoulish proposition to track down Stephie for a reunion show, preferably on the anniversary of the crash. Con would rather gouge out her own eyes than set foot back inside there.

What could have possessed her?

"We needed that gig. But no, it had to turn into the Con show. After your new boyfriend took you out of there, Jasper pulled the plug on the whole thing and had one of his staff DJ for the rest of the night. We were laughed out of there. The band broke up a month later."

Boyfriend? Con's mind was reeling, and Kala's outburst had forced her back down the porch stairs. It took her out of the shadows, and the sunshine lit up her face. Kala stared at her, mouth hanging open.

"What's wrong with you?" Kala asked, all the fire gone from her voice.

Con didn't know where to begin.

"Are you sick?" Kala said.

"No."

"Then what . . . ?" She trailed off, staring hard at Con's bare left arm. Self-consciously, Con tried to cover it with her other arm as if she'd been caught in the nude. In a way, she'd never been more naked in her life. Kala glanced up at her face, then back to the missing tattoos.

"Are you a dupe?" It was Kala's turn to take a step back, her hand reaching blindly for the door.

Dupe was far from the cruelest slang for clones, but it still landed hard. Especially from a friend.

"Yeah, but listen—"

"You should've said. What if you give me cystic fibrosis, or something worse?" Kala opened the door but lingered there on the porch, morbid curiosity overcoming revulsion for the moment. Most people had never seen a clone, not in person. Certainly not one of a friend, and it had clearly rattled Kala.

"Come on, Kala. You can't catch cystic fibrosis."

A conspiracy site had posted a study that claimed to link several spontaneous cases of genetic disease in children to contact with clones. Never mind that genetic disease wasn't transmittable. The study had been debunked as junk science, but polls showed that 58 percent of Americans believed the threat to be real. Several states had laws forbidding clones from working around children.

"That's not what I heard. And actually I need you to get off my porch."

"Seriously?" Con said but retreated farther down the stairs, hands raised in a gesture of compliance.

Once Con was at a safe distance, Kala considered her again. "Does this mean Con is dead?" she asked, her voice quiet and mournful. "Did she die?"

Con knew what she meant, but still, it was hard to admit out loud. "Yeah, I think so."

"How?" Kala might have been furious, but the realization that her friend was dead hit her hard. Death had a way of making old disagreements feel suddenly meaningless.

"I was hoping you knew."

"Me? No, man. Ain't talked to her in forever. Last I heard, she was living down around Richmond."

"Richmond?" The idea that she'd left DC, for Richmond or anywhere else, stunned Con. She'd been trying to escape this city for so long that she'd all but given up on the idea. The gravity of the accident and all she'd lost had fixed her in Zhi's lonely orbit. Depression doing its silent work, gaslighting every idea she had for her future. Go back to school—too much effort. Go home—there was nothing there for her. Start a new band—what kind of disloyal, callous bitch would do such a thing? Two more years had passed that way, in an inertia of self-loathing. And then sometime since her last refresh—the missing eighteen months—she'd moved to Richmond. She'd figured out how to get out of here.

"Yeah, with that guy you brought to Glass House with you on New Year's Eve. Your boyfriend."

"What boyfriend?" Con said, trying to digest the idea that not only had she moved to Richmond but that she'd done it for a boyfriend that hadn't existed five days earlier. There was no way any of that should be true, except Kala's tone told her it was. She had a thousand questions, although Kala clearly had no interest in answering them.

"What is it you actually want?" Kala demanded.

"A place to stay."

"No. No chance."

"Please, Kala. I don't have any place to go. I slept in an alley last night. Please?"

Kala softened but didn't relent. "Why don't you just go back to Richmond?"

"I can't."

"How come?" Kala asked.

"I've never been to Richmond," Con said reluctantly.

"What are you talking about?"

"I've got, like, an eighteen-month gap in my memory. Since the last time I did a refresh. I don't remember moving to Richmond. I don't remember whatever went down with your band. None of it." She was on the edge of tears, as if she were finally coming clean and confessing to a heinous crime. It was as hard a thing as she'd ever had to say.

"See? You're not her. Not really."

"I am," Con said but without conviction. She'd been feeling like an imposter, and this was the proof.

"No, you're her shitty copy. You're not even a person." Kala paused then, seemingly shocked at the vehemence of her words, but it seemed to resolve something in her mind. She went back into her house and slammed the door, leaving Con alone in the yard, stunned and furious.

Growing up, Con had dealt with her share of racism, but generally people in her hometown knew how to dress it up as something else and rarely ever came out and said it. Life and experience had built armor to shield Con against it, but it was another thing entirely to have a friend look her in the eye and tell her she wasn't a person. She wanted to march up the steps and hammer on the door until Kala came back out. Finish what they'd started, but she was rooted to the spot. As if Kala had sucker punched her and knocked the wind out of her.

The front door reopened. Con braced herself, but instead of Kala, it was the guy who'd answered the door in the Knicks jersey. He came halfway down the steps and stopped.

"You Con D'Arcy?"

"Yeah, why?" she said warily.

"Guy was here last night. Looking for you."

The hair on Con's shoulders shifted like a field of grass rippling in a changing wind. "Looking for me? What did you tell him?"

"That I don't know any Con D'Arcy," he said.

"What time was he here?"

Knicks shrugged uncertainly. "Around midnight? I don't know. I was pretty toasty last night. Dude freaked me out."

"Why?"

"Had these eyes, man. Like he was looking at something behind me. Even when he looked right at me. Like he was taking my X-ray."

"What'd he look like? Was his face scarred? Like acne scars?" Con asked.

"Oh yeah, that was him. Left me a number to call if you came by."

So not only did Palingenesis know where she lived, but they knew her friends too. "You going to call it?"

He snorted. "No, man. I'm an unreliable narrator." He hesitated. "You really a clone?"

She nodded reluctantly.

"Is it cool if I get a picture?" He sidled up beside her and snapped a few pictures. It was gross, but what else could she do? She couldn't risk offending him now. He thanked her like she was some kind of celebrity and went back inside.

Before the front door could close, Kala slipped out. She came down the porch steps holding a wad of cash like a ward against evil spirits. It was go-away money, and she thrust it into Con's hand. Con was still in a fighting mood, ready to call her friend every horrible name she knew. But then she thought of that alleyway and which she valued more, her pride or her survival. She took the money.

"Don't come here again," Kala said, unable to look Con in the eyes.

"I won't."

"I'm sorry."

"For which part?"

Kala didn't have an answer and fled into the safety of the house. The door slammed shut. It didn't open again.

CHAPTER EIGHT

Con's first stop was a nearby diner. The money Kala had given her wouldn't get her a room for the night, but if she counted her pennies, it might keep her from starving for a few days. Hopefully that would be time enough to come up with a plan. But first things definitely first. Her brain was staging an aggressive sit-down strike, refusing to do its job until it got fed. The protein shakes had worn out their welcome, and the only word she seemed capable of forming was *bacon*.

After a night on the streets, the air-conditioning felt like heaven. She looked around for somewhere to sit, aware that the normally bustling diner had fallen quiet with her arrival. She lowered her head, feeling the weight of their eyes on her. Was she being paranoid, or could they tell? Had they recognized her for what she was? A waiter blocked her way, scratching the back of his head. He was a young white guy, with the awkward body language of someone who'd never been in a fight and avoided confrontation at all costs.

"Come on," he said with a mixture of embarrassment and exasperation. "You can't come in here."

The air was acutely still, everyone waiting to see how the standoff played out.

"Why not?" she said. Fresh off her encounter with Kala Solomon, she wanted to know how he knew she was a clone.

"Come on," he said again as if why should be obvious.

"I just want something to eat."

"I'm sorry. Can't have you bothering the customers."

The way she looked, the way she probably smelled—he didn't know she was a clone—they thought she was homeless. She felt an unpleasant jolt of humiliation. She wasn't homeless. *Well, what else would you call sleeping in an alley?* the voice in her head that liked to play devil's advocate asked. Maybe this was what being homeless was. Maybe you didn't realize you were homeless until someone treated you that way. One more unpleasant, urban cautionary tale to be stepped over or around.

"I can pay," she said, holding her money up defiantly.

The waiter retreated to his manager, where he pleaded her case. Finally, the manager relented. The waiter returned and showed her to a seat at the end of the counter, away from the other customers.

"My manager says you need to pay up front."

She pushed bills across the counter. The waiter scooped them up, apologized a second time, and asked her what she wanted. The menu listed calories for customers watching their waistlines. Con went the other way, ordering the Filibuster Breakfast, the most caloric item on the menu. Three eggs, two pancakes, bacon, toast, grits, fruit, coffee. And an extra side of bacon.

The waiter shook his head. "No bacon. Our food printer's down."

Disappointed, Con substituted soy sausage.

Laleh had warned her to ease into solid food, but Con was starving and way past half measures. When her food arrived, she ate like a feral castaway. Walking had become more natural since last night, but her hands struggled with the mechanics of a knife and fork.

Strangely, it went better the less attention she paid, so to distract herself, she watched the news on the monitor mounted above the counter. Some people still missed the communal aspect of watching the same channel rather than disappearing into their LFDs. Disappearing would have suited Con fine. Anything to shut out the diner and all the watchful eyes. Still, she hesitated to turn her LFD back on. She'd have to eventually—it was her only lifeline to the larger world—but for now, it could stay in her backpack.

The news felt all too familiar—the same wars dragged on, and the debates ahead of the forthcoming election only served to underline that the country's racial, regional, and socioeconomic divides remained as entrenched as ever. The Independent Secessionist Party looked on the path to winning its first congressional seat. Last night, on the way to Silver Spring, she'd worried that the world would be unrecognizable to her after her eighteen-month absence. That she'd feel like a time traveler in some old movie, lost in a jet-pack future she couldn't comprehend. But, in truth, remarkably little had changed. Mostly it was in the details—a restaurant had shuttered and reopened under new management, a hole in the ground had sprouted a six-story building. It didn't make the differences any less jarring, but at least she didn't have to deal with flying cars.

The most incomprehensible changes appeared to have been reserved for her own life. Somehow in the last year and a half, the original Con D'Arcy had done what she'd been unable to do in the three years prior. It blew Con's mind but also made her strangely proud of her original. Con wished she could have met her so she could ask how she'd found the strength to leave DC behind at last. Of course, that was impossible now. Her original was dead out there somewhere. The need to know returned. And not just how her original had died, but everything, every moment of the last eighteen months. It felt essential to fill in those gaps. If she knew everything, then the paradox of two Constance Ada D'Arcys would resolve itself. Only then would she stop feeling like a charlatan. At least she hoped so.

Since her arrival, the other customers at the diner had given Con a wide berth, but now a man slid onto a stool two over from her. Of Japanese descent, he looked to be somewhere in his midthirties and had brilliantined hair that looked like a sculpted oil slick. He wore a herringbone tweed waistcoat over an impeccable open-necked dress shirt—a little overdressed for a diner in Silver Spring. He turned over the coffee cup in front of him and smiled at Con.

"How's your morning?" he asked in an accent that she couldn't quite place. Southern, if she had to guess, but with all the identifying characteristics carefully sanded down until only the faintest traces remained.

She reached for her backpack. He raised a hand, palm up, to indicate he came in peace.

"Who are you?" she asked.

"My name is Peter Lee."

"And what do you want, Peter Lee?"

"A word. That's all," he said and slid a business card across the counter to her.

It read, "Vernon Gaddis—CEO, Gaddis LLC."

Con raised an eyebrow. She knew the name; everyone did. Vernon Gaddis was the angel investor who'd taken a chance on Abigail Stickling, at the time a young researcher facing ridicule and condemnation from the scientific community for her radical theories. In 2019, they'd founded a small start-up named Palingenesis and gone on to make human cloning a reality. The other relevant detail Con knew about him was that Vernon Gaddis was also a clone.

Three years ago—no, wait, five. Five years ago. Con had to keep reminding herself that it wasn't 2038 anymore. Five years ago, Gaddis and his wife's Gulfstream had crashed in the North Atlantic. Back in Washington, DC, his clone had been activated within seconds. Turned out, though, that his wife wasn't a client and thus had no clone. The new Vernon Gaddis had spent years defending himself against accusations that his original had murdered Cynthia Gaddis, knowing full well his clone would survive the crash. Although no criminal charges were ever filed, the media had lost its collective mind over the unfolding scandal, and the complex optics had forced Gaddis to step down from the company he'd co-founded. Countless think pieces had been written on the issue. Could a clone be charged for a crime committed by its original? Had cloning created a murder loophole? When would Congress write comprehensive, national cloning legislation instead of ceding its leadership role to a patchwork of conflicting state laws? Vernon Gaddis had become a recluse, rarely venturing out in public. After only one night as a clone, Con was beginning to sympathize with his decision.

Curious what he could want with her, she squeezed the top-right corner of the business card between her thumb and forefinger, triggering the embedded video. A middle-aged Black man with snow-white hair appeared on the business card and smiled.

"Hello. My name is Vernon Gaddis." The video segued to a tight, well-produced overview of Gaddis LLC and its core businesses: telecom, real estate, climate therapies, biotechnology, and lobbying, to name but a few. Gaddis LLC, it seemed, had a hand in everything . . . except cloning. There was no mention of Palingenesis. When the video was over, a second recording began, this time a personal message. Vernon Gaddis sat behind a desk, looking somber and thoughtful.

"Constance. I apologize for not reaching out to you sooner. I can only imagine how difficult things have been for you. It would be my privilege to offer you sanctuary. An opportunity to regroup. There are matters that I would discuss with you that I believe will benefit both of us greatly. If you accept my invitation, Peter will bring you to my home. I hope you will consider it. I look forward to meeting you."

The video ended.

"Where exactly is home?" Con asked.

"In Maryland. Charles Island."

"No kidding." Charles Island was a narrow five-mile sliver in the Chesapeake Bay that had become a sanctuary for wealthy elites needing an escape from the grind of DC. Strictly billionaires, mansions, and yachts. Con had sung at a wedding out there once. Eight hundred guests. A white-tie affair. It had paid her rent for three months. Accessible only by a private two-lane bridge, the entire island was a gated community with its own security force and enormous moat, if you wanted to look at it that way. The perfect refuge for the most controversial clone in the United States.

"And Vernon Gaddis is your . . . ?"

"Employer," Peter said.

"Got it. So what does your employer want with me?"

"As he said, there are matters he would discuss with you—"

"That will benefit us both greatly. Yeah, I got that part. What does that mean? If it would benefit him so greatly, why isn't he here himself?"

From his expression, it was clear she'd hit on a sensitive subject. "Mr. Gaddis rarely leaves the island these days, but if you dial the number on his card, he's expecting your call."

Con warily turned the business card over as if it might jump up and bite her. Calling would mean turning her LFD back on, but she had to admit to being more than a little curious about what her aunt's former partner wanted. It was worth the risk. Grudgingly, she fished the LFD out of her backpack, powered it up, and slipped it behind her ear. She saw several missed calls and messages, but they were all from a number she didn't recognize so she ignored them for now. As soon as she started to dial, Peter stood up and moved down the counter out of earshot.

Her LFD rang only once before Gaddis picked up.

"Constance. Vernon Gaddis here. Do you know who I am?" he asked with a false modesty that made her eyes roll.

"You were my aunt's business partner."

"Yes. One of the great honors of my life. It's actually your aunt we need to discuss."

"How's that?" she asked.

"Constance, things have not been right at Palingenesis for a very long time."

"Yeah, I kind of got the guided tour last night," she said.

"Only the tip of the iceberg, I'm afraid. And I also know you've been treated shabbily since. It's terrible, simply terrible."

"How do you know anything about that? You don't know me. And didn't they toss you as CEO after your plane crashed?" It wasn't her at peak tact, but his faux concern rubbed her all kinds of wrong. He was working her. Leading the conversation down a path that he'd prepared in advance. She wanted to see how he'd react once dragged off script.

On the other end of the line, Gaddis drew a sharp breath but then chuckled rather than take offense. He must need her badly.

"That's true," he replied. "I was. But I did retain my position on the board. Would you like to know how they voted about disposing of their Constance D'Arcy situation?"

She really didn't, though she could guess. "A team of men showed up at my old apartment building last night."

That caught his attention, although he didn't sound entirely shocked. "Did they really? She's unbelievable."

"Who?" Con asked.

"Brooke Fenton, of course. My successor."

"She's a piece of work."

"That doesn't begin to cover it. Ironically, I handpicked Brooke. I'm usually a better judge of character. When the board voted to remove me as CEO after the crash, I was actually reassured that she would be filling my shoes. I later learned that she had used the crash as a pretext to maneuver me out. Then she turned around and tried to wrest control of the research laboratory away from Abigail. It was a coup from start to finish, but I was too sick with grief to defend myself at the time."

"So what does this all have to do with me?"

"Precisely what I'd like to know," Gaddis said. "I'd rather not get into the details over the phone. Suffice it to say, in the board meeting, she was uncharacteristically evasive when I pressed her about how you could have been revived after so long. I helped design the systems and protocols governing clone revival. The labs and vaults at Palingenesis comprise one of the most sophisticated Sensitive Compartmented Information Facilities in the world. There are a dozen fail-safes to ensure that a clone isn't revived after its lockout date. It would take an act of God for the entire system to fail this spectacularly. That or an inside job, because Palingenesis's wombs can't be accessed from the outside."

The possibility that Con owed her existence to an act of sabotage put a new spin on things. Laleh had made it sound like simple human error, but what if there was more to it? Could she be involved herself?

"So what is it you want?" she asked.

"I don't know what Brooke is planning, but the mere fact that she has taken such a personal interest in your situation is cause for suspicion. One thing I know for certain, though, is that the board did not authorize a snatch-and-grab operation. The men at your apartment last night were not there at the behest of Palingenesis. Whatever interests Brooke is protecting, they aren't the company's. I'd like to get you somewhere safe until this can be sorted out."

It was a tempting offer. The money Kala had given her wouldn't last long, and Con hadn't even started to think about a place to sleep tonight. While she was mulling over his offer, another call came in from the same unknown number that had been calling all morning. It went to voice mail, but Con realized it was an 804 number. Richmond. Kala had said her original had moved down there with some guy. Suddenly the internal politics of Palingenesis lost all hold on Con's attention.

"I need to call you back," she said.

"Excuse me?" Gaddis said as she hung up the call.

Peter stood up questioningly. She hooked a thumb toward the bathrooms. He nodded and sat back down. His own LFD was already ringing.

Safely locked inside the bathroom, she scrolled through her missed calls. There were several messages from the same 804 number, but before she had a chance to listen to any of them, her LFD rang again.

"Is this the clone of Constance D'Arcy?" asked a man whose voice sounded like it had been aged in a barrel for twelve years.

"Who's this?"

"Darius Clarke. I'm a detective with Richmond PD," he said as though mildly irritated that she didn't already know that. "We received notification from Palingenesis that Constance D'Arcy is deceased. I need to follow up with you. See if we can confirm a few things."

"Confirm what?" She'd been racking her brain for who might be able to tell her what happened to her original. It hadn't occurred to her to go to the police, but who better to provide answers?

"That Constance D'Arcy is deceased."

"You don't know?"

The detective cleared his throat as if he didn't care for the question and it had gotten stuck there. "We don't have a body. Up until the call from Palingenesis, it had been investigated as a missing person."

Con realized that although she'd been obsessing over how her original had died, she hadn't allowed herself to speculate. It had felt taboo and dangerous somehow. But if her original had been missing long enough for the police to get involved, that wasn't a good sign. What had become of her life in the last eighteen months?

"Are you still there?" he asked impatiently.

"So what can you tell me?"

"That's not really how this works. But I can fill you in a little when we meet. My sergeant thinks it could be useful to have a conversation with someone like you."

"Like me?" She didn't care for the way he said that.

"A clone. You have the vic's memories. Who knows her better than you? Not often we get to interview the missing person while they're still missing. It would be helpful to be able to understand her mindset."

"Was I murdered?" It was an unpleasant question to ask.

"Best this is handled in person."

"Okay, but I don't really have any way to get to Richmond."

"No need. I'm in DC now. Should be wrapped up at Palingenesis by eleven, so let's say noon." It was not a question.

Nothing about Detective Clarke's attitude inspired cooperation, and growing up in Lanesboro had made her wary of getting involved with the police. Her interactions had always been fine and courteous when she was with her mother, but when she was alone, it was impossible to predict how she'd be treated. She didn't know Detective Darius Clarke but didn't hold out a lot of hope that he was one of the good ones. He sounded like an officious jerk on a power trip. The same kind she'd encountered when the band had been on the rise—the managers and the promoters, mostly men, who knew they were gatekeepers and that you had no choice but to play their game their way if you wanted to get ahead.

Thing was, he represented an opportunity to fill in a lot of blanks, and she didn't think she had the willpower to say no to him.

"Noon works," she said.

The detective named a dive on Indiana Avenue near Chinatown. Con said she'd be there, but the line was already dead.

Peter Lee was waiting at the counter when she returned. She told him she had to go.

"I'm to tell you that it's a mistake," he said.

"You're not going to try to stop me?"

He smiled. "No, that's not how this works. Wouldn't do any good anyway."

"Are you going to be in trouble with your boss?"

"No, he knew you'd say no. These things have to run their course."

"What things?" she asked.

"Being a clone." It sounded patronizing at first, but there was nothing to suggest that it was anything but a simple statement of fact. He handed her the business card she'd left on the counter. "Keep this. Mr. Gaddis wants you to know his offer stands. Call him when you're ready."

"Tell him not to hold his breath," Con said and started for the door. She turned back when Peter called her name. He had his wallet in his hand and held out several crisp bills.

"What's this for?" she asked.

"Let's just say I am a fan of tough-guy acts."

"Thanks," she said warily but took the money anyway.

"But acting tough only gets you so far. I hope there's something behind it."

"I can hold my own."

He smiled at her and nodded appreciatively. "Be careful out there."

CHAPTER NINE

It had been years since the neighborhood had been Chinatown in anything but name, but the green-and-red Friendship Archway with its seven golden pagodas still greeted Con when she emerged from the Metro. She wound her way through the throng of office workers on their lunch hour, half of whom were engrossed in their LFDs and relied on digital curb warnings to know when to stop at intersections. The trains had been delayed, so she was already running late, but she stopped at a drugstore before she walked down to meet Detective Clarke. She needed a hairbrush and makeup.

Given her meager bankroll, it might have seemed the last thing she should be spending money on, but she'd gotten a good look at herself in the mirror back at the diner. She had questions that only Darius Clarke could answer and couldn't afford to show up looking like . . . well, she hated to use the word, but like a clone. Maybe he was an asshole to everyone, but something in his tone had sounded personal. Cloning was illegal in Virginia, and clones who strayed across state lines had less than no legal standing. If he was anti-clone, he'd be under no obligation to help her. To have a chance, she needed to sell him on the idea that she was a human being despite what Virginia law might claim. The less she looked like a sentient children's toy, the better.

Locking herself in a coffee shop bathroom, she stripped to her underwear and washed in the sink with paper towels and hand soap.

The perfume samples she'd scavenged from the drugstore helped mask the smell of the dumpster a little, but only a little. When Awaken the Ghosts had been on the road, Con had grown accustomed to guerilla personal hygiene. Stephie called it a French bath. Tragically, the three boys in the band hadn't shown much interest in soap. Con remembered the awful way Tommy would smell after a few days cooped up in the van. It had driven her crazy at the time, but now with the benefit of distance, she almost felt nostalgic for the toxic cloud that trailed after the band's keyboardist.

Her hair didn't go nearly as well. The back of her head had fused into clumps in the Palingenesis womb, and she couldn't even get the hairbrush through it. She should have bought a pair of scissors instead. Scratch that, she'd need a machete to make any meaningful progress. Last came makeup, which, again, was a struggle for her hands as she applied foundation and eye shadow to mask the weird perfection of her newborn skin. Muscle memory seemed to be taking the longest to relearn. When she stepped back to assess her progress, she knew her dream of a movie makeover wasn't in the cards. *Not totally tragic* looked to be the best she could do. She hoped it would be enough.

———

She was nearly an hour late to meet the detective from Virginia. The inside of the restaurant was all dark wood and gloomy lighting that made it feel like instant midnight. The lunch rush was in full swing. Every stool at the bar was taken, as were most of the tables, mostly parties of three or four, but several men ate alone. Con realized she didn't know Darius Clarke from Adam. Everyone looked like a cop to her. Probably were, too, since the restaurant was only a few blocks from the courts and MPD headquarters. Either that or the cheap-suit convention was in town.

Toward the back, a Black man in a blue suit waved her over.

"Darius Clarke?" she asked, sliding into the booth across from him.

He nodded, not pausing from his lunch to offer her a hand to shake. "Trouble finding the place?" he asked, mouth full.

"Sorry. Trains were delayed."

"DC," he said with the enthusiasm of a man who'd found an undiagnosed growth on his back.

Up close, she realized he was younger than his voice. No more than thirty. Some people just got a head start on being old bastards, and Darius Clarke seemed ready to be fitted for a rocking chair, a porch, and a view he didn't much care for. His short, meticulously groomed beard drew to a sharp point, and black glasses framed sharp, incisive eyes. It lent him a stern professorial aspect. A harsh grader who took pride in never giving an A.

"What," he asked, brow furrowing, "is that smell?"

Didn't look like the perfume had done the trick after all.

"Ethiopian food," she said, implying she'd had it for lunch.

"What'd you do, bathe in it?" He dropped his fork operatically, appetite apparently gone, and pushed the plate away. Wiping his mouth with a corner of his napkin, he looked her up and down. More than looking. Analyzing.

"Something the matter?" she asked.

"Never seen one of you up close," he said, as if she were an attraction at a carnival and he'd paid for a ticket to gawk at the freak.

His matter-of-fact tone shook her, but at the same time, she preferred he say it to her face. Growing up mixed, it had always been the whispers just out of earshot that got under her skin the most. Whatever it was he was thinking, better to have it out in the open. That way, at least, she knew exactly what she was dealing with. Still, it didn't prevent her temper from flaring. She didn't have a long history of biting her tongue, but she recognized that running her mouth wouldn't get her anywhere. Instead, she gave him what she saw he wanted, lowering her eyes and apologizing a second time for being late. It did the trick. He relaxed now that he thought they'd established who was in charge.

She reached for the menu. "Would it be cool if I got something to eat?" Despite her big breakfast, she was already hungry again. It wouldn't kill the Commonwealth of Virginia to pick up the tab.

He snatched the menu away. "Hey, we're not having lunch. This isn't a date. I need you to answer a couple questions, and then I'm getting back on the road. I'm late as it is."

"Come on," she said, giving him her biggest eyes. "I'll eat fast."

His expression indicated he was distinctly unwooed. "Feel free to order whatever you want. After I'm gone."

He set a recorder on the table between them and recited his name, his badge number, and the time, date, and location.

"Initial interview with the clone of Constance Ada D'Arcy." He said *clone* the way other people said *pedophile*. "How old are you?"

She sat there and said nothing. At least he had the dignity not to repeat his question; she'd give him that much. He stopped the recorder, tongue searching his teeth for any scraps of his lunch. Maybe it wasn't the best idea to antagonize him, but she had the feeling that if she let him bulldoze her, it would become a habit fast.

"I thought you had Ethiopian," he said.

She shrugged. "I'm malnourished."

"Fine." He dropped the menu back in front of her. "What do you want?"

Con flagged down a passing waiter and ordered the first thing she saw on the menu, not wanting to give the son of a bitch the chance to change his mind. It had been a minute since she'd had meat loaf. What was it they said about beggars and choosers?

She reached across the table and started the recording again. "I'm twenty-two. Twenty-four now, I guess."

"No, I mean how old are *you*? How long since Palingenesis brought you online? Is that the correct term? Online?"

The question caught her off guard. "Revived. I don't know exactly. Didn't you ask them?"

He typed a note on his LFD but didn't answer her question. "So it's my understanding that all of Palingenesis's clients have a biometric chip implanted."

"That's right. It notifies Palingenesis of a death event. Gives them a jump on activating the clone. Guessing that's why they knew before you did."

He nodded. "Well, there should also be GPS data associated with Constance D'Arcy's chip. Palingenesis insists they can't access it."

That was true. Several years earlier, the news broke that Palingenesis was collecting and storing GPS data of its clients' whereabouts. It had sparked a furor over privacy concerns. Turned out billionaires didn't like having their movements tracked any more than regular people. To stave off a public-relations crisis and client revolt, Palingenesis had reengineered their chips so that all GPS data older than thirty-six hours was continually erased. After the client died, the final thirty-six hours were preserved and exorbitantly encrypted. Now the only people who could access that information were the clients, designated representatives, or their clones. Con realized why she was really there, and it wasn't so Clarke could interview her to get a feel for Constance D'Arcy.

"You want me to give you the GPS so you can find the body," she said.

"Accurate," he replied. "It would help point us in the right direction."

"How do you think"—Con stumbled over her next word—"she died?"

"Look. No offense to Palingenesis, but we're not in the business of taking anyone's word for it. Until we have a body, I'm not speculating on cause of death."

"So she could still be alive?"

He shrugged. "Palingenesis doesn't think so, but we're not ruling out the possibility. That would be awkward for you, though, huh? Constance D'Arcy pops up alive with you running around pretending to be her. Wonder what they would do with you then. Would be a dangerous precedent."

"I'm not pretending," she whispered, but the feeling of being an imposter returned stronger than ever. He was also right about it being dangerous. The one absolute and sacrosanct law governing cloning was that there never be more than one of anyone. If the original Con D'Arcy turned up alive, then her life would take precedence. Con didn't know how she felt about that—or maybe it would be more accurate to say that she didn't know how to reconcile feeling both ways about it. On the one hand, she wanted more than anything for her original to be safe. On the other, she didn't want to die. After all, she was Con D'Arcy too. One more way her existence was a paradox.

Clarke shrugged again. "So, you going to help us out or what?"

"I could do that maybe. Will you do something for me?"

Clarke frowned. "We're not bargaining here."

It was her turn to shrug. How many club managers had said the same thing over the years? "We're always bargaining."

"I'd think it would be in your interest to help me."

"A girl can have more than one interest."

Clarke rolled his eyes. "What do you want?"

"I want access to everything you learn."

"Absolutely not," Clarke said.

"And if she turns out to be dead, I need you to push through the death certificate and get it into the system as fast as possible."

"Why?" Clarke asked. "Oh, so you can become her, right? Isn't that how it works?"

"I am her," Con said.

"Whatever you say."

"I am."

"Not legally," Clarke needled.

"No, not legally, and I can't access my bank account until then."

"Or get a job," he reminded her.

She didn't like how much he seemed to be enjoying her crisis. "I'll also need you to pack up a few of my things. I really just want my notebooks and guitar. Ship it up to DC. Since it's not safe for clones south of the Potomac."

Clarke sat back. "I'll do what I can on the death certificate. But I can't help you with getting your stuff back."

"Can't or won't?"

"Take your pick. None of it belongs to you."

"What are you talking about?"

"The Commonwealth of Virginia does not acknowledge cloning or clones. Which means you have no legal standing under Virginia law. If Constance D'Arcy is dead, then her estate is the property of her husband. You want anything, take it up with him."

Con felt the blood leave her face in a cold rush. "Her *what*?"

"Her husband," Clarke repeated.

"I'm married?" Con mumbled in shock. Kala had mentioned something about a new boyfriend, but a husband? That was impossible. It was like the detective was describing a complete stranger.

Clarke looked confused. "Well, *you're* not. But yeah, she was, little more than a year now. How do you not know that? I thought they gave you her memories."

"*My* memories," she said defensively.

"Sure. So why don't you know about him?"

"I'm missing some of them," Con admitted.

"How much?"

She barely heard him, instead trying to wrap her mind around what the detective was telling her. Married? How? Since Zhi, she hadn't dated anyone for more than a few weeks. Now she was supposed to believe that she'd met a guy, moved to Richmond, and married him? It was absurd.

"How much?" he repeated.

"The last year and a half."

Clarke let out a long whistle. "You still want to tell me you're her?"

"I'm married," Con said to herself, trying to make it make sense.

Clarke saw her discomfort and kept turning the knife. "Want to see his picture?"

He threw a picture to her LFD, but she blocked it. She already felt overwhelmed without seeing the husband's face. "I don't want to see a goddamn picture."

Clarke smiled for the first time. "Hey, no problem. You don't want to see, I don't blame you. It's not your life anyway. But what do you say? Log in to the encrypted server and unlock the GPS. Do some good?"

"No," she said softly, defiantly, like a hammer wrapped in silk.

Clarke sat forward. "Say what?"

"I give you the GPS. Then what?"

"Then I track down Constance D'Arcy one way or another."

"And leave me high and dry."

Clarke shrugged. "I don't see what that's got to do with anything."

"We see different. Like you said, I guess I need to take it up with my husband." She grabbed her backpack and stood, suddenly needing to be outside. Far from Detective Darius Clarke and his corrosive contempt.

"Where do you think you're going?" Clarke grabbed her by the wrist.

"Let go of me." She tried to pull free, but his grip tightened painfully.

"You know, if we were in Virginia—" He cut himself short.

"Well, we're not. This is DC. I've got rights."

"Rights?" He shook his head and chuckled like she'd told him a joke he'd already heard but that he still found kind of funny. He laid his handcuffs on the table. "You really think anyone's gonna kick up a fuss when they find out what you are? Go ahead, scream, I don't care. Nobody's riding to the rescue of some skinny-ass Gucci."

"Let me go," she repeated.

He pulled her closer. "You know why they call them Guccis, right? 'Cause clones are knockoffs of the real thing. Except you're no Gucci, are you? You're a cheap knockoff of a cheaper original. You're not loaded like the rest of them. Got no money to hide behind. How you think that's going to work out for you?" He let go of her wrist and reached for the check. "You're going to need a friend out here. Might want to keep that in mind."

"Oh, now we're going to be friends?"

"Where'd you sleep last night?" Clarke asked rhetorically. "Might be I could work it so you're a confidential informant for the purposes of this case. That way I could slip you a few bills. Get you off the street for a couple nights."

Con hesitated. By this time tomorrow, she'd be broke again. Maybe she'd get lucky before nightfall and someone would offer her a meal and a place to sleep. Or maybe not. Maybe the Clarkes and Kalas of the world *were* the whole world. If so, she was facing not only another night on the street but a lifetime on the margins. Could she really afford to turn down his offer? But cooperating with him would be nothing more than a short-term fix. A few days and then she'd be right back in this same place. She only had one bargaining chip; she couldn't afford to give it up on the cheap.

"Can I go?" she asked.

"What about your meat loaf?"

"Lost my appetite."

"I still need that GPS," he said.

"And I need my life back. Tell the husband if he wants the GPS, he should call me."

Clarke smiled and shook his head. "I guess what they say about clones is true. You really don't have a soul. Constance D'Arcy is missing, likely dead, and you won't even do the right thing."

"She's not dead," said Con, turning to leave. "I'm right here."

CHAPTER TEN

Con walked until her fury at Darius Clarke had dulled, relieved to disappear among the throngs of tourists taking in the sights on the National Mall. She stopped in the Sculpture Garden at the National Gallery of Art and stood at the foot of a statue of red sheet metal, faded by the years and the elements. It rose above her like a giant insect, but a plaque identified it as *Cheval Rouge (Red Horse)*. She stared up at the statue, trying to see what Alexander Calder had seen when he'd created it in 1974. It didn't look like a horse—in her experience, horses didn't have six legs—but she still thought it was beautiful whatever it was.

In the shade of a towering elm, she found an empty park bench where she could regroup and think things through. Now that she had calmed down some, she really wished she'd taken the damn meat loaf. And why had she been too scared to look at the husband's picture? It was going to make her crazy until she knew more about him. She'd been so rattled that she hadn't even asked his name. But it had been an overwhelming first day—from the lurching panic of discovering she was a clone to learning that the death of her original might not have been natural or accidental. Detective Clarke's contempt had been one more thing than she could bear. And then there was the missing eighteen months and the cancerous self-doubt it was creating. Last night, she'd thought that if she filled in the blanks she would feel like less of an imposter, but so far the opposite was true. With each new revelation, she felt further and further removed from believing she was Con D'Arcy.

This need to know every detail of her missing eighteen months was verging on obsession. How else to explain rejecting Vernon Gaddis's sanctuary? She'd spent one night on the streets without getting robbed or worse, but that had been luck as much as anything. Surviving on a city's streets took skills she didn't possess—skills she wanted very much to avoid acquiring. But forced to choose between a safe place to sleep and pursuing answers from that cop, she hadn't hesitated for a second. And she knew she'd make the same choice again. Being homeless scared the hell out of her, but this half existence of questioning who and what she was scared her far, far more.

If Vernon Gaddis was right and Brooke Fenton had orchestrated Con's revival and escape from Palingenesis, that meant Fenton might also be responsible for the disappearance of the original Con D'Arcy. If she was dead, Con needed to know. If she wasn't, she needed to know that too. No matter the consequences. Everything else was just background noise to her now. And was she really going to wait in DC and rely on Darius Clarke? He hadn't exactly overwhelmed her with confidence in his intentions. So why not go to Richmond herself? She had access to her original's GPS data. All she needed was a car.

She laughed at the hopelessness of her situation. With what Kala and Peter Lee had given her, she was only a few thousand dollars short. So what now?

Even though she knew it was futile, she tried logging in to her private social network. After the behemoth social networks had died off in the twenties—victims of changing legal and cultural privacy concerns—they'd been supplanted by self-managed private social networks. Designed by white-hat, open-source, anti-corporate coders, the new do-it-yourself PSNs were free, easy to set up, decentralized, and had no corporate overlords. Con had read somewhere that there were more than twenty billion private social networks worldwide interconnected in a complex latticework. But her original had changed her credentials in the last eighteen months, and without them, Con couldn't even see her PSN, much less access her personal account.

After that, she spent time working through her contacts, hoping to hunt down a bed for the night. It didn't take long to realize that Kala had been busy since this morning. There was a lot of overlap in their friend groups, and word had spread like wildfire that Constance D'Arcy had died in Virginia and that her clone was looking for a handout. *A handout?* That pissed Con off all over again, although she supposed that Kala had helped her in one regard—there was no way that Palingenesis could simply disappear her now. Too many people knew she existed. But in the short term, her friend had closed a lot of doors before Con even got a chance to knock.

The few people who answered seemed genuinely heartbroken by the news. The consensus was that Con had lived a hard life, and they wished she'd found a way past her grief. It was touching to hear your death mourned, but it didn't feel right that she should hear it. Eulogies were for the survivors, not the departed. Con was in the unique position of being both. They asked her if she knew how she'd died. No one came out and said the word itself, but it was clear that people were worried she'd taken her own life. Con didn't like the idea. She hadn't been that depressed. Or had she? Could that have been what had happened to her?

Everyone had questions, and she could hear them mentally composing the posts they'd share later on social media. How many people could say they knew a clone personally? Con answered as best she could, hoping to earn some goodwill. But when it came to a place to stay, the answer was always a hard no. For some, it was an unmistakable anti-clone bias, but for others, it was simpler than that: their friend was dead, and the idea of letting a living reminder of that loss into their homes was too much.

In frustration, Con tore her LFD from behind her ear and put her head back, staring up at the sky through the canopy of green. There wasn't a breeze on the ground, but the branches up above rippled as if from some untouched hand. When Con looked back down, a white woman was standing a short distance away. The brittle posture was familiar, but it took a moment for her to place the pinched face. Brooke Fenton. Con reached for her backpack and glanced around.

Fenton seemed to read her mind. "I'm alone. I only want to talk."

"Don't you mean delete me?" Con said. If she ran south, she'd be out in the open on the Mall with nowhere to hide, but if she went for Constitution Avenue, there were enough museums and businesses that she might be able to disappear. Depending on how much backup Dr. Fenton had brought.

Fenton shook her head. "We're way past that. You're out in the open now. Richmond PD interviewed you—you're on the record as existing, so deletion is off the table even if I wanted to, which, believe me, I do not."

"I'm a *you* now?" Con said, remembering the casual way that Fenton had ordered her sedated until the board decided how to dispose of her. "I thought I was an *it*."

"I apologize if you were offended," Fenton said. "It was a difficult situation, and I chose my words poorly."

Con made a note of her artful non-apology apology. "How did you find me?"

"Detective Clarke. He was at Palingenesis this morning conducting interviews. He mentioned he was meeting you. I had him followed."

It sounded plausible, but Con still had doubts about her LFD and powered it off just in case.

Fenton drifted closer. "May I sit? Please? Ten minutes."

"It's a free bench," Con replied, trying to sound calm. She held her backpack tightly in both hands.

The two women sat side by side, looking straight ahead. Eventually, Fenton cleared her throat. "I know we got off on the wrong foot, and that you will likely never look on me as a friend, but I believe we can help each other."

"Why? Because those men you sent to my apartment last night missed me?"

"Men?" Fenton looked compellingly puzzled. "What men?"

"Save the Meryl Streep for someone else, I'm not buying it. I don't trust you."

"That's too bad, because you are in a lot of trouble, Constance."

"Alright," Con said, rising. "If we're at the threats part of the conversation, I'm out of here."

"I'm not threatening you," Fenton said. "There was something wrong with your revival."

"Yeah, I heard. I've got real bad lag."

"No, symptoms of extreme lag are psychological in nature. This is something else. This is physiological. We found an anomaly."

"What kind of anomaly?" Con asked, sitting back down on the bench.

"An absence. The log of your download registered a cluster of voids. When we compared it against your stored upload, it didn't match."

Con didn't know what any of that meant other than that it sounded calculated to scare her. Knowing that did nothing to stop it working on her. "What is it?"

"The only thing we know for certain is that it wasn't an error on our end."

"You don't think it was an accident," Con said, thinking back to her conversation with Detective Clarke. What had happened to her original in Virginia?

"Too many things had to go wrong for you to be sitting here today. And I'm afraid human error can't account for all of it. Someone wanted you out of Palingenesis very badly."

"Who?" Con asked, although she knew the answer before Fenton answered. Vernon Gaddis. It wasn't lost on Con how similar a story he had told this morning. "Why would Vernon Gaddis sabotage his own company?"

"He's not trying to sabotage Palingenesis; this is about he and I. Vernon has had a difficult time these last few years. You're familiar with the tragic loss of his wife? It cost him dearly in so many ways, but he has never gotten over having to step down as CEO."

"The way I heard it, you used the plane crash to force him out and try to take control of Abigail Stickling's research laboratory."

"The board forced Vernon out, and they were right to do it," Fenton countered, the resentment in her voice unmistakable. "He thought he could maintain control through me. His little protégé. He actually called me that once to my face. What he really wanted was a puppet. And when I exhibited the least little hint of autonomy, he accused me of betraying him and attempted to have me removed. And as for your aunt's lab, you're damn right I tried to seize control. Can you imagine anything more corrosive for a cutting-edge technology company than to be held hostage by its own research division? Abigail wielded the promise of her inventions like a weapon. She would tease the board with her latest breakthrough and then scurry back to her lab, saying it wasn't ready yet. Or the timing wasn't right. No one dared cross her. The company found itself in the untenable position of begging for scraps from itself. It was madness.

"Vernon Gaddis and Abigail Stickling created something truly revolutionary and came to think of it as an extension of themselves. As far as they were concerned, they were Palingenesis and it couldn't survive without them. They insisted on maintaining an unhealthy amount of control. But when the company needed to grow, their egos wouldn't allow it. It happens so often, it has a name: founder's syndrome. Vernon has spent the last few years resolidifying his hold on the board and undermining my stewardship of the company at every opportunity. I don't know how Vernon did it, but he tampered with your revival and snuck you out of Palingenesis. To what end, I don't know yet."

Con had to admit it was one hell of a compelling story. But then again, so was Vernon Gaddis's version. One of them was a gifted liar. Either way, Con didn't know enough to guess which one was telling the truth, so better not to believe either.

"Why me?" Con asked.

"No offense, but you're poor," Fenton said. "What I mean is that unlike every single other clone in that facility, you aren't worth at least half a billion dollars. You don't have a team of lawyers at your beck and call. It makes you perfect."

"What is it you want from me?" Con asked, cutting to the chase.

"I need to make an upload of your consciousness so I can find out what Vernon did to you."

"Why not just try and grab me again?"

"I didn't try to grab you again, because I didn't try and grab you last night. There would be no point. An unconducive emotional state would make it impossible to image your consciousness. A consciousness can only be uploaded with a client's consent. So I'm here asking for yours."

Interesting. That explained why Fenton was going with a charm offensive. It also put Con in somewhat of a unique position.

"So now we know how I can help you. How are you going to help me?"

Fenton smiled as if Con had just laid down the exact card she needed to make her hand. "You have an unprecedented degree of lag. How is that treating you? Have you begun hallucinating yet?"

"No," Con lied, remembering how real Zhi had sounded. The way her grandmother's slippers had scuffed over the concrete.

"Somehow I don't believe you. I already know from Ms. Askari that you're experiencing apraxia. Muscle memory issues. You couldn't even tie your own shoes, could you? What about slurred speech? Double vision? Proprioceptive disruption?"

"A what-now disruption?"

"Body kinesthesia—trouble keeping your balance, basic coordination, that sort of thing."

"A little bit," Con admitted.

"Did it take you a moment to recognize me? A few minutes ago. Did you have trouble remembering my face?"

Con nodded.

"That's prosopagnosia. Face blindness. There is a whole bouquet of agnosias for you to look forward to. Well, if you're taking the medication that Ms. Askari provided, it will help mask your symptoms for a time. But it is going to get much, much worse."

"Is it going to kill me?" Con asked.

"There are worse things than dying. Believe me."

"Well, you're all sunshine and roses, aren't you?" Con wanted to believe that Fenton was exaggerating, feeding her a steady diet of gloom and doom to get Con to do what Fenton wanted. Somehow she didn't think she was that lucky, though.

"But if you help me, Palingenesis will foot the bill for a new clone. It will take six months to grow one to the appropriate age, but when your new clone is ready, it will be a perfect fit for your consciousness."

A new clone was one hell of a sweetener and underlined Fenton's desperation to stave off Vernon Gaddis's challenge. But even if she trusted Fenton, which Con sincerely did not, the prospect of being her lab rat sounded terrifying. Nor did Con trust Fenton to keep up her end of the bargain once she had what she wanted.

"I'll think about it," Con said in the voice of her sixteen-year-old self who had navigated her mother's increasingly mercurial mood swings by avoiding firm answers on anything. Dr. Fenton didn't seem to appreciate Con's nonchalance and let her temper get the better of her.

"You're a fool."

"Careful now, Doctor. You wouldn't want me in an unconducive emotional state."

Dr. Fenton frowned. "May I at least run a few tests? Take a blood sample."

"Not a chance," Con said. "I don't trust you or Vernon Gaddis."

Fenton's eyes narrowed. "You spoke to Vernon?"

"Yeah, this morning."

"In person?" Fenton said, but Con could see that her mind was racing. She was so pale, she could have had bleach for blood.

"No, he doesn't like to leave his island, apparently."

"Well, I see he's done an exemplary job poisoning the well. Fine, so be it. You're still a fool, but keep taking the medication." Fenton held out her business card. "If you change your mind or your symptoms worsen, please call. Let me help you. It's in both our interests."

Con took the card and tapped it against her LFD to add Fenton's information to her contacts alongside Gaddis. She was accumulating quite the collection today. She didn't think she'd be calling either of them, though. Despite all of Fenton's apocalyptic warnings, there was only one thing Con could bring herself to care about—how had her original died?

Nothing else mattered.

But first, she had a man to see about a car.

CHAPTER ELEVEN

Doors didn't open for another hour, but the line of waiting concertgoers snaked down the block and disappeared around the corner. It was a younger crowd, affluent while trying hard not to look it. Con didn't recognize the name on the marquee but loved the prospect of losing herself in the anonymous cocoon of a live show. It didn't matter the kind of music; what she wouldn't give to dance and sing shoulder to shoulder with people who knew nothing of her life.

Not here, of course. Anywhere but here.

Over the years, Glass House had taken on a mythic quality in her mind. Her last memory of that night was climbing into the van to drive to North Carolina, so, for her, this was where the accident had really happened. The place where her selfishness had set the band's destiny in motion. It was ground hallowed by loss and guilt. Where her future had ended and her real life had begun.

Although she hadn't been back since, Con would have sworn she could describe Glass House faithfully, right down to the studs. Standing across the street, however, she realized it was smaller than she recalled, less grand. Where were the windows? She couldn't even find the parking spot where Zhi had left the van idling while he'd gone to hunt down Tommy. He'd parked under a large tree, but there wasn't a single one on the entire block. Even the marquee was on the wrong side of the building, as if her memories were reflections in a mirror. The single most important moment of her life, and her memory was nothing but a shoddy quilt of different clubs she'd played. What else had she misremembered about Zhi's last night?

Zhi. How was he? As soon as she got her feet under her, she should check in on him. Hopefully her original had visited him; she hated to think he'd been all alone these last eighteen months.

Rather than try her luck at the front, Con went down the alley that ran alongside the club and banged on the stage door. A massive Black bouncer cracked open the door to see what all the commotion was about and seemed genuinely surprised that Con was responsible. She explained who she was and why she wasn't waiting in line with everyone else. He listened impassively, then let the metal door swing shut. After a few minutes, the door reopened and he waved her inside like he was doing her a favor. He said Jasper was busy upstairs and brought her out to the main floor, where he left her to sit at the bar. All around, the staff was hustling to get everything set before the house opened. It made her feel at home, always had, especially on tour when the band played a different venue every night. No two clubs were ever the same, but they all ran on the same high-wire energy. There was nothing like it in the world.

By the time Jasper Benjamin finally came down from his office, the crowd was beginning to stream inside, eager to stake out a spot near the front of the stage. Jasper eased up to the bar beside her, grinning an unctuous salesman's smile. He was one of those white men in their forties who desperately wanted to believe he didn't look forty. The problem lay in the fact that Jasper obviously knew that he did and couldn't live with it. His defining feature had always been the manic desperation of a man feverishly overcompensating. For Jasper, that meant expensive clothes and a sunspot personality that could be seen from orbit. She'd once heard him say, *If you don't own a beautiful painting, at least get yourself an expensive frame.*

Tonight that frame included a slick tangerine sports jacket over a retro Trouble Funk T-shirt, black designer jeans that sparkled in the light, and a pair of red-and-orange Italian leather shoes that probably cost more than her rent. He wore more jewelry than Con had owned in her entire life. It was a lot. The man ought to come with a seizure warning. To complete the effect, behind Jasper loomed a gargantuan white man who made the bouncer look like the kid other kids picked on. She knew his name was Anzor, everyone did. He went where Jasper went, and if even half the stories she'd heard about him were true, he was not a pleasant man, and she didn't much care for the way he was eying her. Like she was the last lobster in the tank and he was picking out dinner.

"Welcome back. Been some days," Jasper said, resting a hand lightly on the small of her back as if she were at risk of toppling off the stool. "Hearing some wild stories about you."

"Oh yeah?" she replied, loud enough to be heard over the rising din.

"Didn't anyone bring you a beverage?" he asked, snapping his fingers to get the bartender's attention. "The lady will have a vodka T."

"I'm fine, really. I don't need a drink."

The bartender set a drink in front of her anyway. Con accepted it with a smile. Better to be appreciative than fight the rising tide of Jasper's hospitality. In her experience, men hell-bent on displaying their generosity resented having it declined and rarely offered a second time. She had a lot riding on that second time.

She took a sip and noticed the way Jasper was looking at her. Not the appraising once-over that men gave women, cataloging perceived imperfections in the blink of an eye. *That* she had long since learned to tune out. No, this was something else. Kala, the detective, and now Jasper Benjamin—when they looked at her it was as if they were trying to decide what kind of spider they'd found in their bathroom. And if it was dangerous.

"What?" It came out more defensive than she'd intended.

He flashed a coy, boyish smile at her. The one he probably saved for when he thought he was being charming. It might actually have worked back when he was young, but now—now it looked practiced and stapled on. "Just wondering if I'd be able to tell. You know . . . if I didn't know."

"And?" Not knowing why she'd asked since she definitely didn't want the answer.

He squinted at her. "I think so. Not sure. You look different, but I don't know that I could say why. So forgive me, but I gotta ask. I thought only rich people could afford clones. You some kind of secret billionaire, slumming down here with the rest of us?"

"Would I be here if I was?" Con asked.

"Got me there. So what's your secret?"

Con wasn't about to get into her connection to Abigail Stickling. "Just lucky, I guess."

Jasper mulled that over, seemingly willing to pretend she had answered his question. "I always thought it would be cool to have a clone, you know? Rumor has it that Palmer Bratt is a clone. Can you imagine?"

Con had heard the same rumor. Palmer Bratt was one of the top-grossing actors in the world. According to the tabloids, she'd been killed accidentally on the set of her movie *Planetarium Station* during a stunt gone wrong. Her camp had issued a strongly worded denial, and the actor had always declined to take questions on the subject, calling the accusation absurd and malicious. Still, the rumors persisted. Amateur internet sleuths pointed to the abrupt dissolution of her two-year marriage to singer Delonte Anders, and certain minuscule changes to a scar on Palmer Bratt's throat that had been there since childhood. It was hard to say whether the mystery had increased or decreased her popularity.

There had been all kinds of films on the subject of human cloning, mostly horror, but not all. Plus television, music, books. Alan Delaney's memoir of his transcendent experience as a clone had been a bestseller in more than thirty countries. The entire concept of human cloning had provoked a massive reaction as the culture tried to work out its complex and often conflicting range of opinions. They loved cloning and hated it. Feared it, objected to it on a variety of grounds, yet also envied it and felt left behind.

Speculating which celebrities were secretly clones had become its own cottage industry. Palingenesis itself remained resolutely silent on the subject, neither confirming nor denying the identities of its clientele. It was speculated that a few desperate celebrities had taken advantage of Palingenesis's strict nondisclosure policy to leak fake stories that they themselves were clones, hoping that the whiff of controversy might revive their flagging careers. In politics, it was a far dirtier game. Smearing opponents as clones was a tried-and-true method of discrediting rivals. Multiple conspiracy theories argued that despite the scandal in '33, the US government still sponsored a classified clone program for key White House personnel. All the prospective candidates, from both parties, in the upcoming presidential election had signed pledges not to accept clone backups should they win in November.

The opening act came on stage and launched into their first number. They were surprisingly good, and the audience packed in tight and heads began to bob appreciatively.

"How's the drink?" Jasper asked, almost yelling in Con's ear to be heard.

"It's good," Con said, taking another small sip to placate him, and discovered it really was. But to be safe, she made herself stop there. Breakfast had been her only meal today—only meal ever, technically—and this body had never experienced alcohol before. She probably had the tolerance of a wet kitten.

Jasper said, "Anyway, can't tell you how bummed out I was when that Weathervane show fell apart. Been trying a long time to get you back here, and we were this close. Man, it was so good to finally see you play again. Really play, I mean."

"What do you mean, 'finally'?" Con asked. She knew for a fact that he'd been to at least a half dozen of her shows.

"I was there that night," he said. "I saw you."

"Saw me? What night?"

Jasper struggled to remember the date. "Sometime after Christmas. You and Weathervane at the Chandelier? I think."

The Chandelier had been the second gig on Kala Solomon's list, the night of the twenty-seventh. It might be ancient history for Jasper, but it was fresh in Con's mind.

"You were . . ." Jasper Benjamin was never at a loss for words, but he trailed off. He could be pushy and loud and irritatingly oblivious, but his saving grace had always been that, at heart, he was a fan first and a club promoter second. When he talked about music, he turned into a big kid who just loved music. "It was one of the greatest shows I ever saw. And I've seen them all. You were like a bomb going off that night. Place was only half full, but no one could take their eyes off of you."

"Okay, easy, killer," Con said, feeling a little too much like buttered bread.

"I'm serious," Jasper said, adopting a serious voice to prove it. "No offense, but I've seen you a lot the last few years, sitting in with one band or another. I always got the impression that you'd rather be just about anyplace else. But something happened that night. It was like a switch had flipped. I only ever saw Awaken the Ghosts that one time you guys played here, but it was like that again. Gave me chills, girl. And then you did that new song during one of the encores." He mimicked an explosion on either side of his head with his hands.

It surprised her that Jasper, for all his bombast, was so observant. She thought she'd done a better job masking how conflicted performing often made her feel. It made her curious to know what song she'd sung.

"Don't know the name," he said. "You came out with just Kala and played some new song you'd been working on. Her on bass, you on guitar. That was it. Haunting. Tried to score the audio off the board op, but alas, he wasn't recording that night."

Con had written so many songs in the past three years that she couldn't begin to guess which one it had been. But the fact that she'd sung any of them was almost more stunning than the news that she'd gotten married. She didn't play old Awaken the Ghosts songs anymore, and she definitely never, ever played her new stuff. What had changed?

"You know I only booked Weathervane for the New Year's Eve show because of you," Jasper said. "Seeing you really go for it? I had to have you play here."

"And I agreed to it?"

Jasper put a hand to his chest as if he'd been mortally wounded. "Yeah, you agreed. Shocked the shit out of me, I'll tell you that."

"So what happened?"

"Couldn't tell you. The band got through sound check fine. But then you kind of lost your shit. I thought that guy you were with was going to take a swing at me. Had to have Anzor here show him the way out. Then, way I heard it, your boy took you back to Virginia with him and you just never came back. Man, Kala Solomon was live ordnance when I told her it was a no-go without you."

"I heard," Con said, understanding now Kala's outrage at her this morning. This husband of Con's was growing more impressive by the moment. She'd barely finished swallowing the outlandish fairy tale about her original falling in love and getting married in the last eighteen months. Now she was supposed to believe that somewhere between December 26 (when she'd done her last refresh) and New Year's Eve, this Romeo had completely upended her life—must have been quite the whirlwind romance. Who was this man among men?

"So what did you want to talk to old Jasper about anyway?" he asked, referring to himself in the third person because of course he did.

"Well, actually, I've got a proposition for you."

"That's funny, so do I."

Con let that go and pressed on. "Are you still interested in me playing Glass House?"

Jasper had just gotten through telling her how much he wanted her to play his club, but now that they were negotiating, he scratched under his chin and squinted as if she were trying to sell green to grass. "I might could be interested in that. Can you get Stephie Martz too?"

"I think she lives out West now," Con said. It was a lie; she had no idea where Stephie lived these days, but it wasn't an option even if she did. The last thing she was going to do was drag anyone else into what needed doing.

"That's too bad," Jasper said. "Two would be better than one, you know? I could really put something together with that. But if it's just you, I think I gotta pass."

"Come on, Jasper. You've had a hard-on to get me to play Glass House again for as long as I've known you. Now I'm saying yes, and you've got cold feet?"

"Well, of course I want you to play," Jasper said. "I'm a fan. But these kids here?" He waved a hand toward the waiting audience. "They don't care the way I do."

"So you're not interested."

"Hey, I didn't say that. Maybe if I could see your set first. Do you have anything coming up anywhere?"

"You know I don't," Con said. "Look, all I need is to borrow a car for a week. I've got some personal business to take care of in Virginia. When I get back, I'll track down Stephie and we'll put together a set. I'll even work for free."

Jasper looked at her like she was crazy. "Borrow a car? Girl, you're not putting the Beatles back together. What do I look like, Hertz? I'm not loaning you a car. But if you really need to make some money, I've got some friends you should talk to."

"What friends?" she said warily.

"Why don't we finish this conversation upstairs in my office where it's quieter?"

Yeah, like she was falling for that one. "Forget it. I'm going."

He put a hand on her arm to stop her. "You gotta understand how unique you are. There's a lot of curiosity out there about clones."

"What are you talking about?" Con said, shaking free.

"Just that there's a lot of money to be made. Lot of men who would pay top dollar for the opportunity to . . ." He trailed off as if not saying it out loud would make it okay.

"Clone fucking," Anzor rumbled, speaking for the first time. "The last taboo."

Con shuddered. "Okay, we're done here."

She looked past Jasper for the fastest way out. Over his shoulder, she glimpsed a familiar, unmoving face. It disappeared momentarily as the crowd left its feet, but on the downbeat, the face reemerged like a jagged rock from the surf. The pockmark-faced man was here. He had one hand cupped over his ear, scanning the crowd for her. How the hell had he tracked her down? Con slid off the stool and pushed away from Jasper, who was imploring her to hear him out. Anzor stepped forward to block her way, but she went low and slipped around a group of women dancing to the music.

Con fought her way forward, swimming against the current of concertgoers. One good thing about being small was that sometimes it made crowds easier to navigate. She glanced back over her shoulder, expecting any moment to see Anzor looming up behind. The scary part was that, despite being in a crowd, she knew that no one would come to her defense. They'd assume security was removing an unruly patron and step back.

Up ahead, the exit sign flickered like a welcome lighthouse. She squeezed past another clump of people—and walked right into the waiting arms of one of Pockmark's men. His hands dug into her shoulders painfully. She looked up at him, but his face was occluded by a corona of crimson lights from above the stages.

"Got her," he said into his LFD, but the music drowned him out. He yelled it again but, again, got no response. Waving his hand over his head, he tried to steer Con ahead of him back toward the pockmark-faced man. She struggled wildly and stomped on his foot, but he was wearing thick military boots and didn't even notice. As expected, the crowd cleared a path for them, not wanting to ruin their good time by getting involved.

Someone, or something, came from the right and smashed into her captor—Anzor, faster than anyone that large had any business moving. Con spun free and fell to the floor. The crowd rippled and parted, creating a void. A third man threw himself into the fray. Anzor was twice their size, but the two men were disciplined and worked in tandem, fanning out around him as he threw wild haymakers. From the floor, Con felt like one of the citizens in an old Godzilla movie watching haplessly as monsters wrecked the city.

The band hadn't stopped playing. A strobe began to fire, which only added to the surreal scene. Con crawled for the stage door and the safety of the crowd, which ebbed and flowed as the fight lurched back and forth. One of Anzor's hammer blows connected with one of the men, launching him briefly into orbit. He landed near Con, rolled nimbly to his feet, and saw her. He grabbed for her leg. She kicked out with her other leg, it connected, and she felt herself come free. She scrambled into the crowd and sprinted down the hallway to the stage door, where the same bouncer who'd let her in earlier blocked her way.

"What?" she demanded, ready to fight even if it was a hopeless cause.

"No reentry."

Con almost laughed. "Don't worry, I'm not coming back."

He shrugged and let her pass.

Con stumbled out into the alley and struck out in a random direction, wanting to put distance between herself and Glass House. She wasn't sure who she was more afraid of catching her—Anzor or the pock-faced man. It was two blocks before she realized she'd lost a shoe in the scrum. *Wonderful.* She knelt to pull a sharp rock from the sole of her foot and then kept walking.

It was hard to admit, but DC might be dead to her. She'd learned as much about her missing eighteen months as she could. The story picked up in Virginia, so that's where she needed to head, despite the danger. Could it be any worse than it was here? She didn't see how, and anyway, she knew deep down that she didn't care. The only question was how to get there. Turning to Jasper Benjamin for help had been a waste of time, but he had given her a certain clarity about the tenuousness of her situation. She wasn't going to stubborn her way to Virginia. She needed help.

She made the call. The phone picked up on the first ring.

"Hello, Con," Peter Lee said, sounding genuinely happy to hear from her. "How are you this evening?"

"Couldn't be better. How are you?"

"Better now. What can I do for you?" he asked.

"Tell your boss I want to make a deal."

"He'll be overjoyed. I'll send a car for you."

CHAPTER TWELVE

Con woke feeling rested for the first time since leaving Palingenesis. It was a relief to be able to think with a clear head again. It was also a relief not smelling like day-old Ethiopian food anymore, courtesy of the best shower of her entire life. Seriously, whoever designed that shower with jets that sprayed water from every direction deserved a Nobel Prize. Even so, it had taken four rounds of shampoo and conditioner before her hair began to feel even remotely clean. It still needed the attention of a gifted stylist, but at least she could run her fingers through it now. Sometimes it was the little things.

She'd arrived on the island last night too late to meet Vernon Gaddis. Peter said he was an early-to-bed, early-to-rise sort of person. She'd been glad for the chance to clean up and sleep first. Now, she sat up in bed and asked the house the time; a cheery British voice answered that it was already midafternoon. No wonder she felt so good. As the curtains rolled open automatically, a lens flare of brilliant sunshine poured into the room.

Her clothes were probably well past salvaging—putting them back on would defeat the purpose of taking a shower in the first place—but Peter had told her to help herself to anything in the closet. What she found was a rack of women's clothes, all brand new, tags still on. A pyramid of shoeboxes was stacked on the floor. Skimming a hand along the hangers, she realized that everything was in her size. It had all been bought for her before she'd even agreed to come. It was a power move, she had to admit, and decided not to dwell on how Vernon Gaddis knew her sizes.

Dressed, she went outside onto the balcony off her bedroom. She wanted to get a look at the property in the daytime. It was another hot, humid day, but a breeze blowing in off the water made it bearable. From the drive in, she knew the residence was built on the far end of the island on a talon of land that curled out into the bay. The house had looked mammoth at night, and leaning out from her third-floor balcony, she saw she hadn't been wrong. Vernon Gaddis lived in a castle. It might be a very, very hypermodern castle, but its weathered black stone gave it an unmistakably medieval vibe. And even though Gaddis lived on an island with its private security, he had still built high walls around his property. All he was missing was a moat and a drawbridge.

Her stomach stirred angrily, reminding her that she hadn't eaten a proper meal since yesterday morning. She asked the house for Peter. It replied that he was in the kitchens and asked if she would like to be shown the way. *Wait, kitchens, plural?* The house guided her, offering directions at each turn, although for the life of her, she couldn't tell where the disembodied voice came from. It led her through the house and down a grand staircase to a marble foyer that reminded her more of a hotel than a private home. From the furniture to the artwork to the design, everything had an impersonal, airbrushed perfection. She stared up at the domed ceiling that soared forty feet overhead. A train-station chandelier hung from a wrought-iron chain as thick as a ship's anchor.

She'd played clubs smaller than this.

The house hadn't misspoken either; there really was more than one kitchen, and each was larger than her old apartment in DC. Peter Lee stood at the counter in one of them reviewing the week's menu with the chef but paused when he saw Con.

"Afternoon. I bet you're hungry."

"I could eat," she said in one of the great understatements of the twenty-first century.

"Breakfast or lunch?"

"Breakfast. Definitely breakfast."

"How does an omelet sound? Coffee. Wheat toast. Grits. A medley of fruit."

"And a side of bacon?" she asked, hoping she didn't sound too much like Oliver Twist. She'd been dreaming about bacon since the broken food printer at the diner.

"A woman after my own heart. All our meat is locally sourced from a sustainable farming collective. Mr. Gaddis is an investor," Peter said, clearing a space for her at a rough-hewn farmer's table piled high with books and papers. It was the first place in the house that actually looked occupied and not carefully staged for a photo op. Peter explained that this was where Mr. Gaddis worked most days. Since his wife's passing, he preferred the bustling energy of the kitchen to the solitude of his office.

"What about his kids?" She remembered reading that Vernon Gaddis and his wife had three children.

The faint outline of an expression crossed Peter's face, but it was gone too quickly for Con to name it. At the kitchen counter, the chef stopped working, knife poised above an onion.

"The children don't live here at the house," Peter explained. There was clearly much more to the story, but his tone made it plain that the subject was not open for discussion.

"So is your boss around? When do I get to meet him?" Con asked.

"Unfortunately, Mr. Gaddis had to go into DC this morning."

"I thought you said he never left the island," she said, frustrated by the delay. She needed to get down to Virginia and didn't have time for any games.

"I said rarely. It was an emergency, but he expects to be home in time for dinner. He hopes you'll join him."

He hopes? She didn't know why people with power had to play it like it was up to you when they had you up against a wall and you both knew it. Maybe it helped them sleep at night.

The chef brought over her breakfast, and she ate in peace while Peter finished his work. She couldn't tell what his job was exactly, only that he seemed good at it. He radiated competence, and she found his presence reassuring. After she had used her toast to clean her plate, he offered to show her around the house.

"Actually, do you have scissors I could borrow?" Con said, gesturing to her hair. "I need to do something about this situation."

Peter laughed unguardedly for the first time since she'd met him. "I can do you one better. Follow me."

He walked briskly, with the purpose of a man who could navigate the house blindfolded if necessary. Con hurried to keep up. They entered a small room that was essentially a one-chair barbershop. It was as well equipped as any salon she had ever been in.

"What's all this?" she asked.

"Mr. Gaddis likes his hair done once a week. We were making a mess of his bathroom floor, so he built this instead."

"You do hair too?"

"I do." Peter spun the barber's chair around for her and gestured for her to sit down.

"Seriously, what exactly is your job title?"

Peter laughed again, and she found she liked when he did. "I think he and I settled on majordomo."

"Which is a what exactly?" It was one of those words that Con knew but had never actually heard said out loud. "Is that like a butler?"

"A majordomo was the head steward in an Italian or Spanish palace. I oversee Mr. Gaddis's affairs, manage the household, keep his life running smoothly."

"And that includes cutting hair?"

"I'm a man of many talents. But fair warning, I haven't cut a woman's hair in a long, long time. As long as you're not looking for high fashion, I think I can manage."

There weren't a lot of people she trusted with her hair, but something about Peter made her take a seat. He let her hair out of its ponytail and cleared his throat apologetically.

"We may have to go a little high and tight."

"How high, how tight?" she asked, although she knew exactly how dire the situation was up there. "You know what, just do what has to be done."

"I usually do."

Over the next thirty minutes, Peter hacked away at everything that wasn't healthy hair and then set to work styling what little was left. He'd been modest—the man was a wizard with a pair of scissors. They talked while he worked, and for a short time, Con let herself believe that life was normal again. She was just out getting her hair done like a million other women. It helped that Peter didn't look at her funny or ask questions about being a clone. She guessed that working for Vernon Gaddis, it just wasn't that interesting a subject anymore. It felt good to talk about ordinary things. She asked how long he'd worked for Gaddis, and he said that he'd started a year after the plane crash. That had been in '35, so that meant nearly four years.

"Where'd you learn to cut hair? That part of the standard majordomo package?" she asked.

"My dad owned a barbershop. Worked there from the time I was seven years old."

"Where was home?"

"Madison Parish. Little town called Tallulah," Peter said.

"You're from Louisiana?" She'd gotten hints of a Southern accent, but she'd never have guessed Louisiana.

Her surprise must have shown because he grinned at her and let his true accent emerge for a moment. "Not a lot of demand in these parts for a Cajun majordomo, cher. I was trained to adapt."

"Whoever it was trained you well."

"Hooah," Peter grunted.

"You were army?" The clothes had thrown her off, but now that she knew, it explained everything about his bearing and manners.

"Seventeen years."

"My dad was army," she said to her own surprise. She never talked about her father. "He was killed in action."

"Mr. Gaddis told me he was a Ranger. I'm sorry for your loss," he said as seriously as if it had happened only yesterday.

"It's okay. I was just a kid," Con said with practiced deflection.

"It's never okay, especially when you're a kid."

The way he said it, Con could feel his pain just below the surface. She said nothing, leaving space for him to go on if he wanted, but instead, he asked her father's name.

"Corporal Antoine D'Arcy. Did you know him?"

He shook his head. "It's a big army. May I ask where?"

"Central America. Mexican-Guatemalan border."

"Operation Southern Vigilance," Peter said with grave familiarity. "That was a cluster from start to finish. We lost a lot of good people down there."

The subject put a damper on their conversation, and Peter worked on in silence. Con rarely thought about her father; he was more an idea than a person to her. She'd only been six when he died, and even before that, he'd been gone more than he'd been home. It didn't help that shortly after Con had gone to live with her grandmother, her mother had purged all traces of Antoine D'Arcy from her house. Con had stopped by to pick up a few things one afternoon when her mother should have been at work, only to find a bonfire raging in the backyard and Mary D'Arcy curled up in a broken-down lounge chair, reading the Bible.

When Peter was finished, he stepped back and held up a mirror. Con caught her breath at the transformation. She had her grandmother's straight black hair but had never worn it this short before. She'd been afraid she was going to wind up looking like a new recruit, but Peter had managed to give her something approximating a pixie. It worked better than she could have hoped. She looked, dare she say it, almost cute. More important, for the first time, she looked like someone. Not herself, not exactly, but someone. Like if someone glanced her way, she wouldn't worry anymore that they were wondering what species she was. To both their surprise, she threw her arms around Peter and hugged him gratefully.

"So I passed?"

"You have no idea. Thank you so much."

"I'm happy you're happy," he said, extracting himself from her grasp.

"Peter, can I ask you a question? Off the record? What's your boss like, for real?" Maybe it was naïve of her to think Peter would give her a straight answer. He worked for Vernon Gaddis, and cutting her hair didn't make them buddies. Still, she found herself trusting him, and that meant something. She rarely trusted anyone this fast.

"Well, that's a complicated question. But I assume you mean can he be relied on?"

"Something like that."

"He can. Does that mean you should? Not sure that's my place to say, really. The man saved my life, so I might not be objective on the subject."

"He saved your life?" she asked.

"You have to understand that Mr. Gaddis's situation is incredibly complex. And rich people, they don't think like you and me. I'm not even sure they live on this planet some of the time. He will surprise me at times, but he has always treated me fairly. Still, in the end, it's up to each of us to look out for our own interests, because no one else will unless their interests align. Do you understand me? That's the best answer I can give you."

"Thank you," she said. "That helps."

With that, Peter excused himself, saying he had work to do and that if she needed anything to ask the house. She spent the rest of the afternoon exploring and thinking about what Peter had told her about aligning interests. One thing was for sure, it was going to be an interesting conversation tonight. Despite Gaddis's hospitality, they weren't friends. Quite the opposite, he just needed something from her. There was also a fifty-fifty chance that everything Brooke Fenton had said was true. She would need to be on her toes.

The house was room after room of perfectly decorated spaces. Each one empty and devoid of any sense of life. It was like walking through a luxury resort after the season was over and all the guests had gone home. Besides dual kitchens, the house also boasted a movie theater; an enormous library that belonged in an old English university; a game room with a fully stocked bar, pool tables, Ping-Pong, and shuffleboard; a full-size gym; a racquetball court; and a climate-controlled wine cellar that held thousands of bottles. She passed through a ballroom so large, it echoed when she walked. But it wasn't until she came to the hospital-grade medical suite that Con's envy began to turn to pity. Peter had told her Gaddis rarely left the island. He hadn't built a barbershop and doctor's office out of convenience. He'd built them so he wouldn't have to leave the safety and privacy of the island. All that money, and he was still trapped. It wasn't a home, it was an A-list prison.

Upstairs, she found his kids' rooms. Each was immaculate and frozen in amber, toys and clothes scattered around where they'd been left. It reminded Con of the way parents sometimes mourned the loss of a child because they couldn't face up to the truth. On one of the boys' desks was an unfinished homework assignment. But Peter had said the children didn't live at the house. The children hadn't been on board the plane, so where were they?

Out the daughter's bedroom window, Con saw a limousine pull into the circular driveway and stop at the front door. Vernon Gaddis got out and walked briskly into the house. She should take a shower and make herself presentable. It was almost time for dinner.

CHAPTER THIRTEEN

A little after eight, Peter showed Con onto a terrace that looked out over the seawalls that kept the island from being reclaimed by the rising Chesapeake Bay. The sun hung low in the western sky and framed the house in a golden halo. Gaddis sat at one end of a table that could easily have hosted thirty. He rose to greet her, wearing an impeccably tailored suit. After her shower, Con had agonized over what to wear. Did she pick something from the rack of new clothes to show her gratitude, or did that make her appear weak? She'd tried on several options, but in the end, she'd gone with the T-shirt and jeans that she'd arrived in, which she'd returned to find cleaned and folded on her bed. She kept on insisting that she was Con D'Arcy, so she might as well act like it.

"Good evening," Gaddis said. "I'm sorry I wasn't here when you woke, but I had to go into DC to put out a fire. Peter took good care of you, I trust? I hear you were brave enough to let him cut your hair."

"Well, he was brave enough to cut it."

Peter smiled at her joke but said nothing. He poured the wine and disappeared back inside the house. Vernon Gaddis raised his glass and waited for Con to do the same.

"Welcome to my home. Thank you for being here."

"Thank you," Con said as they touched glasses. She was anxious to get down to business but knew it would be a mistake to be the first to raise it. A silence opened between them. He smiled, baiting her. Nice try. She was young but she wasn't stupid. Instead, she tried her wine and complimented him although all she really knew about the wine was that it was a white.

"You know, this was your aunt's favorite spot in the house," Gaddis said, breaking the deadlock. "When she stayed here at the island, we would sit out here for hours planning the future of Palingenesis. She loved this view, although it was better before we had to raise the seawalls again."

"It's okay, I've never actually seen the ocean before," Con admitted. "It's beautiful."

"Never? How is that possible? You're from Texas. How far were you from the Gulf? A couple hours?"

"My mom didn't believe in vacations."

"Your mom didn't believe in vacations," Gaddis repeated with an incredulous laugh. "So Abigail wasn't exaggerating about her sister being a piece of work."

Ordinarily, Con didn't care for anyone bad-mouthing her family but her. However, she was willing to let it go in the interest of diplomacy. "My mom. My mom's mom. Probably my mom's mom's mom. Being a piece of work is kind of the family line."

"Abigail might have mentioned that as well. She was very fond of you, though."

"Oh, I bet," Con said too quickly. She had a lot of adjectives she'd use to describe the tone of the letter that'd accompanied the offer of her clone. *Fond* wasn't one of them.

"Who do you think paid for your university?"

"My grandma," Con said warily.

"No, your grandmother only wrote the check. The money came from Abigail. Quietly. So as not to rock you and your mother's boat any further."

Con wanted to deny it again, but she already saw the likelihood of his story. It had always been a mystery where Gamma Jol had come up with the money after Con's mother had forbidden Con to go to school at UT Austin. Gamma had called it her rainy-day money, but now it turned out it had been Con's rich aunt all along.

"Were you able to put it out? The fire, I mean," Con asked to change the subject and get Gaddis off comfortable ground. It seemed to do the trick because his expression darkened.

"No, I'm afraid not. I was removed from the board of Palingenesis today."

"I'm sorry. Was it because of me?"

"There were always going to be consequences for involving myself. I don't know how Brooke knew that you and I spoke. Doesn't matter now, I suppose. She's been looking for an excuse for a long time now." Gaddis refilled his empty wine glass. "Still, even though I knew it was coming, it was harder than I thought it would be. The company I helped found and build from the ground up escorted me out of the building like a common criminal."

"It was me. I told Dr. Fenton that we'd talked." Con saw no reason not to tell him—either he already knew and was testing her, or he would find out eventually. It would be better if it came from her now. "Didn't know it would get you kicked off the board."

"Did you, now," Gaddis said, putting down his glass. "You talked to Fenton after we spoke?"

"Yeah, I saw her."

"You saw her." The distinction between talking and seeing apparently crucial in Gaddis's mind. "So you went back to Palingenesis?"

"No, she came to me."

"In person? She came to you in person," Gaddis said as if she'd just told him the secret of turning lead to gold. "Interesting. And what did Brooke have to say for herself?"

"She said it was you who got me out of Palingenesis. That you're responsible for the anomaly in my download."

"Anomaly?" He sounded genuinely surprised. "What kind of anomaly?"

If it was an act, he was very, very good. Con reminded herself that Brooke Fenton had sounded equally convincing—these people didn't get rich by being open books. She did her best to describe what Fenton had told her about the cluster of voids in her download.

"Son of a bitch," Gaddis said, slamming his fist down on the arm of his chair like a judge with a gavel.

"You know what it is?" Con asked. "Fenton said she had no idea."

"Oh, the hell she doesn't. She's cleverer than I gave her credit for being."

Con waited for him to go on, but Gaddis drifted off in thought and looked out over the bay as if he'd caught sight of a foundering boat away on the horizon. Con stared lasers into the side of his head, willing him to speak. *Tell me.* When that had no effect, she reached for her own glass. If the whole evening was going to be a standoff, then it might be time to find out how well her new body could hold its liquor. Fortunately, Peter made a timely reappearance with dinner. Mixed wild green salad, blue crab bisque, and braised short ribs that looked determined to melt off the bone. She'd only eaten a few hours ago but was already ravenous again. She wondered aloud if she would ever eat or sleep enough again.

"Are you kidding?" Gaddis said with a laugh, all traces of anger magically gone. It was like an exact copy of Vernon Gaddis, gregarious and charming, had tagged into the conversation. "My first month as a clone, I think I slept fourteen hours a day. I wouldn't get out of bed except to eat. Fortunately, Peter wasn't with me yet, so he still has some respect for me."

That felt reassuring to hear. She'd been navigating her new reality entirely on her own, and it was comforting to know that what she was going through was normal.

"How are you feeling? Emotionally?" Gaddis asked now that he'd designated himself her best friend in the world.

"Not great. No one thinks I'm me," Con said, unsure if she should be confiding in the enemy but painfully aware how much she needed to say it to someone who would get it. The irritating part was she felt certain he knew it too.

He nodded sympathetically. "What about you? Who do you think you are?"

"I don't know. It's hard to keep straight in my head."

"I understand completely. I went through the same thing, and I only had two weeks of lag. You have eighteen months. I can't imagine how you must feel."

"I don't even look the same."

Gaddis nodded. "Ordinarily, Palingenesis would have given you the option of adding back your tattoos. Scars. Distinguishing marks. Aged your skin. They have two cosmetic surgeons on retainer. It helps, believe me. Sometimes clients opt for a clean slate, but nine times out of ten, they want to look as much like their original as possible. I sure as hell did, and even then, I struggled."

Con glanced down at her bare left arm. She got that. It would mean everything to look in the mirror and at least recognize the person staring back. "I just feel like I'm losing my mind, you know?"

"I do. And you're far from alone." Gaddis exhaled deeply. His fingers, which were tented together, twisted back and forth. "How much do you actually know about your aunt?"

"Next to nothing," Con admitted.

"She was remarkable. One of a kind. I'm a workaholic, and she made me look like an unemployable slacker. And she was the most brilliant mind I've ever encountered, to boot. Thank God she had no interest in business, or I would have been out of a job. We met at a conference in Boston, spring of '19. She'd done her undergraduate at MIT in quantum computing and had an MD/PhD from Harvard. It was an unusual, heavyweight combination. Her doctorate thesis on human cloning had made a splash, but she'd had no luck attracting investors."

"Why not?"

"She was, as you say, a piece of work. Investors want to know they can control what they're buying." Gaddis smiled at the memory of his former partner. "And Abigail would not be controlled. It frightened a lot of people away. I took a meeting with her as a courtesy to a friend. I had heard the stories and had no expectations that anything would come of it. But then the meeting stretched into dinner. By the time we finished dessert, the entire trajectory of my life had altered. We were going to change the world together. I just never stopped to ask if the world wanted changing.

"When the DoD approached us, it made so much sense. The country's affection for small wars had spread us too thin. By '28, the operational cohesion of our Special Forces units had degraded to the point that SOCOM couldn't meet its international commitments. You have to understand, a single tier-one operator represents years of training and upward of ten million dollars. A sizeable investment to leave vulnerable to an errant bullet." Gaddis snapped his fingers. "But what if Palingenesis could back up those soldiers? Have a KIA back in the field within a matter of weeks and with minimal loss of training or unit integrity? All that invaluable experience and know-how retained rather than tragically lost. And their families wouldn't have lost a mother or a father. We were patriots. It was a win-win all the way around."

"Until they started coming home," Con said, unsure why she was getting a history lesson. It was a story that everyone in America knew by now. In '32, the *Washington Post* had broken the news that a small biotech firm called Palingenesis was providing clone backups for key Special Forces personnel. The news had detonated in the American consciousness, further fracturing an already divided country. The question of what constituted a human life shifted from the hypotheticals of science fiction to the dining room tables of every household in the nation. Traditional political foes found themselves uneasily on the same side of the issue while once unshakable alliances collapsed into warring factions.

It hadn't helped matters that the federal government, mired in its endless bureaucratic quagmire, failed to pass any meaningful legislation on the subject. The optics of voting for legislation declaring that decorated US veterans were not human beings proved to be political suicide. Not a single bill ever came to a vote. That left it to the states to decide for themselves. The first states to pass anti-cloning laws—Illinois, Massachusetts, Georgia among them—simply banned the procedure outright. In the years that followed, other states went further and further as though competing in a national purity test for the mantle of most anti-clone, stripping clones of personhood entirely and straining the limits of the Full Faith and Credit Clause of the Constitution in a way that hadn't been seen since before the Civil War. The rest of the world had taken varying positions on the issue, with the European Union passing a sweeping moratorium on human cloning while China, Korea, and Japan began developing cloning programs of their own. If the rumors were to be believed, the Saudi royal family paid Palingenesis a fortune to maintain its own private cloning clinic in Riyadh.

"Would it surprise you to learn that most of that first generation is gone now?" Gaddis asked.

"Gone? Gone how?"

"The vast majority took their own lives. Those that didn't were ravaged by addiction and depression. And a disheartening number has simply disappeared from the face of the earth. We have no idea where they are now."

"What happened?" Con asked in disbelief. This part of the story she hadn't heard.

"What happened was they were clones. Once they were done serving their country, our government abandoned them. The nation abandoned them. No effort was made to smooth their transition into a world that didn't know they existed. The project was so highly classified that even their own families didn't know the truth. Once the media broke the story, it tore those families apart."

"I had no idea," she said, appetite finally gone.

"No one does, because it's gone largely unreported. It's not in the national interest to dredge it up. The only time we care about veterans is at ball games." Gaddis emptied the last of the bottle into his glass.

"Jesus," Con said quietly even as she felt her anger rise. "And knowing all that, you decided to offer cloning to the general public anyway?"

"Yes, I did," Gaddis answered, taken aback by her challenge. If he thought confessing his sins was the key to her good side, he was in for a rude awakening.

"Why? What the hell were you thinking?"

"I wish there was a nobler answer, but I'm a businessman. I was thinking there was a lot of money to be made. Abigail wanted to hit pause, discuss the ramifications, but there wasn't time for that. Once the media got ahold of the story, I knew I had to move decisively or risk having everything we'd built washed away in the tide of public opinion. I honestly thought that once we overcame their primitivistic skepticism, we'd be able to convince Americans of all the good Palingenesis was doing. We cheat death. Literally. It's been mankind's dream since we left our caves, and Palingenesis made it a reality." Gaddis stopped himself, embarrassed by his own fervor. "You have to understand, in those days, I was evangelical about cloning. I was wrong as I could be."

That surprised her. She didn't take him for a man prone to admitting to mistakes. "So what changed your mind?"

"The plane crash," he answered simply. "Cynthia and I both died. She always supported my work but never had any desire to have a clone herself. So when I was revived at Palingenesis, I was alone. Disoriented. In denial. Sound familiar?"

"Yeah, very."

"I founded Palingenesis, but I didn't understand what it meant to be a clone. I thought I did. I thought I empathized, but I was too in love with its potential. I couldn't see the toll that being a clone took on our clients as anything but an acceptable trade-off. It took dying for me to see how unethical it all was."

"Unethical? So, what . . . you don't think clones are people now?"

Gaddis shook his head. "No, nothing like that. Of course we're people. I've also had plenty of time to consider that question, believe me. It was the one thing I wasn't wrong about when I woke up five years ago."

"So clones are people, but you're against cloning? How does that work?"

"How long have you been a clone? Two days now? How are you enjoying the experience so far?" he asked rhetorically.

Con was saved from answering by Peter, who chose that moment to reemerge from the house, his timing forever impeccable. He leaned in close to whisper in Gaddis's ear. Gaddis's face hardened. The hollow boom of the surf against the seawalls rumbled in the distance.

"They're all here now?" Gaddis asked.

"Yes, sir. In the foyer. Should I send them away?"

Gaddis frowned. "No, that would only make matters worse. Aldous doesn't like to leave the house any more than I do. He'll take it badly if he made a great show of it for nothing. Bring them out."

"Yes, sir," Peter said and went to get them.

"Problem?" Con asked.

"My other fire has arrived," Gaddis said.

"I should go," Con said, moving to rise. "We can finish talking later."

"No, you should stay. This concerns you too now."

Peter let three men out onto the veranda. Even from a distance, Con could see their barely checked anger. They had no patience for standing on ceremony and brushed past Peter. From the look Peter

125

gave Gaddis, he would have gladly thrown all three into the Chesapeake Bay if given the order. Gaddis waved him off even as the men crowded around him. If it had been her, Con would have felt the need to stand up and get some space, but Gaddis sipped his wine and regarded them clinically.

"Gentlemen," he said. "To what do I owe the pleasure?"

"Is it true?" demanded the first man, a tall Sikh whose forehead was harrowed by frown lines.

"Is it?" echoed the second, a plump white man with a patrician nose and country-club jowls.

The third man, also white, said nothing. He was the shortest of the three, but Con found his quiet gravity intimidating. He stood with his hands thrust into his pockets, sports coat swept back stylishly.

"Is what true?" Gaddis said.

"Don't play dumb," said the second man. "James called us. He says you informed him this afternoon that Palingenesis removed you from the board and now you intend to go forward with the appeal. Is it true?"

"Why don't we all sit down?" Gaddis suggested amicably.

"Just answer the question, Vernon. Do you intend to move forward?"

"I do," Gaddis said.

His guests exploded angrily, the pretense of civility eroding rapidly. Only the third man remained silent, although his eyes turned icy behind his benevolent expression. Gaddis sat stoically while they accused him of betrayal.

"We had a deal," the second man said.

"I'm well aware."

"We agreed that if your case made it to the Supreme Court, you would drop the matter first. That was the deal."

"I know, and I'm sorry," Gaddis said.

"You're sorry?" the first man said, slapping the back of his hand against his palm. "That's not good enough. Not nearly good enough. There's too much at stake for all of us."

"Yes," Gaddis said. "We all have something at stake. We're all in this together. That's a lovely sentiment, but I am the one expected to sacrifice everything."

"It's *your* lovely sentiment," the second man said, face so red that Con thought he was going to have a heart attack. "Yours. You've been preaching it since the beginning."

The third man, who until now hadn't spoken, cleared his throat. His colleagues grew silent and looked to him.

"No one is overlooking the impossible price you are paying, my friend," he said with a politician's voice, deep and compassionate.

"They're my children, Aldous," Gaddis said. "You're asking me to give up on my children. Surrender my claim to them. To admit publicly that I wouldn't fight for them to the bitter end. How do you think they will feel knowing their father placed political expedience ahead of them? Could you do it?"

"Vernon, we understand," Aldous replied. "Believe me. We've all suffered. You know that. But you aren't thinking clearly. If this case goes before the court, you will lose. Five to four. Maybe six to three."

"We don't know that for certain," Gaddis said.

"Five to four. Best-case scenario. Garcia will vote with the majority, and you will lose. That's what all of our opposition research tells us. It's a done deal. And then we all lose everything. The Supreme Court will have dealt a death blow to the legal standing of clones in this country. Everything we've worked toward these past five years will be lost. I'm sorry, but this just isn't our moment."

Gaddis offered no rebuttal. He said nothing at all, but Con could see him digging in his heels. She knew the look intimately from growing up with her mother—it was when facts stopped mattering. When the truth became inconvenient, either contradicting her beliefs or becoming an obstacle to what she wanted. Con didn't know what was happening inside Vernon Gaddis's head, but either way, she saw there was no changing his mind.

That didn't deter Aldous from trying. "But if our candidate wins in November, there are two judges in their late seventies. We have a chance to flip the court our way in the next eight years."

"I don't have eight years!" Gaddis snapped.

"I know," Aldous agreed. "It's not fair, but we have to be patient. Pick our spot. You know this."

"Of course he does. It was his plan, after all," the first man said.

Over the next hour, the three men tried every approach they could think of to convince Gaddis. Nothing worked, although by the end, Con would have sided with them had anyone asked her opinion. No one did. She felt like an uninvited guest at a family squabble. Never once did the three men acknowledge her presence. But neither had Gaddis bothered to introduce her, even though he claimed this concerned her. From the conversation, she had guessed that they were all clones, but apparently, Con was the wrong kind of clone. She might as well have been invisible. There was a lesson to be learned from that. Gaddis would let her listen silently, but it took a billion dollars to have a voice. She'd be wise to remember that.

When the three men finally saw there was no talking to Gaddis, they prepared to leave. Their anger had burned off, replaced by a muted sense of disillusionment. Aldous, the undisputed leader, turned back to Gaddis as he buttoned his sports coat.

"You know I'm not one to make idle threats, but if you go through with this, you understand that there will be consequences. You'll leave me no alternative."

"I understand," Gaddis said. "I won't hold it against you."

"Let's talk again soon. I'd hate for you to make an enemy of me."

"I'd like that," Gaddis said, standing to shake each of their hands as though the matter was settled. Con found the whole charade bizarre and didn't get how rich people fought at all. When they were alone again, Gaddis slumped back in his chair and stared out at the bay for a long time. It seemed to be his favorite pose.

"They're not wrong," he said finally. "I will likely lose the case."

"What case?" Con said, adopting a commiserating tone. It was better than the frustration she was actually feeling.

"Right," Gaddis said. "I sometimes forget it's not the center of everyone's world. It's really quite simple when you get down to it. When our plane crashed, Cynthia and I were returning from Paris. It was our wedding anniversary, and Paris was her favorite city on earth. The tragic part of the story is that after our trip, she'd been scheduled to travel to speak at a conference in Barcelona. I'd been meant to return home alone, but a terrorist attack in Spain forced the conference to be rescheduled at the last moment. She flew home with me instead. Otherwise, she'd be alive today. Just one of those random occurrences with unforeseeable consequences." Gaddis paused there, aware that he'd stumbled into more personal territory than he'd intended to share. "Anyway. When we traveled, we often left the children with her brother's family in Virginia. They are the children's godparents, and their children are close in age to ours. We saw each other regularly, and the kids were all thick as thieves. After I was revived by Palingenesis, I sent word for my children to be brought home. I was informed via my brother-in-law's attorney that my children would remain with them in Virginia."

"Why?"

"Because as far as Cynthia's family is concerned, Vernon Gaddis died in the plane crash alongside his wife. They do not acknowledge my existence. I lost my wife. I have not seen or communicated in any way with my children. Now I am on the verge of losing them permanently along with my fortune and everything that I have built."

"Wow," Con said, understanding now his dilemma.

"Virginia's clone laws are unequivocal on this subject. As is Cynthia's brother. As the godparent, he has claimed custody of my three children.

Furthermore, he sued in Virginia court to have the will read, which states that in the event of Cynthia's and my deaths, our estate is to be placed in trust for the children. To be administered by my brother-in-law, because evidently I am a jackass."

"You'd be broke?"

"Destitute. Obviously, I appealed in Virginia and countersued in Maryland court. Maryland ruled in my favor, Virginia in his. Dueling judgments. The consolidated case is headed to the Supreme Court, should it choose to hear the case, which it has signaled it will. Where I am assured that I will lose."

"Which is why your friends are so angry."

"If the Supreme Court rules that I am not Vernon Gaddis, then it will settle the issue of clone personhood at a federal level. Its ruling will supersede all state law and signal the end of legal cloning in the United States. Clones everywhere will be stripped of rights and property. So either I fight for my children with every resource at my disposal, or I sacrifice them in service to the greater good. Which I had more or less resigned myself to doing until today's board meeting."

Con didn't have children, had no real interest in them, but couldn't imagine being forced to make such a choice. "So why the change of heart?"

"Because I don't think any of this is an accident. Something is happening that has been in the works for a long time. I can feel it, but I don't know what it is. Or why."

"So what now?"

"Now we make a deal," Gaddis said. "How does dessert sound?"

CHAPTER FOURTEEN

Dessert was blueberry cobbler and ice cream. Gaddis had a scotch, but Con declined. She was still nursing her first glass of wine and meant to keep it that way. Gaddis pulled his chair close so they could talk quietly. Jacket off, tie loosened, he sat forward conspiratorially and rolled up his sleeves.

"In '32, the *Post* broke the news about cloning, and Palingenesis began offering cloning to the public sector. In the eight years since, both of its founders have been systematically removed from the company they created."

"My aunt killed herself."

"Please." Gaddis snorted. "Abigail Stickling was the least suicidal person I've ever met."

"The media said she was suffering from depression," Con said.

"She was certainly frustrated by setbacks in her work, but she was far from depressed. That was simply Palingenesis's cover story."

"You don't think she killed herself?"

"No, it was definitely Abigail. And yes, I heard all the absurd theories that it was somehow her clone, despite the fact she wasn't medically able to have one herself. Originals and clones are identical in most respects, but there are ways to tell—fingerprints, environmental wear and tear, sun damage. These things cannot be faked. I've no doubt that it was Abigail Stickling who fell from that rooftop. What I've never understood is why."

"You think it's all connected," Con said.

"I know how it sounds. And there were times I thought I was just being paranoid—I'll be the first to admit my imagination has gotten the best of me at times in the five years since Cynthia died—but I never stopped thinking there was something more profound at work than bad luck."

"And you think Brooke Fenton is behind it all?"

"I do now."

"You know she says the same of you," Con said as much to remind herself as to tell Gaddis.

"Of course she does. She needs a fall guy, and I've played into her hands."

"So what is it Fenton wants?"

"When we created the company, I agreed that Abigail would retain final and absolute say on when, and if, her work would be released. It had its drawbacks, but at the end of the day, there was only one Abigail Stickling. From the moment Fenton replaced me as CEO, she went to war with Abigail for control of the research and development labs. She explored every recourse at her disposal to get her hands on the vast treasure trove of intellectual property that Abigail was developing. Nothing worked. When Abigail died, Brooke Fenton marched into the research lab like Hannibal crossing the Alps. And do you know what she found? Absolutely nothing. Abigail had erased everything. Years of research gone. It set Palingenesis back a decade or more. At the time, I thought Abigail was simply too egocentric to leave anything behind that might allow others to follow in her footsteps, to succeed where she had failed. It would have been a very Abigail thing to do."

"But now you're not so sure."

"Now I wonder if any of that's true. Was Abigail's research really erased, or was that also part of Brooke's cover-up? Maybe I'm wrong, but I find it more plausible than the notion that Abigail committed suicide and that eighteen months later her niece was revived despite being fifteen months past the medical lockout deadline. And that the same steward who ostensibly mishandled the lockout in the first place was the very same one who helped sneak you out of the vault."

"You think Laleh Askari was involved?" Con said, thinking back for any hint that Laleh had been lying to her. She hated the idea.

"Well, I'd like to ask her that very question, except she seems to have disappeared."

"So you think Brooke Fenton faked the destruction of Abigail's research and is using my consciousness to steal it from Palingenesis?" Con said, trying to wrap her mind around the idea.

"Yes, I do. But not even the CEO could walk out of Palingenesis with that kind of intellectual property. It's absolutely impossible. She would need a courier. One that had no idea she was even carrying anything of value."

"So you want to make an upload of my consciousness."

"Yes, although to do that we would need access to a Palingenesis clinic, which I can no longer get. What I'd like to do is to take a scan of your head. I have an expert who should be able to tell us whether I'm correct or if my imagination has gotten the better of me. It will take a few days to analyze. In the meantime, you are welcome to remain here as my guest."

"I have a counteroffer."

"Yes, I thought that you might," Gaddis said. "Let's hear it."

"I want a car and enough money to last me a week or two."

"You want to go to Virginia, don't you? Despite the danger, despite the risks, you're prepared to drive down there."

"Yeah, is that stupid?"

"Depends who you ask. Would you tell me why?"

She hesitated to say what was on her mind, knowing how foolish it would sound. "It's hard to explain, but . . . I want to know what happened to her. My original. In the last eighteen months. Like, I need to know."

"Of course you do." Gaddis nodded, a knowing look in his eyes.

"Is it weird how curious I am about her life?" Con asked. "These missing eighteen months? I can't stop thinking about it."

"It would be strange if you could."

"Really?"

"Very much so. It's common to all the clones I've talked with over the last few years. However little lag they experience, there is always this gnawing sense of being incomplete."

"Yes!" Con said, sitting up sharply. She'd been struggling to put a word to what she'd been feeling. Incompleteness. That part of her was missing. Again, she felt relief knowing that she wasn't the only one. "Did it happen to you?"

"I was obsessed," Vernon answered.

"That's how I feel."

"My last refresh was right before we left for Paris. I felt this desperate need to know everything that happened between Cynthia and I. Down to the last detail. Where we went, what we did. Was she happy? I hired private investigators to retrace our movements. Had them speak to hotel and restaurant staffs. Anyone we interacted with. I pored over our text messages to try and gauge our mood. Cynthia was a great photographer, so there was a treasure trove of photos and videos. I looked at everything. Reconstructed the entire trip."

"And did it help?" Con asked.

"Yes and no. I mean, nothing was ever going to be enough, but in the end, I learned enough to feel at peace. I knew that Cynthia had a wonderful trip and that our life together ended on a high note. That helped me to move on."

"I'm sorry," Con said, thinking about the last memories of her life before—waking up on the morning after Christmas, visiting Zhi. A year and a half ago now, yet to her, it was only three days ago.

"I can't imagine how it must be for you," he said.

"What do you mean?"

"I mean, I was only missing two weeks. You are missing a year and a half. And an incredibly eventful year and a half at that—you fell in love, moved, and got married. So many important milestones in your life."

"Is it? My life, I mean," she asked, giving voice to a question that had begun to gnaw at her.

Vernon grew somber and cleared his throat meaningfully. "Of course it is. Whose life is it if not yours? Do you remember your childhood? Your life before?"

"Yes, but—"

"But nothing," Vernon said sternly. "As far as I am concerned, there is no difference between you and your original. Would you say an amnesiac wasn't themselves because they couldn't remember part of their lives? What gives anyone the right to say you're not you? That's for you to say and no one else."

"So you understand why I have to go?"

"I do. Absolutely," Gaddis said sadly. "It's a terrible idea. Clones aren't welcome in Virginia. The last clone that got caught in the state was found hanging from a tree. But I know that none of that matters to you. I know nothing I can say will make you listen to reason. You have my absolute sympathy, but that's why I can't let you do this. If I'm right about what's in your head, then it's the only copy left anywhere in the world. If anything happened to you down there, it would all be lost."

"Fine, if you don't want to help me, maybe Brooke Fenton will. Honestly, I don't trust either of you, but I'm giving you first shot. I'm going to Virginia one way or another. You say you know what I'm going through, well, then you know that this war you got going on between you and Brooke Fenton—I don't care about it, or Palingenesis, or my aunt's research. The only thing that matters to me is finding out what happened to my original. That's it. When I get back, whichever one of you gave me a car can have what's in my head. With my consent, which is the only way you can ever have it."

Gaddis chuckled.

"What's so funny?" Con demanded.

"You remind me of Abigail."

"Do we have a deal?"

"I get a scan of your head before you leave?" Gaddis asked. "And I'd like my doctor to give you a physical before we turn you loose on Virginia."

"Yeah, that I can do."

Vernon Gaddis put out his hand for her to shake. "Then we have a deal."

PART TWO

CROSSING THE RIVER

"I shall learn from myself, be a pupil of myself; I shall get to know myself, the mystery of Siddhartha." He looked around as if he were seeing the world for the first time.

—*Siddhartha*, Hermann Hesse

CHAPTER FIFTEEN

Two days after her dinner with Vernon Gaddis, Con left Charles Island driven by a late-model, two-door electric compact with Virginia plates. It was the color of cold oatmeal and not much to look at, but that's the way she wanted it given where she was headed. The less attention she attracted, the less attention she attracted. In addition to this sweet, sweet ride, Gaddis had also linked her brand-new, out-of-the-box LFD to a bank account that would last her at least a couple of weeks. It was early morning, the sky was clear, and she was in good spirits. The first day after waking in Palingenesis had been a mad scramble to survive. Life reduced to its most basic needs: food, water, shelter. Hard to make a plan when you were hungry, tired, and scared all the time. It had narrowed her focus to navigating safely from point A to point B. Now things felt different. She had a plan. She was on the move.

It was strange, really, how good she felt and how strange it felt to feel good. How self-aware. Awake. After the accident, she had lost all interest in herself, as if making amends for living while her friends had died. Now, she felt her curiosity returning as if she were emerging from the fog of a powerful anesthetic. She had lived those last three years like a negligent tenant in her own skin, paying the rent late and letting things fall apart around her. She felt quite certain that her original had realized the same thing. Only it hadn't taken becoming a clone for her original to wake up and get out of DC. Con needed to know how she had done it.

The car shuddered as it left the Maryland state road and merged onto I-95, the federal highway that ran from Maine to Florida. It startled her, and she gripped the armrests like a life preserver, but it was only the car linking to the interstate traffic-control network, the algorithm that coordinated the millions of vehicles that used the road every day. Automatically, the heavy morning traffic shifted to create a space for Con without a single vehicle slowing down. Her car accelerated to eighty miles an hour, joining the immensely complex game of high-speed Tetris that was the DC morning commute.

She forced herself to let go of the armrest and shook the tension out of her hands. This was only the third car she'd been in since the accident. She reminded herself that it was illegal to self-drive on federal highways. There were plenty of holdouts, sure—purists who clung to notions of the "open road" and resented what they viewed as heavy-handed government oversight—but they hewed stubbornly to secondary roads rather than ever link up to a highway's hive mind. Good, they could have those roads as long as they stayed far away from her.

Her momentary panic did make her stop and wonder what the hell she was doing. Despite all the warnings, despite everything she knew might be waiting for her, here she was crossing the Woodrow Wilson Bridge into Virginia, a state notoriously unsympathetic toward clones. Killing a clone in Virginia wasn't even considered murder. It was considered destruction of property, a class-six felony. She'd rationalized it to herself—that she'd only stay a few days, just long enough to fill in the gaps in her memory. She promised herself not to get greedy. No one knew she was coming. She'd be fine so long as she kept a low profile.

A cheerful sign welcomed her to Virginia, and a tension crept into her chest that would build in the days to come. It was true no one was on the lookout for her there, but if her car should break down by the side of the road, if she stayed at the wrong motel or ate at the wrong restaurant, if someone recognized her—then she'd be in the worst kind of trouble, and she wouldn't see it coming until it was too late. But what scared her most was that none of that made any difference to her. Not even the fact that she didn't have a second clone, and if she died now, she really was dead. Even if she knew a pitchfork mob was waiting for her at the Virginia line with a length of rope, she'd have come anyway. She had no choice. Learning the truth about her missing eighteen months had become an addiction, except she knew there was no rehab in the world that could temper her compulsion. The need to know was calling the shots now.

Down below, the sunshine danced innocently across the Potomac like it was part of a whole different story.

———

Her husband lived on the outskirts of the outskirts of Richmond in a modern development that was indistinguishable from every other upper-middle-class subdivision built in the last fifty years. The most noticeable differences were what was missing. Despite the size of the lots, Con hadn't seen a single swimming pool—victims of ever-tightening water regulations and taxation. In their place were the mandatory water collection tanks and solar panels. Grass lawns had also become smaller since Con was a kid, and about the only thing she liked about the development was how much space was devoted to newly planted trees. Even then, the saplings—probably numbering in the thousands—were too immature to offer any shade, which only reinforced the fact that this was all the invention of a real estate developer and not a real neighborhood.

The car parked itself across the street from her husband's home, and she sat there staring up at the house. She hoped it might give her some feeling for the man who lived there, but it had the institutional sterility that came with planned communities. Every house on the block was nearly, but not entirely, identical to every other house, right down to the mild variations in paint colors, selected no doubt from the approved fascist homeowners-association swatch book. And the houses were all massive to the point of overcompensation. If she hadn't come directly from a real-life castle, she would have been intimidated by the unnecessary size of the things. Fair to say she loathed everything about this place.

Driving here, she'd known it wouldn't be familiar, but she expected to recognize it as a place she could imagine herself—a spiritual affinity if not a practical one. But no, nothing. Having spent the better part of her life trying to escape her small Texas hometown, she couldn't understand anyone who voluntarily exiled themselves to the suburbs. But that's exactly what she had done. This was her home. Where she lived with her husband. A man named Levi Greer. That and this address were all she'd let Vernon Gaddis tell her about him. It had felt too dangerous to know more.

Maybe she should have gone straight to find her original instead. Before leaving Charles Island, she'd logged in to the secure account that stored the encrypted GPS data from Con D'Arcy's biometric chip. As advertised, Palingenesis had only kept the thirty-six hours immediately prior to the "death event." It appeared those hours had been spent at a farm only forty miles south of here. Nor had her original left the farm since. Con wanted to hold out hope that there was a chance her original was still alive, but even her justifiable skepticism of Palingenesis was having trouble explaining it away. That was why she had come here first. Not that her death wasn't important, but it marked the end of the story, and Con didn't want to begin at the end—she wanted to know this woman, to understand how she had lived. Only then would she feel prepared to see how she had died.

That meant putting on her big-girl pants and finding out what was waiting for her behind door number one. Con opened the car door, meaning to get out, but then slammed and locked it, heart rattling like a snare drum. Until now, Levi Greer had remained a silhouette. A cardboard cutout upon which she could pin a thousand possibilities. But he would become real the moment he opened his front door—the answer to the question of whether she really was Constance Ada D'Arcy. What if she didn't feel anything when she met him? What would that tell her about herself? How could she be Con D'Arcy if she didn't love who Con D'Arcy loved?

Enough.

With a final push, she forced herself out of the car and went up the walk before she could talk herself out of it. She rang the bell and stepped back as if she'd lit the fuse on a firework but wasn't sure what would happen when it went off.

A white man in his twenties came to the door, haggard and thin and profoundly weary. The kind of exhaustion that built up like plaque behind your eyes and became a locust hum in your ears. Heavy bags, the texture of old tires, weighted down his eyes, and he hadn't shaved or washed his hair in days, which rose and fell in a raging sea of cowlicks. His vintage Kendrick Lamar T-shirt was covered in interlacing amoeba stains that suggested he hadn't changed clothes in at least a couple days. This was Levi Greer? The Casanova who'd swept her off her feet and wooed her into coming to Virginia. How was that even possible? He was a walking catastrophe. Not that he wasn't handsome in his way. Beneath the scruffy beard were high, pronounced cheekbones, and his green eyes hinted at hidden depth if you just took the time to get to know him. And he had to be a foot taller than her. How had they kissed? She tried to imagine herself in his arms.

Framed in the doorway, Levi Greer glitched at the sight of her, freezing in place, mouth moving silently like a singer who'd stepped out on stage and forgotten the words to the song. She'd been so wrapped up in how she would feel meeting him that she hadn't considered what effect she'd have on him. Was there even a precedent for the clone of your missing, presumed-dead wife turning up at your front door? His expression was unreadable, but beneath the surface, she saw his emotions fighting a pitched battle for the right to dictate his reaction.

"Your hair is so short," he said, staring at her, hard, the way a bartender held a hundred-dollar bill that they suspected might be counterfeit up to the light. "She really had a clone. Unbelievable."

"You didn't know?"

"The police said she did, but I didn't want to believe them. But I guess it was *her* I didn't know." He leaned heavily against the doorframe and folded his arms across his chest. "Man, you look just like her." His eyes danced around her like she was an eclipse that would blind him if he looked at her directly.

"Cool T-shirt," she said for something to say. She'd always been a big fan and regretted never seeing Kendrick Lamar in his prime.

Levi pulled it away from his chest to see what he had on. "Oh, this. Yeah, of course you do. She bought it for me."

She.

Only a few feet separated them, but she could feel the gulf that yawned between them. She'd come to find out if she would feel anything for him. Well, she had her answer. He was a stranger to her, and she felt nothing. No spark. No attraction. Nothing. This wasn't her husband. Her head started to throb as the implications came crashing down around her. A low-pitched sound like an air-raid siren filled her ears, her vision began to narrow, and the string holding all her limbs together frayed and split apart.

She came to lying on a plush blue-and-white sofa that matched the carpet, the curtains, and damn near everything else in the excruciatingly coordinated living room. Had she really fainted? She hadn't fainted since gym class in eighth grade. Realizing that meant she was inside Levi Greer's house, her curiosity got her back into a sitting position. On the end table was a wedding photograph in a silver frame. She picked it up. Her ears and neck got hot like she'd stumbled into someone else's intimate moment. The happy couple was standing on the courthouse steps, arm in arm. Levi Greer and Con D'Arcy. Con didn't even recognize the woman that he had his arms around.

Happy.

Smiling.

In love.

What right did she have to smile that way? It made Con angry, and then jealous, and then the guilt came. Dominoes falling in a row. What about Zhi? How could she have betrayed him this way? But, of course, *she* hadn't betrayed anyone. She didn't really live here, did she? And Levi Greer wasn't really her husband. So who did that make her? What did it make her? She felt tears coming but forced them back down. Not here, not now.

And where the hell was Levi Greer? She stood up carefully, testing to see if her legs were steady enough to hold her. A framed athletic jersey on a nearby wall caught her eye. Curious, she went closer. It was for the Pathogens, the Richmond eSports franchise, and read "GREER" across the back. In the bottom corner of the frame, a photograph showed the team hoisting a trophy over their heads. She saw Levi Greer in the pack. He was grinning, one hand on the trophy, the other holding up one triumphant finger. She'd married a jock? What the hell was going on? She didn't even like sports or play video games. But at least it explained how he could afford a house like this.

Levi Greer appeared in the doorway holding a glass of water. He looked surprised to see her standing. "You're okay."

He handed her the glass, and, embarrassed, she handed him his wedding photograph.

"Is it true?" he asked quietly after she'd emptied the glass. "Is she really dead?"

"I don't know."

"Come on," he said. "Please don't do that. You wouldn't be here if she wasn't. That's how it works, right? So just tell me. I can't take this anymore."

Her head began to throb again. Every time he said *she* instead of *you*, it was like a blow to the side of her head. "That's what Palingenesis says."

"But you haven't actually seen her? She could still be alive."

"It's possible," she admitted.

Instead of being excited by the prospect, he became angry. "So why aren't you helping the police find her? They said you're the only one with access to her GPS coordinates."

"It's complicated."

"It's not complicated," he snapped. "My wife is missing. You're the only one who knows where she is. What's complicated about that?"

"I wanted to meet you first. Hoped we could talk," she said, aware of how selfish it sounded. Her existential crisis suddenly felt insignificant against this man's grief and worry. She didn't think she could live with herself if it turned out her original was still alive, hurt or in danger. Of course, if her original were alive, then Con wouldn't have to live with herself very long. One of the hard-and-fast laws governing cloning in America—under no circumstances could there be two.

"Meet? What for? I thought you had her memories."

"Not all of them." It hurt to admit, especially to him.

That seemed to surprise him, and he took a moment to recalibrate. "How much are you missing?"

"My last refresh was December 26, 2038. I don't know anything after that."

His eyes cleared as he recognized the date. "That's the night I saw her sing for the first time. You don't remember that?"

Con shook her head, already inserting his part of the story into the timeline. That meant that after meeting Levi Greer, she'd moved to Virginia and stopped doing her refreshes. Never even told him about having a clone backup. Why? Didn't she think she needed them anymore? The questions kept mounting, each one a jagged splinter beneath her skin that would only be extracted by answers that Greer seemed less and less willing to provide.

"Well, now we've met," Greer said, voice hard and low. "So what is it you want to talk about that's so important? Why won't you help the police find her?"

"Because I needed to see this, alright?" she said, gesturing at him and the house. "I don't understand. How are we married? How is this my life? I—"

He cut her off, slapping his hands together in front of her face. "It's not your life, *Con*. And we're not married."

Greer took a step forward; she took an involuntary step back—a cruel, ancient dance choreographed by generations of men and women. She tried to read anything in his face that might tell her what he was really about. Was he the kind for whom arguing with a woman led inevitably to violence? Con liked to think she wouldn't have married that sort of man, but some men didn't show themselves until it was too late. If he took another step, then she would know. She set her feet. This was as far as she would go.

But he didn't. He stayed where he was, his expression turning from anger to exhaustion and despair. "I just need to know what happened to her. I can't take this. You don't know what it's like not knowing."

Except she did know and had put this man through hell anyway. Maybe because of the existential threat he represented, she'd resisted thinking of him as a real person up until now. It was cruel of her.

"Please," he implored her. "Tell the police where she is. Whatever you want. I'll do anything."

"I will. I promise," she said. "Can we just talk? After? I have a lot of questions. There are things I need to know too."

He wiped away tears and nodded. "That's all you want?"

That was everything.

CHAPTER SIXTEEN

When Con left Levi Greer, she'd had every intention of keeping her word. She'd even pulled up Darius Clarke's contact and had her finger on the call button. But then the questions started piling up again, and the need to know, like an itch beneath her skin, returned with a vengeance. *Are you really about to call the police?* it accused her. *Did you really risk coming into Virginia just to turn it all over to Darius Clarke?* The moment she told him what he wanted to know, he'd cut her out of the loop. Then she'd never get her answers; there wasn't a doubt in her mind. So she'd given the GPS coordinates to her car and let it drive her here to a small farm in Buffum, an unincorporated community in Dinwiddie County.

It was the middle of the twenty-first century, but she thought Dorothea Lange would recognize this place. The land looked like it had been abandoned since before the Civil War, and a weathered "For Sale" sign hung limply from a stake driven into the ground. The dirt road leading to the boarded-up farmhouse was barred by a rusted gate padlocked with a length of chain. Con told the car to park on the grassy shoulder of State Route 670. It was near noon and a furnace sun rode high and righteous in the cloudless sky. Off to her left, an old grain silo, proud as a sore thumb, stood defiant against the heat, though much of its paint had long since flaked away. Beside the silo stood the skeletal remains of a barn that leaned wearily to the west. Con had seen a hundred farms like it when she was a child. More than a thousand miles separated Virginia and Texas, but loss was loss. Before she'd been old enough to understand the pain behind foreclosures, Con had found the decrepit romance of abandoned buildings beautiful.

Of course, it was easy to find an abandoned farm picturesque at a quarter to twelve on a summer afternoon. Come nightfall, the farm would turn sinister, all runaway shadows and restless dreams, and the tree line that formed a loose semicircle around the property would bloom with specters and myth. Strange how that worked. Buildings didn't know day from night. They didn't change, only the light did, and with the light how she would see them. Better to be long gone before then.

On that note, Con killed the engine. She got out, popped the trunk, and opened the storage compartment. Where the spare tire should have been was the go bag that Peter had packed for her. He hadn't said a word, but she could tell he wasn't a fan of her decision to go to Virginia. Inside the bag was a first-aid kit, food and water, three hundred dollars in cash, a change of clothes, a flashlight, a paper map of Virginia, a second LFD, a survival knife, and pepper spray. *Do you know how to handle firearms?* he'd asked. She'd raised one eyebrow and reminded him that she *was* from Texas. Hunting mule deer with the uncles was an annual Stickling Thanksgiving tradition. That had made Peter chuckle, but he had given her a crash course on the Smith & Wesson Shield 9 mm anyway. At the time, she'd thought it was overkill, but now, looking out at the farmstead, she was grateful that he was a worrier.

She took the water and flashlight, and clipped the gun to her jeans. Then she ducked under the gate and walked up the long, curving dirt road. Was it a good idea coming here alone? Probably not. But simply because a person recognized the law of gravity didn't mean they could ignore it and fly away. The pull to know everything was simply too strong.

Greer had asked if her original could still be alive. Looking around, Con wanted desperately to imagine a happy reason that she might have come here but couldn't think of a single one. Where to start looking? She didn't relish the prospect of bushwhacking across these fields, an overgrown tangle of weeds, thorns, and tall, wild grasses. She could wander around out here for days without stumbling across anything besides wild animals. Did Virginia have poisonous snakes? That would end badly. And then some poor bastard would stumble across two identical dead bodies. Yeah, best if she started indoors.

The silo was a hollow echo chamber. The doors to the barn were padlocked, but she found a gap between two loose boards and squeezed inside. The musty smell of petrified hay greeted her, and the ancient barn groaned like an old man at an unwelcome knock on the door. Slats in the broken roof threw piano keys of light and dark across the floor. Wiping sweat from her brow, she searched upstairs and down for any sign of human activity.

The floorboards above her head creaked. She froze. She'd only just come from up there—she was alone, she told herself—but it was enough to make her break out in a sweat. Shaken, she decided that concluded her search of the barn. She emerged blinking back into the sunshine and stood in the shade against the wall, drinking from a bottle of water until she could hear the hum of the cicadas above the thud of her heartbeat. *That was reckless,* she told herself—*go back to the car and call the police.* This was their job, after all.

Her need to know just laughed. *You're not calling the shots here,* it mocked. *Now finish your water and go check the house.*

The farmhouse sat on a low rise with a view of the property. It was a modest two-story Colonial, psychotic in its rigorous symmetry: twin chimneys at either end, four columns supporting a portico shading the front door, five perfectly spaced windows all boarded shut. Ivy had twined around the columns and spread as far as the second-story windows. There was no way to open the front door without disturbing it, but Con reached through the ivy and tried the handle anyway. The door didn't budge. She couldn't say if that was a relief or not.

She waded around the side of the house through waist-high grass, looking for a way inside. She stopped short when she turned the last corner. The boards across the back door had been pried loose and stacked neatly beside the house, relatively recently, by the look of it. The outer door was held open by a metal bucket filled with old croquet balls. She aimed her flashlight through the filthy screen door and into the gloom of the kitchen. She didn't see anyone, but even an amateur detective like herself couldn't miss the footprints that led across the floor, into the empty dining room, and out of sight.

She glanced back at the woods, which had grown ominous and seemed to have crept closer while her back was turned. She had the uncanny sensation of being watched, and despite the heat, every hair on her body stood up. Which was her being ridiculous. A person couldn't feel someone looking at them. She knew this because she lived in a crowded city. Hundreds of people looked at her every day, and she never felt a thing. So it was absurd for her to be in the middle of a deserted farm, on the threshold of this dead house, and think she could feel someone watching her.

And yet.

"Hello?" she called into the darkness and immediately wished she hadn't. There was no answer but the moldering silence. That was when a smart person would get out of there. Instead, she eased open the screen door, the rusted-out hinges complaining noisily. It felt like a matter of life and death, and that if she didn't keep going, then she might as well lie down right there in the tall grass and die. There was a song there somewhere. If she made it through this, she would think about writing it.

She followed the footprints through the kitchen and out to the front hall, where they went up the wooden stairs to the second floor. She called out again, then climbed the stairs. Her hand kept touching the butt of the gun on her hip, as if reassuring herself that it was still there. The faint smell of overripe fruit grew stronger with each step, and by the time she reached the landing, it was overpowering. A hall branched off in both directions. Doors lined a corridor that was littered with trash as if the owners had fled in a hurry, dropping odds and ends as they went. All the doors were open except for one. Of course it was at the end of the hall. And of course the footprints led to it.

Con looked longingly back down the stairs, hoping to convince herself that she had her answer. She was no expert, but that wasn't rotten fruit making her eyes water. That was the smell of death. For once, it looked like Palingenesis had been right. But she hadn't come all this way only to turn back now. She had to be sure. So she went down the hall, careful to step only in the footprints. It felt important to leave no trace of herself in this place.

At the door, she drew and held a breath before turning the knob. It didn't help. The smell that broke loose was rancid and viscous, a clotted fist that slammed into her. Con staggered back, bent double, and vomited in the hallway. Her vision exploded in orange fireworks, and she had to steady herself against the wall to keep from falling down. When her head finally cleared, she spat in the dust, wiped her mouth with the back of her wrist, and risked another look into the dank room.

Liminal sunlight filtered grudgingly through grimy, cataract windows. Dust hung in the air like spores from some fetid swamp. The discolored yellow wallpaper showed the faded outline of a dresser that had once been pushed up against it. On a bare metal bed frame, under a white sheet, lay a human body. Or what she guessed was a body, but if it was the original Constance D'Arcy under there, then the topography was all wrong. It looked bloated and misshapen. One foot hung out from beneath the sheet, the ankle mottled an ugly, carotid purple. Covering her nose and mouth with the collar of her T-shirt, she stepped over the threshold.

She reached out for the sheet, promising herself to pull it down only far enough to be certain. But when she recognized the eyes, the same eyes that had stared back at her since the time she was tall enough to see in a mirror, she kept going. Trembling, she pulled the sheet past the lips that had kissed Zhi for the first time; past the swirling tattoos that covered her left arm, now hopelessly distorted and warped by decay; past the hands that had learned to play guitar. Only when she saw the scars lacing across that ruined knee did she let go of the ruined sheet.

And the violence etched into her body was appalling. She had been stabbed, again and again. Deep, frenzied gashes, any one of which should have been fatal, but that hadn't been nearly good enough for her killer. And there was a killer. That was undeniable now.

"I'm sorry. I'm so sorry," Con whispered, but whether to herself or the body, she didn't know. Constance Ada D'Arcy was dead.

"Yes, we are," the body agreed.

Con flinched and stumbled backward. Looking around, she saw she wasn't in Virginia any longer. This was her old bedroom back in Lanesboro. Mr. Bob, the stuffed bear that had kept her safe during storms since before she could remember, sat serenely on her pillow. Through the floorboards, she could hear her mother downstairs in the kitchen listening to gospel radio.

"You're not real," Con said. "You can't be."

"Neither are you," the body replied, except now it was Con when she'd been a little girl. "Do you understand that now?"

Con nodded, feeling the sting of tears on her cheeks. All the things she remembered, this was who had actually done them. Not her. "What happened?"

"We died. That's all," the girl explained. "It doesn't matter how."

"I'm not dead," Con said without conviction.

"But you should be. Deep down, you know that."

God help her, she did. "I'm scared."

"I know, but it will be better this way. It's peaceful, I promise. Don't you want to feel at peace again?"

Con nodded. She was so tired.

"But you have to be quick. This may be our only chance," the girl said.

"How?"

"There," the girl said, pointing to the floor by the window. "The broken glass."

Con picked up a shard, dimly wondering why there would be broken glass on her bedroom floor.

"There was a storm," the girl said. "The tree outside broke the window. Momma must have missed some of the glass when she swept up."

That made sense. Bad storms rolled through Lanesboro all the time. Even Mr. Bob was nodding in agreement, and he loved her the most. Con looked down at her wrist.

"You know what to do," the girl said. "We belong together."

That jarred Con out of her stupor. She dropped the broken glass. *Get out of here. Get out now.*

"No," the girl wailed, although already it was turning back into a cadaver. "You're not real. You're nothing."

Con fled down the hall, the hallucination fading with each step. On the landing, she crashed into a wall, but somehow she managed not to trip and fall down the stairs. She heard something clatter to the ground, but she didn't stop to see what it was. She burst through the screen door into the sunshine, hoping the fresh air would wash the smell of that room away, but it was in her head now and she would never forget it.

Her stomach kicked again, and she stumbled into the tall grass and retched until her body grudgingly accepted there was nothing left. Then she slipped gratefully to her knees and rolled onto her side. She lay there panting, listening to the lazy thrum of crickets. A red-and-black ladybug climbed halfway up a leaf before flying away. It seemed real enough, but then so had the girl up in the bedroom. Dr. Fenton had said that Con's condition would worsen, but she hadn't said anything about her hallucinations turning homicidal. She needed to get back to the car where her pills were.

In the distance, she heard the sound of voices. She was still so disoriented that, at first, she didn't register them as real. It wasn't until a pair of men appeared from around the side of the house that she snapped out of it. Both wore boots, green cargo pants, and tactical vests similar to the one she'd found in her dad's old footlocker when she was nine. Her mother had whaled on her when she'd caught Con wearing it. At their belts were sidearms.

It was her first time seeing him in daylight, but Con recognized the taller man instantly—the driver of the SUV outside her old apartment building that first night. The same one who'd shown up at the Glass House when she'd gone to talk to Jasper. She'd know his cragged, pockmarked face anywhere. How had he tracked her here? She'd only been in Virginia for a few hours. Unless Pockmark worked for Gaddis and this was all part of some elaborate setup.

Easing herself onto her stomach, Con prayed that the grass was thick enough to hide her. At the back door, the two men stopped and conferred quietly. Eventually, the younger man disappeared inside the house, leaving her alone with Pockmark. He stepped away from the house in her general direction. Con flattened herself against the ground and held her breath. He toggled his LFD, asking for updates. The answers didn't appear to make him happy.

"Keep looking," he barked.

The younger man returned.

"And?" Pockmark asked.

"Clear, but someone was definitely here. And recently. I've got fresh vomit in the hallway outside the bedroom."

"She tripped the sensors. We already know someone is here," Pockmark said dismissively.

Had they been staking out the farm waiting for her to show up here? Here. Which meant Pockmark knew something that only she was supposed to know—the location of her original's body. Was her body bait? A way to lure her here so they could grab her?

"And this." The young man held up the Smith & Wesson, still in its holster.

Con's hand went to her hip, and she cursed silently. At least now she knew what she'd heard hit the floor in her panic to get out of the house.

"Since when is she armed?" Pockmark said.

"Well, not anymore. Are we sure it's her?"

"We have to assume. Who else would know to come here?"

"Yes, sir," the younger man conceded. "Maybe she already left."

"Without her car? No, she's here."

"Did we get a hit on the car?"

"Registered to a cleaning service in Richmond," Pockmark said.

"Who owns the cleaning service?"

"A plumbing supplier in Arlington. We're still working on who owns that."

"Weird."

"Yes," Pockmark agreed. "Very weird."

"It's a big farm, sir. If she made it to the tree line—"

"Then Rodgers would have scooped her up. No, she's here somewhere. Find her. We can't afford to miss her again. But non-lethals only. She's not to be hurt under any circumstances. Anything happens to her head, that man loses his."

"Understood, s—"

Both their heads craned up toward the sky.

"What the hell is that?" Pockmark demanded, dragging them both against the side of the house.

Con couldn't see what they were looking at without giving herself away, but Pockmark seemed genuinely spooked.

"I don't know, sir. Do we have anything in the air?" the younger man asked.

"Call it in. Find out."

It only took a moment for the younger man to report back. "It's not ours."

Con was so intent on not being seen by the two men that she didn't hear the third man behind her until he grabbed her by the neck and dragged her to a standing position. She yelped and tried to struggle free, but he held her easily.

"Have her, sir."

"Secure her," the younger man said, hurrying over with a set of restraints. "Let's get ready to move."

Pockmark cupped a hand to his ear to isolate his headset. "Say again. We have her in hand. Say again." Whatever it was, Pockmark didn't like it. He tried to argue, but the voice at the other end of the conversation shut him down.

Con felt herself lowered facedown in the grass. The restraints bit into her wrists, and a black bag slipped over her head.

"Stop," Pockmark ordered. "Let her go."

"Sir?" the other men said in unison.

"You heard me. Stand down. We're Oscar Mike. Meet at the rally point in sixty seconds."

The knee came off her back, and she felt the restraints come off. The hood stayed on, though. She heard them retreat but didn't move for a long time. What had just happened? Pockmark and his goons had been after her from the beginning. What had they seen up there that had spooked them badly enough to leave her behind? She rolled over and pulled the hood free. Overhead, the sky was storybook blue, and it took her a minute to spot what was up there—the black speck circling high overhead like a vulture, waiting and watching. A drone.

Who did that belong to, and who did Pockmark work for? He had been insistent that nothing happen to her head, so clearly he knew about the cluster of voids that Vernon Gaddis and Brooke Fenton wanted so badly. But Gaddis had had her at Charles Island and let her go. And back in DC, Fenton had claimed that forcibly taking Con wouldn't work. Well, one of them was lying. Maybe both. But first she needed to get out of there. The problem was she didn't feel safe simply leaving on her own. Pockmark knew her face, knew the car she drove. He would be out there waiting for her.

She looked back up at the sky. The drone was gone.

That did it. She needed help.

She woke her LFD, praying it got any signal out here. One bar. Not much, but it was enough. Pulling up Detective Darius Clarke's contact, she dialed the number and let it ring.

Voluntarily calling the police—was that really what it had come to? In a day of firsts, it wasn't the strangest thing that had happened, but it was up there. At least Levi Greer would finally know the truth.

CHAPTER SEVENTEEN

It wasn't her first time inside a police station interrogation room. In high school, she'd been picked up for trespassing after dark at a swimming pool. The other kids had been let go with a warning, but she and a Latina girl were taken to the station. The police had called her mother, who'd chosen to leave her there all weekend to help cure her daughter of her wild ways. This room wasn't much different from that one. There was no clock and no windows, so Con had no way to gauge how long she'd been here. Part of her wanted to hammer on the door and demand they return her LFD, but she didn't want to give them the satisfaction. And what if they wouldn't? Then all she'd accomplished in calling the police was to trade one potential captor for another.

Up above, an archaic surveillance camera watched silently from the corner of the room.

The cops had descended on the farm like an army. Once Clarke had seen the body inside the farmhouse, he'd escorted Con to a squad car that had transported her to this station, where she'd been locked inside this airless interrogation room. Someone had taken pity on her and brought her a stale Danish and a bottle of water. She'd drunk the water gratefully but only picked at the pastry before pushing it away. Each time she took a bite, her memory offered reminders of what she'd seen inside the farmhouse. A jumble of lurid, flickering images that she couldn't shut out. Opening and reopening the bedroom door at the end of the hall. Her nose and mouth flooding with rot.

But she wasn't in mourning, she was angry. All those images gave her plenty to think through. Like how the body might have been lying peacefully in that bed, but there'd been nothing peaceful about how she'd died. Con hadn't thought about it at the time, but now she realized how undisturbed the room had been. The careful footprints in the dust. No blood anywhere. Whatever had happened, it hadn't happened there. The farmhouse was only the stage. That meant her original had been moved after she'd been murdered. But the last thirty-six hours that the GPS had stored didn't show that. It said she'd been there the whole time. So what did that tell her? How many people would know how to fool Palingenesis's chip? Two names sprang immediately to mind.

She felt so naïve for clinging to the hope that what happened to her original had been an accident. She didn't know whether it was Vernon Gaddis or Brooke Fenton, but one of them had taken an enormous risk sneaking her out of Palingenesis. Why stop there? They wouldn't then wait around for a healthy twenty-four-year-old to die of natural causes. They would've snatched up her original and murdered her, knowing it would trigger her clone's revival. She meant to find out which and make them pay for it. But first, she needed to get out of this room.

The electronic lock deactivated with a mechanical thwonk. Detective Darius Clarke let himself in and took a seat across the table. Her savior. Without acknowledging her, he set to arranging his notebooks and recorder on the table, along with a single cup of coffee that reminded her exactly why she disliked him so much. He looked beat although even that didn't begin to cover it. What he looked like was a man who'd been up too long and seen too much—face unshaved, eyes hooded. He moved in the slow, deliberate way that true exhaustion required. Despite all that, he still seemed strangely alert and focused. She couldn't tell if he was on something or not. No, she decided, he just loved his job. That was his high.

"You going to eat that?" he asked, meaning the Danish.

She pushed it across the table to him. "Sure, help yourself."

He finished it in three lupine bites. "Haven't eaten since breakfast yesterday."

Neither had she, but she wasn't sure she'd ever eat again. Clarke wiped his fingers on his sleeve and cued his recorder. He recited both their names along with his badge number, the date, and the time.

"Is it really four in the morning?" she asked. She'd arrived at the farm before noon. That left a lot of time unaccounted for. How long had she slept?

"It's been a day," he said.

"Where am I?"

"We're at the station in Glen Allen. Virginia State Police, area eight."

She didn't know Virginia well enough for that to narrow it down any. "Can I get my LFD back?"

"Let's get through this first," he said, lifting the lid of his coffee to blow on it. "Then we'll see."

"Get through what? I gave you what you asked for. What else is there?"

He stared impassively at her as if waiting out a recalcitrant child.

"Fine. What do you want to know?" she said, reminding herself that her goal was to get out of there, not butt heads with Clarke. She'd keep it simple, but she'd answer his questions. She wasn't going to give him an excuse to detain her any longer than was absolutely necessary.

"Let's start at the beginning."

"Define *the beginning*?"

He looked down the bridge of his nose at her, warning her not to get cute with him. "You arrive at the farm. What happened next?"

"I searched the barn and the silo first. Didn't seem like anyone had been there in forever."

"And you were alone?" he asked.

"Yeah."

"Okay," Clarke said, making a note. "Then what? The house? What did you see?"

"You know," she said.

"Let me hear it in your words."

"I saw," she said, and faltered as the gruesome slideshow started up again in her mind. "I saw. Her. Like that."

"Dead," he prompted. "What were your impressions?"

"What the hell?" she said, squeezing her eyes shut, trying in vain not to picture it. "That it was bad. Really bad."

"Was it your vomit in the hallway?"

"She was murdered," Con said in her own defense.

"That she was," he said as if it were the first time he had considered the possibility. "It hard for you? To see her like that?"

"What do you think?"

"Beats me. Doesn't it validate your entire existence?"

"Fuck you." It was out of her mouth before she could stop herself. She needed to be more careful; she wasn't in DC anymore. She couldn't afford to get into it with Clarke. This was his kingdom, and he'd already made it clear how he ruled it. Fortunately, he seemed inclined to take her outburst in stride for now.

"So what next?" he asked.

"I ran. Outside. Needed fresh air."

"And then you called me."

"Then I called you," she agreed.

"And you were alone?"

"Yeah, I already said that."

He took his time studying her. She could tell he was trying to decide whether she was holding out on him. Fair enough, she was. She didn't know exactly why she hadn't mentioned Pockmark and his men or the unknown drone that had run them off. Maybe because it sounded batshit crazy even to her and was the kind of twist that might make him hesitant to let her go. He'd asked for the body; she'd delivered it. That was all he was getting from her.

"Just inspired to finally do your civic duty?" he said with undisguised cynicism.

She leaned forward in her seat, seeing no option but to take offense at his insinuation. "What do you want from me? You got what you needed, didn't you?"

He sighed and leaned forward in his own seat, mirroring her, letting her know the degree to which he didn't believe her. "Take me through it again. From the top."

She didn't have a word for how much she loathed him.

For the next few hours, Clarke walked her back and forth through her grisly discovery at the farm, taking a slightly different tack each time, looking for anything that might jog her memory—chronology, sounds, smells, emotions. It was exhausting, like being in a verbal fistfight. Clarke kept trying to punch holes in her story while she did her best to parry and keep things more or less straight. It didn't help that he was very, very good at his job. By the end, even she had doubts about what she was saying—including the parts she knew were true.

It went on so long that she began to suspect that he had an ulterior motive. "Am I a suspect?"

"That what you think? No, we don't have an exact time of death yet, but judging by the decomp of the body, I'd say it's been a while. You're off the hook for that much at least. Constance D'Arcy has been dead since before you were born."

"Clever."

"One hell of an alibi, though," he said.

"So why am I really here? If I'm not—"

"Why were you at Levi Greer's house this morning?" he asked, cutting her off midsentence. It was the first time Clarke had mentioned Greer, and it felt like he was finally getting around to what was actually on his mind.

"To talk."

"You mean make a deal."

"Yeah, I guess. He said if I gave the police the GPS of his wife's location that he would help me . . ." She drifted off, unsure how to put it.

"Become a real girl?"

"Sure," she answered, sidestepping his provocation.

"That must have come as a huge relief. I remember how determined you were in DC. Feisty." He shook a defiant fist as if he found the memory adorable. "So why didn't you hold up your end?"

"What are you talking about? I called you, remember?"

"Sure," Clarke said agreeably. "Eventually. But not right away. First you drove out to the farm. What were you doing out there?"

"I needed to see for myself."

"That she was dead."

She nodded.

"And she was," he prompted. "And then you called me."

She nodded again, tired of talking in circles.

"Why did you sound so scared?"

"I wasn't scared."

"No, I'd say terrified is more accurate. I can play the recording for you," he offered.

"Please don't."

"Who was at the farm with you?"

That caught her off guard. "What?"

"You heard me." Clarke was up and out of his seat, looming over her. "We know someone was there, so don't piss me off by denying it. It was Greer, wasn't it? What else was a part of your deal? What did you do for him out there?"

She finally saw it. What Clarke had been circling this whole time. "You think Levi Greer killed his wife."

"Do I?" Clarke said, interest spiking. "What makes you say that?"

"Because I found a dead body and all you really want to talk about is how Levi Greer was at the farm with me. Tell me I'm wrong."

Clarke glanced up at the camera as if looking for confirmation. "You're not wrong."

She replayed her conversation with Greer. He'd been a lot of things, but she hadn't gotten the feeling he'd killed his wife. And what kind of murderer begged you to lead the police to the body? One who hadn't known his wife had a clone or a GPS chip. He'd have had no choice but to appear super proactive and helpful to cover his ass.

"You really think it's him?" she asked.

"Oh, I know it's him. He's being questioned in Richmond as we speak. Truth is, we've been looking at him since the beginning. He always claimed his wife ran off, but a woman goes missing? Start with the man in her life. Especially if the wife is having an affair."

"An affair?" Con said, genuinely shocked. She'd never cheated in her life, not unless you counted Billy Tomlinson in the sixth grade.

"Looks that way. The GPS data from her vehicle shows Constance D'Arcy was making regular trips to Charlottesville whenever Greer was on the road with the team. She'd stay overnight but never in a hotel. No debit or credit purchases while she was there either—not so much as a stick of gum. Always left her car in the same public garage, including when she disappeared. Almost like she didn't want anyone to know where she was going or who she was seeing."

"That doesn't mean she was having an affair."

"Makes no difference either way. All that matters is what Greer believed. And he sure thought so. Witness statements from his neighbors describe constant fighting in the house. We're in the process of getting a warrant to access his LFD, but text messages between Greer and his teammates don't paint a flattering picture. The wife of one of his teammates who works at a domestic violence shelter says she confronted D'Arcy about bruises on her arm and cheekbone a month ago, but D'Arcy said it was an accident."

"So if you know all this, why do you need me to say he was at the farm?"

"First off, because he was. You know it, and I know it. He missed practice yesterday, called out sick after your visit but wasn't at home all day." Clarke leaned against the edge of the table and flipped through his notebook. "Greer owns two vehicles. A 2039 Mercedes SUV, and a 2012 Ford Mustang Boss 302. Guess which one he took? Here's a hint—it's the thirty-year-old vintage sports car with no auto-drive navigation system. So where was he all day?"

"What does Greer say?"

"Says he drove up into the Shenandoah to do some thinking. Conveniently the part of Virginia with the fewest surveillance cameras. Turned off his LFD too. Said he wanted to be alone. Zero digital footprint. We're checking it out, but no one is going to say they saw him up there."

"Why?" Con asked.

"Because he was at the farm with you," Clarke said with utter certainty. "All the evidence I have is circumstantial, so if he lied and was at the farm with you, then I've got him. What I don't know is why you're protecting him." Clarke sat back down, downshifting into a soothing, reasonable tone of voice. "Look, I was hard on you back in DC, I can admit that. So if you made a deal with Greer to help him tamper with the crime scene or destroy evidence—"

Con shot forward in her seat. "I didn't."

He waved her protestations away. "Relax, it's not you I want. I understand why you thought you had no choice but to deal with Greer. But I am a much better friend to have than Levi Greer, especially where he's going."

"Listen to me, I don't know where he went in his car today, but he wasn't at the farm. I swear."

"Well, who was?" Clarke demanded. "'Cause I've got a partial boot print that says you're lying."

"These men," Con blurted out.

Clarke threw up his hands in disbelief. "Now there are men? What men?"

Reluctantly, Con described Pockmark and his associates to a thoroughly unimpressed Darius Clarke. He glanced up at the camera and gave it a can-you-believe-this-shit look. When she was finished, he rubbed the back of his tired head and cleared his throat.

"So let me get this straight. A team of paramilitary types ambushed you but then let you go because a drone scared them off?"

"Yeah," she answered, aware of how ridiculous it all sounded.

"We've been talking for a while now. How come this is the first I'm hearing about it?"

"I didn't think you'd believe me," Con said.

"And you thought this would drive up your credibility? Come on, you're starting to piss me off."

"It's the truth."

He regarded her for a long time. "It's a good time for a restroom break. Pause recording." Clarke waited until the red light blinked off before he spoke again. "Look, clones can't testify in Virginia court, so don't worry about all that. But my captain believes that a witness statement from you would hold up in support of a warrant application. That's all I need from you. A statement."

"That Greer was at the farm?"

"That's it," Clarke said as if it were as inconsequential as a parking ticket. "I don't know why you're covering for him with this bullshit about some team of soldiers. Are you scared of him? Maybe he got you out there and attacked you? Didn't know his wife had a clone and was looking to relive the kill. Two for one."

"No, nothing like that."

"Then help us secure a warrant for Greer's house. I'm not looking to frame him up. If there's nothing there, then there's nothing there. But if there is, and I know there is, then you've helped us get a murderer off the streets. Either way, I'd be grateful and be in a position to expedite a death certificate. Get you on your way back to DC and a new life. Isn't that what you want? What do you say?"

CHAPTER EIGHTEEN

Con wondered later what she would have said next if there hadn't been a knock at the door. Maybe it was because they'd been at it for hours and she was worn out, but she would have said just about anything to get out of that interrogation room. Including feeding Levi Greer to Detective Clarke. He'd seemed like a big, lost, sad puppy dog when they met, but she was starting to have her doubts about him. He had sure played mister innocent, no mention of a possible affair or that he and her original had been fighting. But then the knock at the door interrupted her, and she recoiled from what she was considering. Clarke glared, like a boxer robbed of a knockout by an untimely bell, at the square-jawed officer who stuck his head into the interrogation room door.

"Detective?" the officer said. "A minute?"

"What do you want? Can't you see I'm in the middle of something here?"

"You're going to want to see this."

Something in his tone caught Clarke's attention. Reluctantly, he told Con to sit tight and followed the officer out into the hall. He was only gone about a minute and returned looking concerned.

"Let's go. We need to move you." When she didn't move quickly enough for his liking, he took her by the arm and led her out the door and to a bank of elevators.

"What's going on?" she asked, resentful at being manhandled.

"Franklin Butler is here."

Con's mouth snapped shut. Whatever threat Darius Clarke might represent, it paled alongside Franklin Butler and his Children of Adam. She didn't like to imagine what they would do should they get their hands on her. It would be open season. All Vernon Gaddis's grim warnings about Virginia would become a reality.

"What does he want?" she asked.

He looked at her as if she were the slowest student in a remedial class. "The body of the murdered wife of a pro athlete was discovered by her clone. Two of the major media networks are already set up outside, and the others will be here soon. What do you think he wants?"

Well, when Clarke put it like that, he might have a point. And as for what Franklin Butler wanted, what did he ever want but attention? And what better place to get it than in Virginia outside a police station holding a clone. Throw in the national media, and the opportunity was tailor-made for his brand of self-aggrandizement and grandstanding. But knowing CoA, it could get dangerous in a hurry—the news would draw every hard-core anti-cloner for a hundred miles.

"How many?" she asked.

"There are only about twenty of those CoA lunatics out there right now, but it'll be a mob scene in under an hour. He's got a portable loudspeaker setup and is already giving speeches."

They got on an elevator. Clarke punched "G," but a hand blocked the doors from closing. A plainclothes Latino detective wedged himself inside. He had the look of a man who knew what happened to messengers bearing bad news.

"What is it, Moreno?" Clarke growled.

"Richmond cut Greer loose."

Clarke cursed acrobatically. "Why? We needed him held."

"He lawyered up. Money talks, man, you know that."

"Greer's going to beat us to the house. How's the warrant application coming?"

"Waiting on your witness," Moreno said to Clarke.

"No time for that now. Go with what we've got. Hope it's enough."

"You got it."

"And post a car at his place. If he runs or tries to take anything out of that house, I want to know about it."

Moreno nodded and stepped back off the elevator. Clarke stared lasers into the closing doors. He and Con rode in silence down to the garage, where three uniformed officers were waiting for them.

"What're we doing?" Con asked.

"It's shift change. We're going to use it to sneak you out. We had your car towed here from the farm. The media won't know it yet, so Bennett here," Clarke said, pointing to a squat, blue-eyed woman whose jaw seemed fused closed, "is going to drive it out."

"Where will I be?" Con asked.

"In the trunk. The other two officers will leave first, so that hopefully the media gets bored and stops reacting to every vehicle coming in or out." Clarke turned to Bennett. "How does it look out there?"

"Local news plus CNN and Fox. The others won't be far behind," she said.

"Vultures."

"Where are they taking me?" Con asked.

"To a motel. It's all arranged. We're going to finish our conversation about these men who were at the farm. Until then, you need to lay low."

Put another way, Clarke would protect her as long as she served a purpose. After that, he'd cut her loose and she'd be on her own again, which meant she needed to assume she was on her own now.

"Thank you," she said, hoping it sounded convincing.

"To protect and serve," Clarke said without a hint of irony and rode the elevator back upstairs.

———

From the dark confines of the trunk, Con listened tensely as they passed through the growing throng of reporters set up outside the station. No one mobbed the car as it left the parking garage, so it seemed that Clarke's ruse had worked. Over a loudspeaker, Franklin Butler was pontificating about the arrogance of the elites and the existential threat of cloning. It brought a roar of agreement that Con couldn't believe was only twenty voices. The fact that CoA had managed to gather so quickly this early in the morning was terrifying. They were like cockroaches waiting for the lights to go out.

Once the car was safely away, she hoped Bennett would pull over and let her sit up front—riding in a trunk was even less glamorous than it sounded—but apparently, Bennett wasn't taking any chances. By the time the car finally rolled to a halt at the motel, Con had been knocked around like a piñata.

Bennett opened the trunk, and Con climbed out, blinking in the morning sunshine, and looked up at the double-decker motel with a green metallic roof that had been retrofitted with boxy, outdated solar paneling. Across the six lanes of traffic, a murderers' row of fast-food joints jostled for attention. An old gas station stood defiantly against the passage of time. Signs directed traffic onto I-95 North or South, but it could have been any one of a thousand small towns off a thousand interstates.

"Room 211," Bennett said, leading her up a concrete staircase to the exposed second floor.

"Do you have my LFD?" Con asked.

"Take it up with Clarke."

Con gestured back toward the fast-food places. "Can I at least get some money for food?"

"Clarke," Bennett said, signaling with her tone that Con should think about wrapping up the question-asking portion of the day. She opened the room with an old-fashioned key card. Of course it was. The musty room looked like it hadn't been redecorated in a hundred years. Clarke had really spared no expense.

Con waited by the door while Bennett checked the bathroom and the closet. Satisfied, the officer dropped the key card on a table but not the key to Con's car.

"So what's the plan?" Con asked.

"Sit tight. Your face is all over the news, but no one knows you're here. You'll be fine as long as you don't wander off. We'll have a unit do a drive-by every hour to check on you." Bennett didn't sound all that concerned about it one way or another. "Clarke will be in touch."

"When?"

"Later," Bennett said, somehow making her nonanswer sound definitive. She turned and left, shutting the door behind her without another word.

Later. Con rolled her eyes and gave the door the finger. They meant to strand her out here. And if she didn't do as she was told, Clarke could keep the keys and the LFD indefinitely. What recourse did she have as a clone? She wondered—had Clarke moved her for her safety or so that he could lean on her any way he chose, away from prying eyes?

She parted the blinds and watched Bennett amble down to the parking lot, where a patrol car was idling. Bennett got in, and the car drove away. When it was out of sight, Con waited five minutes and went down to the parking lot herself. Sitting tight was not high on her list. She wasn't sure where to go now but intended to be long gone before Clarke or anyone else came to check on her. What she wanted was to have it out with Levi Greer. She wasn't about to take Clarke's word for it that the husband was a killer, but the detective had asked some hard questions.

She crouched down beside her car and felt around inside the wheel well, praying the police hadn't found the magnetic box that Peter had hidden there. Her hand closed around it, and she pulled it free.

Opening it with a thumbprint, she shook the spare key into her palm and gave thanks to majordomos everywhere. Peter was fast on his way to becoming her favorite person anywhere. Her backpack was missing from the back seat, but the go bag was still undisturbed in the spare-tire compartment. She fished out her backup LFD and powered it up.

There was a message from Laleh Askari. It was only an hour old, asking if they could meet. That was interesting. After Levi Greer, Laleh was pretty much at the top of Con's to-do list. There were questions that only she could answer. Laleh had put on one hell of a show back at Palingenesis. All that Good Samaritan bullshit about helping Con out of a sense of guilt and responsibility. It had been damn convincing at the time, but now, she felt sure Laleh knew more than she had let on.

When Con texted back to ask where, Laleh must have been waiting because she answered immediately and suggested a public park in Washington. She asked how soon Con could be there. Con's LFD told her it was a little over three hours away, so she said it would take her five. Getting there early and scoping it out sounded like a good idea. According to Gaddis, no one had laid eyes on Laleh since the day she left Palingenesis, so it was awful convenient that she picked now to reach out. Right when Con was out of ideas and out of options.

A less optimistic person might see it as a trap. After all, whoever had put Laleh up to it might have also killed her original. That didn't mean she could stay away.

———

The park was a tree-lined triangle of land at the corner of Florida Avenue and First Street NW. The heat wave had broken momentarily, and people were out enjoying a day of unusually mild weather. Con parked five blocks north of the park and walked the surrounding neighborhood until she knew all the routes back to the car. If she couldn't get back to it, there were three different Metro stops within a ten-block radius. She also made a note of the nearest bikeshare stations should it come to that. It wasn't perfect, but having options made her feel a little better about being a sitting duck out here.

When she was satisfied, she bought a coffee and sat in the shop's window watching for anything out of the ordinary. While she waited, she checked her feed for the news. Bennett hadn't been exaggerating. There wasn't a ton up yet about the murder of Con D'Arcy, mostly local outlets, but every single story featured a big photo of the original Con. One had even dug up concert footage of Awaken the Ghosts. The articles all hewed to the same basic narrative—the body of the original Constance D'Arcy, wife of Richmond Pathogens star Levi Greer, had been discovered by her clone. The police would not confirm if Greer was a suspect, but unnamed sources inside the department called him a person of interest. The clone was said to be cooperating with detectives but had not been made available to speak to the press.

Con wondered whether this qualified as cooperation. She didn't remember taking that photo, but at least her hair had been long until Peter cut it. To be safe, though, she would need to buy sunglasses and a hat if she hoped to go unrecognized.

Some men were playing horseshoes in the park. It reminded her of her father. He'd died when she was so young that she sometimes wondered if she remembered him at all. Or if she only knew him second-hand, a collage assembled from photographs and stories she'd heard told about him after his death. But this memory she recognized immediately as hers and hers alone—Antoine D'Arcy had loved horseshoes. At family cookouts, he would set up shop at the pit with a ready horseshoe in one hand and a cigar in the other. He'd shoo her away if she made a fuss—this was grown-up time, he'd say—so she knew to sit real quiet if she wanted to watch. Whenever he threw a ringer, which in her memory he did every time, he'd catch her eye and wink. As if she were his secret good luck charm. It was the most relaxed she ever saw him. Her father never laughed at home, rarely even smiled. Things with Con's mother were always one wrong word away from a fight. But after a few beers in the Texas sunshine, the armor he'd accumulated over repeated deployments would fall away. He would laugh and tell stories like the other fathers, and she saw the outline of the young, charismatic man who had joined the army at eighteen.

It was a good memory, and she felt reassured by it. She might not be the Con D'Arcy who'd been there that day, but she was the Con D'Arcy who was here now remembering it. The overalls she'd worn. The plate of barbecue sitting in the grass beside her. The sweet smell of her dad's cigar, and how the fathers would curse and then glance around to make sure they hadn't been overheard. It was all a part of her. That was undeniable and had to count for something. She sipped her coffee and thought about her dad some more. Her dad. There was power in that.

Laleh showed up a few minutes early. She got out of a rideshare and crossed the park to the fountain. Con watched for any sign that she'd brought company but didn't get that vibe. Maybe it was the way Laleh kept glancing back over her shoulder as though she was the one who should be worried about being followed. Still, Con waited fifteen minutes before leaving the coffee shop and crossing the street. She circled around to the back of the park, coming up behind Laleh, who had found an empty park bench. Gone was her confidence; Laleh's head was tilted down like she'd been caught doing something she shouldn't. Despite sitting in a park surrounded by families in the middle of a sunny afternoon, when Con sat down, Laleh flinched like Con had jumped out at her from a dark alley at two in the morning.

"What's new, Laleh?" Con asked.

"Con," Laleh said. "How are you? Are you alright?"

"Don't," Con warned. She had less than no interest in Laleh's concern for her well-being. "Are we alone?"

"I think so. Don't think I was followed."

That wasn't what Con had meant, but it was interesting that was what Laleh thought. Maybe this wasn't a trap after all. Laleh sure didn't act like someone who felt in control of the situation.

"Why did you call me?" Con asked.

"I saw the news about your original. I'm so sorry."

"Did you see what was done to her? How she died?" Con demanded.

Laleh looked ill. "I didn't know what was going to happen. I swear. That's why I'm here. I didn't know."

"Bullshit. Who was it? Who put you up to it? Fenton or Gaddis?"

"I don't know which one. It was all anonymous and encrypted."

"But you think it was one of them?" Con said.

"Yes. Whoever it was, they knew Palingenesis inside and out. They knew the layout. Our procedures. They knew things that only someone on the inside would know."

"And they just wanted you to tamper with the lockout?"

"Yes, I'm so sorry," Laleh said.

"Stop. I don't care," Con said, growing impatient with Laleh's self-pitying tone. "You understand me? I don't care if you're sorry. So just tell me what happened. When were you approached?"

Laleh nodded, eyes rimmed with tears. *Wonderful.*

"March of last year," Laleh said. "You were nearing the ninety-day lockout. I'd tried reaching out to your original several times to schedule a refresh, but she never responded. Then I got the offer. Override your lockout. I'd worked there seven years and didn't even know it could be done. But they showed me how."

"And you did it." Con didn't know why she cared but found herself asking anyway. "Why?"

"For my younger brother. He's sick. Cancer, but they found it too late. Money was placed in an offshore account to pay for a clone."

That was a small fortune. Con thought she should almost be flattered. "And his clone wouldn't have cancer."

"It's unlikely, and anyway, we would know to screen for it this time. You had stopped doing refreshes, so what difference did it make? I didn't know what they were going to do."

"But you didn't think about it any too hard, did you?"

"No, I did not," Laleh said, some of her old poise returning. "I've spent years watching billionaires cheating death while complaining about what a hardship it was to have to come in once a month to do a refresh. Why should they live while my brother dies a slow, horrible death?"

It made it somehow better, knowing that Laleh hadn't been motivated purely by greed. That didn't mean Con was ready to absolve her. She'd been contacted more than a year ago—the first link in the chain that had led to Con D'Arcy's murder. Con moved on before she said exactly that. "And then what happened?"

"Nothing. That was it. I thought I was done. Until about three weeks ago."

"What happened three weeks ago?"

"Your original showed up," Laleh said.

"She did what?" Con said, her skin going cold.

"She was waiting for me one night when I got home. She was scared and anxious. Said she had gotten herself in over her head and was in danger. She was afraid that something bad might happen to her and needed my help."

"She knew that you'd tampered with the lockout?"

"She seemed to know everything. Where the money was. All of it."

"How?" Con asked in disbelief.

"She said there was a battle being waged for control of the company. I think somehow she had gotten involved with Vernon Gaddis."

"She told you that?"

"Not explicitly, no. But when I mentioned his name, she reacted strangely. Like he frightened her."

"She knew she was going to die," Con said, slumping back against the park bench. All along, she'd assumed that her original was an innocent victim.

"I think so. That was the last I ever saw of her. Then she went missing and her death event triggered your revival."

"I need to talk to Levi Greer," Con said.

"They arrested him. It popped up on my feed as I pulled up here."

Con cursed. Clarke might be a son of a bitch, but he seemed plenty good at his job. Well, Levi Greer might be a murderer, but if he was, someone was pulling his strings same as Laleh Askari. There were too many coincidences to think otherwise.

"I have to go," Laleh said.

"What will you do now?"

"I fly to England tonight. I have family in Manchester."

———

After leaving Washington, Con told the car to take her back to Levi Greer's home. If the police had arrested him, there was a chance they'd be gone and that the house's identification system would mistake Con for her original and let her in. She was dying to have a look around and get a feel for how her original had lived. But when she got there, she found a police car parked in the driveway and the front door barred by yellow caution tape.

With nothing to be done until morning, she went back to the motel for the night. She stopped in at the manager's office, curious to know if Detective Clarke had left word. A tired white woman in her sixties looked up from a dog-eared book of sudoku puzzles.

"We don't log messages. This ain't the Beverly Wilshire."

It was a fair point. And despite the motel's half-hearted approach to record keeping, she doubted Clarke had been by. Why would he? With Levi Greer behind bars, she'd probably dropped way down his list of priorities. Possibly off of it. With a bit of luck, he didn't even know that she'd played hooky.

Back up in her room, she put on the news and ran a shower. The death of Con D'Arcy was now national news. She sat on the edge of the bed, wrapped in a towel, and flipped to all the news networks to be sure. One channel showed footage of police searching the farm while a reporter described the gruesome discovery of Levi Greer's wife. A wedding photograph of the happy couple appeared in one corner of the screen. For contrast, Con supposed. She'd also be good with them referring to her as something other than a wife. On another channel, a heated roundtable discussion raged over the ethical treatment of clones. To her surprise, there was even some sympathy for her situation among the panelists. The fact that she was of "limited means" seemed to work in her favor—a polite way of saying broke-ass poor. It was nice to hear something positive, but it wasn't lost on her that there wasn't a single clone on the panel. When the discussion turned to Levi Greer, the panel wasn't nearly so gentle.

Curious, she reached for her LFD to learn a little more about the man she might have married. Most of what she found covered his athletic career. Turned out the Richmond Pathogens were an expansion team that had made the playoffs for the first time last season. Levi was credited with being a big part of the team's success and had come in third in MVP balloting. Not surprisingly, his public persona aside, personal biographical details were scarce—little that might tell her what kind of man he was. Like most of their generation, he'd clearly rejected the obsession with living life online that had gripped the dawn of the social-media age. But based on the handful of interviews he'd granted over the years, she pieced together that Greer was a twenty-six-year-old Virginia native with perhaps the world's largest collection of hoodies. He'd bounced around the Department of Social Services' foster system as a child. It wasn't an experience he ever discussed publicly, but reading between the lines, Con could tell that it had been a brutal time in his life. The happy ending to the story, though, was that when Levi Greer was eleven, he'd been placed with a family in Richmond that had been a good fit and shepherded him through to college. After he signed his first professional contract, he'd quietly started a charity to provide tutoring and college counseling for foster children.

It made for one hell of a compelling story. She wanted to like him. He came off as humble and self-aware, and it was easy to see why he'd been so popular with fans. But now that he'd been accused of murder, the media was using that same narrative to cast him as a controlling abuser with a dark side.

Con put her LFD on the nightstand to charge and lay there in the dark for a long time wondering what her original had gotten herself into. She'd known she was in danger, and she'd known about Laleh. That meant she had to know who was orchestrating the whole thing. But *how* she knew, that was the real question. Con was missing something essential. Hopefully, Levi Greer knew more than he had told her. Tomorrow, she would pay him a visit in jail.

CHAPTER NINETEEN

One at a time, the visitors passed through a full-body scanner and were patted down. Con had been worried that someone at the jail might recognize her, but her presence didn't seem to raise any eyebrows among the guards. She and the other visitors were let into a utilitarian meeting area of brute metal tables and chairs all welded crudely to the floor. The visitors spread out around the room to give themselves the illusion of privacy. They'd all had to check their LFDs on arrival, so there was nothing to do but sit and wait. An hour ticked by, then another.

Just when Con started to get concerned, a sad claxon sounded. At the back of the meeting room, a door opened. Prisoners in orange jumpsuits shuffled out. Last was Levi Greer. Where the rest of the prisoners wore only handcuffs, his hands and ankles were yoked with chain to a thick belt at his waist. When she'd met him, he'd looked exhausted. Now he looked about as beaten down as she'd ever seen a man.

A guard led him over by the elbow, but when Levi saw who was waiting for him, he drew back. For a moment, Con thought he would simply turn around and retreat to his cell. But then either curiosity or the inertia of the guard dragging him forward got the better of him, and he let himself be seated opposite her.

"You want to hear something pathetic?" Levi said, drawing a deep breath. "I kept telling myself that the police were lying. You know?

Screwing with my head. Some kind of game. It had to be, right? But you saw her? With your own eyes? It's really true?"

"It's true."

Levi leaned heavily against the table as if he needed help carrying the weight of her words. His shoulders begin to shake. Con searched his face for any sign it was an act. She needed more than an Oscar-worthy performance to be convinced. So she sat there feeling like God's own bitch and let him cry himself out.

"What are you doing here?" he asked, lowering his face to dry his eyes with the heel of his hand.

"We had a deal."

"Oh right. Yeah, we did." His voice flat, affectless, drained of any fight. "What do you want to know?"

"Why didn't you ask me for the GPS coordinates?"

That hadn't been what he'd expected. "What do you mean?"

"I mean, your wife is missing. And you don't once ask for them."

"I told you to give them to the police."

"Yeah, you did. But if it was me? And someone I loved was missing?" She was thinking about Zhi now, imagining if he'd gone missing for a week or longer. How she'd react if someone showed up who knew where he was. "No way I tell you to take it to the cops. I wouldn't have let you out of my sight until I had the GPS. I'd have put a gun to your head if that's what it took. But you let me walk back out of your house like you'd ordered Girl Scout cookies. And then the detective said you went for a drive or some shit?"

"Yeah, I did. Up into the Shenandoah like I said. David—the man who adopted me—used to take me up there to decompress whenever I needed to get away from things."

"You have to know how that sounds," she said.

"Oh, you think I don't know?" he said, showing her his shackled wrists. "Did you ever read *Macbeth* in high school? This Scottish king, he has one of his rivals murdered, guy named Banquo. Then Banquo's ghost starts haunting the king. Doesn't say anything. Banquo, he just stands there. Staring. Judging. Kind of like how you're looking at me now. Except I didn't do it. But I still got to deal with her damned ghost accusing me of hurting her."

"I want to believe that."

"I didn't kill her."

"So what happened?" Con asked.

"Damned if I know. Why do you think I drove up to the mountains yesterday? None of it makes any sense. The first year? Best year of my life. She was in such a sad place when we met. But after a few months, she really came out of it and seemed happy. At least, I thought she was, I don't know. Everything just seemed on the upswing. Things were really clicking for me with the team. She was busy with her music, writing all these new songs. And we got married. Didn't make a big deal of it, just went to the courthouse. Sort of the last thing either of us expected, but it felt right. We were even talking about se'ling the house and moving downtown. Man, she hated the burbs, but I guess you know that better than me, right?"

It was like catching a few stray bars of music and trying to imagine the entire song. Her need to know the story in more detail was unbearable. But visiting hours were brief, and she had too many urgent questions to indulge her curiosity now.

"What changed?" she asked.

"Nothing. Everything? She just became distant. If I asked, she always said everything was fine. Things were real busy with the team, and eventually I stopped asking. I know I wasn't paying attention the way I should have been, but I thought when the season was over that we'd go somewhere. Get back on track, you know? Now, I find out she'd been taking all these trips to Charlottesville while I was on the road."

"Was she having an affair?"

"I don't know," Levi said, voice rising. "The way the police describe it to me, they're talking about someone else's life. Like she's hiding bruises from people, and the neighbors saying we fought all the time."

"You didn't?"

"No, never. Part of me wishes we had. Maybe if we'd had it out, she'd still be here. I just didn't try hard enough. Or maybe I never had a chance. What do you think? You're her. Did she ever love me?"

Con didn't have an answer, so she didn't offer one. They sat there in the indistinguishable murmur of nearby conversations. It was a terrible irony. They were each haunted by the same questions: Who was Con D'Arcy, and why had she married Levi Greer? Con knew who she'd been before meeting him, while Greer only knew her afterward.

"So, what do I call you? Just can't be calling you Con, you know? That would mess with my head."

Since the beginning, she'd been fighting to convince everyone that she was Con D'Arcy. But it was more complicated than that. She was and she wasn't. She was some of that person—they shared so much— but no matter how many questions she asked, no matter how much she learned about her missing eighteen months, they were never going to be *her* eighteen months. Any more than the original Con D'Arcy could know what she'd been through in the last few days.

"How about Constance?" she suggested.

"You hate that name."

"It's weird that you know that."

"What's not weird about this?" he said. "Alright, Constance it is."

He smiled at her then for the first time since she'd met him, a bemused, crooked smile at the sheer absurdity of his situation. She saw what her original must have seen in Levi Greer: a sweet, quiet man who had been through hell as a kid and come out more or less intact. Well, he was back there now, and try as she might, she couldn't talk herself into his having had anything to do with it.

"So, what else do you want to know?"

"If you didn't kill her, who did?"

"Isn't that the cops' job?"

"The cops think it's you; I don't. You really want to roll the dice that they'll come around?"

"Fair point," he conceded.

"I don't think she was having an affair."

"How can you possibly know that?"

"Because I wouldn't."

"Damn," he murmured like a prayer. "Fine. So who did kill her?"

She asked if his wife had ever mentioned Brooke Fenton or Vernon Gaddis, but he only knew the name Vernon Gaddis as "the cloning guy." He asked what they had to do with it, and against her better judgment, she told him everything she knew. By the time she finished, his expression was one of wary disbelief.

"You have to know how that sounds," he said, throwing her words back at her.

"I'm aware. Tell me about Charlottesville."

Levi exhaled like he'd breathed in smoke. "After she disappeared, the police traced her car to a garage in Charlottesville near the UVA campus. According to the car's navigation history, that's where she always parked when she went down there. Which she did a lot over the last year. Always while I was on the road with the team. She'd stay down there, sometimes two or three days at a stretch. Never said a word about it to me."

"Did she have any friends in Charlottesville?"

"You tell me."

Constance shook her head. She'd never been to Charlottesville in her life.

"The cops canvassed around the garage but came up empty. I've driven down there twice now since she disappeared," Levi said. "Thought maybe I'd know where she'd gone if I saw it for myself, but it's just shops and restaurants and stuff. I don't know what I thought I'd find. It's not like I knew her."

"You really think that?"

"I didn't even know she had a clone. Didn't know she was going to Charlottesville. Only thing I do know is she was planning on leaving for good."

"If she'd been going down there so much, what makes you think this last time was any different?" she asked.

"Because after you left the other day, I went through the room she used as a music studio and found some things missing. Let me ask you this, if you were leaving somewhere, what're the two things you wouldn't leave behind?"

Constance nodded, understanding. "My guitar and my notebooks."

"Exactly. She even took the little purple Christmas tree. Cops weren't so interested in that theory, though," Levi said. "You ever feel like you don't know why anything is happening?"

"Only since I was six."

"When your dad died," Levi said. "She talked a lot about that. I wanted to invite her mom—your mom—to the wedding, but Con wouldn't have it."

"Wouldn't have been your wedding anymore. Would have been the Mary D'Arcy show, trust me."

"That's just what she said," Levi said. "Man, this is so damn weird. Like, my wife is dead. But . . ."

"But here I am."

"What am I supposed to do with all this?" he said, jabbing himself hard in the chest with four fingers.

"Can I ask how you two met?"

"You really don't know?"

"No, I have no memory of you at all. She met you and stopped doing her refreshes. You don't have to talk about it if you don't want."

"No, it's okay. I've been thinking about it a lot lately. The team was in DC for a versus against the Filibusters. If we won, we'd make the playoffs for the first time. We did. A group of us went out to celebrate. It was the day after Christmas. We wound up at this club in Shaw. Con was singing with Weathervane. Couldn't take my eyes off her. She had a way on stage. A presence. I didn't meet her that night, but I made an excuse and didn't take the team bus back to Richmond just so I could see her sing again the next night. Thought that'd be it, but the show was at a tiny little club, and she wound up next to me at the bar after the show. Got to talking. Never stopped. You know those moments when you can feel something happening, but you're too in it to know what it is? Like you're on the train going a hundred miles an hour, not watching a train go a hundred miles an hour, so you've got no perspective on it."

She did. That's exactly how she would have described meeting Zhi.

He continued. "I stayed up at her place. We sat around this fake little purple Christmas tree and just talked until it was time to go to the next show."

"I loved that tree," Con said.

"Well, she brought it with her when she moved down here. Said it was her good luck charm and that it had brought me to her or something. We were pretty corny, I'm not going to lie. She even played me some of the new songs she'd been working on, although she swore me to secrecy."

"She did?" That surprised Con even more than the tree and told her a lot about how her original must have felt about Levi Greer. She had never played her songs for anyone. Ever. She didn't know what had gone wrong in their marriage, but if her original trusted Levi Greer enough to share those songs with him, then she'd loved him once.

"Then that crazy New Year's Eve show at Glass House. She had that awful fight with Kala and that prick manager threatening to sue if she didn't go on. I was halfway to knocking his teeth in. Con wouldn't stop crying. Like I legit thought I was going to have to take her to the hospital."

"What happened that night?" Con asked.

Levi's face fell. "You seriously don't know, do you?"

"Know what?"

"Zhi's parents called. He'd died that morning."

Con became very aware of her own breathing and of the electronic whine that filled her ears. Levi was talking but she couldn't hear him anymore.

"I have to go," she said, trying to swallow down what felt like a knotted rope being dragged up her throat. She needed to get outside in the fresh air before she was sick.

Darius Clarke was waiting for her on the jailhouse steps. He was leaning beside the door but pushed off the brick wall and glided up alongside her like a frigate preparing to board a crippled schooner. All she wanted was to reach her car before she started to cry. Somehow she'd managed to hold it back so far, but every step she took, she could feel her makeshift levee begin to give way to a grim hysteria. She thought she'd already grieved for Zhi, but apparently that had just been the opening act. The headliner was itching to take the stage. Then an unexpected thing happened. She looked at Darius Clarke, and the urge to cry went away as if it had never been there at all. Whatever else happened, she would not cry in front of this man.

"I could have sworn I left you at a motel," the detective said with a bemused smile.

CHAPTER TWENTY

"I had things to do," Con said.

"Yeah, I saw that," Clarke said. "Very touching."

Con stopped halfway down the steps, catching his meaning. What she'd written off as inefficiency had actually been the jail buying Clarke time to get there.

"You were watching."

"Course I was watching. They notified me as soon as you checked in here. You really think a clone gets into a Virginia jail otherwise? It was a good idea too. Wish I'd thought of it. We could have fed you questions to keep him talking. Wasted opportunity if you ask me. Not every day you get the chance to confront a killer with his victim. Have to hand it to him, though. That was one hell of a performance. For my money, he's wasting himself playing video games. Should get his ass out to Hollywood. They love lying bastards who can cry on cue out there."

"He didn't kill her."

"Right, it was your mystery men at the farmhouse. And they're working for who again?"

"I'm not sure yet."

"That's always the best part of a good conspiracy theory," Clarke said, his condescension cloaking his words like low-hanging clouds.

"I really don't think he did it," she said but made no real effort to convince him. If he'd eavesdropped on her conversation with Levi Greer and still didn't believe her, there was nothing left that would convince him.

"He did it," Clarke said with absolute certainty. "Want to know why I didn't need your witness statement to get a search warrant for his place? Because that farm where you found the body, well, turns out that was Levi Greer's foster home growing up. And the room where you found his wife's body, that was the bedroom where the old man used to work him over. The foster parents are monsters. Guess no one wanted to live in that house after word got out what happened there."

Clarke loaned a file to her LFD and stood silently while she swiped through the pages of Levi Greer's case file. It painted a vivid portrait of cruelty at the hands of his foster parents, who were both currently serving lengthy jail sentences for a host of criminal charges. The pictures of his childhood bedroom looked little different than it did now. She froze on a series of photographs documenting the horrific bruising on young Levi Greer's torso.

"He was seven, eight years old at the time those pictures were taken. Hate to think about the long-term effect on a kid that young."

"Aren't those files sealed?" Con remembered reading that in one of the articles she'd found about him. She didn't love the thought of using someone's childhood trauma against them.

"That they are," Clarke said. "So, tell me how anybody but him knew about that house?"

Con returned the loaned file. She'd seen enough. "Money," she said.

"Stop already. Whoever killed Constance D'Arcy knew a lot about Levi Greer's life. Intimate, personal things. Take that in conjunction with his erratic behavior in the last few months. Neighbors report loud arguments from the Greer house in the weeks prior to her disappearance, and text messages between Greer and several friends indicate that he was worried his wife was having an affair. All those trips to Charlottesville."

"She wasn't having an affair."

Clarke shrugged. "In the end, I don't care one way or another. Only matters what he thought. Doesn't give anyone the right to do what he did."

"What he's accused of," Constance corrected. "You still don't—"

"We have the murder weapon," Clarke interrupted. "We haven't told the press yet, but we found it during the search of his house. Ceremonial air force dagger hidden beneath a floorboard in the basement. It had been cleaned, but a field kit found traces of her blood type in a crack in the handle. It's being tested now, but it'll come back a match."

"But—"

"He did it," Clarke said. "He had motive and opportunity. He can't provide a verifiable alibi for the day of his wife's disappearance. I know he put on a good show in there, but they all do. Why do you think I'm such a cynical son of a bitch?"

"Why are you telling me all this?" Con asked.

"Because somehow this little crusade of yours has made you news. We had press calling the station asking to interview you. They're fixing to make you the face of cloning in America. I'm giving you the facts so if you do get it into your head to talk to the media, you'll do the right thing and keep Levi Greer's name out of your mouth. I know I've been an asshole, but that doesn't make Levi Greer innocent. It's always the husband. A jury should take about five minutes deliberating this one, believe me. But if you start up talking about corporations and conspiracy theories and whatnot, you're going to muddy what are otherwise crystal-clear waters. Crystal fucking clear. And I can't have that. A woman is dead, and the man who did it is locked up in there."

She didn't have the heart to tell him that all his little presentation had accomplished was to impress upon her the sophistication of the effort to frame Levi for murder. A woman was dead, but he had the wrong person. Greer was nothing but the fall guy.

"Don't worry. I'm not interested in being anyone's *face*," she said.

"The media has a history of deciding that kind of thing for itself."

"Fine, but I'm not talking to anyone."

"Good to hear, because I want you out of Virginia today," Clarke said. "It's too dangerous for you here."

"How's that?" she asked.

"Now the media has made a symbol out of you, who else do you think is going to want to make you a symbol?"

"Children of Adam," she said, realizing Clarke was right. The CoA was always going to be a threat, but now she would be its number-one priority.

"If they catch up with you, I guarantee you won't enjoy the experience. Better for both of us if you get back across the Potomac before they find you. You hearing me?"

"Yeah," she said, although that wasn't where she was headed. Talking to Levi, she'd already decided that she needed to see Charlottesville for herself.

"You hearing me?" Clarke asked a second time, clearly underwhelmed by her answer.

"Yeah, I hear you."

"Good. Now get the hell up out of here before I lose my famous charm and good humor. If you're still here come sunup, you're on your own. Interfere with my investigation again, and I'll deliver you to the Children of Adam personally."

CHAPTER TWENTY-ONE

Charlottesville was only seventy miles west of Richmond, but the car wouldn't make it on its remaining charge. Con found a nearby station and headed there first. When she arrived, the car pulled into one of the four bays. She got out and paid at the automated kiosk while a hydraulic lift raised her car. Battery life had improved dramatically from when she was a kid, but charging still took forever. The car companies had eventually wised up and switched to interchangeable batteries. So rather than plug in and charge for hours, drivers could simply pull in and have the battery swapped out for a fresh one in a matter of minutes.

Con waited beneath the canopy and allowed herself to think about Zhi. It was hard to fathom that he'd been gone for a year and a half when she remembered so clearly sitting at his bedside only a few days ago. She didn't know why, but now that the shock of first hearing had passed, the urge to cry had passed with it. Not that it didn't break her heart, but so much had happened to her that she felt at a strange remove from that part of her life. One of her had already mourned his death, did she have to go through it as well? Of course that made her feel guilty all over again for not falling apart the way maybe she felt she should.

Con looked up from her thoughts to see Peter Lee. Gone was his suit, replaced with a T-shirt and heavy-duty work pants and boots.

Somehow she'd missed how muscular the man was back on Charles Island. And not a sculpted, movie-star physique but powerful, utilitarian muscle that looked like it had been built with a specific job in mind. The gun holstered on his hip hinted at what that job might have been. She took a step away from him. She'd really liked Peter. He was one of the main reasons she didn't want to believe Gaddis was behind framing Levi Greer for murder. But showing up here, like this, made her wonder if she'd read Peter Lee all wrong.

He raised his hands. "Can we talk?"

"It's a free country," she said, although it had never felt less like one. "Are you following me?"

"The car's GPS," he explained.

Of course they'd been tracking her movements. The car didn't belong to her. It had been naïve of her not to have known that from the start. "I have an LFD, you know?"

"Mr. Gaddis felt this was too important for a call. You hanging in there?"

"It's been a strange couple of days, you know?" she said, but refused to be sidetracked by Peter's soothing everything's-gonna-be-fine voice. This wasn't a damn yoga class. "What's with the gun, Peter? Seriously. What exactly is your job?"

Peter looked down at it as if he'd forgotten it was there. "I am Mr. Gaddis's majordomo. I speak for, look to, and protect Mr. Gaddis's interests. Whatever those may be."

"Does that include shooting people?" Con asked.

"Not so far, but this is Virginia and the day's not over. We're not exactly welcome here, are we?"

Con's eyes narrowed. "We're?"

"First gen. West Point, class of '21."

She'd had no inkling that Peter was a clone and found that reassuring. "How'd you wind up working for Gaddis? Special Forces to majordomo seems like a strange career path."

"Well, that's a long story," he said and then took so long choosing his next words that she wondered if he'd ever told it. "My original caught a bullet in Havana during the invasion in '30. I was activated or whatever they're calling it these days. Everything worked flawlessly. Life went on. Then the *Times* and *Post* broke that damn story in '32. Let's just say my family did not take the news well that I was a clone."

"They didn't know for two years?"

"Couldn't tell them. Whole thing was classified up the ass. But I knew that when I signed up for the program. Got no one to blame but myself." He shrugged. "My girl just turned sixteen. Would've been nice to have been there."

Behind his laconic understatement, Con saw a pain so severe that the only way to survive would be to lock it away and ignore it for as long as possible.

"Don't suppose I blame them," Peter said. "They should've been told. I chose my country over my family. Had no right to expect any different."

"So, Gaddis hired you?" She recalled the guilt in Gaddis's voice talking about the fate of the first generation of clones. Was Peter some kind of penance?

"Well, that doesn't really begin to cover it. Saved my life first. When he found me, I was living in Tupelo under a fake name. I was in a bad way for a few years there. Drugs," Peter said stoically. "Mr. Gaddis paid to get me cleaned up. Hired me in '36. I've worked for him ever since. Should have told you in Maryland. Just not something I talk about if I can avoid it."

"Can I ask you something?" When he didn't say no, she continued. "If you had it to do over again, would you?"

"Would I take the clone, you mean? Or would I have preferred to die in Cuba and be done with it? Suppose I go back and forth. Some days being dead doesn't sound so bad."

"What about now? Do you have another clone?"

Peter chuckled. "Being a majordomo doesn't pay as well as you seem to think."

"Fair, but what if your boss offered you one?"

He didn't take but a moment to answer. "No. I'm through with all that. Next time I die, I want that to be the last time. What about you?"

"I'm still adjusting to this clone, don't know if I'd want to start all over."

"I get that," Peter said. "Did you hear about that guy up in New York? Killed his wife, then ate a bullet. Police arrest his clone for murder. Clone has no memory of the crime, obviously. Claims he never even thought about killing her, but no way to know for sure. At the trial, his lawyer argued that a clone shouldn't be held responsible for the actions of their original. Prosecution argued that would create a free pass for people to commit crimes without consequences."

"What did the jury say?"

"Found him guilty in under an hour. It's being appealed. Makes me think, though. That it would be nice not remembering. Things got real dark there for a while. The army probably still has my last upload in storage. Technically, it's my property. Sometimes I think it would be nice to not remember any of the things I did in this body. So maybe, I'd go back and start over. Wipe the slate clean."

"But wouldn't you risk going through all those same things anyway?"

"I don't know. Are you going through the same things your original did?"

She thought about her unexpectedly muted reaction to the news of Zhi's death, especially compared to her original's. Her total lack of attraction to Levi Greer. It had troubled her at first; she thought maybe it proved that she wasn't really herself. But maybe that relationship depended on the precise alchemy of those lost days between Christmas and New Year's Eve. Love wasn't a given, it was something that took timing and no small amount of luck.

"Not all," she said.

"Exactly. But, still, I know I wouldn't. It took me a long time to block out the people telling me I wasn't me. But I am Peter Lee. *This* Peter Lee. It was a hard-earned clarity, and I'm not interested in making another one of me have to learn that same lesson. That'd be a brutal kind of reincarnation, you know what I mean?"

She did and again found herself trusting him. Though she reminded herself that trust shouldn't extend to Vernon Gaddis. Peter worked for him; they weren't partners. If Gaddis was behind all of this, keeping Peter in the dark might be useful for winning the trust of gullible twenty-four-year-old musicians. For instance.

"So what are you here to tell me that was too important for the phone?" she asked.

"Mr. Gaddis would like a word," Peter said, pointing down the street.

"He's here? In Virginia?"

"That is how it usually works," Peter said, dry as a fistful of sand.

That shocked her. Gaddis had made it clear that it would take an act of God for him to cross the Potomac. The news hadn't mentioned any second comings, so she was more than a little curious to know why he was here. Still, the vivid memory of discovering her own body in the farmhouse and of Levi Greer locked in a jail cell for a crime she felt sure he hadn't committed made her hesitate. The person who had orchestrated that was capable of anything.

"What if I don't want to talk to him?" she asked.

"I think you're going to want to hear this for yourself," Peter said. "But I'm not going to force you to do anything you don't want, if that's what you're asking."

One of these days, her curiosity was going to get her into serious trouble, and there wouldn't be a drone handy to get her out of it. She hoped today wasn't that day as she followed Peter. Her car would park itself after the battery change.

He led her to the parking lot behind an old fast-food burger joint a few doors down. Gaddis might have broken his cardinal rule coming to Virginia, but if anyone thought to cause trouble for him, he'd brought his own private army along to cause a little in return. Flanking an idling limo were two gigantic black SUVs. Unnaturally large men in dark suits formed a perimeter. At least two carried rifles on slings like the ones her father had worn in the pictures with his unit.

"Mr. Gaddis is taking a big personal risk coming down here to see you," Peter said and held open the door for Con, who climbed inside. Across from her sat Vernon Gaddis and a middle-aged white woman in a severe power suit. She couldn't have been more than five feet even but didn't look like anyone to take lightly. She typed steadily on a laptop balanced on her knees and didn't look up or acknowledge Con.

"This is one of my attorneys, Karen Harper. I asked her to sit in."

"Does she speak?"

"Where appropriate," Gaddis said and tapped on the window, gazing up at the logo mounted atop a tall pole overlooking the restaurant. "You like burgers?"

"I'm from Texas," she said, although, in truth, it had been years since she'd had one. Burgers from a food printer just never tasted right, and most burger chains had either shut down or pivoted to new gimmicks. There were those who decried the decline of the cheeseburger as a tragedy, but most people simply couldn't afford to pay those kinds of prices for genuine ground beef.

"When I was a kid, there were more than fifty thousand burger places in this country," Gaddis said. "Every corner, every airport, every ballpark. Burgers, burgers, burgers. As American as apple pie. Now you hardly see them anymore, and it makes me angry and sad. Which is idiotic. I couldn't tell you the last time I had one. So why do I care so much? Why is it that the more I change, the more I need everything around me to stay the same? It's a perverse design flaw in our species. That even something as inconsequential as a cheeseburger, which doesn't affect my life one iota, still threatens my understanding of the world. Ironic, isn't it?"

"You did invent cloning."

"Well, your aunt did the inventing, but I sure sold it. I suppose that makes me the Ray Kroc of cloning. I sold America one of the most profound changes in human history and am frustrated and disappointed by the country's inability to adapt. Yet my feelings are hurt that people aren't eating enough cheeseburgers. That takes a special kind of hypocrisy, don't you think? But here we sit, the cheeseburgers of Virginia."

"I got the impression you'd never set foot here again," Con said.

"There have been developments."

"What developments?"

"I want you to come back to the island with me. It's not safe here." Gaddis paused and corrected himself. "Well, it was never safe, but now it's way beyond that."

"I have things left to do. I'm not finished here."

"We had a deal. You wanted to know what happened to your original. Now you do. The police have a suspect in custody. What's left?"

"Levi didn't do it."

"Levi?" Gaddis said, seemingly surprised to hear her use his first name. "The husband had ample motive, opportunity, and the details of the crime are very personal to him. The fact that he has a childhood connection to that farm is damning. There's also a surplus of evidence against him. The murder weapon, for one."

"How exactly do you know all that?" Con demanded. According to Clarke, none of it was public knowledge yet.

"I'm worth three billion dollars," Gaddis said, deeming it a more than adequate explanation. Con supposed it was—that kind of money bought access to almost anything. Or anyone. Buying Laleh Askari a clone for her brother would be pocket change to Vernon Gaddis. He could also know all this because he had framed Levi Greer and needed Con to believe the lie.

"How nice for you," Con said.

"But I don't need a fortune to know it's not safe for you in Virginia. So give me one good reason why you wouldn't come back to Maryland with me?"

"Because my original was murdered to activate me. Levi Greer was framed so there would be someone to blame. It was either Fenton or it was you. You both want whatever's in my head. That much is obvious, even though you both get cute about it and won't just tell me what it is."

To her surprise, Gaddis laughed to himself as if realizing his predicament. "So because I need your consent to make an upload of your consciousness, the more I offer my help—"

"The less I trust you. Yeah, that's about it."

Gaddis took a moment, weighing his options. He glanced at his lawyer, who nodded. Then he said, "The scan we took before you left. I have the results."

"And?" Con didn't much like the way his voice had deepened.

"When Brooke told you about seeing a cluster of voids in the log of your download, it jogged my memory. One of the projects that Abigail was working on at the time of her death was a technique for inserting accessible data into an upload. Augmented consciousness, she called it. Instant expertise."

"I'm sorry, that sounds like science fiction to me," Con said, aware that was ironic coming from a human clone.

"Half of science these days is finally catching up to the whims and dreams of writers from the 1950s," Gaddis said. "Theoretically, it should have worked. The brain has plenty of unused space, but Abigail could never make an effective addition without corrupting the download and causing fatal complications in the host brain. For complex reasons, the sensors that logged downloads couldn't interpret Abigail's augmentations, and they read as empty space. A cluster of voids, if you will."

Con drew in a sharp breath, catching on. "Which would mean you were right. My aunt didn't delete her research."

"Which brings us back to Brooke Fenton," he said with the disdain usually reserved for rare cancers. "She was the only person to confirm this so-called erasure. My guess is when she realized the scope of Abigail's research, she decided to hide it and claim Abigail destroyed it before her supposed suicide. It's been right there all this time. Brooke has simply been biding her time for the opportunity to tiptoe it out."

"But why would she steal from her own company?" Con asked.

"Because no one makes movies about the Tim Cooks of this world."

"Who's Tim Cook?"

"The CEO of Apple after Steve Jobs died. Did a damn fine job too. But it was never *his* company. Brooke always aspired to a Steve Jobs kind of greatness but knows now she'll never have it. I think she'll be looking to sell to the highest bidder. The Chinese would be my guess. They've been playing catchup for ten years and would give Brooke the deed to Hong Kong Island for Abigail's research, since it would certainly leapfrog them past anything we have currently."

"So Brooke Fenton murdered Con D'Arcy so that I could carry Abigail's lost research out of Palingenesis in my head. I really am her unwitting courier, just like you said. And that's this cluster-of-voids thing in my head. Do I have that about straight?"

Gaddis handed her a tablet. "That and it's killing you."

Wonderful. She scrolled slowly through the doctor's analysis of her scan. Much of it was technical, but Con understood the bottom line. She came to an image of her scan; beside it for comparison purposes was the scan of a neurotypical download. Hers was much darker, with slashes of empty space. The cluster of voids.

Gaddis said, "Whatever Brooke inserted has corrupted your download. Your brain is attacking it the way the body might reject an organ transplant."

"How long do I have?" Con returned the tablet and sunk back, adjusting to the weight of her new reality. She imagined that later she'd have all kinds of emotions about it, but for now, she felt only a spreading numbness. All this time, she'd been fighting for a life that would be no life at all. It felt like a prank, a practical joke scribbled by a lazy, unjust universe. Well, at least now she didn't have to worry so much about being driven insane by the lag.

"We simply don't know. You have some time left. Six months? Perhaps longer with the proper medical care. Again, we're in uncharted territory here, so it's impossible to say with any degree of certainty. The good news is that medication can mask most of the symptoms until the end. The bad news is that the end will be swift and come with almost no warning." Almost as an afterthought, Gaddis added, "I'm sorry."

Con nodded. "Thanks."

"With that in mind, there is a possible solution," Gaddis said.

"What kind of solution?"

"We grow you a new clone. One that correctly matches the age of your last upload, thus eliminating the lag you've been experiencing. The other good news is that whatever Brooke Fenton inserted is not a part of your last upload. That means an uncorrupted copy of your consciousness still exists on the quantum servers at Palingenesis."

That was the second time she'd been offered a clone. She was tempted to ask for one hundred million dollars on top of it. Somehow she didn't think Gaddis would blink. He had danced around the precise nature of her aunt's research, but he knew exactly what she'd been working on and wanted it for himself. Con could hear the greed in his voice. That wasn't why she was going to turn him down, though.

"I'm guessing that means you can't move this consciousness into a new clone," she asked, knowing the answer.

"I'm afraid not. The damage is already done. All we'd be doing is moving your corrupted download from one body to another. The outcome would be the same."

She knew it would sound absurd to explain it to anyone else. Maybe only Peter would understand. Even though it had only been a few days, so much had changed. She saw herself differently now, and the idea of starting this journey again felt terrible. And anyway, it wouldn't be her starting over. It would be a different Con waking up thinking it was the day after Christmas with not one but two predecessors to obsess over.

No. She wouldn't give up whatever was in her head, and she wouldn't take a new clone. She would finish this journey on her own. There were still questions she needed to answer. Starting with why the original Con D'Arcy went to Laleh Askari for help. How did she know she was in danger? And what did that mean?

"I'm going to Charlottesville," Con said.

Vernon Gaddis nodded with grave disappointment. "And how will you get there?"

"I'll walk if I have to."

Gaddis pressed the heel of his palm against his forehead as if it were in danger of cracking open. "You are the most stubborn woman. When I said you reminded me of your aunt, I didn't mean for you to take it to heart."

"But if you let me keep the car and stay out of my way, I'll give you what you want when I'm done."

Gaddis thought it over. "I want it in writing."

"Well, I assume you brought the lawyer for a reason."

CHAPTER
TWENTY-TWO

The parking garage her original used on her clandestine visits to Charlottesville was on Water Street only a few blocks from the University of Virginia campus. Students wouldn't return until the end of August, and the college town dozed contentedly in the June sunshine. Con parked and walked down to the sidewalk, where she looked up and down the street. It had felt important to come here. To retrace her original's steps. See what she must have seen. Hear what she must have heard. But standing on the curb, it felt like a fool's errand. She had no leads, not so much as a place to start. Nothing but this irrational certainty that if there was something here to find, she would be the one to find it.

That was the theory anyway. So, what now?

Well, the police had canvassed every business within a five-block radius but had stopped there. Understandable. At the time, Con D'Arcy had only been a missing person and not yet a murder victim. It wouldn't have been a top priority, and now that Clarke had a suspect in custody, why would they bother looking any further? But their search had clearly assumed that her original parked here to be close to her destination. Con pulled up a map on her LFD. The next closest public garage was more than fifteen blocks away, and there wasn't any overnight street parking without a resident sticker. What if her original hadn't parked here because it was convenient but because it was the only alternative to getting towed? If so, the police had simply given up too soon.

Con created grids on her LFD's map, expanding the search area by another five blocks. It was a daunting amount of ground to cover, but pleased to have a plan, she struck out toward the campus for no better reason than it looked pretty in that direction. She spent hours walking through neighborhoods of ancient, low-slung brick buildings, stopping at every business to ask if they had seen someone who looked, well, just like her. The question raised a few eyebrows, so as a cover, she invented a twin sister. It worked. Too well. A missing twin had a tragic allure that sparked people's curiosity, and she'd had to improvise an entire backstory for her imaginary sibling just to satisfy the endless questions.

By early evening, her optimism had given way to the sinking realization that police work was tedious as hell. It would take a week to canvass the entire area, and even then, she would need dumb luck to stumble across anyone who remembered her original. If she hoped to find anything she needed to start thinking like a detective. Problem was, she was a musician, and there simply wasn't a whole lot of overlap in the two skill sets. What did she hope to see that trained professionals had missed? Then she remembered something that Darius Clarke said to her at their first meeting in DC—that it wasn't often that a detective got to interview a missing person while they were still missing. How it would help him understand Constance D'Arcy's mindset.

She'd been thinking about this all wrong.

She didn't need to interview the victim; she was the victim. She might be missing the last eighteen months, but she was still Con D'Arcy. So, what did she know that the police didn't? Well, for one thing, her original wasn't having an affair. No chance. She was far from perfect, but that just wasn't how she did things. So who or what had kept her returning to Charlottesville over and over again? What was the draw to this place? Hoping something would jump out at her, Con created a list of all the businesses within a fifteen-block radius of the parking garage. The vast majority were restaurants and bars. About a million dry cleaners. Drugstores. Banks. Barbershops. Nail salons. Gyms. Coffee shops. Bike shops. Liquor stores. Head shops. The usual college-town stuff, and nothing that couldn't be found in Richmond where her original lived. She wasn't driving an hour out of her way to do her dry-cleaning.

Then something caught her eye: Young Americans Music. It was only eleven blocks from the garage. Online reviews said it sold guitars and other instruments. It also offered lessons to all ages. A small recording studio was available for rent. Con scratched the back of her head and grinned to herself. A recording studio named for a David Bowie song? Could there be anything more Con D'Arcy in the whole wide world? Levi had mentioned that her guitar and music were missing from his house. To him, that meant his wife had left him, but what if music had been the purpose of her trips to Charlottesville all along?

———

Young Americans Music sat at the corner of a quiet, tree-lined intersection permanently closed to vehicle traffic. It gave the street a calm, bohemian vibe, and now that the sun was setting, people strolled down the middle of the street and early birds were looking over menus at outdoor tables. Con paused to let a family of three cycle past before crossing the street to the shop. Over the front door, a shingle hung from an ornate wrought-iron bracket. The iconic lightning bolt from the cover of *Aladdin Sane* lanced out from the capital *Y*. Con appreciated the flourish even if "Young Americans" wasn't actually from that album.

A welcoming bell tinkled cheerfully when she pushed through the door. It was cool and dark inside the shop. Con felt immediately at home and imagined that her original would have felt the same. An old Roberta Flack album played quietly in the background. A gorgeous Fazioli baby grand piano took up the front window. A gray cat with amber eyes lay across the lid watching Con indifferently. Guitars of every description lined the walls from floor to ceiling. Beneath them, amplifiers were arranged in orderly rows. Con paused to admire a vintage 1965 Gibson twelve-string. All in all, it was an impressively curated collection of instruments. The owner knew their business.

At the back of the store, a Latina woman stood behind the counter ringing up a teenage boy with a shock of neon-blue hair and a guitar case slung across his back. In her late twenties or early thirties, the woman had a kind, gentle face and a smile that could have powered every guitar in the shop. The way they chatted, Con could tell the boy was a regular customer.

"See you next week, Tony," the woman said, handing him a bag of sheet music. "Keep practicing. It's starting to sound really good."

"Thanks, Elena," the boy said, and left the store beaming.

How could he not? The woman was fresh-bottled joy. Who wouldn't want to crowd around her and absorb some of that positivity? Con was puttering near a display case of ukuleles, which brought back memories of learning to play on a lavender one given to her by Gamma Jol, small enough to fit her five-year-old hands. She would have killed for a teacher like this woman, or any teacher at all, really.

Finished with her student, the woman at the counter turned to ask if Con needed any help. She fell silent, and a look of recognition passed across her face.

"I wasn't sure if we'd be seeing you," she said, her smile turning melancholy.

"You know me?" Con asked, feeling a thrill at her familiarity.

"I do," Elena said. "We were friends."

"We were?"

"I thought so anyway." Elena walked to the front of the store, locked the door, and flipped the sign from "Open" to "Closed." "Come on. She's back in the studio. She'll be anxious to see you."

"Who?" Con asked but followed Elena through a door and down a hall past two music rooms and a cluttered office. They went out into a small, private courtyard. The floor was worn cobblestone, and an unruly jungle of plants grew from planters built into the courtyard's high brick walls. A tattered hammock hung between two trees, while a hodgepodge of furniture formed a circle around a stone firepit. A girl in a floral sundress, no more than twelve, sat picking out notes on a guitar. She stopped when she heard them and looked up shyly from beneath an explosion of curly black hair.

"Hi, Con," she said.

"Hi?" Con replied, wondering if this was who wanted to see her. Everyone seemed to know her here.

"Dahlia," Elena said. "Go set the table and start a pot of water on the stove. I'll be upstairs in a minute."

"Yes, Mamá," the girl said, putting aside her guitar. "For how many?"

Elena gave Con a curious look. "Four. I think. Fingers crossed."

"Yes, Mamá," the girl said with her mother's irrepressible smile and scampered off inside.

"Beautiful girl," Con said.

"Thank you," Elena said. "Proof that good can come from even the worst decisions."

At the back of the courtyard was an old two-story carriage house. Elena paused with her hand on the doorknob.

"She's been in here all day. Ever since we heard the news. Be a little gentle with her?"

"Of course," Con said as if she knew who Elena meant.

They went into the control room of a small music studio. Overlapping Persian rugs covered the floor. Two plush couches piled high with pillows sat back from a recording console. It wasn't high-end equipment, used by the look of it, but it was professional and well maintained. Through the rectangular window separating the control room and the live room, Con saw a woman playing a piano with her back to them. Over the monitors, she heard a familiar tune, an old Awaken the Ghosts song called "Incidental Perdition." It was the first song Con had ever written, although the band rarely played it live. Chills ran up her spine.

Elena went to the console and pressed the talk button. "Hey, you were right. She's here."

The piano stopped, but the woman didn't move. Con found herself holding her breath. Finally, the woman gathered herself and stood up from the piano. Con couldn't see her face. The soundproofed door between the two rooms opened, and the woman stepped through.

"Stephie?" Con said in stunned disbelief. Stephie Martz was about the last person in the world she'd expected to see, but now, it all made a kind of sense. Of course this would have been where her original had been going. Making amends to Stephie had been one of those things that Con had been meaning to get around to for three years but then always found an excuse to put it off. She felt strangely proud of her original that she'd actually done it. And happy for her too. Con wished that she'd been the one to do it.

"I didn't expect you so soon," Stephie said. "Was just playing one of your old songs. And here you are, like magic."

"I haven't heard that song in years."

"Me neither," Stephie said. "Popped into my head this morning, and I've been messing with it all day."

"Your hair is so long," Con said, suddenly on the edge of tears.

"I grew it out. Yours is so short."

Con's hand went to her head. "It was a mess. Stephie, I—"

Stephie shook her head and closed the distance between them. She put her arms around Con, pulling her close. It came as a shock to Con's system, and her arms hung limp at her side. This was the first time anyone had touched her. Really touched her. She hadn't realized how badly she needed it. Even if it was only because of a horrible misunderstanding, it felt indescribably good. But it was a misunderstanding; it was all based on a lie. Con tried to pull away, but Stephie hugged her all the tighter.

"I'm not her," Con whispered.

"I know."

With that, Con began to cry, softly at first, then hard and ragged like a landslide, clinging to her friend.

Stephie just held her and said nothing at all.

CHAPTER
TWENTY-THREE

Con kept out of the way while Stephie and Elena finished making dinner. Dahlia set the kitchen table, a wooden oval with mismatched chairs, and then showed Con where to sit. They were in the apartment above the music shop. Con had a thousand questions, but there would be time for that later. Right now, she felt content to sit and huddle close to the warm glow of this family. It gave her time to process the fact that Stephie had been living only a few hours from DC all this time. She was from San Antonio, and Con always assumed she'd followed Hugh's body home to Texas. But no, here Stephie was, happy and in love.

When the food was ready, everyone sat and Elena held out her hands for grace. The table lowered its eyes, even Stephie, which surprised Con. In college, they'd bonded over escaping the suffocating expectations of their intensely religious parents. Stephie was about the last person Con would have expected to find their way back to God. She wondered if maybe Stephie was only going along to make Elena happy, but when Elena finished saying grace in Spanish, Stephie lingered for a moment, eyes closed, to say a private amen. When Stephie looked up, she noticed Con watching her and smiled as if she'd been caught going through Con's purse.

Grace over, the table sprang to life. Salad and garlic bread were passed around. Stephie picked out music, and the opening track of *The Bends* began to play. Con looked over at her old bandmate. First grace and now Radiohead, a band that Stephie notoriously loathed. Con had spent most of freshman year trying to convince her of her abject wrongness. Once it became clear that Stephie wouldn't change her mind, it degenerated into Con rickrolling her with Radiohead songs whenever and wherever possible. Con's masterstroke came at a show in Dallas when the band launched into a pre-rehearsed cover of "Just" during an encore. Con had winked mischievously at Stephie, who had burst out laughing and given Con a defiant middle finger, then was left with little choice but to play along.

Now it was Stephie's turn to wink at Con. Her friend raised her wine glass in a toast. Con couldn't have said why an old inside joke made her want to cry, and for a moment, her eyes got hot. Stephie just smiled and shook her head as if to say that everything was going to be alright. Con believed her. They touched glasses over the table, and she felt all her anxiety about not being wanted melt away.

"What?" Dahlia wanted to know, with a child's intuition that she was being left out of something.

"Old inside joke," Con said, but when she saw that wasn't going to satisfy the girl, she told her the whole story.

"And this is Radiohead?" Dahlia asked about the music when Con was finished. "It's alright, I guess. Bit sad."

"See!" Stephie said, pouncing triumphantly.

"Dahlia," Con said, laughing. "How're you going to do me like that when we just met?"

"We just met?" Dahlia said, her face falling. "So, like, you really don't remember me?"

"I'm sorry. I don't. I'm not her, not exactly."

"Because you're, like, a clone? Is that it?" Dahlia asked with a child's total absence of tact.

"Dahlia Irma Diaz!" Elena said.

"What? That's what it said online," Dahlia said. "Is that wrong?"

"I apologize," Elena said. "Dahlia was very attached to . . . her. She took it hard when Con stopped visiting."

"It's really alright," Con said and turned to Dahlia. "Is there anything else you want to ask?"

Dahlia glanced at her mother, who nodded sternly for her daughter to ask her questions but to tread very lightly.

"Why did you stop coming around?" the girl asked.

"I honestly don't know. That's what I'm trying to find out myself," Con said.

"She was cool," Dahlia said, clearly unsettled by the idea. "I wish you remembered me."

"Me too," Con said and meant it. Not only because she would feel more complete, but because she wished she had gotten to know them the way her original had. There was a pleasure in getting to know people that you could tell you were going to like, but Elena and Dahlia had already been through that with her. It wouldn't be the same a second time, and it made Con jealous.

"But how could you forget?" Dahlia asked.

"I know it's hard to wrap your head around, but it's not that I forgot you. It's more like . . . that was someone else who happened to be a lot like me."

"But not the same," Dahlia said. "Is that why you keep saying you aren't her? Can you tell the difference?"

"Only because there's stuff about her that I can't know. Recent stuff. Otherwise, I'm the same person."

Dahlia didn't seem satisfied with that explanation. "So, I mean, why does it have to be one or the other? Why can't you be both? Her but not her. Her but also you?"

"It's complicated," Con said. But she found the girl's untroubled acceptance of her peculiar duality comforting. Sometimes children had a way of knowing when not to make more of a thing than it had to be.

"So? What's wrong with that? Complicated is only bad to the kind of people who need things to be simple."

"Maybe you're right."

Dahlia shrugged and, weighty philosophical insights dispensed, attacked her spaghetti like a hungry Viking. Elena and Stephie shared a proud look, and Stephie told the story of how she'd come to live in Charlottesville and own a music shop. Turned out, her aunt was a law professor at UVA. After the accident, the aunt had taken Stephie in and given her time and space to heal. Stephie told Con that between the grief of losing Hugh and the guilt at surviving the crash, she had barely gotten out of bed the first month. She talked about Hugh, not without pain, but with a fluency that only time could bring.

Elena reached out to sweep a strand of Stephie's hair back but didn't interrupt.

Stephie said, "My aunt had a son. There was a piano in the living room, and he wouldn't leave it alone. I started teaching him just so he would treat it with a little respect. There's only so long you can lie in bed feeling sorry for yourself while an eight-year-old clangs away at a Steinway. Turned out I was pretty good at it. That's where the idea for the store originated."

When everyone was finished eating, Dahlia cleared the table and did the dishes without being asked. That was not how Con remembered things going when she was twelve.

"She's a good kid," Con said.

Elena beamed at the praise, but said, "Ah, she's showing off. She can be a handful too."

"No, I can't," Dahlia called from the kitchen, and everyone laughed.

"How did you two meet?" Con asked.

Stephie put her hand over Elena's. The two women looked at each other as if silently agreeing who got to tell the story.

Apparently, they decided Stephie would, because she said, "I placed an ad for a guitar teacher."

"You play?" Con asked Elena.

"Eight instruments," Stephie said. "She's ridiculous."

Elena shooed away the praise. "My father taught me, and I studied music in school. But if I knew this one had ulterior motives, I would've kept job hunting."

Stephie feigned outrage. "Oh, *I* had ulterior motives?"

Elena shrugged—exactly the way her daughter did—but couldn't keep that irrepressible smile from her face. "Well, that is the way I remember it."

"Three years now," Stephie said. "My evil plan worked."

Elena kissed Stephie good night, and excused herself for the evening, saying she was tired and would go to bed early. "Will I see you in the morning?" she asked Con.

"If that would be alright with you," Con said.

"I insist," Elena said. "I'll have Dahlia make up the guest bedroom for you."

"Thank you."

Elena hugged her tightly. "It is good to meet you. I'm glad that you found us again."

Stephie took the bottle of wine and led Con out to the courtyard. Even though it was still very warm, Stephie made what she claimed was a "small fire to keep the bugs away." Con got comfortable on one of the couches. Stephie came back from tending her bonfire and flopped down beside her. They kicked off their shoes and put their feet up on the edge of the firepit.

"Hell of a life, huh?" Stephie said.

"They're amazing. Well done, you."

"Thanks. Yeah, I don't know what I would do without them."

The apology tumbled out of Con before she could stop it. Bottled up for three years, once it started, she couldn't have stopped it if she wanted to. And she didn't want to. It was a rush and a relief to own up to everything. The crash. Being a terrible friend. Shutting Stephie out of her life. Tears poured out of her, and she trembled with fear. There weren't many people left who made her feel vulnerable, and Stephie was first among them.

But there was no need. Con saw nothing but understanding from Stephie, who was crying now too. What a pair they were. Cutting off her best friend had been one more way to punish herself.

Stephie took Con's hand in hers. "I listened to you talking to Dahlia. How you weren't Con and all that crap? It's funny because, what you just said? She said all of that to me a year ago when she showed up at the store. Almost word for word. I mean, it's unbelievable."

"Really?"

"Verbatim," Stephie said.

"Did you forgive her?"

"Con, there's nothing to forgive. Look. First, the crash wasn't your fault."

"Of course it was. If I hadn't pushed Zhi to go on to Raleigh—if we'd stayed the night in DC like Tommy wanted—none of this would have happened."

"If you hadn't pushed? Come on, Con. The only opinion that mattered in our band was Zhi's. Period. I loved him like a brother, but he was a grade-A prima donna. You know how he was if he didn't get his way, and what he wanted that night was to go to Raleigh. He was also the one who insisted on manually driving us all over the country in that piece-of-shit van. Maybe you're responsible for helping him always get his way. Okay, but me and Hugh always went along to get along. It was lazy and chickenshit; I was just sick of arguing with Zhi all the time, so I picked my battles. The wrong battles, it turns out, and that's on me. I saw how exhausted Zhi was that night. I didn't have to get in the van. None of us did. It sucks, but we all helped foster our collective dysfunction. We were always going on to Raleigh. You don't get to martyr yourself over it."

"How can you be so Zen about all this?"

"Because I've had this conversation once already. And I wasn't so Zen about it the first time, believe me," Stephie said. "Look. If you need to be forgiven—and I only say this because she did—well, you are. But I hope you'll forgive me back. I cut you out as much as you did me. I regret it, but maybe we both needed time off to heal? I don't know. But I was glad to see you again last year, and I'm glad to see you now."

"Even if it means she's dead?"

"Like you said upstairs, it's complicated. But none of that's your fault, so, yeah, I'm glad." Stephie stood. "Come on, I want to show you something."

They went back into the studio, where they sat side by side at the console in the control room. Stephie powered on the board and played Con a song. It was a good track, spare but melodic with a driving guitar line anchoring it. Stephie brought up the bass a touch, and Con's head began to nod appreciatively.

"This is good," she said.

Stephie found that funny. "Well, she wrote it, so I'm not surprised you like it."

"Really?" Con said, listening more closely. "Man, I'm full of myself even when I don't know it."

"No, you're not. She was so inspired while she was here. I've never seen someone so locked in."

They sat there while Stephie played track after track, all in varying stages of completion. Some Con didn't know, but others she recognized as songs she'd written since the crash. The ones she'd never been able to bring herself to record. It was overwhelming to hear them taken from scribblings in a notebook to full-fledged songs. One sounded exactly how she'd imagined in her head, but others had evolved in new directions. Stephie's influence was unmistakable. She had never been a songwriter herself but had a gift for always improving a work in progress.

Con squeezed her friend's arm. It was thrilling and incredibly disconcerting all at once. The hardest part was hearing her own voice singing words that she'd written but had no memory of singing.

Stephie paused the music. "Sorry."

"It's not your fault. It's just confusing." Con pantomimed her head exploding. "Part of me is even jealous that I didn't get to work on them with you. How messed up is that?"

"Part of me is angry we never finished them. How messed up is *that*? My best friend died, and I'm upset about some stupid music."

"I think that's what we all do, though. Find ways to make sense of"—Con waved her hand vaguely in the air—"all this. For weirdos like us, it's music."

Stephie laughed and leaned against Con appreciatively.

Con asked, "Kind of on that subject, but do you know what happened to my notebooks or guitar? They weren't at her husband's place."

"Yeah, sure," Stephie said, pointing through the window. "In there."

"Seriously?"

Con went into the live room and saw her things stored neatly under a table. She sat cross-legged on the floor. Reverently, she opened the case and took out the guitar. She tuned it and tried to strum a C chord, but it didn't come out right. In her mind, she knew what to play, but her fingers struggled to follow along. Eventually, she got her fingers in place, but she had to look at her hand and tell each finger where to go, like a child learning her first chords. Or a clone remembering how to walk again.

Stephie followed her into the live room and sat at the bench of a world-weary Hammond B3 organ attached to a Leslie speaker cabinet. She listened while Con struggled through the chord progression of "North Dakota," an old Lyle Lovett song. Texas country was the only kind of music her mother would tolerate, and Con had taught herself hundreds of old songs so she could practice without catching hell: Tish Hinojosa, Nanci Griffith, Townes Van Zandt, Terri Hendrix, and so many others. It was a surprise yet no surprise at all that she would return to them now to remind herself how to play. Always start at the beginning, her gamma had said, otherwise a body is apt to get lost.

Third time through, Con's fingers moved less stubbornly. Stephie switched on the Hammond, holding the run toggle for ten seconds before flipping the start switch. She filled in around the edges of Con's halting guitar with honeyed chords that gave Con the courage to look away from the strings and keep playing by touch and memory. Together, they began to sing, Stephie taking the Rickie Lee Jones part, her breathless, ethereal soprano blending with Con's rougher alto. It felt like old times, and Con would have given anything to stay in the middle of that song forever. But when the end came, she let it fade away, tapping out the final syncopated rhythm—a castaway's heartbeat—on the body of the guitar.

The room fell silent, neither of them wanting to be the first to break the spell. Con looked down at the guitar—her guitar—and felt vindicated at what it meant. Her original hadn't been coming to Charlottesville because she was having an affair. Nor had she sneaked her guitar and music out of Levi Greer's house because she was leaving him. She'd been coming to Charlottesville to record music with Stephie.

"So she just walked in the door one day?" Con asked.

Stephie laughed. "Pretty much. I was working the counter, and she strolled in like she'd been coming in every day for years. Said she'd married a guy in Richmond and wanted to make things right with us."

That sounded like her old self—straightforward and direct. She missed that version of Con D'Arcy. "When was that exactly?"

Stephie thought it over. "A year, give or take."

"And she was really over Zhi?" Con said, standing and putting the guitar back in its case.

"No," Stephie said simply. "But I think she was starting to make her peace with knowing she'd never really get over it. Zhi had passed that New Year's Eve, and she'd only met Levi a few days earlier. She talked about being in this moment when her grief was telling her that she had no right to be happy. How close she'd come to picking some stupid fight as an excuse to blow it up before it even got started. We talked a lot about that—whether we were allowed to move on. I know I don't ever want to forget Hugh. He's a part of me, part of this amazing time in my life. But he's a part of my past. Elena is my future. I think Hugh would have liked her."

"Do you have any idea why my original wouldn't tell her husband she was coming here?"

"She needed to finish this music, but I think she felt guilty about it too. I'm a part of her old life. A connection to Zhi. I know she loved her husband, but everything was his, you know? His house. His stuff. His friends. They didn't start a life together so much as she joined his life already in progress. I think that was partly why she reached out to me—to reconnect with something that was just hers."

"Thank you for helping her," Con said. "How did she seem to you at the end?"

"Couldn't begin to tell you. We haven't seen her since she stopped coming around six months ago, but she was sure as hell strange that last day."

"Six months?" But the police had found her car in Charlottesville after her original went missing, and GPS records showed her making regular visits in the last few months. If she'd stopped visiting Stephie, then why had she kept coming? "Police think her husband killed her because she was having an affair with someone in Charlottesville."

"Here? No way. When she was here, we worked." Stephie thought back. "But that last day, she was anxious about something. She'd been traveling with her husband, so I was looking forward to getting back to work. Right away, I knew something was wrong."

"Wrong how?" Con asked.

"Just wrong. She felt off to me. Remote. Said she'd gotten involved with something and couldn't come around anymore. I tried to get her to tell me, but she said it wasn't safe. Asked me to respect her wishes and not to contact her. It hurt; I'm not going to lie. We'd just reconciled, and then she was gone again. She was scared to death."

"How could you tell?"

Stephie pointed to the guitar and music. "Because she left those. Asked me to keep an eye on them for her. Just in case, she said. That was when I knew that it was really bad, whatever it was."

Con agreed. She couldn't even imagine the circumstances in which she'd willingly part with her guitar. Her original had gone to Laleh Askari for help a few weeks before she died, but if she was already afraid for her life six months ago, that changed the timeline significantly.

"Then she left, and never came back," Stephie said.

"Yes, she did," Dahlia said softly.

Stephie and Con turned to see the twelve-year-old leaning in the doorway in her pajamas. They had no idea how long she'd been listening.

"You saw her?" Stephie said. "When?"

"Two weeks ago. It was really weird."

"How so?"

"She ignored me."

"Ignored you how?" Stephie asked.

"I didn't get to say goodbye, so I thought it would be nice, you know? But she walked right by me like she didn't even know me."

"Where was this?" Con asked.

"On Water Street," Dahlia said.

That was where her original always parked her car. Con asked the girl if she saw what direction her original was headed.

"I know more than that. I know where she went. I followed her," Dahlia said defiantly.

"Followed her where?" Con asked, kneeling in front of the girl.

"I don't know the address," Dahlia said.

"Yeah, but can you show me tomorrow?"

Dahlia looked at Stephie. "Can I?"

"That's a question for your mom."

Dahlia disappeared like she'd been shot out of a cannon.

"I was hoping you would stay awhile," Stephie said. "That's selfish, I know."

"I wish I could. You have no idea."

"Oh, I have some, but I get it. Just remember our door is always open," Stephie said and hugged her when she stood. "Don't forget us."

CHAPTER
TWENTY-FOUR

In the morning, Dahlia led Con to a quiet residential street in Belmont, a neighborhood on the southwestern edge of Charlottesville. The first thing that jumped out at her was all the empty parking spots, not to mention that every town house had a driveway and garage. On two good legs, it was twenty minutes by foot from Water Street. It might have made sense for her original to park there while visiting Stephie, but with her bad knee, there was only one reason to walk that far—she hadn't wanted any record of exactly where she was going.

They took a casual stroll down the sidewalk, and Dahlia nudged her as they passed the town house that she'd seen Con's original enter. It stood unremarkably in the middle of the block, a taupe house with taupe trim, a taupe front door, and taupe curtains. Exactly like the rest of the block. Con asked Dahlia how she could be sure this was the right house, and the girl pointed out a bed of red flowers on either side of the front door.

"Those are dahlias. They're the national flower of Mexico."

The house was dark, all the shades drawn, no vehicle in the driveway, no signs of life at all. Even though her original had been dead for more than a week now, the front garden was immaculately maintained, and the small strip of grass between the sidewalk and curb had recently been mowed. Though the same could be said of every other house on the street. Maybe a yard service maintained it? Or maybe someone had been here since.

"Did you see if she rang the doorbell?" Con asked.

"No, the house let her in."

"You're sure it was the house and not a person?"

Dahlia nodded. "I heard the chime."

That was interesting. If someone had gone to the trouble of adding her original to the house's exception list, that meant it hadn't been a one-time visit. If her original had rented it, the police would know, so whose house was it? Why had she been coming here for the last six months?

"Did you see anyone else come or go?" Con asked.

"No. I hung around for a little bit, but then friends texted, and I went to meet them."

"Why didn't you tell your mom?"

"I don't know. The way Con pretended not to recognize me. Like I meant nothing to her. I don't know. I just didn't want to tell anyone," Dahlia said with barely disguised hurt. "Why did she do that?"

"I don't know. Maybe she was trying to protect you." Con hoped that was what it was, and it seemed to cheer Dahlia up a little.

At the end of the block, they turned the corner and stopped. Con thanked Dahlia and told her to go home. The girl pleaded with Con to let her help, but Con reminded her that Elena would kill them both if Dahlia didn't go straight home. Reluctantly, Dahlia agreed and threw her arms around Con, hugged her fiercely, then walked away fast without looking back. Con watched until the girl was out of sight. Whatever got her original killed, she was nearing its center, and couldn't take the chance that Dahlia might double back. It was what Con would have done at that age, but then Dahlia had a much different relationship with the grown-ups in her life. It was amazing what feeling safe did for your outlook.

Clones weren't identical to their originals, but Con doubted that the average home security system was designed with that in mind. Across the street, an older white man working in his garden paused and waved to her as she went up the walk to the town house. She waved back. Maybe it was the misleading security of daylight, but she felt safe. If anyone was home, she would just scream until a neighbor called the police. That qualified as a plan, didn't it?

She went up the walk to the house. It chimed gently in recognition as the front door unlatched. Dahlia hadn't been wrong; the house had her original's biometric profile. Con gave the door a push. It swung silently open into a dark entry hall. *Wonderful.*

"Hello?" she said and winced when she got no answer.

When was she going to learn to quit doing that? She should just save time and tie a cowbell around her neck and be done with it. She stood there on the threshold, apologizing for all the names she'd called people in horror movies who had done what she was about to do. Because as much as she was enjoying the sunshine, any answers she hoped to find were inside.

She stepped through the doorway and, after a lengthy debate, closed the door behind her. Overhead motion-activated lights flickered on automatically. The house was jarringly cold, and she asked the house the temperature. *Fifty-eight degrees.* Zhi had always run hot, but even he would turn into a popsicle in here. And her original wouldn't have lasted five minutes.

Rubbing her hands on her bare arms for warmth, she went down the hall to the living room. It was empty, and the wall-to-wall carpet was new. The smell of disinfectant and fresh paint hung heavy in the air. Under normal circumstances, she'd have guessed that someone was getting ready to sell, but this felt like something else. This house had been scrubbed down to the foundation. Whatever trace of her original Con had hoped to find was long gone. Had that been the point?

In the kitchen, she found a pallet of bottled water. The plastic had been torn back, and a dozen bottles were missing. A partially eaten carton of Szechuan beef sat in the refrigerator, relatively fresh from the smell of it. On the counter was a stack of mail. Con leafed through it, but it was all junk mail addressed unhelpfully to *occupant*. Upstairs, there were three bedrooms. The first two were as spotlessly empty as the downstairs. In the third, she found a twin-size mattress on the floor, pushed against the wall. A spindly reading lamp rested on a makeshift table of books—a new biography of Mark Zuckerberg, a history of the Gilded Age thicker than her calf, and a dog-eared copy of *The Fountainhead*. Because it was the only sign, other than bottled water and cold Chinese, that anyone had been here, she treated it the way an archaeologist might an ancient ruin. She stripped the bedding in case anything was trapped between sheets and blanket. Flipping the mattress, she felt around the baseboards. Nothing. She thumbed through the pages of the books, hoping to find—what? A handwritten confession in the margins? Sure, why not? But no, the books were as unmarked as the house.

Frustrated, she squatted on the edge of the mattress, trying to make any sense out of it. Somehow she doubted her original had been shacking up in an empty townhome catching up on her reading for six months. More likely all the furniture had been removed before the house had been cleaned and painted. She reminded herself that her original hadn't died at the farmhouse. Was she sitting in the middle of her own crime scene?

Unnerved, she went back downstairs to the kitchen and called Darius Clarke. It went to voice mail after one ring. That was fine with her. She left him a message suggesting he pay a visit to Young Americans Music and talk to Stephie Martz. She also gave him the address of the town house and described what she'd found, and not found, there. Then as an afterthought, she said that if she didn't hear back from him, she'd take the story to the media. Hopefully that would convince him that she was serious.

But what was happening here? In frustration, she went through all the drawers and cabinets a second time. Next steps were running short. She supposed she could find out who owned the house—that would be a place to start. And there was the gardener across the street. She could ask him if he'd seen anything. If that didn't work out, she'd just start knocking on the neighbors' doors until she found someone who had. And if none of that worked, she could just wait here for someone to come back for their Ayn Rand. She leaned against the kitchen counter and looked down the hall toward the front entrance.

There was a door off to the side that she'd missed.

How the hell had she done that? With all the adrenaline, she'd apparently been too zeroed in on someone jumping out at her to notice anything important like, say, a whole extra door. That was reassuring.

The door opened into a single-car garage, a concrete slab empty apart from a small trash bag and four dark-blue bags laid out in a row against the back wall. Each bag was about six feet long and made of durable plastic. It was disconcerting to know what a thing was without ever having seen one in real life. But from a lifetime of movies and television, she knew immediately that the four mishappen lumps were body bags, and that none were empty. The only questions were who was inside and whether she had the nerve to look. Well, she knew the answer to the second one already.

Kneeling, she unzipped the first bag. Slowly and only far enough to turn down the flap so she could see the face. She didn't recognize the man, but he looked oddly peaceful. Curiosity getting the better of her, she unzipped the bag the rest of the way. He'd been stripped naked and scrubbed with bleach. Other than being dead, she couldn't see anything wrong with him. And the smell of decay wasn't making her gag the way it had at the farmhouse. He'd died recently. That was why the thermostat was set so low. The house was a literal meat locker.

She paused to untie the trash bag. Inside were the missing water bottles from the pallet in the kitchen. They were all bone dry. She sniffed one but didn't smell anything. Had there been something in them besides water? Shivering, she unzipped the next two body bags—two more dead men, scrubbed and bleached. Violence was one thing, but this was somehow worse. It was all so clinical and detached. These men had been treated like packaged meat at a supermarket.

The last body bag, well, that was a different story, and it made Con suddenly afraid in a way that she hadn't been before. This face she recognized immediately. It had been chasing her, haunting her, since the night she'd left Palingenesis. The pockmark-faced man was dead. Someone had murdered him and his team. She should have been relieved that she didn't have to worry about him anymore, but she wasn't. At least she'd known his face. Now she wouldn't know who was coming after her.

She needed to get out of there. That her original had been coming here of her own free will frequently enough to be recognized by the house's security was profoundly unnerving. These deaths proved just how involved she'd been before whatever was going on had gotten her killed. But first she needed to send pictures to Darius Clarke. Unless he could magically connect these murders to Levi Greer, currently in jail, then the case against him started to fall apart. At least that's what she hoped it meant as she straddled the first body to take its picture.

The door to the house swung open behind her.

Slowly, Con glanced back to see a burly white man in a tank top that emphasized his rough, pig-iron shoulders and biceps. He filled the doorway like he'd been cut to order. Con turned to face him and stepped away from the bodies.

"Who the hell are you?" he demanded but didn't wait for an answer. Reaching out, he tapped the garage door button with surprising delicacy. For a crazy moment, Con thought he was opening the door to let her out. But as the retractable door rumbled up, she saw the tires of a pickup truck waiting to back into the garage.

He wasn't letting her out, he was letting his friends in.

A second white man ducked under the door while it was still opening. He was big too, but it was hard to tell where the beer ended and the muscle began. He looked from his partner to Con and back to his partner. "Who's that?"

The man in the doorway shrugged. "We ain't been introduced."

"Who're you?" the second man asked her, then called over her shoulder. "John. You're going to want to see this."

The garage door finished its lazy climb. A third man climbed out of the pickup truck. He was white, too, and older, his black beard leavened with gray. He moved gingerly, favoring one leg. The other two men deferred to him, looking to him for answers. He was slow to offer them, and stood awhile gazing at Con and scratching at the back of his hand. It drew Con's eye to the tattoo on his forearm—a black umbrella.

These men were Children of Adam.

Everything slowed to a panicked, syncopated drumbeat. She wanted to ask for a time-out so she could figure out how the Children of Adam knew about this town house. How they were connected to her original. Across the street, the gardener fired up a leaf blower and everything rushed back to full speed. She was going to die if she didn't get out of here.

"Jesus, boys, don't you know who that is?" John said with a hint of disappointment.

"Who?" the two men said in unison.

"That's the clone that's been all over the news."

The two men looked at Con with renewed interest.

"Let's just take it easy," Con said, walking slowly toward the older man. His gimpy leg made him the best of her bad options.

"What's she doing here?" the second man asked.

"Isn't that a question?" John replied. He signaled the burly man by the door, who pressed the garage door button a second time. Overhead, the motor ground to life and the door began to lower.

Con broke for the street, screaming for help. She didn't make it.

CHAPTER TWENTY-FIVE

Con came to stretched out on an orange leather couch that was as cracked and blistered as an old man's foot. Gingerly, she eased herself into a sitting position and squeezed her eyes closed until the nausea passed. She didn't remember the end of her failed escape attempt, only that the gardener never even glanced up from his leaf blower. She had no idea which of the Children of Adam goons had knocked her out, but the welt on the back of her head felt wet and soft and tender. A deep breath to clear her head succeeded only in filling her lungs with the stale, listless stench of ten thousand cigarettes. Stumbling into the bathroom, she cupped her hand under the faucet and drank until her headache began to recede. What she could use were the pills from her backpack, but for all she knew, it was still in the garage. And of course they'd taken her LFD.

They'd moved her from the town house and stashed her in a narrow, windowless room with a black-and-white-checkerboard floor. Exposed pipes crisscrossed the low ceiling. The hodgepodge of ramshackle furniture made her wonder if it was a storage room. She ran her fingers across the writing on the wall beside the cracked bathroom mirror, realizing where she was.

The Griefers—2/22/34 D., Louie, Gin

The Keanu Reeves Experience—8/3/39
Doof Warriors—11/15/37

It went on and on like that over all the walls, thick swirls of primordial graffiti—band names, autographs, cryptic messages in a thousand different inks and hands. Crude doodles drawn by bored musicians waiting to go on stage. Con had a fairly encyclopedic knowledge of bands, but only recognized a few of the names on the walls. Still, she knew them even if she didn't *know* them—jaded, tired, sick of the grind, sick of each other. Ten hours in a van before loading onto another cramped stage with substandard electrics, then penned down here until it was time to play for a semi-hostile crowd of thirty inebriated strangers. The walls were a memorial to the thousands of forgotten bands that never quite made it. She could guess the kind of club she was in—small, sketchy, a hole-in-the-wall with more fire code violations than beers on tap.

The irony wasn't lost on her that she was being held prisoner in some dingy basement greenroom. Her captors weren't fans looking for a command performance, though.

Pressing her ear to the locked door, she heard the muffled sounds of voices and music. She pounded on it until her fist ached, but no one came. The door appeared to be the one sturdily made thing about the room. She slumped back down on the couch to wait. It gave her a chance to go back to the ill-timed question that had popped into her head in the garage—what were the Children of Adam doing at that town house? Because they hadn't followed her there. They'd been every bit as surprised to see her as she'd been to see them. And the burly one had come in through the house to open the garage, which meant either the house had recognized him or he'd had a key. Con rubbed her face in frustration. She didn't like it, but the town house tied her original to both the Children of Adam and to Pockmark and his team. What she didn't know was how, but she knew there wouldn't be an answer she was going to like a whole lot.

From the other side of the door, she heard a growing commotion. Con rushed back to the door. Pounding feet were coming this way. Men arguing. Not quite at blows, but from the way their voices were pitched, the promise of violence was in the air. Then one voice, a clarion baritone, rose above them all.

"Where is she?"

Everyone else fell silent.

"Where?" the voice demanded.

If someone answered, Con didn't hear it, but a key turning in the lock caused her to back away from the door. The older man at the garage, the one called John, opened it. He looked none too happy, as if he'd gone to the dentist for a cleaning but stayed for a root canal. Behind him, men lined the walls of a narrow, gloomy hallway that ended in a narrow, gloomy staircase. She couldn't make out their faces, but their anger, raw and blistering, was like staring into an open furnace.

A white man in a three-piece suit stepped into the gap in the doorway. He stood toe to toe with John if not eye to eye. Nearly a foot shorter, he still managed somehow to loom over John, who seemed to shrink back.

"Wait upstairs," the man in the suit said.

"Now come on. We found her."

"You did, John. You did. But that's not really the issue, is it? Was your chapter specifically told to stop doing jobs off the books?"

"Yeah," John admitted grudgingly.

"Were you told personally, by me, to keep a low profile until things cooled off?"

John nodded and glared at Con as if his troubles were her doing.

"Yet you did it anyway. Well, now I have to clean it up. Take your boys and wait upstairs."

Reluctantly, John and his followers tramped back up the stairs like moody teenagers whose parents had come home early and broken up the party. When they were gone, the man in the suit closed the door and made a slow, deliberate lap around the room like a lead singer prowling the stage while his band struck the opening chords. He didn't look her way or even seem aware that he wasn't alone. The fact that he was famous only made the performance that much more surreal. He pulled a chair up close to her and sat. From a pocket, he removed a small device the size of her pinky. He powered it up and placed it on the low coffee table that separated them. When the light blinked from red to green, he finally acknowledged her presence.

"There," he said. "That's better."

"Surveillance suppressor?" she asked, although she'd never heard of gear that small. Law enforcement had been pushing to ban personal audio and video recording blockers for the better part of a decade, but industry lobbyists and the ACLU had fought them every step of the way.

"For any friends who might want to record a keepsake of our conversation," the man said, gesturing abstractly to the walls and ceiling. "Do you know who I am?"

She rolled her eyes at him. He was Franklin Butler: founder, leader, spokesperson, and self-appointed messiah of the Children of Adam. She thought from his videos that he would be taller. Older too. In person, he didn't look anywhere close to forty-two, and she understood why he had grown the beard. It had to be a challenge to lead a hate group with the face of a cherubic Boy Scout.

"Good," Butler said. "We don't have time for lengthy introductions. And for the record, I know you as well. Hard not to, given how the media has obsessed over you. Clone solving the murder of her original. Compelling stuff."

In a previous life, before becoming the face of the anti-clone movement, Franklin Butler had been a rising star at the University of Chicago in the Department of Philosophy. Was that why he talked like a patriarch in an old black-and-white movie?

"Why am I here?" she asked, although what she meant was *Why am I not already dead?* Franklin Butler's position on clones was well documented. There was a standing bounty for any clone caught south of the Potomac River, and in the past five years, at least eight clones who'd strayed into the wrong state had been murdered—*put down*, in the parlance of the CoA—and, of course, none of the eight had been prosecuted as homicides. One of the killers had actually been convicted, but only for destruction of property. He'd received a token fine. Franklin Butler had reveled publicly in that decision. So, despite his refined, civilized patina, Con knew exactly what his presence meant for her chances of walking out of here alive.

"Ironically, I have precisely the same question," Butler said. "Why am *I* here?"

"Hey, *you* kidnapped *me*."

"Well, as the facts will bear out, I did not."

"Those assholes had CoA tattoos. That means they answer to you."

Butler laughed derisively. "Were it only that cut and dried. Were you hurt or mistreated in any way?"

That was an unexpected question. Beneath his bluster, though, she thought he seemed on edge. Nervous. It made her curious but wary. "Apart from the kidnapping?"

"Apart from that," he allowed.

"No," she said. "But I could eat."

"So could I, now that you mention it." Butler took a handkerchief from his pocket and unfolded it on the table. Almonds spilled out. He picked one out and popped it into his mouth. "Please. Be my guest."

She left them untouched.

"If I meant you any harm, you'd already be harmed," he said, managing to sound offended that his grand gesture had been rebuffed.

She took one and made a show of eating it. "There. Happy?"

"Ecstatic."

"Why am I here?" she asked a second time.

"The reason you are here and not hanging from a tree the way Big John intends is that, an hour ago, I received a message from the CoA's largest single donor requesting that I personally intercede to prevent anything drastic from occurring to you. You're welcome, by the way. This donor has always insisted on absolute discretion and anonymity. I've never met them nor know their identity. Given the generosity of the sums involved, I was perfectly content with the arrangement since, until now, he or she never asked for any considerations. Well, I am no longer content."

"What do you want from me? I don't know who your investor is," Con said, although she wondered if that was true.

"Vernon Gaddis has taken quite an interest in you."

"You think your anonymous investor is Vernon Gaddis? That's the dumbest thing I've ever heard. He hates the CoA with a passion."

"And we, him," Butler confirmed. "But humor me. Vernon Gaddis has already ridden to your rescue once, yes? Swooping in like some medieval knight-errant at your hour of greatest need. Honestly, the whole thing should come with its own classical score. Why wouldn't he do it again? Or do you have another wealthy benefactor I should know about?"

"He's not my benefactor," Con said, careful not to mention Brooke Fenton, who would only incite Butler's worst impulses. In the last few years, Butler had spun out one conspiracy theory after another detailing the sinister motives behind the existence of clones. His followers ate it up—the more outlandish, the better. What would happen if a natural-born conspiracy-monger learned that her head contained Abigail Stickling's lost research? What wouldn't he do to keep it away from either Vernon Gaddis or Brooke Fenton?

"Out of curiosity, why is Gaddis underwriting your little tour of Virginia?"

"Abigail Stickling was my aunt," she said, hoping the revelation would satisfy him. While what she wanted to ask was how the hell he knew so much about it.

"Yes, I know," Butler replied. "The problem with that explanation is that he despised Abigail Stickling. And she him."

"What?" Con said, unable to hide her surprise.

"Oh yes, the story goes they fought like cats and dogs. Especially in the last few years. Differing visions for the future of Palingenesis. Your aunt forced the board to choose between them, and they wisely sided with her. Money is easy to come by, you see, but genius . . . well, you can't simply fundraise genius. So, the board elected to ride with the one who got them there and gave her absolute control over the research division. Gaddis was legendarily bitter about it. Being outmaneuvered by a lab coat with no interest in politics or people was not an easy pill for a narcist to swallow, I'd imagine."

That was not at all the impression Gaddis had given her. He'd painted himself as her aunt's one true ally at Palingenesis and cast Brooke Fenton as the enemy. Once again, Con found herself questioning all of her assumptions. She also saw why Butler had been such a magnetic young professor. The trick, she realized, was that he hadn't come straight out and said it, instead teasing at an answer while gently scoffing at more straightforward explanations, implying that only a fool would be taken in so simply. But that was Butler's gift—making people question themselves and persuading them to accept his viewpoint as their own. He'd built two careers on it.

"I didn't know that," she said.

"Why would you?" Butler asked. "It's hardly the image Palingenesis wishes to project. But don't tell me Vernon Gaddis risked crossing into Virginia out of loyalty to the memory of Abigail Stickling."

"Look, I'm just trying to figure out what happened to my original. That's all."

"Ah yes, your original. Another thorny question. Why do you think Constance D'Arcy was murdered?" Butler asked. "The prevailing theory is that the husband did it, jealous of her infidelity. It's at least plausible. Husbands murdering wives is a cottage industry in this country, but the four dead bodies in Charlottesville suggest there's more to it than that."

"Why? CoA put them there," Con shot back.

"No, Big John was just hired to clean up."

"By who?" Con said.

"He doesn't know. Another anonymous party, which is where a less credulous man would start to see a pattern. Who were those men anyway?"

"I have no idea," Con said, which at least had the advantage of being true.

"So why were you at that town house?"

"Why was Children of Adam?"

"Touché." Butler sighed and reached for the almonds. "Were you good at math in school?"

"More of an English and arts person."

"That's right, you were in that little band, weren't you?" he said. "Math was easy for me. Flew through it in high school. Algebra, geometry, trig. Just made sense to my brain. Teachers would dock me points for not showing my work, because I could see the answers in my head."

"Congratulations?" Con said, not sure where he was going with this.

A rumble in his throat acknowledged her sarcasm. "And then along came calculus. My nemesis. Textbooks turned to gibberish. I went from an A student to a pest who needed every concept explained a dozen times. I had hit 'the wall,' as old Mr. Blake generously explained. It was the first time anything had been hard for me, academically speaking. Through sheer force of will, I ground out a C in the class, but math was never intuitive to me again. I hated that feeling. Knowing that I would never see the big picture no matter how hard I worked. I say this because I am having that same feeling again now."

"What do you want from me?"

"I want to know who is pulling my strings."

"It's not a good feeling, is it?" she asked, feeling a fleeting camaraderic with him. They had exactly the same question and, possibly, the same answer.

"Who is it?"

"I don't know."

"Tell me," Butler roared, scattering the almonds across the floor. "I walk out that door, there will be nothing between you and the thirty men waiting to end your miserable existence."

"I don't know!" Con roared back. She was well aware that it didn't matter one way or another if he wasn't convinced. Crying and pleading ignorance was always an option; men like Franklin Butler fed on fear, so a woman crying in a locked basement would be like crack to him. The only problem was she couldn't seem to muster any tears. Ironic, since there'd been no shortage of them in the last few years. But all she felt now was irritation. A deep, pervasive anger. It would have to do. "Maybe it is Gaddis. I don't know. Why don't you ask him? I'm just presumptuous meat, right, like all clones? Why would anyone tell me anything?"

Butler recoiled, caught off guard at the ferocity of her reply. It felt good to put him on his heels, so good that she wanted to make him choke on it.

"I'm sick of it. You and Gaddis and the police. You're all the same. Here's an idea. Why don't you sort it out among yourselves and leave me out of it, you psycho?"

Reddening, Butler held up a cautioning finger. "You should remember where you are."

"Like I could forget. Look, I don't know why Gaddis is helping me. If he's your anonymous donor, he sure as shit didn't share it with me. So, why don't we just get this over with, huh? I'm tired."

Butler let a long moment pass, then nodded. "I think I would have liked Constance D'Arcy. I'm sorry she died." He rose and went to the door.

"Where are you going?" she said, sure that she'd pushed him too far and scared what that would bring.

"I'm going to go have a little chat with your host," he said cryptically.

"About what?"

"I'm going to take your advice."

"What does that mean?" she asked, but the door had already swung shut.

CHAPTER
TWENTY-SIX

Con hunted the greenroom for anything that she could use as a weapon. She didn't know what advice Butler thought she'd given him, and it sounded too much like a veiled threat for comfort. She'd been in enough negotiations to know when she'd overplayed her hand. But they weren't haggling over the terms of a recording contract; this was her life, and Franklin Butler was a man who didn't believe she deserved one. Bluffing and losing wasn't an option. She was trying to loosen the arm on one of the chairs to use as a club when the door opened and Butler returned. She flinched away from him, but all he did was gather the remaining almonds into his handkerchief and slip it back in his pocket. Almost as an afterthought, he beckoned for her to follow.

"Where are we going?" she asked, not moving.

"Does it matter? Unless you'd prefer to stay here?"

She really didn't.

"Whatever happens," he said, "I need you to keep your mouth shut and your head down. Do you hear me? Any urge you have to run that smart mouth of yours? Smother it."

"Why? What's going to happen?"

"Taking you out of here is not proving a popular decision."

"Do you run things or don't you?" Con said.

"As I said, it's not that simple. My leadership is not quite as ironclad as the media paints it. Children of Adam is more a loose confederation of independent groups than a single top-down organization. And even then, there are always fringe elements who accuse me of being too moderate, too soft. It took some serious horse-trading before Big John agreed to let you go."

They went down the hallway and up a narrow flight of stairs, emerging onto a bare postage-stamp stage. The surrounding walls were brick, blackened with age and papered over by a collage of overlapping band stickers and decals. Looking out into the audience, Con had to shade her eyes from the overhead Fresnels, which belched slabs of carmine light across the stage. The club was long and narrow like a budget coffin. Booths lined windowless walls, and a scattering of particleboard tables formed a semicircle around the pit at the foot of the stage. The walls were covered in a hectic mass of license plates, signs, and gewgaws as if a tornado had blown through, and rather than clean up, the owner had simply nailed everything up. Men, perhaps as many as twenty, stood around the bar drinking and arguing. There was an impatient, empty-handed energy to them that made Con's jaw tighten. When the men saw Franklin Butler and Con, they stopped arguing among themselves and turned as one to face the stage. Con had performed in enough clubs to recognize a hostile crowd when she saw one. She'd also been on enough stages to recognize stage fright, and Butler was sweating. How hard was he willing to push this before he gave her up to save himself?

"Maybe you should give them a song," Butler said, forcing a hollow chuckle in a failed bid to sound confident.

"Isn't there a stage door? A back way out of here?"

"Any way but out the front door, I'm finished and you're dead. Do you understand?"

She understood that Butler believed he needed to play chicken with an angry bar full of drunk bigots. Alpha dogs couldn't very well slip out the back. Not if they hoped to ever call the shots again. She also understood that her life now depended on keeping her mouth shut while this white man did the talking. As metaphors went, it was a little on the nose for her tastes, but if that's what it took, that's what it took.

"It'll be fine," he said, although she couldn't decide which of them he was trying to convince.

"Will it?"

Butler glared down at her, clearly disappointed by her lack of team spirit, and marched to the front of the club as if expecting the men to wilt in his presence. When they reached the bar, the waiting men didn't give an inch. Butler could have tried to push his way through, but even Con knew that in the unspoken dynamics of men that would spell disaster. The men stared him down, a wall of cooling-tower eyes and clenched jaws. Up close, Con saw there were more like thirty of them, a mixture of races and ages. She thought it was nice how hatred could bring people together.

"John?" Butler called out. "I thought we had a deal. Are we really doing this?"

"This is bullshit, Franklin," John's voice replied from behind the wall of men. There was a rumble of agreement. Whatever deal had been struck did not appear to have gone over well with the rank and file. Franklin Butler wasn't the only one whose standing was on the line.

"It's the way it has to be, John."

"So you say."

"That's right, that's what I say," Butler said loudly to make sure everyone heard him, his voice laden with grave disappointment. "And I would have thought that what I say would carry a little more weight at this point."

"But we have her now," John pressed. "With all the media attention she's getting? We should capitalize on that. No one invited you here. She needs to be made an example of."

"String her up!" a voice called out, provoking a roar of approval.

Con felt herself begin to shake and couldn't will herself to stop. It wasn't fear exactly, although she was definitely afraid. But when neither fight nor flight was an option, there was nowhere for the adrenaline to go. She felt it pooling up inside her like a toxic spill. Her only hope was that they couldn't see it in the dim lights. The hell if she would give them the satisfaction.

Butler's voice somehow rose above the competing din. "And your initiative will be an asset to the national committee, John. I know they will be as excited as I am to welcome you. But unfortunately, the big picture takes precedence."

"Fuck the big picture," a voice snarled from the back.

"Fuck the big picture?" Butler said, relaxing now that he had an argument to make. "My friends. There is no picture but the big picture. Our friends in the Virginia police give CoA chapters a lot of latitude to operate freely. They turn a blind eye to your, shall we say, extralegal activities. However, that loyalty is a two-way street, and the fact of the matter is our allies in the department consider this thing"—Butler gestured dismissively to Con—"integral to their investigation. Under any other circumstances, I would tie the noose myself. You all know that. But how fast will our support dry up if we take matters into our own hands before they are done?"

Butler paused to let that sink in. This time, no voices rose to interrupt. Sensing he was swaying them to his side, he laid it on thick. "To be honest, this entire chapter deserves recognition. You're the shock troops of the CoA. And that begins with your leader, John Highsmith."

That earned a rousing cheer, and Butler smiled magnanimously. The men turned, parting slightly, and Con caught sight of Big John Highsmith, who stood behind the bar with the look of a man who couldn't decide if he'd just won or lost. Butler pointed at him, letting everyone know exactly who *the man* was, and began to applaud. The men joined in heartily. Con thought it would lose a little something if she joined in and kept her hands at her side.

"John?" Butler called out when the noise died down. "What's it to be? This is your place. The decision's yours. Do we give it back to the police or fetch a rope?"

The club hung there in silence while John weighed up his options, the pause between tracks, everyone wondering what the next song would be.

"Alright, let them through," John said, relenting.

He had sway, because the men parted like a rough sea. Butler didn't hesitate and led her through the gap before Big John could have second thoughts. These men might have consented to let her go, but Con felt their eyes on her, ferocious in their appetite and fury. They muttered familiar slurs under their breath, and some new ones.

"We'll be coming for you, zirc," a voice hissed in her ear. She flinched but kept her eyes fixed on the front door, feet moving.

They passed through the gauntlet and out the door into the parking lot of a prehistoric strip mall. Vacant signs hung in the windows of half the storefronts. Whatever painted lines had once separated spots had long since faded to spectral outlines, and the jumble of old cars were parked haphazardly like a mouthful of bad teeth. A pale half-moon hung in the night sky. Con looked back at the bar they'd just vacated. It was called the Fencepost, which Con thought was a better name than it deserved.

"Well, that was a disaster," Butler said, looking rattled and pale. He signaled to a sleek white Mercedes, which flared to life and pulled up alongside them. "I had to promise that jackass a seat on the steering committee to get you out of there in one piece."

"Why?" Con asked, relieved, and a little surprised, to be breathing fresh air.

"Everyone has their price," Butler said. "John Highsmith wants respect, which he has no prayer of earning on his own. I don't know if he believed my story that we couldn't afford to alienate Virginia police, but he knew he had to play along. His body would be found in a ditch if he cost the chapter the meth trade."

As if on cue, men began to pour out of the bar, laughing and jeering, restless with the need to inflict harm. All it would take was a spark. They might have allowed her to go, but she'd seen men feed on each other this way before, inciting themselves toward a violence that they weren't capable of alone. A beer bottle arced over the car and smashed on the concrete. The men roared and surged forward, emboldened by their own daring. Butler implored her to get in.

Con didn't.

"Are you kidding me? Get in the car!" Butler said, getting in himself before he turned around and pleaded with her. "I didn't shackle myself with John Highsmith to watch you get dismembered on a sidewalk."

"Where are we going?" she asked. Now she was out of the bar, she was much less inclined to blindly follow Butler.

"To get some answers. That's what you came to Virginia for, isn't it?"

It was, but Con still didn't budge. "How do I know your answers will be my answers?"

"Because my donor knew John Highsmith had you before I did. I'm being paid handsomely to get you out of there. Aren't you curious how and why?"

She was. And if Butler was being honest, then his anonymous donor and the individual who'd hired John Highsmith to dispose of the dead bodies at the town house were likely one and the same. That was the person Con needed to meet. Looked like she was sticking with Butler a little while longer. She bundled into the back seat beside him.

"Emergency," Butler told the car.

The doors locked, and the car peeled out of the parking lot so fast that Con had to hold on not to be thrown against Butler. No, thank you, there wasn't enough soap in the world for that. The front seat was empty. Butler had come alone, clearly prizing secrecy above security.

He was braver than she'd given him credit for being—either that or more desperate.

Beside her, Butler was already on his LFD.

"It's done. I have her. Yes. Yes. Yes," he said, becoming angrier with each affirmative. When he finally came to a negative, he said it with the pleasure of cutting into a perfectly cooked steak. "No, change of plan. I'm doubling my finder's fee. Yes, doubled. And I want to meet."

Con listened to herself being haggled over.

"I don't care what we agreed. Do you know how much political capital I squandered today playing your errand boy? I looked like a fool in front of my own people. I don't give a damn about your precious anonymity. This is nonnegotiable. If you want her, then bring me my money. Tonight. Otherwise, I'll drop her right back where I found her, and those boys will have themselves a barbecue right there in the parking lot."

Butler listened intently and then hung up, regarding Con with newfound curiosity.

"What is so important about you?" he asked rhetorically.

"Nothing."

"Well, certainly not nothing. Far from nothing. That was my whale on the phone. A few hours ago, this person offered me five million dollars for your safe return. I just doubled the price, and they didn't even blink. I insisted on meeting, and they didn't hesitate."

The car came to a light, and they sat in silence. When the light turned green, Butler squinted knowingly at her.

"How interesting."

"What?" Con asked.

"We're well away from that mob, but you know what?"

"What?"

"You didn't try and get out. You're not restrained. No one is holding a gun on you, yet you didn't even try your door." Butler thought through the implications.

"And you walked into that bar alone. I'm not the only one taking risks here."

Butler shook his head tiredly. "Pieces are being moved around the board, and I'm not even sure what game it is we're playing."

Welcome to my world. "If you don't know the game, what makes you think you're one of the players? Doesn't that make you one of the pieces?"

Butler didn't care for that idea one bit. "What are you suggesting? That we're both pawns?"

Con shrugged at him as if to suggest his very question was tiresome. "On the bright side, at least now you know the game."

CHAPTER TWENTY-SEVEN

They drove south toward the North Carolina border before turning west along the John H. Kerr Reservoir, skirting the edge of the waterway. The sedan rode nearly silent, slaloming through the turns on the dark country road. Butler, in the dim glow of the car's interior, stared straight ahead, probably lost in thought about how to spend ten million dollars. His price for ferrying her across this uncrossable divide. She didn't think she'd be coming back, but felt neither sad nor afraid. She was here on her own terms, and that brought a certain calm that had been missing. The car slowed and turned off onto a gravel road. They had arrived.

The partial moon broke from behind the clouds and shone across the water, casting a spectral glow on a phalanx of enormous black towers rising up alongside the dam. Narrower at the base, the towers widened like giant megaphones turned up at the ambivalent night sky. Con could feel the churn of the massive turbines through the floor of the car. She had never seen a carbon-recapture plant in real life, but like everyone else, she knew all about them. As a child of the twenty-first century, she vacillated between hope that so-called climate therapies could undo the damage done by her ancestors and cynicism that it was anything other than a Band-Aid at this point.

"It's massive," she said, awestruck.

"Fourth largest on the East Coast," Butler confirmed. "One guess who owns it."

"Gaddis," Con answered, feeling the knot tightening.

"Indeed," Butler said, opening the center console and removing a locked wooden box. From it, he took a small pistol that looked as if it had never been fired. He tried to insert the magazine backward, but maybe that was because it was dark. Maybe.

"You have a gun? Why didn't you bring it into the bar with you?" Con asked.

"Can you imagine what would've happened if I'd pulled a gun on those people?"

He had a point, but *those people?* That was an interesting way to talk about his devoted followers.

The car stopped in the dale between two of the towers. It shut off its headlights, but Butler turned them back on, muttering about it being too dark for his taste. His nerves had returned, and he sat there waiting, gun in one hand and sipping from a flask with the other. Apparently after the almond fiasco, he wasn't in a sharing mood and didn't offer her a taste. That suited her fine; she wanted a clear head for whatever came next.

A light, misting rain began to fall.

"You know, you are the first clone I've ever met," Butler said.

"Oh? And did I live down to expectations?"

"You seem fine. A bit of a bitch, but I doubt that has anything to do with you being a clone."

"Well, you didn't catch me on a good day."

"Touché," he replied and toasted her with his flask.

"So you've really never met a clone before?"

"Is this the part where you are incredulous that someone can hate someone they've never met? I'll save you the time. I don't hate clones. I hate the idea of clones."

"That's not the impression you give in your speeches."

"Well, since when have nuanced arguments ever worked in America?" Butler asked. "I make the case in a manner I know people will respond to."

"It's irresponsible."

"No, it's human cloning that is irresponsible. It was Abigail Stickling and Vernon Gaddis who were irresponsible. A prodigal twentysomething-year-old grad student doesn't get to unilaterally rewrite the fundamental nature of our species simply because she had an epiphany. Science belongs to the people. Particularly science that has the potential to change their lives."

"People can decide for themselves whether they want to adopt a new technology or not."

Butler snorted dismissively. "No, they absolutely cannot. People have always been too quick to adopt whatever appears to make their lives easier in the short term. Humans are very good at inventing solutions and very, very bad at anticipating consequences." He gazed up at the towers. "And just look how that has worked out for us."

"So what are the negative consequences of cloning?"

"What are the positives?" Butler retorted. "For hundreds of millions of years, life on earth has followed a simple pattern—everything that is born will die. And then twenty years ago, along came Abigail Stickling to change all that. I simply feel that maybe there should have been more discussion before unleashing it on the world."

"Clones still die. She just found a way to prolong life a little. She never solved immortality."

"Yes, and thank God she jumped off that roof before she did. Otherwise, we . . ." Butler drifted off midsentence as a car came around the nearest tower, circling them before rolling to a stop some twenty feet away. Nothing happened. Both cars sat there idling like awkward teenagers at a school dance. Butler took one long last swig from his flask and put it in the seat pocket. Then he combed his fingers nervously through his hair as if he were about to do an on-camera interview.

"So . . . ," Con said. "We going to go talk to them or what?"

"In a minute, in a minute," Butler said. Like a lot of academics, he appeared to prefer theory to practice and wasn't particularly eager to get out of the car.

"I mean, we came all this way." Con couldn't help herself.

"Please. Stop," Butler implored, but he took the hint and finally got out of the car. Con followed after him. He opened an umbrella and walked out between the two cars to where the headlights crosshatched brightest. Con stood a short distance away in the rain. Huddling beneath a black umbrella with the founder of Children of Adam seemed to be asking for trouble.

"The moment of truth," Butler muttered.

Con hoped he was right. The truth was the best she could hope for out of this.

The passenger door of the other car opened, and it was a testament to the seductiveness of Butler's arguments that Con was genuinely surprised when it wasn't Vernon Gaddis who opened it. Instead, Dr. Brooke Fenton, CEO of Palingenesis, got out of the car, cinching her raincoat tight against the rain. Butler glanced toward Con, registering his own surprise at having had it so wrong.

"Hello, Doctor," Butler said, turning his attention to Fenton, his voice dipped in acid. "This feels long overdue."

"You brought the girl, I see," Dr. Fenton said.

"Good to my word as always. I must admit, I've spent years speculating about your identity. Never in my wildest dreams did I expect that it would be the CEO of Palingenesis."

"What are you talking about?" Dr. Fenton said.

Caught up in the pageantry of his own performance, Butler was slow to understand her confusion. "Let's not be obtuse with one another, shall we? Not after so long. Just tell me why? What's your angle?"

"I'm just here for the girl," she said.

Maybe it was only from having dealt with her, but Con didn't think Dr. Fenton was playing dumb. She looked mystified, brow furrowed as if she were trying to follow a conversation in a language she only half knew. Either she really was playing dumb, which made no sense at this point, or Dr. Fenton genuinely didn't know what Franklin Butler was talking about.

"She's not your anonymous donor," Con said to Butler.

"I most certainly am not," Fenton said, indignant at the very idea.

Butler gave them both a puzzled look and asked Fenton what she was doing here.

"Because you called me."

"I did what?" Butler said.

"You said you had the girl. You said you would release her for ten million. That is why I am here."

He paused, the idea filtering leisurely through his mind like a coin rattling down a Plinko board. Con began to laugh.

"What is so funny?" Dr. Fenton demanded.

"You both got played," Con said.

They both stared at her incredulously.

"What are you talking about?" Butler asked.

"Your anonymous donor struck a deal with you and sent Fenton in their place."

"No, I spoke directly to him on video," Fenton said.

"Well, you got deepfaked good," Con said.

Fenton was shaking her head like something unpleasant had landed in her hair and was nesting there. "What? No. Impossible. I have anti-deepfake software installed. It would have known if it was a simulated video call."

"Well, apparently you need an upgrade, Doctor," Butler said, warming to Con's theory. "Because we've never spoken before."

"Then who?" Fenton demanded.

Butler glared at Con, his turn to gloat. "My guess would be Vernon Gaddis."

"You're insane. Gaddis is the one who took her out of Palingenesis in the first place. He's been stymying my efforts to bring her back ever since. Why on earth would he tell me where to find her now?"

"I haven't the faintest," Butler admitted. "That's why I asked for this meeting, but the old bastard outmaneuvered me yet again. He got to remain in the shadows, get us to do his dirty work for him, and he saved himself ten million dollars. Assuming you have my money, that is."

"I have the money. Are you willing to turn her over to me?"

"I'm not his prisoner," Con said, feeling it was important to make that clear even as they haggled over her.

"Yes, I see that," Dr. Fenton said. "What exactly am I paying you for? What's stopping me from simply taking her?"

"It's a long drive back to DC, Doctor," Butler said, favoring her with a friendly smile and letting the implications of his threat settle like fine ash. "Do you have my money?"

"Of course I have it," Dr. Fenton said. "Now do you wish to make a deal or are we simply here to enjoy the rain?"

"Yes, to that in a moment, but while I have you, there's one other matter we should discuss."

"And what is that?" Dr. Fenton said with a tired sigh.

"Vernon Gaddis and his case before the Supreme Court. He's going to lose."

"Yes, I'm well aware of his legal difficulties."

"I'd think that would concern you. If the court rules against him, and it will, it marks the beginning of the end of human cloning in this country. You will be out of business."

"As will you."

"Exactly. That's why it's in both our interests that he drop the case before it comes to that."

Con and Dr. Fenton both looked at Butler with bewildered curiosity. Ever the narcissist, he stood basking in the confusion he'd sown.

"Please. Your life's work is the abolition of human cloning," Dr. Fenton said.

"Yes, Doctor, but"—Butler paused for effect—"it can't very well be my *life's* work if it is abolished."

"I don't understand," Dr. Fenton said. Con shared the same sentiment.

"In this country, power doesn't derive from defeating a threat; true power comes from the fear of the threat. And maintaining power requires a continuing threat. No one worries about causes that are already decided. When was the last time someone wrote a check to defeat prohibition?"

"You don't actually give a shit about cloning," Con said in dawning amazement. "Everything you said in the car was bullshit."

"Don't turn naïve just when I was beginning to have a modicum of respect for you," Butler said. "Of course I care about it. However, at this time, I find cloning to be a useful evil."

"What are you proposing exactly?" Dr. Fenton said.

"Vernon Gaddis and his kamikaze lawsuit threaten the status quo. I, for one, have no interest in spending the next ten years repositioning myself as the face of a different movement. I've invested too much time and effort. How about you, Doctor? Ready to start over after Palingenesis is shut down?"

"I'm listening."

"I propose an alliance. Strictly under the table, obviously. In public, I will continue to vilify you as a scourge upon the human race. As you will me. But in private, we pool our resources and find a way to halt this suit. It would be a win for both of us."

"Gaddis will never give up his family," Con said.

"I am inclined to agree with the girl," Fenton said.

"As am I," Butler said. "We may need to be very encouraging indeed. But there's simply no other way, not unless you want to see the valuation of Palingenesis drop to nothing."

Dr. Fenton took a long time answering. There was no doubt that she despised Franklin Butler, and the thought of accepting his offer clearly turned her stomach. But when she spoke, it appeared that pragmatism won out over principle. Con wondered if it was ever any other way.

"I think something can be worked out," Dr. Fenton said.

"Good. Then I'll be in touch," he said and threw his banking information from his LFD to hers. "If you'll transfer the funds in the cryptocurrency of your choice, I'll be on my way."

While Fenton did as she was asked, Con asked Butler if she could make a suggestion. Butler seemed amused at the idea and gestured for her to go on.

"What if, instead, you encouraged the in-laws to throw the case? Let Gaddis win," Con said.

"Why on earth would I do that?"

"You said power derives from the threat itself. Imagine the power you would have if the federal government recognized the legality of human cloning."

Butler stood there a long time, face frozen in the last expression he'd made, too deep in thought to even reset to neutral. "Gaddis's brother-in-law would never go for it. To do that, I would need to buy a Supreme Court judge, maybe two. I would—"

"If only you had ten million dollars burning a hole in your pocket," Con interrupted.

A smile crept across his face. "And what's in it for you?"

"Existence," she said simply. "It would be a win for both of us."

He looked at her and laughed. "You do enjoy quoting me back to me, don't you? It was truly good to meet you, Constance D'Arcy."

Con couldn't say the same so said nothing at all.

"Be careful with the good doctor," Butler said. "Don't turn your back on her."

"Oh, I'm aware."

Butler offered his pistol to her, but she made no move to take it. She was going to ride the train to the end of the line, and if she got cold feet, she didn't want anything that would help her get off it early.

Butler regarded her somberly, all of his artifice and showmanship fading away momentarily. "And yet you go voluntarily. I don't know whether to admire or pity you. I hope you find the answers you're searching for."

"You're really strange, you know that?"

"Shh. Our little secret," he said with a sly wink, and having confirmed that the money was in his account, he opened the back door and left without another word.

Con watched his sedan until it was out of sight. When it was gone, she looked across to Dr. Fenton, who waited impatiently in the rain, which was beginning to drive in off the lake.

"So, what now?" Con asked.

"Back to DC."

"What's in DC?"

"My lab. So we can get to the bottom of what is happening," Dr. Fenton said.

"You rushed down with ten million to buy me back from the CoA? That's some next-level customer service, Brooke."

"Yes, obviously there is more at stake than that. But it all starts with your head. Gaddis is using your head as a hard drive. We knew theoretically it was possible, but it seems he has taken it from the hypothetical to the practical."

Con let Fenton keep talking, not bothering to tell her that Gaddis had already explained all this. She was curious if the two versions would differ. They didn't.

"So what do you think is in there?" Con asked when Fenton was done.

"There's no way to know for sure. Your aunt was working on a variety of new applications of cloning. She really was quite brilliant. Everything from enhanced consciousness to treatments for dementia to cures for a host of genetic brain disorders. Her struggle with Wilson's disease made that a particularly personal crusade. Any one of them would be worth a fortune on the open market. But you know what I believe it is?" There was an innocence and excitement on her face that Con had never seen before.

"What?"

"Immortality," Fenton said. "It was your aunt's dream. What she aspired to—her life's work—was nothing short of solving death. But she was always limited by the mind-body dilemma. No matter what approach she tried, the consciousness of a sixty-year-old can only be downloaded into a clone that's genetically and chronologically identical to its original—like for like. Any attempt to download an older consciousness into a younger clone met with catastrophic failure. I think it drove her a little mad toward the end. She knew that when you cut through its sales pitch and artful jargon, all Palingenesis really offered was half measures. A temporary reprieve against what remained the unavoidability of death. No matter how many clones our clients keep, eventually old age claims them as it always had. She felt like a failure. For a long time, I believed that was why she took her own life."

"You think she solved it," Con said. The implications were staggering. She wondered whether Franklin Butler would still be happy with his ten million dollars. If Fenton was right, then he'd made the worst deal since the Louisiana Purchase.

"I can't think of anything else worth the trouble Vernon Gaddis has gone to."

"Unless it's you who's gone to the trouble," Con countered.

"I know you don't trust me, but regardless, I believe we can help each other."

Someone began clapping slowly in the darkness.

A woman's voice—a weirdly familiar woman's voice that made every hair on Con's body stand up—spoke. "Well done, Dr. Fenton."

They both looked toward the voice. A figure emerged from the gloom like a spirit summoned by an uneasy séance.

"I really didn't think you were clever enough to figure it out," the voice said. "Serves me right for underestimating you."

Then the damnedest thing happened. The figure stepped into the light. In the woman's hand was a small gun. It was pointed in the general direction of Brooke Fenton, but Con didn't get the impression it would play favorites.

"Hello, everyone," Constance D'Arcy said with a sundown smile. "I'm the other shoe."

PART THREE

THE MOUNTAIN

Life is obstinate and clings closest where it is most hated.

—*Frankenstein*, Mary Shelley

CHAPTER TWENTY-EIGHT

Since her revival inside Palingenesis, Con had viewed her own corpse, met the man who would have been her husband, heard her songs sung in a voice that was hers yet not. Again and again and again, she'd been told who she was and who she wasn't. What she was and what she wasn't. It had made her question whether she was nothing more than a medical parlor trick fooled by the seamlessness of its own illusion. Her mistake had been in needing the answer to be simple: she was *the* Con D'Arcy or she wasn't. A binary yes or no. It had taken a child to remind her that complexity wasn't necessarily something to fear. A definition of herself, one that allowed her to accept both who she'd been and who she was now, had begun to come into focus.

And then another Constance D'Arcy had strolled out of the dark holding a gun. The punch line to a long, grim joke told by an unsmiling comedian. Fenton wasn't having an easier time of it. The doctor stood there, mouth agape like someone seeing a dinosaur for the first time in a Steven Spielberg movie. The way a person did when confronted with something they believed impossible.

"Hello, Brooke," the other Constance D'Arcy said.

The sound of her name jarred Fenton from her bewildered stupor. "How is this possible?"

The other Constance D'Arcy simply shrugged and circled the doctor.

"Answer me!" Fenton demanded. "That son of a bitch built a cloning womb? Where were you created? Do you know how many laws you've both broken?"

The other Constance D'Arcy gave her a pitying look. "I'm afraid there isn't time to play twenty questions. Besides, it doesn't matter. You won't remember any of this tomorrow."

Con stared at this other Constance D'Arcy—who hadn't so much as looked at her, by the way—and fought a rising tantrum. One of the few things she'd thought she knew for certain was that her original was dead and that made her the only Constance Ada D'Arcy. So what did it mean that this other Con had a perfect sleeve of tattoos running down her left arm? Not for the last time, Con wished she had accepted Stephie's invitation and stayed in Charlottesville. Anything would be better than this.

"What do you want?" Fenton said.

"I'm here for her, same as you," the other Constance D'Arcy said.

"So I was right. Abigail didn't destroy her research."

"Of course not. And it's been right there in Palingenesis all this time. If only you'd been an actual scientist and not a feckless bureaucrat passing off another's genius as your own, you might have recognized what was right under your nose."

"What's in the clone's head? What did Abigail discover?"

"The key to everything," the other Constance D'Arcy said.

"Whatever he's paying you," Fenton said, "I'll double it, triple it. Just name your price."

The other Constance laughed. "It's not for sale. We just wanted you to know what has slipped through your fingers." She leveled the gun on the doctor.

"What are you going to do? Kill me? What good will that do? I have a clone, you idiot. I'll still—"

"Remind me," the other Constance D'Arcy interrupted. "You refresh your upload when? The first of every month, isn't it? Such an admirably predictable life you live. Well, it's near the end of June. That adds up to a month of lag for you."

Fenton blanched.

"How will your clone figure out what happened, I wonder? Four weeks ago, none of this had even begun. And it's not like an ambitious hack like you would risk leaving a paper trail. Does anyone even know about your meeting with Franklin Butler? No. You couldn't risk that, could you? Then you'd have had to share." The other Constance D'Arcy smirked, enjoying plucking the wings off her new fly. "Lag can be a cruel mistress, Brooke. My guess is your clone will lose her mind trying to understand why you died here tonight."

"Please," Fenton said, putting her hands out for mercy.

"As if you wouldn't do the same in my place," the other Constance D'Arcy said and pulled the trigger.

The shot sailed wide of its mark. Fenton stumbled back, eyes panicked ovals. Her heels caught in the gravel, and she fell gracelessly onto her back.

"Dammit," the other Constance D'Arcy said, glaring at the gun as if it were at fault. She strode over to where the doctor lay babbling, begging for her life. A second gunshot cut Fenton short, but the other Constance D'Arcy kept firing until the doctor lay still.

By the time it occurred to Con that maybe she should run, the other Constance D'Arcy had swung the gun her way. Not that it actually mattered. Con knew she wasn't going anywhere. She'd come too far for answers that at last felt within reach. She looked down at the body of Fenton bleeding into the gravel, then up at the other Constance D'Arcy, who was still pointing a gun at her. She was aware that her shoulders were shaking and that she couldn't stop them. She wondered abstractly if this was what shock felt like.

"Calm down," the other Constance D'Arcy chided, checking herself to make sure she hadn't gotten any blood on her clothes.

"You killed her." It was upsetting enough seeing herself kill someone, but the calculating, detached way the other Constance D'Arcy talked was almost worse.

"At this very moment back in DC, Fenton's clone is already being prepped for its download. She has a long life ahead of her wondering what the hell happened, which is less than the bitch deserves." The other Constance D'Arcy heaved the gun in the direction of the lake, but it never even hit the water—the police would find it in about five minutes. When she peeled off a pair of latex gloves, Con realized that was the whole point.

"You're setting up Franklin Butler."

The other Constance D'Arcy nodded as if that should be obvious. "It will sow a little useful confusion. Plus, when people get a load of the video I shot earlier, there will be endless questions about why the CEO of Palingenesis was meeting secretly with the mouthpiece of Children of Adam. Two birds with one stone as far as I can see."

"It was you posing as Gaddis on that call. You orchestrated this meeting."

"Well, I couldn't very well show up to pay your ransom. Can you imagine Franklin Butler's face? It would have made his tiny little head explode." The other Constance D'Arcy apparently found the thought charming.

"What happened to you?" Con asked.

"We should go."

"Who was that in the farmhouse?" Certain baseline questions needed to be answered before Con was going anywhere.

"We don't have time for this," the other Constance D'Arcy said. She drew a second gun and pointed it at Con.

Con found that nothing but funny. "You really should have pointed that at me a week ago back when I still gave a shit."

"Believe me, we tried."

"You can't threaten me anymore. I'm past that."

"You're right." The other Constance D'Arcy put the gun away. "But I won't need to, will I? Not knowing is like a burning coal in your clenched fist, isn't it? And only the truth will allow you finally to put it out."

"Are you my original or another clone of us?"

"I'm not your original."

That was a comfort. Con didn't much like this version of herself. "Then who made you?"

"Come and see."

"Answer my question," Con said.

"Come and see," the other Constance D'Arcy repeated and walked out to the roadway, disappearing into the darkness like an apparition from a Shakespearean drama that had said all it would say.

Con followed, as they both knew she would.

A car pulled up, silent as Charon's ferry. The two Cons got in.

CHAPTER
TWENTY-NINE

They drove in darkness along deserted country roads with no names. First north to Lynchburg, where the car turned west along the James River. As they climbed the Blue Ridge Mountains, dawn broke through a low halo of clouds that clung to the trees like a tattered shawl. Leaving the highway, the car began to wind along a series of mountain roads. Trees pressed in on both sides, all but blotting out the sky, as if the road were a crack in the earth that the forest yearned to seal up. No homes were visible from the road, only unpaved turnoffs marked by mailboxes and signs warning "Private Property." If that didn't make the owners' attitude toward uninvited guests clear enough, many turnoffs were also barred by heavy chains that hung between tree stumps. Con had been lost now for miles. It didn't bother her. This had felt like a one-way trip for a while now, and she was at peace with that. She was tired but not sad—the end of a long journey that had begun without a clear destination. It was a relief to have one at last.

When the other Constance D'Arcy sat up and looked expectantly out the window, Con guessed they must be getting close. The car slowed and turned off at a nondescript dirt road. No mailbox or signs of any kind, just an overgrown gash in the forest that someone could pass every day for a year without noticing. Tree branches scraped both sides of the car, urging them to turn back before it was too late. They kept on, bumping slowly up the rutted dirt road like an old-timey roller coaster dragging its victims to the top of the big drop.

A quarter mile up the road, the car stopped at a tall security fence topped with razor wire. The fence had been painted forest green and was all but invisible until you were almost on top of it. A caution sign announced that the fence was electrified, and Con saw a dozen cameras and sensors—someone was profoundly serious about their privacy. When the gate didn't automatically open, the other Constance D'Arcy sighed irritably and left the car. She approached the gate and addressed one of the cameras.

"I know you're listening. You have no right to keep me out," she said and gestured back at the car triumphantly. "I have her, so you've got to deal with me eventually. Quit being obstinate."

The gate unlocked and swung inward with an audible shudder.

"Someone's in a mood," the other Constance D'Arcy said, getting back into the car. Beneath her dismissive tone, though, Con heard apprehension. Not that it made the least difference now. She should have been afraid, but what she felt was closer to a giddy, childlike excitement. Excitement and impatience. The answers were waiting on the other side, and she just needed everyone to pick up the pace.

Another quarter of a mile up the road, they entered a sunny clearing at the base of a rock face of ancient greenstone. Water cascaded into a small pond that fed into a stream that snaked away down the mountain. Set flush against the rock was a small peach house. One story with a modest front porch. Two weather-beaten Adirondack chairs waited invitingly on either side of a wooden crate turned makeshift table. It was picturesque and quaint, and about the last thing Con expected to find behind all that carefully designed security. The equivalent of opening a bank vault to find a penny. She would have felt disappointed if not for the solar array on the far side of the house reminding her that there was much more to the cottage than a nice view and a cozy place to read a book. It looked large enough to power a city block, let alone

one remote mountain cottage. Exactly how much voltage was being pumped through that fence?

As the car parked itself outside a detached garage, four headless sentry rDogs loped into view, metal skins a woodland camouflage. Apart from four legs, they didn't actually look anything like a flesh-and-blood dog, but their patrol and hunting algorithms were modeled after the pack behaviors of North American gray wolves. Con had seen demonstration videos of rDogs herding and subduing trespassers. Even online, their ruthless efficiency always shocked her. She remembered that there were both military and civilian models but couldn't tell which these were. She hoped not to find out.

The rDogs surrounded the car, two on each side. The other Constance D'Arcy cracked a window and ordered them to heel. Immediately, the four machines flattened themselves to the ground in an alert crouch. The other Constance D'Arcy seemed surprised that they'd obeyed her and didn't seem in any great hurry to get out of the car.

"Are we going?" Con said, opening her door.

"Wait," the other Constance D'Arcy said, studying the unmoving rDogs.

"For what? They did what you wanted, didn't they? It's fine." Con had come this far. What were four killer robot dogs in the grand scheme of things?

"Just wait. Let me think," the other Constance D'Arcy said, pointing her gun at Con.

Con got out of the car anyway. "What did I tell you about that? Give me a break."

The other Constance D'Arcy cursed and had no choice but to follow. Giving the rDogs a wide berth, they circled the car to the front of the cottage. As they passed the pond, Con saw the flash of orange-and-red koi. It reminded her of the pond in the lobby of Palingenesis where she'd sat only a handful of days ago, although, in reality, it had been eighteen months going on a lifetime.

When they reached the bottom of the porch stairs, the front door opened and a white woman in her midfifties stepped out into the sunshine.

"Welcome home," Abigail Stickling said, looking remarkably fit for someone who had leapt to her death on Christmas night eighteen months ago.

All ideas required assumptions, and Con had been making the wrong ones from the very beginning—that her aunt was dead and it was her former partners fighting to control her legacy. Turned out, Abigail Stickling still had something to say about it. Con found some small comfort in the fact that she'd been right in a way. It *had* taken a founder of Palingenesis to pull all this off. She'd just guessed the wrong one.

"Oh, is this what welcome looks like?" the other Constance D'Arcy said, the hurt in her voice barely disguised.

"Now calm down. Don't overreact," Abigail said.

"You had no right to keep me out. None. This is as much mine as it is yours."

In the morning sunshine, Con could finally get a good look at her twin. She'd never much liked seeing recordings of herself, and watching a real live Constance D'Arcy was a lot to absorb. Everything about her was familiar yet unpleasantly foreign. How could two people who were so much alike be so different?

Abigail seemed genuinely offended by the accusation. "I merely took steps during the crisis to protect this place. That was always paramount."

"Don't be obtuse. The only reason you opened the gate is because I got to her first."

"You killed Pruitt and his entire team," Abigail scolded. "Four men. Without consulting with me. It's as if you've lost sight of everything that's important."

So Pockmark's name was Pruitt. In the midst of this peculiar argument, Con had a name to put to that grim face. She wondered if even he'd known who he was working for.

"We've been over and over this," the other Constance D'Arcy said. "They were seen by Vernon's drone at the farm. How long before he tracked them down? What then? There wasn't time for a symposium. I had to act."

"We do not kill people," Abigail said.

"Well, that's simply not true."

"We don't intentionally kill people," Abigail amended with a frown that suggested that this was an irrelevant point that had been settled long ago. "That was a regrettable mistake. You know as well as I that Cynthia wasn't supposed to be aboard that plane."

Cynthia. Con's ears perked up at the name. Her aunt had just claimed responsibility for Vernon Gaddis's plane going down in the North Atlantic. That was nearly five years ago and had sent dominoes toppling that would cost Vernon Gaddis his children and force him out as CEO of Palingenesis. It had set him against Brooke Fenton and Fenton against him. How long had her aunt been planning for today?

"You can stand there carping about the ends and the means until you're blue in the face, but I got the job done," the other Constance D'Arcy argued. "And in the process cauterized our Brooke Fenton problem and gave us leverage over Franklin Butler."

"You're delusional if you think it is that simple."

"See? That's the problem," the other Constance D'Arcy said. "You sit here in the mountains where everything is theoretical and abstract. I've been out there. Doing the dirty work. *Our* dirty work."

"Theoretical and abstract?" Abigail said, voice rising above practiced detachment for the first time. "How dare you? You think being trapped here is theoretical? Alone, year after year?"

"Yes, I'm well aware of your many sacrifices," the other Constance D'Arcy said, voice painted with sarcasm.

"I think we're done here," Abigail said and turned her attention to Con, expression shifting moods like she had changed the channel. "Hello, my dear, how are you?"

"I have a few questions." That didn't begin to cover it.

"I can imagine. How much has she told you?"

"Only that I'd get answers."

"Amazing the things we risk to have them, isn't it?" Abigail marveled. "Why don't you come inside? We have much to discuss."

The other Constance D'Arcy pulled the gun from her jacket pocket. "Don't you dare ignore me. Have you been listening?"

"The question is, have you been listening?" Abigail asked with a schoolteacher's weary disappointment toward an inattentive student.

Con followed Abigail's eyes and flinched. While the two women argued, the rDogs had stalked up behind them like whispers. Panicked, the other Constance D'Arcy ordered them to heel again, but this time, they didn't obey. They fanned out around her. The last few minutes had been a trap. She had only been granted control of the rDogs long enough to convince her she was safe.

"You traitorous bitch," the other Constance D'Arcy said.

"Takes one to know one," Abigail replied without rancor. "One single step, and they will respond with lethal force. I'm sorry it has to end this way. You've left me no other choice."

The other Constance D'Arcy laughed bitterly and pointed her gun at Abigail. "Call them off."

"Please. We both know what a terrible shot you are. And even if you get lucky and kill me, they will tear you apart before I hit the ground. So put the gun down. Let's at least end this like civilized people."

"That's my reward? Euthanasia?"

"It will be absolutely painless, you know that."

"It's not fair," the other Constance D'Arcy cried.

Abigail softened. "I know this is difficult. But it was always going to be this way. It was why we made you. You know that."

The other Constance D'Arcy cast about at the rDogs, looking for a way out.

Abigail said to Con, "My dear, why don't you come stand by me. You are perfectly safe. My sentries won't react to you."

Con felt no kinship to her aunt, but she felt even less to the other Constance D'Arcy. They might look alike, but that was all they shared anymore. The pleasure the other Constance D'Arcy had taken in tormenting and murdering Fenton had horrified Con. She was happy to be away from her and took a step toward the cottage.

The other Constance D'Arcy lunged at her like a cornered snake. She wrapped an arm around Con's neck, dragging her back. The rDogs flexed but didn't attack. Con felt the gun pressed to her head.

"Call them off," the other Constance D'Arcy warned. "I might not be able to hit you, but even I can't miss from here."

Abigail took a step down the stairs, a hand held out. "Don't. She is the key to everything we've worked for. Are you insane?"

Con saw genuine fear on her face.

The rDogs crept closer.

"Call them off!" the other Constance D'Arcy yelled, driving the barrel of the gun into Con's temple. "Remember that dirty work I was talking about? Well, this is it."

"You know it doesn't matter which one of us it is," Abigail implored. She was on the verge of tears.

"Then prove it. Call them off. I swear I will kill her otherwise. All of our work will be lost forever."

On the porch, Abigail swayed like a sapling in the breeze. Con could see her considering her options and finding none to her liking.

"Heel," Abigail called out to the rDogs, which returned to a waiting crouch. "You win. Now point the gun somewhere else, please."

"Not until you turn over complete access to me," the other Constance D'Arcy said.

Abigail acquiesced and typed a command in the air on her LFD; the other Constance D'Arcy matched her typing on Con's shoulder, back and forth.

When they were done, the other Constance D'Arcy called out, "Hunt."

The rDogs rose and scattered silently into the woods.

"Satisfied?" Abigail asked.

"Throw your LFD into the grass."

Abigail did as she was told, seething at having been outmaneuvered. The other Constance D'Arcy released her hold on Con, who stumbled away, happy to get some distance from both of them. The other Constance D'Arcy went up the steps, closing the distance between herself and Abigail, the gun never wavering.

Abigail said, "This is precisely why I had no choice but to lock you out. There's been a divergence and not for the better. I know if you would just take a deep breath and think it through, you'll agree that your recent actions testify to the truth of that."

"To the contrary, my recent actions are precisely why it should be me." Then she turned to Con. "Shall we head inside?"

"I'm good right here," Con said.

"I thought you wanted answers."

"All you've given me is more questions and a headache, not answers."

"And they lie within."

"How about don't talk like a fortune cookie? You promised me answers—answer this. How can there be another one of me?"

"Is that what she told you?" Abigail said, raising a curious eyebrow. "That's she's Constance D'Arcy?"

"She didn't have to tell me anything. Look at her," Con said.

"Well, looks aren't everything," Abigail said.

"Who the hell is she, then?" Con said, an uneasy prickling on the back of her neck accompanying her question.

"She's Abigail Stickling," Abigail said.

Con looked at the other Constance D'Arcy again, her mind spinning wildly like reels in an old slot machine. "Then who are you?"

"We're both Abigail Stickling."

CHAPTER THIRTY

Con felt sick and as angry as she'd ever been in her life. The kind of violent, instantaneous reaction that high school chemistry teachers showed off the first week of class to wow their students. Only it was happening in her chest, and the longer she stared at the other Constance D'Arcy knowing who was actually inside, the angrier she became. Her vision became pixelated, and she sat down hard in the grass. It was her own family who had done this to her.

Up on the porch, the two Abigails were locked in intense discussion—a pair of witches in the doorway of this gingerbread house deep in the woods.

"I beg you to reconsider," Abigail was saying. "This next phase is so delicate, and you've changed so much."

The other Constance D'Arcy, who wasn't Constance D'Arcy at all, answered, "Of course I've changed. You don't know what it was like. To you, he's just a name. I lived with him. Knowing what was coming. But I got the job done."

"Him?" Con repeated, her voice a thin, cold razor. There was only one man that could be. She climbed back to her feet. However angry she had been before was nothing compared to now. "It was you living with Levi?"

The women were too engrossed in their argument to hear or acknowledge her question.

"Was it you?" Con screamed, this time getting their attention. The two Abigails stopped and stared at her. Side by side, their mannerisms, even in completely different bodies, were eerily similar.

"See?" Abigail said with clinical detachment. "You've upset her."

"Was what me?" the other Constance D'Arcy asked, although it was messing with Con's head to think of her that way anymore. Instead, she spontaneously christened her Cabigail. A dreadful hybrid, like those celebrity couples the media would fuse into a single name once they stopped being individuals. That's how Con saw Cabigail now, as a thief and God only knew what else. Con's feet were moving now, carrying her up the stairs straight toward Cabigail. Her hands gathered in pressed fists.

"That's far enough," Cabigail said, raising her gun.

Con brushed the gun aside like it was nothing and drove Cabigail back against the house. "It was you living with Levi Greer?"

"Get your hands off me," Cabigail said, although it sounded more like a question than a demand.

"Please stop. Both of you," Abigail pleaded.

"Was it you?" Con repeated.

"Yes. It was me."

"For how long? Was it always you?"

"Six months," Cabigail said. "I took her place six months ago."

Six months. That was when Stephie said Con had told her she couldn't come around anymore. Except it had been Cabigail. Con could see it now. All that bullshit about having trouble at home had been a cover story. There was no trouble at home and never had been. Then she'd kept making regular trips to Charlottesville to keep up the suggestion of an affair. That's why Con hadn't recognized Dahlia that day on Water Street. Because it hadn't been Con at all.

"Why?" she asked.

"It's easier to frame someone from the inside," Cabigail said as if it were the most natural decision in the world.

"No, I mean, why frame him?"

"There couldn't be any loose ends," Abigail said simply. "Con D'Arcy couldn't simply disappear. There had to be someone to blame."

"You're monsters, both of you," Con said. "And where was the real Con all this time?"

"Right here. She stayed here with me," Abigail said as though Con's original had driven up here for a nice, cozy visit. Niece and aunt catching up after some years, sitting on the cottage porch trading stories. But all Con could see was her original's mutilated body in that moldering farmhouse. Stepping in close, she put her forehead to Cabigail's, trying to drive her back like a crooked nail.

"Did you kill her?"

"Yes," Abigail said. "We did. But with her consent."

Con's head jerked toward Abigail. "You lie."

"It's true," Cabigail said.

"Why don't we go inside?" Abigail said, opening the door and smiling hospitably. "Let us explain."

Con looked from one woman to the other. "What's the point? I'm never going to give you what's in my head. Not ever."

"You will," Cabigail said.

"After we explain," Abigail finished.

"Never going to happen," Con spat.

"Your original said something similar," Abigail said.

"Please. Let us explain," Cabigail said.

Con let go of Cabigail. "Yeah, okay. This I have to hear."

The three women went into the cottage and closed the door on the outside world. This was why she was here, wasn't it? To hear the end of the story, even if it wasn't the story she wished she'd lived.

The door led into a dark, cluttered living room with ceilings low enough that even Con could almost touch them. Bookcases overflowed with old paperback mysteries, games, and about a hundred jigsaw puzzles. A stone fireplace that looked as if it had been carved out of the side of the mountain dominated the back wall. Its mantel was covered in knickknacks and what, to the naked eye, looked like junk. An ancient plasma television older than Con was mounted on one wall opposite a threadbare couch covered with a patchwork quilt. Off to the left was a narrow galley kitchen, and through the only other door, Con saw a cramped bedroom.

It reminded her of one of those rustic cabin getaways that city people rented to escape the bustle for a long weekend. Hard to imagine anyone living here year-round, much less one of the most brilliant minds of the twenty-first century. Abigail—the one who actually looked like Abigail Stickling—had said she'd been here for years. Con looked around the cottage. If there were two Abigails, then her aunt had made a clone. Where, though? Because it hadn't been in that kitchen.

"No one actually lives here, do they?" Con said. "This is all just set dressing."

"Very good." Abigail nodded approvingly. "We call this the show home."

"Camouflage in the event anyone got curious enough to take a serious look at the property. All they'd find is this old eyesore," said Cabigail.

"So, where's the real deal?" Con asked.

In answer, Cabigail placed her palm on one of the stones in the mantel of the fireplace. It slid back to reveal a state-of-the-art security station and a shallow rectangular indentation that seemed to serve no purpose. Cabigail entered her biometrics. After a moment, Con felt a low rumble beneath her feet. Behind them, the front door locked of its own accord, and then the fireplace retracted smoothly back into the wall. Lights ticked on, revealing a wide passageway that sloped down into the mountain.

"Hey, a secret lair," Con said. "Very on brand, you guys."

"I've missed her sense of humor," Abigail said.

"Best not to talk about that," Cabigail suggested.

"You're right. You're right," Abigail agreed. Now that things seemed settled between them, the two Abigails had turned oddly civil.

"Come along," Cabigail said. "Let us give you the nickel tour."

The passageway was longer than Con expected, at least one hundred feet long, down into the heart of the mountain. Abigail explained that it was built in a natural cave system that had been enlarged as necessary. They came to a second security door, which required yet more biometrics. It let them into a bright, spacious, and determinedly spartan living space and kitchen—the antithesis of the cottage above. False windows were set into the walls, which Abigail explained simulated both the time of day and the current weather outside. The illusion was immersive. If Con didn't know better, she'd have had no way to tell she was underground.

"So, when it's raining outside?" Con asked.

"It's raining in here," Abigail confirmed. "If we 'opened' the windows, you'd even hear birds chirping, crickets at night. A small thing, but it's important to feel connected to the outside world."

"How long did all this take to finish?" Con asked, looking down the two hallways that led away into the complex.

Abigail took a seat at one end of a long dining table. "Well, nothing is ever really finished. There are always improvements to be made. Upgrades. Work goes slowly when you have to cover your tracks. Everything had to be outsourced. We've used close to three hundred subcontractors, each hired through a different holding company. The logistics alone were enough to drive a person to drink. But to your question, primary construction began in '33. Yes?" Abigail looked to Cabigail for confirmation. "That would make it seven years ago now. The complex has been habitable for five."

Seven years. Two years before Vernon Gaddis's plane crash. Con looked around, almost admiring the terrible and deliberate purpose with which her aunt had planned for today. She finally understood why the entire family had been given clones. It hadn't been to rub their faces in Abigail's success. That had all just been a sideshow. Only Con had mattered. And in the wake of her accident, she had predictably accepted the gift. It made her wonder how much of her last three years had been manipulated by her aunt. How long had she been a rat running her aunt's long-form maze? How much of what she thought she knew was true, and how much was part of the Abigails' design? Even her lag had played its part, driving Con forward recklessly. A windup machine in thrall to her broken programming, she had delivered herself, willingly, right to her aunt's doorstep.

"So what's the story? I thought you couldn't have a clone," Con said.

"Well, no, I couldn't back in '27," Abigail said, as Cabigail sat down beside her, her hand resting lightly on the table so no one would forget who had the gun. "The excess copper buildup in the brain characteristic of Wilson's disease played absolute havoc on uploads. It was impossible to get a clean image. Took until '33 to solve it. As diversions go, though, it proved just about perfect."

"And you decided to hide that discovery from Palingenesis," Con said, sitting at the far end of the table where she could see both of them.

"By then, the company had demonstrated that it was an unreliable steward of my vision," Abigail said. "I no longer felt beholden to share my progress with Vernon."

"Which, I'm guessing, is also why you never told anyone that you solved the mind-body problem. You have, right? I'm guessing that wasn't just a lie to torment Brooke Fenton. Seeing as how you're in my body and all."

Cabigail looked down at herself and chuckled. "Good point. But, yes, I've . . ." Cabigail paused and looked apologetically at Abigail. "We've come a long way since '27. Back then, the mind-body paradox appeared insurmountable. We could clone a human being, but only like for like. Same body. Same age. Which was fine as far as it went, but that was never the goal. We kept at it for years. But no matter what we tried, the lag between clone and original was always the limiting factor. And forget about moving a consciousness from one body to another. That had a survival rate of zero."

"And yet here you are."

"You know how long we've been waiting to tell someone? It's not easy to keep a secret like this. Some days I just want to burst from excitement." Cabigail's eyes blazed like twin lighthouses. "You understand what this means, don't you? The best Palingenesis can offer is half measures—an insurance policy against death. But its clients would continue to age and eventually die. Now, the true immortality of the human conscience is within our grasp. With your help, we can make it a reality."

"You really did it," Con said, still struggling to wrap her mind around the enormity of what that meant. If Abigail could transfer her consciousness to a younger body, then she could theoretically live forever, playing hopscotch from one new body to the next for a thousand years. It would rewrite what it meant to be human.

"Well, not yet, no," Cabigail qualified. "We've had limited success with jumps between close genetic relations—an aunt and her niece, for example—but even this pairing has a shelf life. But it should give me enough time to perfect the process."

"How long?" Con asked.

"Ten years, give or take," Cabigail said with a sly smile. "If you grant me access to the rest of my work."

"That's what's stored in my head."

"Yes. Years of research and data. The research lab at Palingenesis possesses computational power to run modeling simulations that would take me a hundred years elsewhere. Unfortunately, there was no easy way to remove that data without raising alarms. Palingenesis is one of the most secure information facilities in the world. I should know. I designed it. A hermetically closed system with no connection to the outside world. Nothing goes in and nothing goes out. Let's just say

I needed to think creatively to claim my research without raising red flags."

"The mass in my scan is literally killing me," Con said.

"We are aware of that."

"But you can fix it, can't you?" Con said.

"Of course. At this point, Palingenesis is generations behind."

"And let me guess, you'll only fix what you broke if I give you what's in my head. That's the deal, isn't it?"

"In part. I'm sorry we had to go to such lengths, but you understand now what is at stake."

Con did and for perspective, rattled off those lengths to keep fresh in her mind the harm her aunts had inflicted to get what they wanted. Besides Brooke Fenton's death, they had already confessed to killing Cynthia and Vernon Gaddis and the four men in the town house in Charlottesville. They had kidnapped Constance D'Arcy (Con wasn't buying any of their with-her-consent bullshit), stolen her body, and masqueraded as her for six months to frame Levi Greer for her murder. It was a grotesque violation. All so they could live forever. Con reckoned people had killed for less. She was sorely tempted to follow their bad example.

Instead, she tried her best to sum it all up. "So you built this place, made a clone of yourself, and convinced her to commit suicide so you could steal your own invention."

"No, you misunderstand," Abigail said.

Con looked at Abigail quizzically.

"*I* am the clone," Abigail said.

"What?" Just when Con thought she was starting to see the big picture, she got thrown a curveball.

"It was the original Abigail Stickling who jumped off the roof of the Monroe Hotel. Abigail here is her clone," Cabigail continued. "A necessary evil, but for the world to believe that Abigail Stickling was truly dead, the illusion had to be perfect. It was inevitable that the apparent suicide of the mother of human cloning would be greeted with extreme skepticism. Clones are not physically identical to their originals."

"Besides," Abigail said. "She and I both recognized that our consciousness would be better served in a newer body. Hers had fifty-plus years of wear and tear on it. There was never any question, really."

"It had to be her body," they said together.

"It was very hard," Abigail said. "We had grown quite close. I miss her."

"You miss yourself?" Con said.

"I suppose that does sound a bit narcissistic. Originally, I was only supposed to be a test of the equipment. But then we realized how much more could be accomplished if there were two of us. We worked together for several years until it was her time. What can I say? She was good company. It can get very lonely down here."

Cabigail patted Abigail's arm. Apart from the gun in her other hand, it seemed almost affectionate. A small reconciliation. Abigail smiled and squeezed her hand gratefully.

"Why did you wait so long?" Con asked. "Why the eighteen months?"

"Because your original fell in love," Cabigail said.

"What a disaster," Abigail agreed. "We meant to make contact with your original in January after New Year's. Always such a grim month."

Cabigail said, "We spent a year planning the suicide of a depressed young woman overwhelmed by personal tragedy. But then out of the blue, in swooped Levi Greer, and suddenly your original was in love and had moved to Richmond. We had to scrap everything and go back to the drawing board."

"It took us eighteen months to lay a convincing groundwork for her murder," Abigail said. "Levi Greer's history with the farmhouse was just a lucky find. It all came together perfectly."

Con recoiled at the callous pride in Abigail's voice. As if her aunt had solved the Sunday crossword. She wanted to argue that Levi Greer wasn't a loose end, that he was an innocent man and what they'd done was evil. But there was no point. The Abigails had spent the last seven years hatching their master plan. They weren't about to be talked out of it now. They both had the eyes of converts. True believers. Her mother had those same eyes, although Con doubted that the Abigails would appreciate the comparison.

Instead, she said, "I want you to know now that all your planning was for nothing. I'm never giving you what you put in my head."

"Your original said something similar," Abigail said.

"You kidnapped her."

"Yes, at first," Abigail admitted. "But once we explained—"

"Yeah, yeah, she agreed to let you stab her to death with a big smile on her face."

"That was all postmortem. She didn't suffer," Cabigail said in a tone meant to convey what an essential difference that made.

"She had a life. She was in love," Con protested.

"Even so," Abigail said. "She still agreed."

"It's never going to happen," Con said, conscious of how unimpressed the Abigails were by her threat.

Abigail and Cabigail looked at each other and reached a silent consensus.

"We have to accelerate the timetable," Abigail said. "Show her everything today."

"We were going to give her a few weeks to acclimate," Cabigail said, discussing Con as if she were a child who couldn't follow adult conversations.

"With Vernon sniffing around out there, it's a luxury we can't afford. Otherwise, we're going to run out of time," Abigail said. "It has to be now."

"Vernon." Cabigail said the name like an ancient curse. "Nothing has gone right."

"It's time for tea," Abigail said.

The suggestion seemed to demoralize Cabigail. "No, not yet. It's too soon."

"It's time," Abigail said soothingly.

"What if I need you?" Cabigail asked. "What if she refuses?"

"Convince her. Everything depends on it," Abigail said. Outside, they'd been threatening to kill each other, but that all seemed forgotten now; the two Abigail Sticklings were strangely affectionate and gentle. "You were right out there, I think," Abigail said. "You're better equipped to handle things from here. You can do it."

Cabigail nodded dejectedly. "It's just that we've been looking forward to this for so long. I hate that you're going to miss it."

"I won't," Abigail said, squeezing her hand again. "Because you'll be there. This is the plan. This has always been the plan. Nothing else matters."

Cabigail nodded and stood up. "I'll get the tea."

After Cabigail went into the kitchen, Con looked across the table at her aunt. "How long have you been down here?"

"Always."

"What does that mean, always?"

"I've never left the mountain," Abigail answered. "It would have ruined the effect if Abigail Stickling was seen going to the opera at the Kennedy Center."

"I can't believe my aunt would commit suicide," Con said, still shocked by the idea of one of the most notorious egos of the twenty-first century voluntarily ending her life.

"Well, she didn't," Abigail said.

"She jumped off a roof," Con replied.

"And yet here I am. Two of us, in fact," Abigail said, gesturing toward the kitchen. "So how could Abigail Stickling have committed suicide? You of all people should appreciate that."

"You know it's more complicated than that," Con snapped, realizing this was how the Abigails had given themselves permission to kill

Vernon Gaddis, Brooke Fenton, and the original Constance D'Arcy. By their twisted logic, it couldn't be murder if the victim had a clone. Only the accidental death of Cynthia Gaddis gave them any pause. Not that it had stopped them. Cabigail had graduated to premeditated murder, killing Pockmark and his entire team.

"Is it?" Abigail asked rhetorically. "If I'm talking to Constance D'Arcy, how can I have murdered her?"

"The dead body, for one."

"Ah yes, the body," Abigail said like a professor who had finished greeting the class and was ready for the lecture to begin. "The tyranny of the body. Let me ask you this—if a soldier loses a limb in combat, should we declare him dead? No, that seems a little premature. How about two limbs? Three? How about all four? Is it time for a funeral?"

"No, obviously."

"Of course not. We may impute some poetic importance to the human heart, but it is called brain death for a reason. Our humanity has always resided in our minds. The body is only a vessel and an extraordinarily fragile one at that. My work liberates us from that limitation."

"I'll never give it to you," Con repeated.

"You will."

"Yeah, I've heard. But you're not selling me so far."

"Well, we haven't gotten to the good part yet," Abigail said with the tease of a born storyteller.

"What's the good part?" Con asked, wary but curious.

"Where we make your dream come true."

"You have nothing I want," Con said.

"Your original said that too."

CHAPTER
THIRTY-ONE

Cabigail returned from the kitchen with a floral tray and set out three mugs and spoons, a teapot, milk, sugar, and a small plate of cookies. It was all so peculiarly civilized. Pouring water into the first cup, Cabigail stirred in milk and sugar, fussing over it until it was just so. Then she placed it with a ceremonial flourish in front of Abigail. Abigail lifted the cup to her nose with both hands and breathed it in.

"Chamomile. How apropos."

Cabigail prepared the other two mugs and slid one in the direction of Con. Con left it untouched; even if she liked tea, she didn't trust Cabigail enough to drink anything she made. Pockmark and his team hadn't died of natural causes.

"She doesn't drink tea yet," Abigail reminded her.

"True, that's true," Cabigail said, then asked Con if she would like something different.

"I'm fine," Con said. "What is happening here?"

Abigail took a tentative sip. "Do you remember the last time we saw each other?"

"My father's funeral."

"How is the tea?" Cabigail asked.

"Perfect," Abigail replied, then to Con: "That's right. Your father's funeral. September 7, 2022. Antoine D'Arcy was the most stoic human being I've ever met. The weight he bore. I honestly couldn't say which was the more unforgiving taskmaster—the US Army or your mother. I don't know anyone who could have taken it for as long as he did. And he never said a word. Never complained. Did his tours and carried the weight. In many ways, he was her anchor. The one thing keeping her from indulging her demons. I was heartbroken when he was killed in that absurd war."

"Is that why you made a scene?"

"*I* made a scene?" Cabigail said, glancing at Abigail, who rolled her eyes. "Is that how the family tells it? Be honest, in your lifetime did anyone ever *start* a scene with your mother?"

Con had to admit she had a solid point. One of the risks of being anywhere in public with her mother was the high chance of drama. Con couldn't remember a single time that her mother wasn't feuding with someone in the family or at her church. Even as a little girl, she understood on some level that her mother was always the instigator. It was certainly that way between the two of them. She remembered once, without a trace of irony, her mother demanding to know why God cursed her with such a combative child.

"So, what set her off?" Con asked.

"I told her that I was sorry that I wasn't in time," Abigail said and sipped her tea. Each time she did, Cabigail nodded approvingly.

"In time for what?" Con asked.

"To save your father. Vernon and I founded Palingenesis in the spring of '19. We made huge strides in the intervening three years. The dream of human cloning was within reach. I could see the way forward. All I needed was time and funding, both of which I knew Vernon would get me. He is a genius with such things." Abigail paused to reflect and take a big drink from her mug. "I think I always had Antoine in the back of my mind. That I'd be able to give soldiers like him a second chance. But I was too late."

"That's what the big fight was about?"

"It was foolish of me. I was aware Mary had become more seriously involved with her church. I knew she disapproved of my work. But I hadn't really been home in years, and it wasn't until that moment at the funeral that I realized that I had become the enemy. So, I left and never came back. We have that much in common at least," Abigail said, clearly hoping to find common ground. When Con only stared her down, she kept on with her story. "But five years later, when Palingenesis won its first contract with the DoD to provide clone backups for key military personnel, I thought of your father. It was the proudest moment of my career. Just goes to show you what a naïve fool I was."

"Naïve how?"

"Scientists are trained to find answers. Locked in a laboratory, the real world has a way of becoming an abstraction. All that matters is solving the puzzle. Real-world applications are someone else's problem, but I had this fantasy that my work would be used to help give working-class people in high-risk professions a second chance. People like your father. I never stopped to think of the billionaires who would line up, eager to buy themselves more time. But Vernon did. He always knew that our work with the military was only to gain a toehold. His leaking the news to the *Times* and the *Post*? A stroke of genius."

"That was him?" Con said with a surprise that was already fading as the words came out of her mouth.

Cabigail cut in. "Who else? Once the story was out in the open, the demand created itself. Oh, I objected, but I was easily dealt with—in all things political, I was an infant. Just another idealistic scientist with her head in the clouds. Let's just say, I am a very quick study."

Again, Con saw the scope and sophistication of her aunts' plan. "It was you who maneuvered his clone off the Palingenesis board, not Brooke Fenton."

"Well, she did the maneuvering. I simply whispered in her ear that having a clone enmeshed in a legal challenge to his fortune with his heirs was bad for business."

"After you murdered his original."

"A person with a clone—" Cabigail said tiredly.

"Cannot be killed," Con finished. "Yeah, yeah, I heard you the first dozen times."

Abigail finished her tea and set the mug down clumsily. It toppled on its side and a little tea dribbled onto the table. Her eyes went wide as if trying to bring them into focus.

"I think it's starting," Abigail said, slurring over the last word. "I wonder if this is how Socrates felt."

"What did you do to her?" Con asked Cabigail, pushing her own tea farther away.

"Please don't hold it against her. There can't be two of us for what comes next," Abigail said.

"She poisoned you."

"Yes, I know," Abigail said.

"So you're just going to let yourself die?" Con said.

"Not as long as she is here," Abigail said and squeezed Cabigail's hand.

"You're both insane," Con said, but the two Abigails weren't paying her any attention.

"Why don't I go lie down?" Abigail suggested.

Cabigail agreed and took Abigail by the elbow to help her up from her seat. Abigail's legs buckled, but Cabigail caught her before she fell.

"Would you help me get her to the lab, please?" Cabigail asked Con.

Con put an arm around Abigail's waist and helped walk her down the hall. Not out of any real concern for Abigail, though, she was just curious to see the lab. And to see what happened next. She wanted to believe their confidence that she'd give them what was locked in her head was just more of their mind games, but she needed to know for sure. Well, she needed them to try and convince her. Then she'd know the truth about her original. And whatever it was, she suspected it would be in her aunt's laboratory.

Where the rest of the complex was resolutely minimalist, the labs were packed with medical equipment and computers. Con couldn't identify most of it, but she recognized a CT scanner against one wall. A spectrophotometer. Two examination tables. There was also an upload chair, although the Abigails' chair was much more utilitarian, without any of the creature comforts that went into the Palingenesis five-star spa experience. Con counted three wombs similar to the ones Palingenesis used to store clones. Two sat empty. The third held an inanimate clone of Abigail Stickling. The backup to the backup to the backup, if Con had her math right.

"Do you want to rest in the office?" Cabigail asked.

"No, just take me to the tray. It will be a pain to move me after I'm gone."

Cabigail nodded at the good sense of that. Together, they wound their way to the back of the lab. Abigail's head dropped to her chest, and her breathing became thick and labored. Her feet gave out and dragged behind them on the floor. As they approached the far wall, twin metal doors parted to reveal a blackened chamber. A flat metal tray on a track rolled out and shuddered to a halt.

"What is this thing?" Con asked.

"An incinerator," Cabigail said.

"Why the hell do you have an incinerator?"

Cabigail looked at it, then back to Con. "Isn't that kind of self-explanatory?"

"You cremate a lot of bodies?"

"Too many to count over the years. They are the byproduct of our research. Now, if you don't mind, would you lift her legs? I'm not strong enough to get her up by myself."

"She's not dead," Con said.

"I know," Cabigail said with genuine sadness. "It'll only be a few minutes now."

They managed to wrestle Abigail up onto the tray, miraculously without dropping her. Con leaned against the wall, panting from the exertion.

Abigail's eyes fluttered open. "Are you there?"

"I'm here," Cabigail said, taking her hand. "Do you need anything?"

"No, it won't be long. I can feel it."

"So, I was thinking," Cabigail said. "When did you do your last refresh?"

"Yesterday evening. Why?"

"Well. When this is all over, and I've finally solved the mind-body problem . . . maybe I could bring you back. Would you like that?"

"You would do that for me?" Abigail said, brightening at the thought.

"Why not? If everything works the way we believe, it will be easy enough to hide two of us from the world."

"That will be so nice. Thank you," Abigail said.

"I'll miss you until then," Cabigail said and brushed the hair from Abigail's forehead.

"We will have so much to catch up on," Abigail said.

"And all the time in the world to catch up on it."

"Until then," Abigail said and closed her eyes for the last time.

Cabigail stood there holding her hand until Abigail stopped breathing. Then she started the incinerator. No parting words, no moment of silent reflection. All the sentiment of taking out the recycling. The tray retracted back inside the wall. The metal doors closed. Cabigail punched a second button, and the incinerator roared to life.

"I don't understand," Con said, stepping back from the heat.

"I thought we'd been over that," Cabigail said.

"No, I mean, why build this place at all? Why didn't you just finish your work at Palingenesis? Why go to these insane lengths? You spent seven years planning to steal your own invention from your own company. Was it just greed? Are you that selfish?"

"Selfish? You think I'm the selfish one."

"What else would you call what you've done? All so you could keep immortality all to yourself."

Cabigail shook her head in disbelief at how badly she'd been misunderstood. "What do you think would happen if Vernon Gaddis or Brooke Fenton got control of my work?"

"They'd sell it."

"We agree on something at last," Cabigail said. "And how much do you think Palingenesis could charge for immortality?"

"Whatever they want."

"Precisely. Only this time, Palingenesis wouldn't be selling an insurance policy, it would be rewriting the underlying rules of how our species functions. A techno-evolutionary leap unlike anything that's preceded it. But one that is evenly distributed. It would create an overclass of unthinkably wealthy and powerful individuals who would never die," Cabigail said, pausing for dramatic effect. "And we have a name for such beings."

"They'd be gods," Con said in awe.

"You understand now why I couldn't risk Palingenesis ever finding out."

"But you did risk it," Con retorted. "You could've destroyed your research. What makes you think you deserve immortality any more than Palingenesis?"

"It *is* my discovery."

"Exactly. What you did, you did out of selfishness."

"Given enough time, I will be able to make the processes available to all."

Con sneered. "Spare me your champion-of-humanity routine. You killed my original so you could live forever."

Cabigail's face clouded. "You're really not going to let that go, are you?"

"It doesn't seem like it, does it?"

"You truly are your mother's daughter," Cabigail said.

At any other moment in her life, Con would have taken that comment badly. But standing there in the violent heat of the incinerator, she wore it as a badge of honor. She was Mary Stickling's daughter, for better and for worse.

"So convince me," Con said. "You keep saying I'll willingly give you what's in my head once you explain. Well, how about we get on with it, then? 'Cause so far the answer is still absolutely not."

"This wasn't how it was supposed to be," Cabigail said almost apologetically. "You were supposed to have time to rest and acclimate before I showed you, but Vernon's involvement has rendered all of that unfeasible."

"Before you show me what?"

"There's a question I've been meaning to ask," Cabigail said, glossing over Con's own question. "That first night you left Palingenesis. Where did you get the money to get on the Metro? My team was meant to take you once you found out your LFD wasn't connected to a bank anymore and returned up the escalator. By the time we realized something had gone wrong, you were halfway home."

Con thought back. It felt like a lifetime ago now. "A cop took pity on me. He let me through the turnstile."

"Unbelievable," Cabigail said with a sardonic laugh. "My entire career is predicated on the belief that I could account for all the variables. That all it took was planning and intellect, and there was nothing that couldn't be anticipated and controlled. And I failed to account for the possibility that you might charm a police officer into doing you a favor. And because of my well-documented arrogance, Vernon met you.

And now his head is filled with all sorts of suspicions and theories. The one thing I most wanted to avoid."

"And here we are," Con said.

"Here we are," Cabigail replied, seeming to make up her mind about something. "Come along. There's something I want to show you."

CHAPTER
THIRTY-TWO

"Show me what?" Con asked, trailing warily after Cabigail.

They came to a locked door, which accepted Cabigail's credentials. The locks disengaged audibly, but Cabigail hesitated before opening the door. "A few ground rules before you go inside."

"Aren't you coming with me?" Con said.

"Better if he only sees one Con D'Arcy at a time."

"Who?" Con asked, suddenly very aware of the beating of her heart and the chill running the length of her spine.

"Keep in mind that he is very sensitive to external stimuli, so no loud noises or sudden movements. Do your best to remain calm. He doesn't do well with emotional peaks. Try to speak slowly and clearly." Cabigail held the door open, and Con peered into a simple antechamber. At the far end was a plain wooden door that looked conspicuously out of place in her aunt's hypermodern underground complex. "Also, no mention of the date or how much time has passed. As far as he is concerned, it is still 2037. It will upset him if you challenge that belief."

"What have you done?" Con said but took a halting step into the antechamber. Once, in high school, a girl had crept up behind her in the hallway and coldcocked her in the ear. Con hadn't lost consciousness, but for the next day, she'd felt underwater, as if two strong hands were holding her head just below the surface. That was how she felt now. Cabigail was still talking, but it sounded muffled and far away, drowned out by the words that played over and over in a perverse Möbius strip.

Better if he only sees one Con D'Arcy at a time.

Better if he only sees one Con D'Arcy at a time.

Better if he only sees one Con D'Arcy at a time.

Con had been adamant that her original would never agree to any of this. There was nothing that could persuade her. But now, she wondered. Had her aunt offered the one thing that Con would willingly die for? She reached the wooden door and looked back at Cabigail, who smiled reassuringly and waved her on.

"You'll do fine. I'll be in my office when you're finished. We'll talk then."

Con turned the doorknob and opened the last door.

Inside was a small, dimly lit room—twin bed, dresser, two chairs. A rudimentary table sat beneath a window that, even though they were deep underground, had a panoramic view of the mountains. On the table was a half-finished jigsaw puzzle of Jimi Hendrix kneeling before his burning guitar.

On the bed, a man lay on his side with his back to her. Con covered her mouth with her hand in a timeless gesture of dread.

"What have you done?" she whispered through her fingers as the man rolled over and sat up on the edge of the bed. A choked moan escaped her, and then tears came like the sudden Texas storms that would roar out of the desert, sending families scrambling for high ground.

It was Zhi. Even though he had died more than a year ago, it was her Zhi.

He scratched his shaved head sleepily. His feet were bare. A loose white T-shirt couldn't hide how thin he was. Hospital scrubs with an elastic waist hung low on his hips. He didn't look surprised to see her, but when he smiled, it was only with half his face. The other side sagged like a sail that had lost the wind, the way her uncle Frank's face had after his stroke.

"I was starting to worry that you weren't coming back," Zhi said, his voice strangely childlike.

"Of course I was," she said. Zhi thought she was the original Con D'Arcy, and she played along, remembering what her aunt had said about not challenging his beliefs.

"Why are you crying?" he asked. "Did I do something wrong?"

"No, nothing. I'm just happy to see you," she said, stifling her tears and forcing a smile. The truth, of course, was infinitely more complex. This was all she had dreamed about for more than three years. So why did she feel so divided now?

She wanted to throw her arms around him but was afraid. Instead, she asked, "How are you?"

"Doc says I'm doing good. She won't say when I can leave, but I can tell I'm getting close. Asked if maybe I could take a walk on the grounds soon, but she says I have to work harder at my physical therapy. Man, I hate it, though."

She realized Zhi thought he had survived the accident. He didn't know he was a clone at all. "Me too," Con said, beating back her tears again.

"How's your knee?" he asked.

"Better," she said. "Much better."

"I'm so sorry."

"For what?" Con said, on alert.

"I changed the music," he said and looked down at the floor, ashamed.

It took Con a moment to orient to what he was trying to tell her. "What music?"

Zhi seemed to lose his train of thought and reached for a walker. It was only when he dragged himself into a standing position that Con saw how truly damaged he was. She watched him wheel himself over to the table, right leg moving only haltingly while his right hand fumbled to keep a grip on the handlebar of the walker. She knew he meant the crash and fought back the urge to press him to remember. When you carried an unanswered question for long enough, at some point, a hint of the truth wasn't enough. She needed to hear him say it, but at the same time, what did she hope to get out of it? Was that how she wanted to spend this time with him?

"Did you see the puzzle? I'm almost done." He rolled over to the table and eased himself slowly into a chair.

"Yeah, it's coming along great," she agreed.

"You used to shred 'Voodoo Chile.' Man, I loved playing with you so much." He smiled his half smile.

"Me too," she said softly.

All the talk seemed to have worn him out, and Zhi barely spoke again. She'd never known him to sit still for so long. He'd always been pure kinetic energy, leaping from one project to the next to the next, but they sat at the table for more than an hour while he worked patiently on his puzzle. When he found a piece that fit, he let out a little whoop of joy and smiled brokenly at Con. Watching him, there were moments when she saw the old Zhi—sharp, proud, intense. But they were fleeting glimpses of the sun, and just as quickly, the clouds rolled back, dulling his eyes as he worked diligently on his puzzle. This wasn't Zhi, she thought, knowing how uncharitable and hypocritical that made her. But then he saw where another piece fit, and Zhi would emerge again just long enough to make her question herself. Eventually, Zhi said he needed to rest. He wheeled himself back to bed and lay down in a series of methodical, old-man steps. Con saw him shivering and covered him with a blanket.

"Will you play for me? Doc gave me that guitar, but I can't anymore," he said, showing her his atrophied right hand.

Con brought the guitar over to the bed and tuned up as best she could. Her hands were having their own difficulties. When things sounded decent, she still hadn't settled on what to play. How ironic was that? Her thoughts went back to that first night in college when they'd sat up all night trading songs and passing a different guitar back and forth. She knew every song he'd played and every song she'd played for him. Both trying to impress the other with their knowledge and taste—the good-natured competitiveness that had marked their relationship. She remembered the song he'd sung when she caught herself falling in love with him.

She sat on the edge of the bed and played it for him now. An old Big Star track called "Thirteen." It was a simple, hopeful little tune about young love. Zhi recognized it and mouthed the words silently as she sang. She thought about their life together. The life that was and the one that might have been. It was a familiar, well-traveled rabbit hole. There'd been a time that she'd taken comfort in the pain to be found there. She didn't feel that way anymore. Now she just felt glad that she had known him and that he'd been in her life.

When she finished, he reached out and took her hand. "Come back tomorrow?"

"I promise," she lied.

He smiled up at her and rolled over on his side. She sat there quietly until he was asleep. She didn't cry anymore.

Con found Cabigail in a huge office connected to the lab, working at a broad mahogany desk piled high with papers. The walls were lined with bookcases that stretched from floor to ceiling. Con had never seen so many books outside of a library. In the background, an old Wilco album, *Yankee Foxtrot Hotel*, played because of course. With a curse, she dragged Cabigail out of the chair and forced her against the wall, forearm up under her chin, choking her.

"Didn't we already do this?" Cabigail spluttered.

"What did you do?" Con roared.

"It's a work in progress."

"His name is Zhi Duan. He's not an it."

"Yes, his name is Zhi Duan, and you should be thanking me."

"How? How did you get his upload?" Con demanded.

Cabigail twisted her head side to side, searching for a breath. "From Johns Hopkins. I arranged through back channels to have him signed up for a study on long-term-care patients. I licensed a modified version of my scanner to the university for a few years. Consciousness mapping was a boon to their understanding of traumatic brain injuries. It was simple enough to obtain bloodwork and a copy of his scan from their study. I've been working with his clones ever since."

Con remembered the nurse at Zhi's long-term-care facility mentioning Zhi having just returned from Hopkins. That had been the day after Christmas eighteen months ago. She remembered feeling momentarily hopeful, and then foolish and stupid. How much worse it was knowing now that it had been her aunt all along, pulling the levers of her plan and baiting her trap. Because that was all Zhi was to her aunt—bait. Con leaned harder against her aunt's throat and for a wild moment believed that she might kill her. A clearheaded bloodlust surged like drain cleaner through her veins.

Cabigail struggled, slapping weakly at Con's arm.

Con saw her aunt's eyes go wide and unfocused. It scared her how badly she wanted to finish it. But then she thought of where she was. Without her aunt, there was no way out of here. She wouldn't even be able to get back through the door to Zhi, who couldn't possibly fend for himself. He would die alone and frightened.

Her arm went slack.

Cabigail slipped from her grasp and slid to the floor. Con stood over her while her aunt panted for breath.

"You've been working with his clones? Clones, plural?" Con said.

"Yes," Cabigail said, touching her neck. "The one you met is the third. I've also run innumerable simulations. Each iteration brings me closer."

"Closer to what?"

"To bringing him back the way he was, of course. In the case of traumatic brain injuries, making a precise image of a human consciousness had been impossible. But my epiphany on how to solve the mind-body problem produced some spectacular ancillary benefits. Like the possibility of repairing and reconstructing damaged uploads. But as I said, it's a work in progress—this last download caused micro-strokes that are responsible for his physical challenges. But he's come so far this time. You have no idea."

"And what happens to all the old Zhis?" Con asked, afraid of the answer.

"Oh, don't be naïve. He's a lab culture. Genetic material in a very large petri dish. A means to an end."

Con recoiled. "If we're human, he's human."

"Only the consciousness matters," Cabigail snapped. "I only showed you so you'd understand what's possible. What could be achieved if I had full access to what's locked inside your head."

So, that was it. The terrible bargain that her original had struck with Abigail Stickling. She had traded her life for the possibility of giving Zhi his life back. It wasn't that Con didn't understand. She knew she'd have made the same bargain. How many times since the accident had she begged the universe for the chance to trade places with Zhi? What broke her heart, though, was that she'd thought her original had made it out. Finally achieved escape velocity from the guilt. It had given Con hope to know that her original had started a new life—met someone, fallen in love, made amends with Stephie, even begun making her own music. And still, when the chance came to save Zhi, she had sacrificed everything.

"Why didn't you just leave her alone? She was happy."

"This is more important than happiness," Cabigail said. "She understood that. Now may I get off the floor?"

Con realized she was standing over her aunt, fists balled. She backed away to give Cabigail room to stand up. Her aunt climbed to her feet, brushing herself off dramatically.

"And you really think you can do it?" Con asked. "Make Zhi whole again?"

"It's going to take some time, but I'll get there," Cabigail answered with absolute certainty.

"So, in your perfect world, what happens now?"

"If you consent, I make an upload of your consciousness and extract my research. Then I get back to work."

"And then I have some tea. That the idea?"

"No, actually, then I do," Cabigail said.

Con was taken aback. "How does that work?"

"Even if you give me my research today, everything I've described is still ten years away. I need to get to work. Unimpeded. And I can't do it in this body."

"Well, you can't go back to being Abigail."

"Exactly. Abigail Stickling is dead, and she needs to stay that way. To finish what I started, I have to become my niece, Constance D'Arcy. That's why I need your body."

"You already have one of those," Con pointed out.

"No, I need your body. Your exact body," Cabigail said calmly as if giving directions to a scenic overlook. "I only passed as you because no one was looking too closely. But Vernon and Palingenesis are suspicious now and will be watching like hawks. If the clone of Con D'Arcy doesn't exactly match their records—which means no tattoos, among other things," she said, lifting her arm, "they will figure out what I've done."

"The fingerprints."

"All the unique biometrics. Everything that I've done, everything that I've sacrificed, every hard choice I've made, means nothing if the illusion isn't seamless."

"So, how does that work? You'll just overwrite me with you?" Con said, feeling a little sick at the thought.

"In essence."

"And if I agree to all this, you'll finish what you started with Zhi? Make him whole again? That's what you promised my original?"

"I gave her my word."

"And you just expect me to take this all on faith?"

"No, I don't. Because I'll bring both you and Zhi back," Cabigail said. "And not your upload from eighteen months ago the way Vernon offered. Your current, up-to-date consciousness. With none of the ill effects you're currently suffering."

"Really?" Was she even entertaining the idea? She'd turned down Gaddis and Fenton because it would have meant losing everything she'd experienced since her revival. It had only been a few days, but each one felt essential to who she was now. Yet another Con D'Arcy starting out on this same journey held no appeal to her. But if her aunt could fix this version of herself and bring back Zhi too . . . wasn't that everything she wanted? "So when is this all supposed to happen? Ten years from now when you've finished your work? And where am I going to be until then, stored in a computer? What if something goes wrong?"

"There is a risk in any journey. Airplanes crash. Ships sink. Vans jump medians. The question to you is whether the destination is worth the risk. And remember, it will all pass for you in an instant. Think of it like suspended animation. You're aboard a colony ship traveling to a new world, and when you wake up, you'll start a new life."

"And I'll be me again?" Con asked. "This me."

"If you wish. Once I've solved the mind-body problem, anything will be possible. I certainly don't intend to remain in the body of my niece. No offense, but it's a little peculiar."

"No shit. Who will you become?"

"Whomever I wish. Perhaps I'll try being a man first. It would be nice to have everything easy for a change. Who knows? That's the beauty of what we can accomplish here. Can you imagine it? Lifetimes spent experiencing the full range of human potential. And the same goes for you and Zhi. You could spend a thousand lifetimes together."

"Is that what nature intended?" Con said, trying to wrap her mind around the possibilities. "It just seems so unnatural."

"Well, first of all, nature has no intentions. Nature is simply a personification of a complex system that ancient peoples were overawed by. And secondly, there is no such thing as unnatural."

"Of course there is. A car. An airplane," Con countered.

"A car? Please. A car is the most natural thing in the world."

"How? You don't find cars in nature."

"Of course you do. Tens of millions of them," Cabigail said.

"That's not nature, that's Detroit."

"Are you arguing that humankind is itself unnatural?"

"No, but—" Con said.

"The anthill doesn't exist without the ant. But if a human builds a house, according to you, that is unnatural? It's nothing more than a semantic contrivance to make us feel special. Some native insecurity of our species, I suppose. Human beings have exactly one thing going for us—our minds. We're neither the fastest nor the strongest. Adapting the environment to our needs is what's natural for us. What nature intended, if you prefer. We are nature's greatest builders. It is what we have always done. It's what I have done. It's pure hubris to label our nature unnatural."

"I think you're making an argument to suit your needs."

"Yes," Abigail said with a wry smile. "Look at me, adapting the world to my needs. How unnatural."

"What if I say no?"

Cabigail considered the question. "I convince you to say yes. Do you think I came all this way without having a backup plan? But what do you have to lose when you have everything to gain? Your body is rejecting your download. You're dying."

"Because of you," Con said. "I'm dying because of you."

"I know it's scary, but I can fix it if you let me. I can fix everything. The question is, will you let me?"

"Yes," she said simply and not because she was afraid to die. She had found a bravery that she hadn't known existed. The truth was it felt good to be alive again. This life, not some hypothetical "better life" ten years from now. She wanted the here and now. She wanted more time with Stephie. She wanted to play music again, to feel passion again. But if she turned down her aunt, then her original would have sacrificed her life for nothing. She felt a sisterly solidarity with the first Con D'Arcy who was placed in this impossible situation and forced to choose. Con couldn't betray her sacrifice that way.

Cabigail's face was pure relief and triumph.

"On one condition," Con said.

"Name it."

"Levi Greer goes free." There was no chance she was going through with this if it meant Levi spent his life in prison.

Cabigail looked anything but happy. "That's not a good idea."

"Can you make it happen? Yes or no."

Grudgingly, Cabigail nodded. "Yes."

"Then we have a deal."

"I can live with that."

An alarm began to sound throughout the complex. Cabigail's attention disappeared into her LFD, a frown spreading across her self-satisfied face like a toxic spill.

"What is it?" Con asked.

"It would appear we have a visitor."

CHAPTER THIRTY-THREE

"Peter Lee," Cabigail said from the porch of the cottage. The gun was once more in her hand, pointed down at the deck. "You're a very long way from home."

Vernon Gaddis's majordomo lay in a ragged, bloodied heap at the bottom of the steps. Peter's clothes were torn and mud splattered. One side of his face was battered as if it had gone twelve rounds with the fender of a pickup. Surrounding him, three of the robot sentries formed a loose perimeter. One had burn marks along its flank. The fourth rDog was nowhere to be seen. It appeared the former soldier still had plenty of fight left in him.

"Peter, what are you doing here?" Con asked. She had followed an angry Cabigail to the surface and had to shade her eyes against the sun, which now sat high overhead, casting rippling shadows across the mountains.

"That you, Con?" he said, wrestling himself into a sitting position using his one good arm; the other he cradled protectively against his chest. "I followed Brooke Fenton from DC. Followed you from there."

"You shouldn't have come here," Con said.

"Now you tell me."

"Does Vernon know you're here?" Cabigail asked.

Through his one good eye, Peter stared up at them both placidly while taking stock of his injuries. "I'm sorry, who are you again? I know I'm concussed, but there appear to be two of you."

"This is going to be more of an I-ask-the-questions-you-answer-them relationship. That is, if you'd like something for the pain."

"Yeah," Peter acknowledged. "He knows I'm here."

"And what does he know about this place?"

"Only that Con was brought here by car, and that there is a perimeter security fence around this property that has no earthly business being out in these woods."

"And he told you to break in?" Cabigail asked.

"No, that I did on my own. Thought maybe Con could use some help."

"The girl is lucky to have you," Cabigail said dryly.

"Well," Peter said. "It was four on one."

"And what are Vernon's intentions?" Cabigail asked.

Peter gave the question some thought. "The man doesn't necessarily confide in me, but I imagine he's digging into who owns this place. And when he doesn't hear from me, he'll come knocking."

"I see. Are you able to walk?" Cabigail asked.

"Not far," Peter replied.

"There's not far to go," Cabigail said. "Are you armed?"

Peter said no, but Cabigail ordered one of the rDogs to scan him for weapons. Satisfied, she asked Con to help him inside. Con went down the stairs and knelt beside Peter. Up close, she realized his injuries were much more severe than his stoicism permitted him to let on.

"You doing alright?" he asked.

She took his hand. "I'm so sorry."

"Here I had thoughts I'd be saving you." Peter coughed blood onto his chin. "Should've known better."

"Con," Cabigail called down. "We don't have much time, and probably best not to linger outside."

Con helped Peter to his feet. He put an arm around her shoulders, and she supported his weight as best she could. Together, they hobbled up the stairs.

On her LFD, Abigail ordered two of the remaining rDogs to scatter back into the forest, but the third fell in behind Peter and Con, stalking up the stairs like a herding dog bringing in a lost sheep.

"What the hell have you gotten into here?" Peter asked Con under his breath.

"You wouldn't believe me if I told you."

"I am a decorated US soldier, you know."

He was trying to keep his spirits up, and Con forced a smile at his joke. They limped into the cottage and down the passageway into the complex.

"Okay, you were right," Peter admitted, looking around. "I don't believe this."

They made it to the lab before Peter lost consciousness. His legs gave way, and the best Con could do was ease him to the floor. She sat and cradled his head in her lap. His breathing was a jagged wheeze, wet and labored. The rDog went into a crouch at his feet, watching him with its smooth, eyeless face. Con looked to her aunt, imploring her to help him.

Cabigail stood there deep in thought as if trying to solve a complex mathematical formula. "I'm sorry. There's really nothing I can do. This is a lab, not a hospital."

"Then we have to take him to one," Con insisted.

Cabigail entered her biometrics to unlock a cabinet. "Out of the question. He's seen too much. But he has a clone at Palingenesis. He'll be fine."

Con knew that was a lie. Peter had explicitly told her that he never wanted another clone. She watched her aunt take out a syringe and a small, clear vial.

"What the hell's that?" Con asked.

"It's for the pain," Cabigail assured her. "We can at least make him comfortable."

Con didn't believe her. "He was a first-gen clone."

"I know who he is," Cabigail snapped, drawing up a dose from the vial and tapping the syringe with a practiced finger. "Now hold him still."

Cabigail put the syringe between her teeth and knelt to roll up the remnants of Peter's tattered sleeve. Con continued pleading for him, but her aunt wasn't listening anymore, her expression distant and resolved. Con recognized it. Cabigail had had the same look on her face standing over Brooke Fenton's body. Had it been any different when she killed Pockmark and his team? Maybe Cynthia Gaddis had been an accident, but her actions since had stripped away any morality Abigail Stickling might once have had. What lay beneath was cold and cruel and despicable. Peter was destined for the incinerator if she did nothing. Con was certain of that much.

"If he dies, you can forget our deal," Con said.

Cabigail glared at her niece. "Listen to me, girl. Vernon knows about this place now. That doesn't give us much time. He'll be on his way. We have too much to do before he arrives. There isn't the luxury of saving this trespasser."

Cabigail took Peter's arm, but before she could find a vein, Con grabbed her by the wrist. Rather than angry, Cabigail looked simply disappointed. The two women struggled, as evenly matched as two people could ever be. But Cabigail had the high ground, and Con could feel herself losing the battle for leverage.

"Let. Go," Cabigail commanded from between clenched teeth.

"Stop."

Cabigail grunted from the exertion, teeth drawn back in a snarl. "This is the only way."

Peter's head slipped off Con's thigh and cracked on the floor. It jolted him back to consciousness and his eyes flew open. Grabbing

Cabigail by the wrist and elbow, he twisted her arm back and used her own strength against her, driving the syringe up into her own chest.

Cabigail toppled back, grasping for the syringe.

In one motion, the forgotten rDog leapt, landing on Peter and pinning him to the ground. There was a horrendous tearing sound. A shearing collapse. Peter let out a terrible scream. His legs kicked out once, and then didn't move again. Con scrambled away, but the rDog paid no attention to her. It assessed its target coldly and trotted away to its master, where it once again crouched patiently.

Cabigail yanked out the syringe and threw it skittering across the floor. Her face turning blue, she began to shiver as if night had fallen and the temperature was dropping.

"What was in the syringe?" Con asked, although she had no doubt it was the same drug that had killed both Abigail and Con's original. How quickly it did its work when injected so close to the heart.

Instead of answering, Cabigail stabbed a finger in the direction of the nearest cabinet. "I need a syringe and a vial of Klenadone."

Con went on autopilot and scrambled to her feet, her instinct to help temporarily overriding her fury. She ran to where Cabigail was pointing.

"A green label. Hurry," Cabigail called out weakly.

"It's locked," Con yelled, yanking on the handle. "I can't get in."

Cabigail nodded and typed something on her LFD. When she was done, she told Con to enter her biometrics and try again.

This time, the cabinet opened.

Everything had a green label. Con pawed through the shelves until she found the Klenadone. She took it and a syringe to her aunt, who lay on her back, struggling for breath. Cabigail checked the label and nodded, thrusting it back into Con's hands.

"Hurry," Cabigail said, voice growing fainter with each passing moment.

Con had never injected anyone before, but she'd just seen her aunt do it, so mimicked the same steps. Tapping was to remove any air bubbles—she didn't know how she knew that, probably from a movie. Then her eyes fell on Peter's broken body, and she paused, the syringe hovering above her aunt. Peter was like Con's father. A soldier. The kind of person that her aunt claimed she was protecting all this for. If her aunt could sacrifice him, who would ever be immune from her ruthless self-interest? Her aunt had spoken so eloquently of the dangers should Gaddis or Fenton gain control of her research. Con realized it was nothing compared to what would happen if Abigail Stickling was allowed to keep it for herself.

What happened when someone with a god complex became one?

Across the lab, Con saw the womb holding yet another waiting clone of her aunt. Maybe it was time to put her aunt's theory to the test. Con set the syringe down on the floor. It wasn't murder if the person had a clone, was it? She hoped her aunt would appreciate the irony. Gently, Con plucked the LFD from behind Cabigail's ear. She didn't know how much access to the complex her aunt had given her, but she wasn't about to risk losing it.

Cabigail protested but could barely lift her arm to stop her. Instead, she let her head fall toward the rDog. Con realized almost too late what her aunt meant to do and clamped a hand over Cabigail's mouth. Her aunt bucked with all her waning strength, thrashing hopelessly, trying to get free. But the poison had spread too far, and she was too weak to throw Con off now. Right to the end, Con could hear her trying to shout muffled commands to the rDog. Con watched in terror for any sign it understood, but the rDog never so much as flinched, sitting motionless by its master's side while Con smothered her.

When Abigail Stickling was dead, Con fell back on the floor and lay there until she didn't have to concentrate simply on breathing in and out. She climbed unsteadily to her feet and stumbled over to the door leading to Zhi's room. What she did next hinged on whether her aunt had had the presence of mind to limit her access to the medical cabinets. If the door didn't open, then Con would be trapped down here forever. But not alone, because her aunt's clone was already being prepped in its womb for download.

Con's hands shook as she entered her biometrics, and she held her breath while the door took an eternity thinking about it. But then the lock turned from red to green. The door swung open.

She went down the hall and cracked his bedroom door. Zhi was lying on his back in bed, but when she got closer, she saw he wasn't sleeping. His eyes were open, staring glassily up at the ceiling. He'd been dead for a little while now. Her aunt must have triggered something remotely. Once he'd served his purpose, she'd euthanized him like the laboratory experiment he was to her. Con closed his eyes and sat on the edge of the bed the way she'd done on countless occasions visiting him in the hospital. But for the first time, she felt only relief that he wouldn't wake up to this nightmare. How strange that she'd come all this way only to wind up where she'd begun.

She took his hand in hers and said a final goodbye. Then she went out to the lab and pulled the plug on her aunt's new clone. Did that qualify as murder? After seeing Zhi, she really didn't give a damn.

CHAPTER
THIRTY-FOUR

When Con emerged into the living room of the cottage, the enormous fireplace closed of its own volition, sealing up the underground complex behind her. Con couldn't even find the seams in the wall with her fingers. That was probably for the best. In the kitchen, she took a glass from a cupboard and filled it with water, relieved that the cottage wasn't entirely for show. Leaning against the counter, she gulped it down and looked out the window.

A car sat idling out front.

At first she assumed it must be Gaddis, but how had he gotten past the gate? And the last two rDogs were nowhere to be seen, which meant that the car and its occupants must be trusted by her aunt. What would that make them to Con? She cast around for a weapon and found a dull kitchen knife in a drawer. How far was she going to get with that?

She went back to the window. The car hadn't moved, but she caught a glimpse of a bald white head peeking out from above one of the Adirondack chairs. Someone was sitting on the porch enjoying the view. When she cracked the front door a few inches, a white man stood to greet her. He was convincingly tall, with a patrician bearing that Con associated with movies from the twentieth century. He had to be at least sixty but looked tennis fit in his crisp blue suit.

"Hello, Miss D'Arcy."

"You know me?" Con said, ready at the first hint of danger to shut the door.

"Only from your picture," he said, running his fingers across the remnants of his hair as if smoothing a blanket too small for the bed it covered.

"And who are you again?"

"Oh, I apologize. Where are my manners?" he replied, extending a manicured hand. "My name is William Small. I'm a senior partner at Daniels Lovell in DC. I am Abigail Stickling's personal attorney and continue to represent certain of her lingering interests."

"Well, you sure talk like a lawyer," she said, opening the door and shaking his hand.

"Occupational hazard," he acknowledged. "I'm quite harmless otherwise."

"How long have you been sitting out here?"

The man looked at his watch with pursed lips. "Not long. I knocked but no one was home," he said, although she had clearly come from inside the cottage. "Not to worry. My instructions were to wait."

"For?"

"You."

"How? How did you know I'd be here?" Con asked.

"I'm afraid I'm not free to discuss that."

"When were you told to come?"

"I'm not able to discuss that either. May I come inside?" he said, picking up a briefcase from between his feet. "We have a great deal to go over."

Con let him into the house. He asked for a glass of water, and she brought it to him in the living room. He was standing in the doorway to the bedroom, shaking his head.

"You know, I was Abigail's attorney for almost twenty years. She was always so vague about this place. At the firm, we used to speculate what could be up here that she would spend so much time here. Especially toward the end. Hector will be so disappointed."

"Why?"

"He has this crazy theory she'd built a secret laboratory. Calls it her fortress of solitude. But no, it's just a shack. I mean, look at all this junk. Can you imagine anything more absurd than Abigail Stickling doing a jigsaw puzzle?"

"My aunt was a very eccentric woman," Con said.

"Preaching to the choir there," he said, looking around again. "The woman was worth close to a billion dollars, and this was where she chose to spend her time. If I live to be one hundred, I will never understand what goes through the heads of the very rich."

At first, she'd taken his ignorance for an act. A role player in her aunt's sprawling charade. But as he'd talked, Con realized that he'd been kept in the dark too. When you meant to steal the secret to immortality, no one could know. There was no amount of money that would buy his silence if he knew the truth. What was the old adage about the only way two people could keep a secret was if one of them was dead? No one could ever know. That had been Abigail Stickling's plan all along.

Con asked, "So, what's this about? Why did you drive all this way to see me?"

"Well," he began, opening his briefcase and arranging documents on the coffee table. "As you may or may not know, upon her death a year and a half ago, your aunt's estate was placed in a sealed trust that came with very specific instructions for how and when it should be opened. Only myself; Hector Alonzo, the managing partner at Daniels Lovell; and Anne Friedman in Boston knew its terms."

He paused dramatically, and Con had the impression that he had been rehearsing this moment for a long time.

"Its terms . . . ?" Con said helpfully. Apparently, she had a line here.

"Allow me to be the first to congratulate you," the lawyer said grandly. "You are the sole heir of Abigail Stickling. She left you everything."

Con felt her mouth fall open, and for the life of her, she was unable to close it again.

He seemed to enjoy her silence, mistaking it for delight and shock. After years of work, it probably felt good to be there at the end, the bearer of good news, believing he'd played a part in changing her life so completely. But what the lawyer mistook for happiness was Con realizing the full breadth of her aunt's intentions. Abigail Stickling hadn't left everything to her niece; she'd left everything to herself. If everything had gone to plan, it would be Abigail Stickling sitting here in Con's body with her fortune returned to her and no one the wiser.

"When was this will written?" Con asked.

"Well, Ms. Stickling's will went through many iterations, but this last version was completed only a few days before . . ." He trailed off, too polite to use the word *suicide*.

"How long was I the heir?"

The lawyer shifted in his seat and reached for his water. "Unfortunately, I'm not at liberty to share that either."

Con glanced at the fireplace and what lay beyond it. Stopping her aunt's download might have been premature. Her penance would be never getting the answers to all of her questions. Some of which would torment her until her dying day. Fortunately, depending how you looked at it, that day wasn't that far away. Con had cost herself the only chance she had at fixing the damage to her download. She hadn't thought about it in those terms in the heat of the moment, but now found she wasn't scared. And however and whenever the end came, she wouldn't be broke when it did.

For the next two hours, she signed and initialed document after document. The lawyer talked the entire time, laying out the breadth of Abigail Stickling's holdings and the complexities of her diverse portfolio of real estate, stocks, and businesses. Con, who had been poor her entire life, found it overwhelming. Much of the legalese she only understood in general terms, and he recommended hiring a financial adviser.

"You will also want to retain the services of at least one lawyer at your earliest convenience," he said.

"Are you available, Bill? Or is that one of those conflicts-of-interest deals?"

He seemed taken aback by that. "No, it's not, and yes, I could be. But perhaps it would be best to look around? One should not make hasty decisions in these matters."

"No. My aunt trusted you. That's good enough for me." Perhaps her logic was twisted, but it was the truth. William Small didn't know anything about his client's scheme yet had done everything her aunt had asked of him. Loyally and without question. Even today, under the most bizarre of circumstances, he had followed his client's wishes to the letter. It was the best audition that Con could imagine.

He smiled. "In that case, it would be my pleasure."

"Do I have to retain you? Is there something I need to do?"

"You just did," he answered with a grin. She thought she was going to like him. She'd never had a lawyer before.

"Cool. In that case, I have a couple of things I need you to do right away."

"Oh?" he said, reaching for a legal pad. "Fire away."

She described Levi Greer's situation. With her aunt gone, there was no simple way to clear his name. She told her new lawyer that she wanted the best legal team that money could buy. Bill didn't see it as a problem. They stood and shook hands.

"Thank you," she said.

"Of course. Do you need a ride back to Washington?"

"No, I have a car."

"Good enough," he said, gathering up his things into his briefcase. "Oh, I almost forgot. A present from your aunt." He handed her a small rectangular box wrapped in red-and-gold nutcracker paper. He waited, eager to see what was inside the box he'd kept for a year and a half. When Con made no move to open it, he looked disappointed and shook her hand again. "Then I will see you soon. Make an appointment. Come by the offices. In the meantime, I'll begin assembling a legal team for your review. And we will get right to work on a transfer of person-hood. Shouldn't take more than a few weeks."

She went out on the porch with him and waited until his car passed out of sight on its way down the mountain. Then she went back inside and unwrapped the package, curious to know what her aunt had given herself. Inside was a simple cardboard box. Inside that was a heavy rect-angle of clear polymer with two prongs on each side. It almost looked like a faceplate, but there was nothing engraved on its perfectly smooth surface. Where had she seen that shape before? She remembered the strange indentation below the biometric reader set in to the fireplace. The faceplate was about that size.

When she tested it to see if it fit, the faceplate snapped neatly into place as if magnetized. After a moment, it began to glow with a simple instruction.

Initiate Self-Destruct?

The last step in her aunt's plan, covering her tracks by burying the underground laboratory under a mountain. Once she had assumed the role of a newly wealthy Constance D'Arcy, she'd have been free to build a laboratory anywhere on earth and wouldn't have to remain hid-den from the world. For all Con knew, the new laboratory was already underway somewhere. But what to do about the old one?

Con's finger hovered over the "Initiate" button.

Was there any reason not to blow the place to hell? The key to her aunt's research might be locked in Con's head, but Abigail had re-created important parts of it. All stored on the laboratory's servers. Gaddis would find it eventually. He might already be on his way to crack the place open like an ancient burial mound. Hell, Con might do it herself one day. Right at this moment, she felt clear in her mind that, even in the right hands, the damage her aunt's research would do would be incalculable. But what about as her body and mind continued to sever ties and drift inexorably apart? Would she be so principled then? She could already hear the counterargument forming—how she should wait and see if she felt the same in a few months. The laboratory was secure, and not even Gaddis knew how to get inside. So why rush into a decision?

It made perfect sense, so she pressed the button.

60 Seconds.

It began to count down.

Sixty seconds? That wasn't enough time. Con tapped the faceplate again, but no option to abort appeared.

45 Seconds.

Con backed away and went for the door. Yanking it open, she nearly lost her balance and fell, half expecting security to have locked her inside. But the door opened easily, and she spilled down the stairs. She ran about ten feet before pulling to an abrupt halt. Two thoughts occurred to her simultaneously, which taken together added up to one overriding sentiment: no running away.

Either the faceplate was a trap—a middle finger from beyond the grave—in which case there would be nowhere Con could run in sixty seconds that would be safe from Abigail's revenge, or else her aunt had designed the self-destruct so that no running was necessary. Either way, Con wasn't going to spend the last thirty seconds of her life running like an animal.

Curious, she turned back to the cottage and put her hands on her hips. Whatever happened, she wanted to see it coming. She thought she'd earned that much.

She waited.

It wouldn't be long now.

PART FOUR

Awaken the Ghosts

On the other hand, what I like my music to do to me is awaken the ghosts inside of me. Not the demons, you understand, but the ghosts. There, I'm using that old language again. I don't believe in demons. I don't think there is such a thing. Or evil. I don't believe in some force outside of ourselves that creates bad things. I just think of it as all dysfunctionalism of one kind of [sic] another. No Satan, no devil. The devil only really appears in the New Testament. He makes a couple of casual appearances in the Old, but only as an irritating obstacle. We create so many circles on this straight line we're told we're traveling. The truth is of course is [sic] that there is no journey. We are arriving and departing all at the same time.

—David Bowie

CHAPTER
THIRTY-FIVE

Con held the final chord until it faded to silence and then held her hand up to the light. It trembled faintly, and she flexed her fingers, trying to shake it off. Her hands did that now whenever she played for any length of time. The tremors had gradually worsened these last few weeks, but if she rested at night and followed her team of doctors' elaborate regime, it was mostly manageable.

She glanced over at the little purple Christmas tree, which was a permanent resident in the studio. It had become her good luck charm that she touched every morning before she started work for the day. It twinkled at her supportively.

"Everything okay in there?" Stephie asked over the intercom.

Con looked through the glass at Stephie and Dahlia sitting at the console. "Yeah, my hands are a little sore."

"Not surprised, you've been at it for ten hours. Need a break?"

This was their arrangement—Con lied about how she was feeling and Stephie pretended to believe her. When Con first moved in, she'd told her friend about the diagnosis. She reckoned that Stephie and Elena had a right to know what they were getting themselves into, but it only made them more insistent that Con come to stay with them. She'd begged them not to treat her any differently, though. Whatever time she had left wouldn't be spent treated like an invalid. She had too much she wanted to get done first.

That included undoing the damage caused by her aunt. The first thing she'd done after retaining the legal services of William Small was have him assemble the best defense team that money could buy. She'd bankrolled Levi Greer's bail, but neither Detective Clarke nor the Commonwealth of Virginia seemed inclined to drop the charges. Tomorrow, Con had to drive over to Richmond to discuss deposing her in the event she wasn't physically able to testify at the trial. That would cost her most of the day.

"Couple more takes?" Con asked. "It's still not there."

"Are you crazy?" Dahlia cut in. The young girl had been helping out in the studio, even filling in when Stephie was busy in the store. She had the makings of a talented board operator. "That totally slings. What's it called?"

"'Dahlia Is a Badass.' In D minor," Con said with a grin. She'd never had a little sister but found it suited her. Dahlia made the devil's horns with her fingers and stuck her tongue out.

"One more?" Con asked, compromising even though Stephie had already agreed. Her perfectionist streak would never not get the best of her, and Con felt guilty for dragging Stephie along on this tour of her obsessiveness.

"Do as many as you like, fool," Stephie replied. "But are you still good to watch the store this afternoon? We've got parent-teacher conferences with this one."

"No problem."

"You sure? We can always close for a few hours. Really not a big deal," Stephie said, hesitant to leave Con alone after the first of the seizures.

"Are you kidding? I will sell three guitars before dinner."

"Three?" Dahlia said skeptically.

"Count it, girl."

"Alright, then," Stephie said. "Ready to lay it down again?"

Con gave her hand an encouraging squeeze. "Ready."

———

The shop was a ghost town all afternoon. All she managed to sell was the sheet music for Joni Mitchell's *Blue* and a ten-pack of guitar picks. The only way she was selling three guitars was if she bought them herself. She could certainly afford it now, but it felt like cheating. It was actually nice to have the time alone and gave her time to work on the lyrics to a new song. These days, they were coming almost faster than she could write them down. Sometimes new melodies came so easily that it felt as if she were transcribing notes that someone else was playing to her. She was hardly a spiritual person, but it had made her feel connected to Zhi and her old life.

Midafternoon, three teenagers came in out of the rain to check out the amplifiers. Con recognized them. Two of them were Stephie and Elena's students and often hung around the shop after school. All semester, they'd been trying to start a band but couldn't find a bassist, agree on their sound, or settle on a name. They'd spent the last few months rehearsing as a nameless trio. Con remembered forming her first band—the High Plains. They'd lasted nine whole days before breaking up over artistic differences, and also because they had nowhere to practice. Con smiled to herself at the memory. Rock and roll.

From behind the counter, she listened to the teens argue about who was the best pianist—capital-*E* ever. Names flew back and forth across the shop. One boy insisted it was Elton John or Ray Charles. The girl made an impassioned case for Stevie Wonder. The other boy said either Trent Reznor or Matt Bellamy would kick all their asses, sparking a fresh round of debate. It made Con nostalgic for those long hours in the back of the van, passed in pointless but passionate bull sessions about the greatest this or the all-time that.

She could think about Awaken the Ghosts, and the people in it, fondly again. Remembering had become an important ritual for her and Stephie—two old veterans of the wars memorializing their fallen brothers. After finishing in the studio, they'd sit up late into the night reminiscing and telling tall tales about those days. The time Tommy quit the band for a week because someone ate his oatmeal. Superserious and highbrow Hugh's not so supersecret love of old-school Britney Spears. Zhi's penchant for impassioned soliloquies and Tommy's habit of derailing Zhi's train of thought with seemingly innocent questions that Stephie suspected weren't nearly as innocent as they seemed.

It felt good to have those stories back, to be able to speak their names without crying. Even Zhi, who she had loved and lost, found and then lost all over again. Before she died, she hoped his memory would bring her joy again. She didn't know if she could get there, but it was important to try. That was, hopefully, what the new album would help her do—if she ever finished it.

"Con, who you got?" the girl asked. For whatever reason, Con had a weird credibility with all the kids who frequented the shop. Maybe it was because she rarely left the studio and that mysterious obsessiveness made her cool with kids desperate for something to be obsessed about. She appreciated how little any of them seemed to care that she was a clone. It made her hopeful for the future.

"Yeah, who?" the Trent Reznor fan said.

"And don't say Bowie," the girl admonished. "You say Bowie for everything."

Con gave the girl a guilty-as-charged shrug, and the teens all laughed.

"Well," Con said thoughtfully, remembering old arguments in the back of the van. "My old friend Tommy Diop would have said Billy Preston."

"Who?" the first boy demanded.

"The fifth Beatle. Played that great electric piano on 'Don't Let Me Down,'" the girl said, rolling her eyes, which did not go over big with the boys.

"But who do you think?" the Trent Reznor fan asked, which quieted the others.

"Well, for my money, it was Tommy Diop. Man, could he play."

"Who's that?" they all asked.

"He was in a band called Awaken the Ghosts," Con said, picturing the delighted grin on Tommy's face whenever he played. Even during their most serious songs, which drove Zhi around the bend.

The kids looked among themselves, none recognizing the name. It wasn't surprising, but still, Con felt a little sad. Zhi Duan, Hugh Balzan, Tommy Diop—her friends, her bandmates. They'd lived. They'd dreamed. They'd died. And already their memory was fading. Con thought about setting the teenagers straight, but for what? Most of life is lived to be forgotten. That was the way of things, cruel though it felt when it was your life that would be lost.

Still, she figured there was always a chance that one of these kids would go home and look up the band. Then, curious or even bored, they would listen to a few of the old songs. Maybe like them enough to share them with friends. Or maybe they were teenagers with other things to worry about, and they'd forget this conversation the moment they left the store. Either way, it had no effect on the lives that her friends had led. If you lived your life to be remembered when you were gone, you were wasting your time.

When the kids left, Con went back to her notebook. The album she'd been envisioning since the crash had grown far beyond its initial scope. She'd pared the song list down to two twelve-track collections. The first was composed of songs that her original had written and recorded before her death. The second twelve were all songs influenced by her experience since her download. She thought the two halves worked well together, bookends on the twin lives she'd led. Hopefully people would listen with an open mind. She still had a childlike belief in music's ability to bridge even the bitterest divides.

With a little luck, she'd live long enough to hear it played from start to finish. If not, she trusted Stephie to finish it for her. There was so much left to do—she hadn't even settled on a title. For a while, she'd toyed with *Coda*, but that felt a little on the nose. Then *Constants*, but she didn't want her final contribution to the world to be a bad pun. Lately, she'd been thinking about calling it *Awaken the Ghosts*, but she hadn't run it by Stephie, who should have a say. Why were titles so hard?

When the shopkeeper's bell above the front door jingled, Con glanced up to see if the customer looked the sort to buy three guitars. Well, he could certainly afford it, but she didn't take him for the musical type.

"Hello, Mr. Gaddis. I was wondering when you'd show up," she said.

"Hello, Constance," he said, shaking off the rain. "Honestly, I've been meaning to get down here sooner, but things have been so busy. Brooke took a leave of absence from the company, and the board asked me to step in for her."

Con put down her pen but didn't stand up from the stool behind the counter. It felt important to remain still and let him come to her. "Strange to see you this far south without an armed escort."

"Well, a lot has changed," Gaddis said.

"Congratulations on winning your case."

"Thank you, but it's really all our case, isn't it?" Gaddis replied with the gravitas of a seasoned politician, but she supposed it was true. In a stunning five-to-four decision, the Supreme Court had ruled for the plaintiff in the case *Gaddis v. Virginia*. In finding that the clone of Vernon Gaddis was also the person Vernon Gaddis, it had swept aside the patchwork of state anti-clone laws and extended federal protections to all clones. The decision had thrown the country into an uproar that seemed far from being over. Children of Adam had seen its membership rolls triple virtually overnight. Con hadn't heard from Franklin Butler, not even a thank-you note for the idea. He was everywhere these days in full crusader and firebrand mode, vowing not to rest until the travesty of this ruling was overturned, and the original sin of human cloning was cleansed from America's soul. There were even whispers of a run for president in '44.

"Bet your friends forgave you for not dropping it now," she said.

"It is remarkable how much one resounding victory can paper over old grievances. You seem to be thriving," he said, looking around the shop. She couldn't decide if he was serious or being condescending. She found she didn't care either way.

"I'm doing fine. How are your kids?" she asked.

He held his hands, palms up, as if comparing the weight of two things. "The boys still refuse to speak to me."

"I'm sorry. That's got to be hard."

"It is, but I am having lunch with my daughter next week," he said, voice filled with hope but tinged with caution. "These things take time. I only wish I had more of it."

"Yeah, that's going around," Con said, ignoring the implication behind his words.

"Indeed. I saw your lawyers dissolved our contract."

"Didn't feel I lived up to my end of the bargain."

"I'd certainly agree with you there. But you don't need me to buy you a clone anymore, do you?" Gaddis said.

"No, I'm pretty well fixed in that department now."

Gaddis chuckled. "Yes, it's been quite a reversal of fortune for both of us. But it makes me curious why you haven't. We both know your medical situation."

"I have my reasons," Con said, turning her attention to straightening the counter.

He watched her in curiosity. "You're really just going to let yourself die?"

"It's been working for people for thousands of years," Con said.

"But it doesn't have to anymore. Not for someone of your means."

"You didn't come all the way down here to ask after my health." She found his concern for her well-being irritating.

"No, I did not," Gaddis admitted.

"So, get to it. What do you want?"

"I want to know who killed Brooke Fenton."

Cabigail had never released her recording of the meeting between Fenton and Butler, and the police still had no suspects in her death. Butler would never know how different things might be for him if she had.

"Didn't Peter tell you?" Con had assumed that Gaddis knew at least that much.

"He arrived too late for anything but the aftermath. He saw you get into a car with a young woman but was too far away to identify her. Who was she?"

Con blank-faced him as though she'd spontaneously forgotten the English language. When he saw she wouldn't answer, he leaned heavily on the counter as though testing to see if it would bear his weight should he decided to hurdle it. He seemed to change his mind, though, and his frown disappeared, replaced by a hospitable smile. "What happened in that mountain? That was a spectacular cave-in."

"Loudest thing I ever heard. And I was in a band."

"If it were to be excavated, what would we find, I wonder?" Gaddis said.

"Well, that's private property and about a million tons of rock, so that's not going to happen."

"Abigail Stickling's private property until you inherited her estate. What happened up there? What are you hiding?" he demanded.

"Maybe you'd know what happened if you'd gone yourself instead of sending Peter," Con said, realizing for the first time the depth of her anger toward him. "You know, you still haven't asked me about him."

Gaddis's expression darkened once more. "I assume Peter is dead. He was a good friend. He deserved better. Is that why you're building that organization in his name? Some kind of penance."

That's exactly what it was, but Con didn't respond or react to Gaddis's provocation. One of the first things she had elected to do with her newfound wealth was found a nonprofit organization that would provide outreach and counseling to the first-generation clones, veterans like Peter who were still struggling to adapt. She hoped he would approve.

"I owe him," she said simply.

"That's very noble of you."

"Well, someone needed to be," Con said, slipping off her stool and heading for the front of the store. "Now, I'm sorry, but I need to lock up."

"Of course. I didn't mean to keep you. I just wanted you to know that I've had teams combing through Palingenesis's computers for months. I have a pretty good idea what's in your head."

Con didn't break stride and kept her voice resolutely neutral. "Oh?"

"You're not even a little bit curious?"

She held the door open for him and stepped onto the sidewalk. The rain had broken for a moment. "It was good to see you again."

"Apparently you are not." He paused in the open doorway. "Or is it only because you already know?"

"What is it you want from me?"

"That's Palingenesis's intellectual property in your head. I can get a court order to force you to return what's ours."

"And my lawyers will have you tied up in court until long after I am gone."

"If it's even there anymore," Gaddis said. "Is that what Abigail bought with her fortune?"

"My aunt's dead."

"Yes, so I keep telling myself. Do you have time for a story?" Gaddis asked and then told it without waiting for an answer. "An old friend of mine was in Seoul on business last week. He called me with the most curious story."

She looked up and down the street, waiting for him to go on. If he thought she was going to play him in, well, he was out of his damned mind.

"He said he saw the spitting image of Abigail in the Namdaemun Market."

Con felt the hair on the back of her neck prickle.

"Strolled right by him. Clear as day, he said. He tried to follow her but lost her in the crowd. Swears up and down it was her. I had to persuade him that was impossible. There are only so many faces in the world. Eventually they have to start repeating."

"A look-alike," she agreed, unsure which of them she was hoping to convince. She had terminated the clone of Abigail in the mountain, but what if she had only triggered yet another clone stored somewhere off-site? Say South Korea. It had been pure hubris to think her aunt hadn't anticipated something going catastrophically wrong. This was a woman with a backup plan for everything—even herself.

"Exactly. That's exactly what I told my friend," Gaddis said. "But it's a reminder of what a strange world we live in now. So hard to ever say when something is really over anymore. Things we think are dead and buried can come back to haunt us now."

"I'll keep that in mind. Goodbye, Mr. Gaddis," Con said and stepped back into the shop. "I hope lunch with your daughter goes well."

"Please. Think about what you're doing. It's the greatest advance in the history of our species. It's a gift. It belongs to the world."

"I thought you said it belonged to Palingenesis," she said and shut the door in his face.

From the window, she watched him cross the street to his waiting car. Was immortality really an advance, and if so, toward what? She thought she'd prevented it from getting out. Now she realized all she'd done was delay its arrival. Whether her aunt was alive or not made no difference. Now that Vernon Gaddis suspected that immortality was attainable, he would devote himself to finding the answer. Abigail Stickling was a genius, but there would be others who would stand on the shoulders of her work to glimpse what she had discovered. One day, the mind-body paradox would be solved again. It was inevitable. Con saw that now, but she wouldn't be the one to unleash it on the world. What had Vernon Gaddis called it? A gift? Well, she had very different ideas about gift giving.

———

Elena, Stephie, and Dahlia returned a little after five with two large pizzas—Dahlia's reward for the glowing reports from her teachers. She made a big show of counting the guitars in the shop and then lavished Con with a heartbroken face that could have been seen from orbit.

"Can I still have some pizza?" Con asked.

Dahlia pretended to think about it long and hard.

They went out to the courtyard. Elena ran upstairs for drinks, and they sat around the firepit and ate. The evening stretched out. A few friends arrived with wine. Elena arranged a pyramid of logs in the firepit and lit the kindling. The call went out, and still more friends arrived, bearing all sorts of food and drink. Con looked up and realized there had to be thirty people laughing and drinking and telling stories. That was how things usually went when Stephie and Elena entertained— nothing was ever planned, people just showed up until it was a party.

Con camped out by the firepit for most of the night, talking and enjoying the warm glow of human company. Abigail Stickling felt like a distant memory. She dismissed Gaddis's story as cheap scare tactics.

And if she were alive, what could she do to her from South Korea that she hadn't been able to do in southern Virginia?

Someone asked Stephie if she would play. She declined, but by then it had already begun to circulate that she had agreed.

"Come on, give us a song!" someone yelled out happily, which was greeted with laughter and cheers.

"They're calling your name, *mi amor*," Elena said, resting her head on Stephie's shoulder.

"I'm not getting up there alone," Stephie said, looking over at Con.

"Oh no, no. No," Con said, and then, in case anyone had missed it the first three times: "No."

Dahlia, perched on the arm of her mother's chair, was grinning at her. "You so are."

"Why are you still up?" Con asked. "Isn't it past your bedtime?"

"Straight A's," Dahlia said. "Fact."

"What do you say?" Stephie said, taking Con's hand and giving it a firm squeeze. "I will if you will."

Con looked from Stephie to Elena to Dahlia and back to her oldest friend. How could she say no to any of these people? "One song."

"One song," Stephie agreed. "Your choice."

Acknowledgments

One of the first lessons you learn as an author is that if you have a good idea while falling asleep, get up and write it down before you do. Because if you don't, then in the morning, all you'll have left is a faint chalk outline of that idea and the melancholic certainty that it was the best one you'll ever have.

One night, nearly five years ago now, I was in that lovely halfway house between consciousness and sleep when a simple thought occurred to me: Wouldn't it be cool if someone had to investigate their own death? I remembered the old Edmond O'Brien movie, *D.O.A.*, in which he had to figure out who had poisoned him before he died. And I was sure there had to be hundreds of supernatural stories about the dead searching for answers, but how could someone living be in a position to solve their own murder?

I stared at the ceiling for a while until I wondered: What if the hero were a clone of the murdered person with all their memories except those of the murder itself? I executed a flawless movie sit-bolt-upright-in-bed eureka moment and somehow managed to make it to my desk without injuring myself. I spent the rest of the night jotting down pages and pages of world-building notes and wrote the first draft of what is now chapter four. Then I put it all in the proverbial bottom drawer and went back to work on the second Gibson Vaughn book. It would be four more books before I felt ready to return to *Constance*.

When I finally did return to my notes, it took a host of generous and talented people to help me flesh out and finish the book that you're holding. It is fair to say I could not have done it without them, and so, my heartfelt thanks . . .

To my agent and friend, David Hale Smith, and his colleagues at InkWell Management Literary Agency.

To my editors, Megha Parekh and Grace Doyle, and to everyone at Thomas & Mercer who worked on this book.

To Steve Konkoly, Joe Hart, and Ed Stackler for reading an early draft and helping point me in the right direction.

To Nadine Nettmann for her boundless patience as I repeatedly spun out the cotton balls of possible plotlines crowding my head.

To Johnny Shaw who read a partial draft when I was struggling to see the ending and helped me get back on track.

To Elizabeth Little for somehow carving out time to read a draft of the manuscript and offer some essential late-game suggestions.

To Katie Lahnstein for helping to imagine how legal protections for clones might, or might not, function; to Lee Kovarsky for explaining how a clone-related lawsuit would make its way to the Supreme Court; and to Steve Feldhaus for his expertise on trusts and wills. Any mistakes or liberties taken are mine, not theirs.

To Lara Atella for her suggestions on the neural-psychological repercussions that cloning might have on the human brain. Again, any mistakes or liberties are mine.

To Tim Lyons and Melissa Wolverton for advice on all things music and band related.

To Aaron Bachmann for his cartological knowledge of Charlottesville, Virginia.

To Mike Tyner for projecting how security and privacy might function twenty years from now.

To Matt Misiorowski for his engineering insights, particularly in the potential directions of electric-vehicle design.

To Boneza Hanchock for her invaluable work as the book's primary sensitivity reader and for helping me do justice to Con's experience.

To Valerie Klemczewski for helping me locate Con's edge and for never letting me soften her.

To Eric Schwerin, Nathan Hughes, Karen Hughes, Giovanna Baffico, Jess Lourey, Matt Iden, D.M. Pulley—you're all the best.

And to Vanessa Brimner, first and foremost.

About the Author

Photo © 2017 Douglas Sonders

Matthew FitzSimmons is the author of the *Wall Street Journal* bestselling Gibson Vaughn series, which includes *Origami Man, Debris Line, Cold Harbor, Poisonfeather,* and *The Short Drop*. Born in Illinois and raised in London, he now lives in Washington, DC, where he taught English literature and theater at a private high school for more than a decade. For more information, visit him at www.matthewfitzsimmons.com.